THE TURN OF THE SCREW

AN AUTHORITATIVE TEXT
BACKGROUNDS AND SOURCES
ESSAYS IN CRITICISM

W.W. NORTON & COMPANY, INC.
also publishes

THE NORTON ANTHOLOGY OF AMERICAN LITERATURE
edited by Nina Baym et al.

THE NORTON ANTHOLOGY OF ENGLISH LITERATURE
edited by M. H. Abrams et al.

THE NORTON ANTHOLOGY OF LITERATURE BY WOMEN
edited by Sandra M. Gilbert and Susan Gubar

THE NORTON ANTHOLOGY OF MODERN POETRY
edited by Richard Ellmann and Robert O'Clair

THE NORTON ANTHOLOGY OF POETRY
edited by Alexander W. Allison et al.

THE NORTON ANTHOLOGY OF SHORT FICTION
edited by R. V. Cassill

THE NORTON ANTHOLOGY OF WORLD MASTERPIECES
edited by Maynard Mack et al.

THE NORTON FACSIMILE OF
THE FIRST FOLIO OF SHAKESPEARE
prepared by Charlton Hinman

THE NORTON INTRODUCTION TO LITERATURE
edited by Carl E. Bain, Jerome Beaty, and J. Paul Hunter

THE NORTON INTRODUCTION TO THE SHORT NOVEL
edited by Jerome Beaty

THE NORTON READER
edited by Arthur M. Eastman et al.

THE NORTON SAMPLER
edited by Thomas Cooley

⇛ A NORTON CRITICAL EDITION ⇚

HENRY JAMES

THE TURN OF THE SCREW

AN AUTHORITATIVE TEXT
BACKGROUNDS AND SOURCES
ESSAYS IN CRITICISM

⇛⇚

Edited by

ROBERT KIMBROUGH

UNIVERSITY OF WISCONSIN

W · W · NORTON & COMPANY

New York · London

ISBN 0-393-04275-8 Cloth Edition

ISBN 0-393-09669-6 Paper Edition

W. W. Norton & Company, Inc., 500 Fifth Avenue, New York, N.Y. 10110

PRINTED IN THE UNITED STATES OF AMERICA

1 2 3 4 5 6 7 8 9 0

Contents

Preface

The Text of *The Turn of the Screw*

The Turn of the Screw   1
Textual History   89
Textual Notes   91

Background and Sources

JAMES ON THE GHOST-STORY

A Review (1865) ["Mysteries * * * at Our Own Doors"]   97
A Notebook Entry (1888) ["Subject for a Ghost-Story"]   99
A Notebook Entry (1888) ["Another Theme of the Same Kind"]   100
To G. B. Shaw (1909) ["The Imagination * * * Leads a Life of Its Own"]   100
From a Preface (1909) ["The Question * * * of the Supernatural"]   101

JAMES ON THE TURN OF THE SCREW

A Notebook Entry (1894–1895) ["Grose"]   106
A Notebook Entry (1895) ["Note Here the Ghost-Story"]   106
To Alice James (1897) ["Finished My Little Book"]   107
To A. C. Benson (1898) ["Of the Ghostly and Ghastly"]   108
To Paul Bourget (1898) ["A Little Volume Just Published"]   109
To Dr. Waldstein (1898) ["That Wanton Little Tale"]   110
To H. G. Wells (1898) ["The Thing Is Essentially a Pot-Boiler"]   111
To F. W. H. Myers (1898) ["The T. of the S. Is a Very Mechanical Matter"]   112

To W. D. Howells (1900) ["Another Duplex Book
Like the 'Two Magics' "]   113
A Notebook Entry (1900) ["Something As Simple As
The Turn of the Screw"]   114
To W. D. Howells (1900) ["A Little 'Tale of
Terror' "]   116
To W. D. Howells (1902) ["A Story of the '8 to 10
Thousand Words' "]   117
The New York Preface (1908) ["An Exercise of the
Imagination"]   118

OTHER SUGGESTED SOURCES

Robert Lee Wolff · The Genesis of "The Turn of
the Screw"   125
Francis X. Roellinger · Psychical Research and
"The Turn of the Screw"   132
Miriam Allott · Mrs. Gaskell's "The Old Nurse's
Story": A Link Between "Wuthering Heights" and
"The Turn of the Screw"   142
Oscar Cargill · *The Turn of the Screw* and Alice
James   145

Essays in Criticism

EARLY REACTIONS: 1898–1923

The New York Times · Magic of Evil and Love   169
The Outlook · ["The Story * * * Is Distinctly
Repulsive"]   171
The Bookman · Mr. James's New Book   172
John D. Barry · On Books at Christmas   173
The Critic · The Recent Work of Henry James   173
The Independent · ["Most Hopelessly Evil Story"]   175
The Chautauquan · ["Psychic Phenomena"]   175
Oliver Elton · ["Facts, or Delusions"]   176
Walter de la Mare · ["Evidence of a Subliminal
World"]   177
William Lyon Phelps · [The "Iron Scot"
Stenographer]   178
Virginia Woolf · ["Henry James's Ghosts"]   179
F. L. Pattee · ["The Record of a Clinic"]   180

MAJOR CRITICISM: 1924–57

Harold C. Goddard · A Pre-Freudian Reading of
The Turn of the Screw   181

Edna Kenton · Henry James to the Ruminant Reader:
The Turn of the Screw 209

Martina Slaughter · Edmund Wilson and *The Turn
of the Screw* 211

Robert Heilman · "The Turn of the Screw" as Poem 214

Leon Edel · The Point of View 228

RECENT CRITICISM

Ignace Feuerlicht · "Erlkönig" and *The Turn of the
Screw* 235

Eric Solomon · The Return of the Screw 237

Mark Spilka · Turning the Freudian Screw: How
Not to Do It 245

S. P. Rosenbaum · A Note on John La Farge's Illustration for Henry James's *The Turn of the Screw* 254

John J. Enck · *The Turn of the Screw* & the Turn
of the Century 259

Robert Ginsberg · ["James's Criticism of James"] 269

Bibliography 274

Preface

"I take up my *own* pen again—the pen of all my old unforgettable efforts and sacred struggles. To myself—today—I need say no more. Large and full and high the future still opens. It is now indeed that I may do the work of my life. And I will." So Henry James addressed himself in January, 1895, finally realizing after five years of frustration that the theater was not congenial to his talents. His "work" was to be the writing of novels—long narratives, slowly unfolding through the focal point of a central consciousness. He hoped that short pieces—pot-boilers, tales, magazine stuff—were as much behind him as were his plays. He did not want even to have to serialize his long works, but he had to eat. Thus the next five years of his artistic life were curiously mixed: he was forced to depend on the magazines (only one tale and a novelette appeared first in book form), yet most of his writing was highly experimental, exploring the ways and means of mastering what would become the style and technique of his "major phase." Because of his continuing fame as the author of the immensely popular *Daisy Miller* (1878), James had no trouble placing his material, but this five-year period of transition cost him his wide audience. After 1900, the only novel first tied to serial publication was *The Ambassadors*, but that appeared in a literary magazine, not a popular one.

The Turn of the Screw is both typical of this period and yet exceptional. On the one hand, though commissioned by a popular magazine, it reflects James's moving toward his later phase of the involuted style and the technique of the restricted point of view; on the other hand, like *Daisy Miller*, it was immediately, successfully popular. "Why?" has been the critical question asked ever since. Is the tale merely "sensational," the plot simply forcing itself on us? Or is the process the reverse, the tale as it unfolds evoking responses from deep within us? Each reader must decide for himself.

The first section of the present volume contains the only critical edition of *The Turn of the Screw* ever published and is the first modern text to follow the New York Edition, the one which had James's final authority. Annotation of the text is light, and entirely reportorial, critical judgments being left to the reader. One aspect of the notes, however, should be emphasized: because the tale first appeared divided into five parts and twelve installments, these breaks have been recorded, for they provide a special rhythm and structure for that particular version of the tale. Following the text is a note on Textual History, which in turn is followed by a full selection of Textual Notes.

The Backgrounds and Sources section contains mainly statements from James's notebooks, letters, essays, and prefaces both on the ghost-story in general and *The Turn of the Screw* in particular, but does include as well four articles which suggest sources for the tale beyond those acknowledged by James. The three subsections of Essays in Criticism differ one from another: the first is a sampling of the early reactions to *The Turn of the Screw*; the second contains some of the landmarks of criticism which have surrounded the tale; and the last reveals a variety of recent, fresh approaches to James's story. Because a number of interesting essays on the tale, more than could be reprinted here, have lately appeared, the fourth part of the Bibliography is rather full, is arranged chronologically, and is annotated. Even so, this and the other three parts of the Bibliography are only selected. The first part indicates where some other bibliographies may be located; the second provides a list of good general introductions to James; the third concentrates on technical studies; and the fourth, as indicated, is devoted to studies of *The Turn of the Screw*.

In establishing and editing the text, in studying James, and in bringing together a selection of critical essays, I have received help from several quarters, for which I am most grateful. But special thanks are owed. Singly, I wish to thank Professor John J. Enck, Professor S. P. Rosenbaum, and Miss Martina Slaughter, each of whom kindly consented to write essays which are published here for the first time. Collectively, I wish to thank the ladies of the Department of English and of the Institute for Research in the Humanities of the University of Wisconsin, who patiently transformed an illegible manuscript into a legible typescript. Particularly, I wish to thank Professor Enck for his generosity at all stages in sharing with me his finer knowledge of James.

ROBERT KIMBROUGH

Madison, Wisconsin

The Text of
The Turn of the Screw

The Turn of the Screw

The story had held us, round the fire, sufficiently breathless, but except the obvious remark that it was gruesome, as on Christmas Eve in an old house a strange tale should essentially be, I remember no comment uttered till somebody happened to note it as the only case he had met in which such a visitation had fallen on a child. The case, I may mention, was that of an apparition in just such an old house as had gathered us for the occasion—an appearance, of a dreadful kind, to a little boy sleeping in the room with his mother and waking her up in the terror of it; waking her not to dissipate his dread and soothe him to sleep again, but to encounter also herself, before she had succeeded in doing so, the same sight that had shocked him. It was this observation that drew from Douglas—not immediately, but later in the evening—a reply that had the interesting consequence to which I call attention. Some one else told a story not particularly effective, which I saw he was not following. This I took for a sign that he had himself something to produce and that we should only have to wait. We waited in fact till two nights later; but that same evening, before we scattered, he brought out what was in his mind.

"I quite agree—in regard to Griffin's ghost, or whatever it was—that its appearing first to the little boy, at so tender an age, adds a particular touch. But it's not the first occurrence of its charming kind that I know to have been concerned with a child. If the child gives the effect another turn of the screw, what do you say to *two* children—?"

"We say of course," somebody exclaimed, "that two children give two turns! Also that we want to hear about them."

I can see Douglas there before the fire, to which he had got up to present his back, looking down at this converser with his hands in his pockets. "Nobody but me, till now, has ever heard. It 's quite too horrible." This was naturally declared by several voices to give the thing the utmost price, and our friend, with quiet art, prepared his triumph by turning his eyes over the rest of us and going on: "It 's beyond everything. Nothing at all that I know touches it."

"For sheer terror?" I remember asking.

He seemed to say it was n't so simple as that; to be really at a loss how to qualify it. He passed his hand over his eyes, made a

1

little wincing grimace. "For dreadful—dreadfulness!"

"Oh how delicious!" cried one of the women.

He took no notice of her; he looked at me, but as if, instead of me, he saw what he spoke of. "For general uncanny ugliness and horror and pain."

"Well then," I said, "just sit right down and begin."

He turned round to the fire, gave a kick to a log, watched it an instant. Then as he faced us again: "I can't begin. I shall have to send to town." There was a unanimous groan at this, and much reproach; after which, in his preoccupied way, he explained. "The story 's written. It 's in a locked drawer—it has not been out for years. I could write to my man and enclose the key; he could send down the packet as he finds it." It was to me in particular that he appeared to propound this—appeared almost to appeal for aid not to hesitate. He had broken a thickness of ice, the formation of many a winter; had had his reasons for a long silence. The others resented postponement, but it was just his scruples that charmed me. I adjured him to write by the first post and to agree with us for an early hearing; then I asked him if the experience in question had been his own. To this his answer was prompt. "Oh thank God, no!"

"And is the record yours? You took the thing down?"

"Nothing but the impression. I took that *here*"—he tapped his heart. "I 've never lost it."

"Then your manuscript—?"

"Is in old faded ink and in the most beautiful hand." He hung fire again. "A woman's. She has been dead these twenty years. She sent me the pages in question before she died." They were all listening now, and of course there was somebody to be arch, or at any rate to draw the inference. But if he put the inference by without a smile it was also without irritation. "She was a most charming person, but she was ten years older than I. She was my sister's governess," he quietly said. "She was the most agreeable woman I 've ever known in her position; she 'd have been worthy of any whatever. It was long ago, and this episode was long before. I was at Trinity, and I found her at home on my coming down the second summer. I was much there that year—it was a beautiful one; and we had, in her off-hours, some strolls and talks in the garden— talks in which she struck me as awfully clever and nice. Oh yes; don't grin: I liked her extremely and am glad to this day to think she liked me too. If she had n't she would n't have told me. She had never told any one. It was n't simply that she said so, but that I knew she had n't. I was sure; I could see. You'll easily judge why when you hear."

"Because the thing had been such a scare?"

He continued to fix me. "You'll easily judge," he repeated: "*you* will."

I fixed him too. "I see. She was in love."

He laughed for the first time. "You *are* acute. Yes, she was in love. That is she *had* been. That came out—she couldn't tell her story without its coming out. I saw it, and she saw I saw it; but neither of us spoke of it. I remember the time and the place—the corner of the lawn, the shade of the great beeches and the long hot summer afternoon. It wasn't a scene for a shudder; but oh—!" He quitted the fire and dropped back into his chair.

"You'll receive the packet Thursday morning?" I said.

"Probably not till the second post."

"Well then; after dinner—"

"You'll all meet me here?" He looked us round again. "Isn't anybody going?" It was almost the tone of hope.

"Everybody will stay!"

"*I* will—and *I* will!" cried the ladies whose departure had been fixed. Mrs. Griffin, however, expressed the need for a little more light. "Who was it she was in love with?"

"The story will tell," I took upon myself to reply.

"Oh I can't wait for the story!"

"The story *won't* tell," said Douglas; "not in any literal vulgar way."

"More's the pity then. That's the only way I ever understand."

"Won't *you* tell, Douglas?" somebody else required.

He sprang to his feet again. "Yes—to-morrow. Now I must go to bed. Good-night." And, quickly catching up a candlestick, he left us slightly bewildered. From our end of the great brown hall we heard his step on the stair; whereupon Mrs. Griffin spoke. "Well, if I don't know who she was in love with I know who *he* was."

"She was ten years older," said her husband.

"*Raison de plus* [1]—at that age! But it's rather nice, his long reticence."

"Forty years!" Griffin put in.

"With this outbreak at last."

"The outbreak," I returned, "will make a tremendous occasion of Thursday night"; and every one so agreed with me that in the light of it we lost all attention for everything else. The last story, however incomplete and like the mere opening of a serial, had been told; we handshook and "candlestuck," as somebody said, and went to bed.

I knew the next day that a letter containing the key had, by the first post, gone off to his London apartments; but in spite of—or

1. All the more reason.

perhaps just on account of—the eventual diffusion of this knowledge we quite let him alone till after dinner, till such an hour of the evening in fact as might best accord with the kind of emotion on which our hopes were fixed. Then he became as communicative as we could desire, and indeed gave us his best reason for being so. We had it from him again before the fire in the hall, as we had had our mild wonders of the previous night. It appeared that the narrative he had promised to read us really required for a proper intelligence a few words of prologue. Let me say here distinctly, to have done with it, that this narrative, from an exact transcript of my own made much later, is what I shall presently give. Poor Douglas, before his death—when it was in sight—committed to me the manuscript that reached him on the third of these days and that, on the same spot, with immense effect, he began to read to our hushed little circle on the night of the fourth. The departing ladies who had said they would stay did n't, of course, thank heaven, stay: they departed, in consequence of arrangements made, in a rage of curiosity, as they professed, produced by the touches with which he had already worked us up. But that only made his little final auditory more compact and select, kept it, round the hearth, subject to a common thrill.

The first of these touches conveyed that the written statement took up the tale at a point after it had, in a manner, begun. The fact to be in possession of was therefore that his old friend, the youngest of several daughters of a poor country parson, had at the age of twenty, on taking service for the first time in the school-room, come up to London, in trepidation, to answer in person an advertisement that had already placed her in brief correspondence with the advertiser. This person proved, on her presenting herself for judgment at a house in Harley Street that impressed her as vast and imposing—this prospective patron proved a gentleman, a bachelor in the prime of life, such a figure as had never risen, save in a dream or an old novel, before a fluttered anxious girl out of a Hampshire vicarage. One could easily fix his type; it never, happily, dies out. He was handsome and bold and pleasant, off-hand and gay and kind. He struck her, inevitably, as gallant and splendid, but what took her most of all and gave her the courage she afterwards showed was that he put the whole thing to her as a favour, an obligation he should gratefully incur. She figured him as rich, but as fearfully extravagant—saw him all in a glow of high fashion, of good looks, of expensive habits, of charming ways with women. He had for his town residence a big house filled with the spoils of travel and the trophies of the chase; but it was to his country home, an old family place in Essex, that he wished her immediately to proceed.[2]

2. Harley Street was a fashionable residential area at the "time" of the story; Hampshire lies SW of London; Essex, NE.

He had been left, by the death of his parents in India, guardian to a small nephew and a small niece, children of a younger, a military brother whom he had lost two years before. These children were, by the strangest of chances for a man in his position—a lone man without the right sort of experience or a grain of patience—very heavy on his hands. It had all been a great worry and, on his own part doubtless, a series of blunders, but he immensely pitied the poor chicks and had done all he could; had in particular sent them down to his other house, the proper place for them being of course the country, and kept them there from the first with the best people he could find to look after them, parting even with his own servants to wait on them and going down himself, whenever he might, to see how they were doing. The awkward thing was that they had practically no other relations and that his own affairs took up all his time. He had put them in possession of Bly, which was healthy and secure, and had placed at the head of their little establishment—but belowstairs only—an excellent woman, Mrs. Grose, whom he was sure his visitor would like and who had formerly been maid to his mother. She was now housekeeper and was also acting for the time as superintendent to the little girl, of whom, without children of her own, she was by good luck extremely fond. There were plenty of people to help, but of course the young lady who should go down as governess would be in supreme authority. She would also have, in holidays, to look after the small boy, who had been for a term at school—young as he was to be sent, but what else could be done?—and who, as the holidays were about to begin, would be back from one day to the other. There had been for the two children at first a young lady whom they had had the misfortune to lose. She had done for them quite beautifully—she was a most respectable person—till her death, the great awkwardness of which had, precisely, left no alternative but the school for little Miles. Mrs. Grose, since then, in the way of manners and things, had done as she could for Flora; and there were, further, a cook, a housemaid, a dairywoman, an old pony, an old groom and an old gardener, all likewise thoroughly respectable.

So far had Douglas presented his picture when some one put a question. "And what did the former governess die of? Of so much respectability?"

Our friend's answer was prompt. "That will come out. I don't anticipate."

"Pardon me—I thought that was just what you *are* doing."

"In her successor's place," I suggested, "I should have wished to learn if the office brought with it—"

"Necessary danger to life?" Douglas completed my thought. "She did wish to learn, and she did learn. You shall hear to-morrow what she learnt. Meanwhile of course the prospect struck her as slightly grim. She was young, untried, nervous: it was a vision of serious duties and little company, of really great loneliness. She hesitated —took a couple of days to consult and consider. But the salary offered much exceeded her modest measure, and on a second interview she faced the music, she engaged." And Douglas, with this, made a pause that, for the benefit of the company, moved me to throw in—

"The moral of which was of course the seduction exercised by the splendid young man. She succumbed to it."

He got up and, as he had done the night before, went to the fire, gave a stir to a log with his foot, then stood a moment with his back to us. "She saw him only twice."

"Yes, but that's just the beauty of her passion."

A little to my surprise, on this, Douglas turned round to me. "It *was* the beauty of it. There were others," he went on, "who had n't succumbed. He told her frankly all his difficulty—that for several applicants the conditions had been prohibitive. They were somehow simply afraid. It sounded dull—it sounded strange; and all the more so because of his main condition."

"Which was—?"

"That she should never trouble him—but never, never: neither appeal nor complain nor write about anything; only meet all questions herself, receive all moneys from his solicitor, take the whole thing over and let him alone. She promised to do this, and she mentioned to me that when, for a moment, disburdened, delighted, he held her hand, thanking her for the sacrifice, she already felt rewarded."

"But was that all her reward?" one of the ladies asked.

"She never saw him again."

"Oh!" said the lady; which, as our friend immediately again left us, was the only other word of importance contributed to the subject till, the next night, by the corner of the hearth, in the best chair, he opened the faded red cover of a thin old-fashioned gilt-edged album. The whole thing took indeed more nights than one, but on the first occasion the same lady put another question. "What 's your title?"

"I have n't one."

"Oh I have!" I said. But Douglas, without heeding me, had begun to read with a fine clearness that was like a rendering to the ear of the beauty of his author's hand.[3]

I

I remember the whole beginning as a succession of flights and drops, a little see-saw of the right throbs and the wrong. After rising,

---

3. The first of twelve installments which ran in *Collier's Weekly* in 1898 ended here (see Textual History).

in town, to meet his appeal I had at all events a couple of very bad days—found all my doubts bristle again, felt indeed sure I had made a mistake. In this state of mind I spent the long hours of bumping swinging coach that carried me to the stopping-place at which I was to be met by a vehicle from the house. This convenience, I was told, had been ordered, and I found, toward the close of the June afternoon, a commodious fly in waiting for me. Driving at that hour, on a lovely day, through a country the summer sweetness of which served as a friendly welcome, my fortitude revived and, as we turned into the avenue, took a flight that was probably but a proof of the point to which it had sunk. I suppose I had expected, or had dreaded, something so dreary that what greeted me was a good surprise. I remember as a thoroughly pleasant impression the broad clear front, its open windows and fresh curtains and the pair of maids looking out; I remember the lawn and the bright flowers and the crunch of my wheels on the gravel and the clustered tree-tops over which the rooks circled and cawed in the golden sky. The scene had a greatness that made a different affair from my own scant home, and there immediately appeared at the door, with a little girl in her hand, a civil person who dropped me as decent a curtsey as if I had been the mistress or a distinguished visitor. I had received in Harley Street a narrower notion of the place, and that, as I recalled it, made me think the proprietor still more of a gentleman, suggested that what I was to enjoy might be a matter beyond his promise.

I had no drop again till the next day, for I was carried triumphantly through the following hours by my introduction to the younger of my pupils. The little girl who accompanied Mrs. Grose affected me on the spot as a creature too charming not to make it a great fortune to have to do with her. She was the most beautiful child I had ever seen, and I afterwards wondered why my employer had n't made more of a point to me of this. I slept little that night —I was too much excited; and this astonished me too, I recollect, remained with me, adding to my sense of the liberality with which I was treated. The large impressive room, one of the best in the house, the great state bed, as I almost felt it, the figured full draperies, the long glasses in which, for the first time, I could see myself from head to foot, all struck me—like the wonderful appeal of my small charge—as so many things thrown in. It was thrown in as well, from the first moment, that I should get on with Mrs. Grose in a relation over which, on my way, in the coach, I fear I had rather brooded. The one appearance indeed that in this early outlook might have made me shrink again was that of her being so inordinately glad to see me. I felt within half an hour that she was so glad—stout simple plain clean wholesome woman—as to be positively on her guard against showing it too much. I wondered even then a little why she should wish *not* to show it, and that, with reflexion, with suspicion, might of course have made me uneasy.

But it was a comfort that there could be no uneasiness in a connexion with anything so beatific as the radiant image of my little girl, the vision of whose angelic beauty had probably more than anything else to do with the restlessness that, before morning, made me several times rise and wander about my room to take in the whole picture and prospect; to watch from my open window the faint summer dawn, to look at such stretches of the rest of the house as I could catch, and to listen, while in the fading dusk the first birds began to twitter, for the possible recurrence of a sound or two, less natural and not without but within, that I had fancied I heard. There had been a moment when I believed I recognised, faint and far, the cry of a child; there had been another when I found myself just consciously starting as at the passage, before my door, of a light footstep. But these fancies were not marked enough not to be thrown off, and it is only in the light, or the gloom, I should rather say, of other and subsequent matters that they now come back to me. To watch, teach, "form" little Flora would too evidently be the making of a happy and useful life. It had been agreed between us downstairs that after this first occasion I should have her as a matter of course at night, her small white bed being already arranged, to that end, in my room. What I had undertaken was the whole care of her, and she had remained just this last time with Mrs. Grose only as an effect of our consideration for my inevitable strangeness and her natural timidity. In spite of this timidity—which the child herself, in the oddest way in the world, had been perfectly frank and brave about, allowing it, without a sign of uncomfortable consciousness, with the deep sweet serenity indeed of one of Raphael's holy infants,[4] to be discussed, to be imputed to her and to determine us —I felt quite sure she would presently like me. It was part of what I already liked Mrs. Grose herself for, the pleasure I could see her feel in my admiration and wonder as I sat at supper with four tall candles and with my pupil, in a high chair and a bib, brightly facing me between them over bread and milk. There were naturally things that in Flora's presence could pass between us only as prodigious and gratified looks, obscure and roundabout allusions.

"And the little boy—does he look like her? Is he too so very remarkable?"

One would n't, it was already conveyed between us, too grossly flatter a child. "Oh Miss, *most* remarkable. If you think well of this one!"—and she stood there with a plate in her hand, beaming at our companion, who looked from one of us to the other with placid heavenly eyes that contained nothing to check us.

"Yes; if I do—?"

4. Raphael (1483–1520), Italian painter in the High Renaissance, renowned for his religious works.

"You *will* be carried away by the little gentleman!"

"Well, that, I think, is what I came for—to be carried away. I 'm afraid, however," I remember feeling the impulse to add, "I 'm rather easily carried away. I was carried away in London!"

I can still see Mrs. Grose's broad face as she took this in. "In Harley Street?"

"In Harley Street."

"Well, Miss, you 're not the first—and you won't be the last."

"Oh I 've no pretensions," I could laugh, "to being the only one. My other pupil, at any rate, as I understand, comes back to-morrow?"

"Not to-morrow—Friday, Miss. He arrives, as you did, by the coach, under care of the guard,[5] and is to be met by the same carriage."

I forthwith wanted to know if the proper as well as the pleasant and friendly thing would n't therefore be that on the arrival of the public conveyance I should await him with his little sister; a proposition to which Mrs. Grose assented so heartily that I somehow took her manner as a kind of comforting pledge—never falsified, thank heaven!—that we should on every question be quite at one. Oh she was glad I was there!

What I felt the next day was, I suppose, nothing that could be fairly called a reaction from the cheer of my arrival; it was probably at the most only a slight oppression produced by a fuller measure of the scale, as I walked round them, gazed up at them, took them in, of my new circumstances. They had, as it were, an extent and mass for which I had not been prepared and in the presence of which I found myself, freshly, a little scared not less than a little proud. Regular lessons, in this agitation, certainly suffered some wrong; I reflected that my first duty was, by the gentlest arts I could contrive, to win the child into the sense of knowing me. I spent the day with her out of doors; I arranged with her, to her great satisfaction, that it should be she, she only, who might show me the place. She showed it step by step and room by room and secret by secret, with droll delightful childish talk about it and with the result, in half an hour, of our becoming tremendous friends. Young as she was I was struck, throughout our little tour, with her confidence and courage, with the way, in empty chambers and dull corridors, on crooked staircases that made me pause and even on the summit of an old machicolated square tower [6] that made me dizzy, her morning music, her disposition to tell me so many more things than she asked, rang out and led me on. I have not seen Bly since the day I left it, and I dare say that to my present older and more informed eyes it would show a very reduced importance. But as my little conductress, with her hair

5. Mail guard.
6. Designed like a castle turret with firing apertures, or battlements.

of gold and her frock of blue, danced before me round corners and pattered down passages, I had the view of a castle of romance inhabited by a rosy sprite, such a place as would somehow, for diversion of the young idea, take all colour out of story-books and fairy-tales. Was n't it just a story-book over which I had fallen a-doze and a-dream? No; it was a big ugly antique but convenient house, embodying a few features of a building still older, half-displaced and half-utilised, in which I had the fancy of our being almost as lost as a handful of passengers in a great drifting ship. Well, I was strangely at the helm!

II

This came home to me when, two days later, I drove over with Flora to meet, as Mrs. Grose said, the little gentleman; and all the more for an incident that, presenting itself the second evening, had deeply disconcerted me. The first day had been, on the whole, as I have expressed, reassuring; but I was to see it wind up to a change of note. The postbag that evening—it came late—contained a letter for me which, however, in the hand of my employer, I found to be composed but of a few words enclosing another, addressed to himself, with a seal still unbroken. "This, I recognise, is from the head-master, and the head-master 's an awful bore. Read him please; deal with him; but mind you don't report. Not a word. I 'm off!" I broke the seal with a great effort—so great a one that I was a long time coming to it; took the unopened missive at last up to my room and only attacked it just before going to bed. I had better have let it wait till morning, for it gave me a second sleepless night. With no counsel to take, the next day, I was full of distress; and it finally got so the better of me that I determined to open myself at least to Mrs. Grose.

"What does it mean? The child's dismissed his school."

She gave me a look that I remarked at the moment; then, visibly, with a quick blankness, seemed to try to take it back. "But are n't they all—?"

"Sent home—yes. But only for the holidays. Miles may never go back at all."

Consciously, under my attention, she reddened. "They won't take him?"

"They absolutely decline."

At this she raised her eyes, which she had turned from me; I saw them fill with good tears. "What has he done?"

I cast about; then I judged best simply to hand her my document —which, however, had the effect of making her, without taking it, simply put her hands behind her. She shook her head sadly. "Such things are not for me, Miss."

My counsellor could n't read! I winced at my mistake, which I attentuated as I could, and opened the letter again to repeat it to her; then, faltering in the act and folding it up once more, I put it back in my pocket. "Is he really *bad?*"

The tears were still in her eyes. "Do the gentlemen say so?"

"They go into no particulars. They simply express their regret that it should be impossible to keep him. That can have but one meaning." Mrs. Grose listened with dumb emotion; she forbore to ask me what this meaning might be; so that, presently, to put the thing with some coherence and with the mere aid of her presence to my own mind, I went on: "That he 's an injury to the others."

At this, with one of the quick turns of simple folk, she suddenly flamed up. "Master Miles!—*him* an injury?"

There was such a flood of good faith in it that, though I had not yet seen the child, my very fears made me jump to the absurdity of the idea. I found myself, to meet my friend the better, offering it, on the spot, sarcastically. "To his poor little innocent mates!"

"It's too dreadful," cried Mrs. Grose, "to say such cruel things! Why he's scarce ten years old."

"Yes, yes; it would be incredible."

She was evidently grateful for such a profession. "See him, Miss, first. *Then* believe it!" I felt forthwith a new impatience to see him; it was the beginning of a curiosity that, all the next hours, was to deepen almost to pain. Mrs. Grose was aware, I could judge, of what she had produced in me, and she followed it up with assurance. "You might as well believe it of the little lady. Bless her," she added the next moment—"*look* at her!"

I turned and saw that Flora, whom, ten minutes before, I had established in the schoolroom with a sheet of white paper, a pencil and a copy of nice "round O's," now presented herself to view at the open door. She expressed in her little way an extraordinary detachment from disagreeable duties, looking at me, however, with a great childish light that seemed to offer it as a mere result of the affection she had conceived for my person, which had rendered necessary that she should follow me. I needed nothing more than this to feel the full force of Mrs. Grose's comparison, and, catching my pupil in my arms, covered her with kisses in which there was a sob of atonement.

None the less, the rest of the day, I watched for further occasion to approach my colleague, especially as, toward evening, I began to fancy she rather sought to avoid me. I overtook her, I remember, on the staircase; we went down together and at the bottom I detained her, holding her there with a hand on her arm. "I take what you said to me at noon as a declaration that *you 've* never known him to be bad."

She threw back her head; she had clearly by this time, and very honestly, adopted an attitude. "Oh never known him—I don't pretend *that!*"

I was upset again. "Then you *have* known him—?"

"Yes indeed, Miss, thank God!"

On reflexion I accepted this. "You mean that a boy who never is—?"

"Is no boy for *me!*"

I held her tighter. "You like them with the spirit to be naughty?" Then, keeping pace with her answer, "So do I!" I eagerly brought out. "But not to the degree to contaminate—"

"To contaminate?"—my big word left her at a loss.

I explained it. "To corrupt."

She stared, taking my meaning in; but it produced in her an odd laugh. "Are you afraid he 'll corrupt *you?*" She put the question with such a fine bold humour that with a laugh, a little silly doubtless, to match her own, I gave way for the time to the apprehension of ridicule.

But the next day, as the hour for my drive approached, I cropped up in another place. "What was the lady who was here before?"

"The last governess? She was also young and pretty—almost as young and almost as pretty, Miss, even as you."

"Ah then I hope her youth and her beauty helped her!" I recollect throwing off. "He seems to like us young and pretty!"

"Oh he *did*," Mrs. Grose assented: "it was the way he liked every one!" She had no sooner spoken indeed than she caught herself up. "I mean that 's *his* way—the master's."

I was struck. "But of whom did you speak first?"

She looked blank, but she coloured. "Why of *him*."

"Of the master?"

"Of who else?"

There was so obviously no one else that the next moment I had lost my impression of her having accidentally said more than she meant; and I merely asked what I wanted to know. "Did *she* see anything in the boy—?"

"That was n't right? She never told me."

I had a scruple, but I overcame it. "Was she careful—particular?"

Mrs. Grose appeared to try to be conscientious. "About some things—yes."

"But not about all?"

Again she considered. "Well, Miss—she 's gone. I won't tell tales."

"I quite understand your feeling," I hastened to reply; but I thought it after an instant not opposed to this concession to pursue: "Did she die here?"

"No—she went off."

I don't know what there was in this brevity of Mrs. Grose's that struck me as ambiguous. "Went off to die?" Mrs. Grose looked straight out of the window, but I felt that, hypothetically, I had a right to know what young persons engaged for Bly were expected to do. "She was taken ill, you mean, and went home?"

"She was not taken ill, so far as appeared, in this house. She left it, at the end of the year, to go home, as she said, for a short holiday, to which the time she had put in had certainly given her a right. We had then a young woman—a nursemaid who had stayed on and who was a good girl and clever; and *she* took the children altogether for the interval. But our young lady never came back, and at the very moment I was expecting her I heard from the master that she was dead."

I turned this over. "But of what?"

"He never told me! But please, Miss," said Mrs. Grose, "I must get to my work." [7]

III

Her thus turning her back on me was fortunately not, for my just preoccupations, a snub that could check the growth of our mutual esteem. We met, after I had brought home little Miles, more intimately than ever on the ground of my stupefaction, my general emotion: so monstrous was I then ready to pronounce it that such a child as had now been revealed to me should be under an interdict. I was a little late on the scene of his arrival, and I felt, as he stood wistfully looking out for me before the door of the inn at which the coach had put him down, that I had seen him on the instant, without and within, in the great glow of freshness, the same positive fragrance of purity, in which I had from the first moment seen his little sister. He was incredibly beautiful, and Mrs. Grose had put her finger on it: everything but a sort of passion of tenderness for him was swept away by his presence. What I then and there took him to my heart for was something divine that I have never found to the same degree in any child— his indescribable little air of knowing nothing in the world but love. It would have been impossible to carry a bad name with a greater sweetness of innocence, and by the time I had got back to Bly with him I remained merely bewildered—so far, that is, as I was not outraged—by the sense of the horrible letter locked up in one of the drawers of my room. As soon as I could compass a private word with Mrs. Grose I declared to her that it was grotesque.

She promptly understood me. "You mean the cruel charge—?"

7. Second weekly installment ended here.

"It does n't live an instant. My dear woman, *look* at him!"

She smiled at my pretension to have discovered his charm. "I assure you, Miss, I do nothing else! What will you say then?" she immediately added.

"In answer to the letter?" I had made up my mind. "Nothing at all."

"And to his uncle?"

I was incisive. "Nothing at all."

"And to the boy himself?"

I was wonderful. "Nothing at all."

She gave with her apron a great wipe to her mouth. "Then I 'll stand by you. We 'll see it out."

"We 'll see it out!" I ardently echoed, giving her my hand to make it a vow.

She held me there a moment, then whisked up her apron again with her detached hand. "Would you mind, Miss, if I used the freedom—"

"To kiss me? No!" I took the good creature in my arms and after we had embraced like sisters felt still more fortified and indignant.

This at all events was for the time: a time so full that as I recall the way it went it reminds me of all the art I now need to make it a little distinct. What I look back at with amazement is the situation I accepted. I had undertaken, with my companion, to see it out, and I was under a charm apparently that could smooth away the extent and the far and difficult connexions of such an effort. I was lifted aloft on a great wave of infatuation and pity. I found it simple, in my ignorance, my confusion and perhaps my conceit, to assume that I could deal with a boy whose education for the world was all on the point of beginning. I am unable even to remember at this day what proposal I framed for the end of his holidays and the resumption of his studies. Lessons with me indeed, that charming summer, we all had a theory that he was to have; but I now feel that for weeks the lessons must have been rather my own. I learnt something—at first certainly— that had not been one of the teachings of my small smothered life; learnt to be amused, and even amusing, and not to think for the morrow. It was the first time, in a manner, that I had known space and air and freedom, all the music of summer and all the mystery of nature. And then there was consideration—and consideration was sweet. Oh it was a trap—not designed but deep—to my imagination, to my delicacy, perhaps to my vanity; to whatever in me was most excitable. The best way to picture it all is to say that I was off my guard. They gave me so little trouble—they were of a gentleness so extraordinary. I used to speculate—but even this with a dim disconnectedness—as to how the rough future (for all futures are rough!) would handle them and might bruise them. They had the bloom of health and happiness; and yet, as if I had been in charge of a pair of little grandees, of princes of the blood, for whom everything, to be right, would have to be fenced about and ordered and arranged, the only form that in my fancy the after-years could take for them was that of a romantic, a really royal extension of the garden and the park. It may be of course above all that what suddenly broke into this gives the previous time a charm of stillness—that hush in which something gathers or crouches. The change was actually like the spring of a beast.

In the first weeks the days were long; they often, at their finest, gave me what I used to call my own hour, the hour when, for my pupils, tea-time and bed-time having come and gone, I had before my final retirement a small interval alone. Much as I liked my companions this hour was the thing in the day I liked most; and I liked it best of all when, as the light faded—or rather, I should say, the day lingered and the last calls of the last birds sounded, in a flushed sky, from the old trees—I could take a turn into the grounds and enjoy, almost with a sense of property that amused and flattered me, the beauty and dignity of the place. It was a pleasure at these moments to feel myself tranquil and justified; doubtless perhaps also to reflect that by my discretion, my quiet good sense and general high propriety, I was giving pleasure—if he ever thought of it!—to the person to whose pressure I had yielded. What I was doing was what he had earnestly hoped and directly asked of me, and that I *could*, after all, do it proved even a greater joy than I had expected. I dare say I fancied myself in short a remarkable young woman and took comfort in the faith that this would more publicly appear. Well, I needed to be remarkable to offer a front to the remarkable things that presently gave their first sign.

It was plump, one afternoon, in the middle of my very hour: the children were tucked away and I had come out for my stroll. One of the thoughts that, as I don't in the least shrink now from noting, used to be with me in these wanderings was that it would be as charming as a charming story suddenly to meet some one. Some one would appear there at the turn of a path and would stand before me and smile and approve. I did n't ask more than that—I only asked that he should *know*; and the only way to be sure he knew would be to see it, and the kind light of it, in his handsome face. That was exactly present to me—by which I mean the face was—when, on the first of these occasions, at the end of a long June day, I stopped short on emerging from one of the plantations and coming into view of the house. What arrested me on the spot—and with a shock much greater than any vision had allowed for—was the sense that my imagination had, in a flash, turned real. He did stand there!—but high up, beyond the lawn and at the very top of the tower to which, on that first morning, little Flora had conducted me. This tower was one of a pair— square incongruous crenellated structures [8]—that were distinguished, for some reason, though I could see little difference, as the new and the old. They flanked opposite ends of the house and were probably architectural absurdities, redeemed in a measure indeed by not being wholly disengaged nor of a height too pretentious, dating, in their gingerbread antiquity, from a romantic revival that was already a respectable past. I admired them, had fancies about them, for we could all profit in a degree, especially when they loomed through the dusk, by the grandeur of their actual battlements; yet it was not at such an elevation that the figure I had so often invoked seemed most in place.

It produced in me, this figure, in the clear twilight, I remember, two distinct gasps of emotion, which were, sharply, the shock of my first and that of my second surprise. My second was a violent perception of the mistake of my first: the man who met my eyes was not the person I had precipitately supposed. There came to me thus a bewilderment of vision of which, after these years, there is no living view that I can hope to give. An unknown man in a lonely place is a permitted object of fear to a young woman privately bred; and the figure that faced me was—a few more seconds assured me—as little any one else I knew as it was the image that had been in my mind. I had not seen it in Harley Street—I had not seen it anywhere. The place moreover, in the strangest way in the world, had on the instant and by the very fact of its appearance become a solitude. To me at least, making my statement here with a deliberation with which I have never made it, the whole feeling of the moment returns. It was as if, while I took in, what I did take in, all the rest of the scene had been stricken with death. I can hear again, as I write, the intense hush in which the sounds of evening dropped. The rooks stopped cawing in the golden sky and the friendly hour lost for the unspeakable minute all its voice. But there was no other change in nature, unless indeed it were a change that I saw with a stranger sharpness. The gold was still in the sky, the clearness in the air, and the man who looked at me over the battlements was as definite as a picture in a frame. That's how I thought, with extraordinary quickness, of each person he might have been and that he was n't. We were confronted across our distance quite long enough for me to ask myself with intensity who then he was and to feel, as an effect of my inability to say,

8. See note 6, above.

a wonder that in a few seconds more became intense.

The great question, or one of these, is afterwards, I know, with regard to certain matters, the question of how long they have lasted. Well, this matter of mine, think what you will of it, lasted while I caught at a dozen possibilities, none of which made a difference for the better, that I could see, in there having been in the house —and for how long, above all?—a person of whom I was in ignorance. It lasted while I just bridled a little with the sense of how my office seemed to require that there should be no such ignorance and no such person. It lasted while this visitant, at all events— and there was a touch of the strange freedom, as I remember, in the sign of familiarity of his wearing no hat—seemed to fix me, from his position, with just the question, just the scrutiny through the fading light, that his own presence provoked. We were too far apart to call to each other, but there was a moment at which, at shorter range, some challenge between us, breaking the hush, would have been the right result of our straight mutual stare. He was in one of the angles, the one away from the house, very erect, as it struck me, and with both hands on the ledge. So I saw him as I see the letters I form on this page; then, exactly, after a minute, as if to add to the spectacle, he slowly changed his place—passed, looking at me hard all the while, to the opposite corner of the platform. Yes, it was intense to me that during this transit he never took his eyes from me, and I can see at this moment the way his hand, as he went, moved from one of the crenellations to the next. He stopped at the other corner, but less long, and even as he turned away still markedly fixed me. He turned away; that was all I knew.[9]

IV

It was not that I did n't wait, on this occasion, for more, since I was as deeply rooted as shaken. Was there a "secret" at Bly— a mystery of Udolpho or an insane, an unmentionable relative kept in unsuspected confinement? [1] I can't say how long I turned it over, or how long, in a confusion of curiosity and dread, I remained where I had had my collision; I only recall that when I re-entered the house darkness had quite closed in. Agitation, in the interval, certainly had held me and driven me, for I must, in circling about the place, have walked three miles; but I was to be later on so much more overwhelmed that this mere dawn of alarm was a comparatively human chill. The most singular part of it in fact —singular as the rest had been—was the part I became, in the

9. Third weekly installment and "Part First" ended here.
1. *The Mysteries of Udolpho* (1794) by Anne Radcliffe (1764–1823), a ghost-novel in which the heroine is carried off to a lonely castle in the Apennines; the alternative describes the situation which confronts the governess-heroine of Charlotte Brontë's *Jane Eyre* (1847).

hall, aware of in meeting Mrs. Grose. This picture comes back to me in the general train—the impression, as I received it on my return, of the wide white panelled space, bright in the lamplight and with its portraits and red carpet, and of the good surprised look of my friend, which immediately told me she had missed me. It came to me straightway, under her contact, that, with plain heartiness, mere relieved anxiety at my appearance, she knew nothing whatever that could bear upon the incident I had there ready for her. I had not suspected in advance that her comfortable face would pull me up, and I somehow measured the importance of what I had seen by my thus finding myself hesitate to mention it. Scarce anything in the whole history seems to me so odd as this fact that my real beginning of fear was one, as I may say, with the instinct of sparing my companion. On the spot, accordingly, in the pleasant hall and with her eyes on me, I, for a reason that I could n't then have phrased, achieved an inward revolution—offered a vague pretext for my lateness and, with the plea of the beauty of the night and of the heavy dew and wet feet, went as soon as possible to my room.

Here it was another affair; here, for many days after, it was a queer affair enough. There were hours, from day to day—or at least there were moments, snatched even from clear duties—when I had to shut myself up to think. It was n't so much yet that I was more nervous than I could bear to be as that I was remarkably afraid of becoming so; for the truth I had now to turn over was simply and clearly the truth that I could arrive at no account whatever of the visitor with whom I had been so inexplicably and yet, as it seemed to me, so intimately concerned. It took me little time to see that I might easily sound, without forms of enquiry and without exciting remark, any domestic complication. The shock I had suffered must have sharpened all my senses;. I felt sure, at the end of three days and as the result of mere closer attention, that I had not been practised upon by the servants nor made the object of any "game." Of whatever it was that I knew nothing was known around me. There was but one sane inference: some one had taken a liberty rather monstrous. That was what, repeatedly, I dipped into my room and locked the door to say to myself. We had been, collectively, subject to an intrusion; some unscrupulous traveller, curious in old houses, had made his way in unobserved, enjoyed the prospect from the best point of view and then stolen out as he came. If he had given me such a bold hard stare, that was but a part of his indiscretion. The good thing, after all, was that we should surely see no more of him.

This was not so good a thing, I admit, as not to leave me to judge that what, essentially, made nothing else much signify was

simply my charming work. My charming work was just my life
with Miles and Flora, and through nothing· could I so like it as
through feeling that to throw myself into it was to throw myself
out of my trouble. The attraction of my small charges was a constant joy, leading me to wonder afresh at the vanity of my original
fears, the distaste I had begun by entertaining for the probable
grey prose of my office. There was to be no grey prose, it appeared,
and no long grind; so how could work not be charming that
presented itself as daily beauty? It was all the romance of the
nursery and the poetry of the schoolroom. I don't mean by this
of course that we studied only fiction and verse; I mean that I can
express no otherwise the sort of interest my companions inspired.
How can I describe that except by saying that instead of growing
deadly used to them—and it 's a marvel for a governess: I call
the sisterhood to witness!—I made constant fresh discoveries. There
was one direction, assuredly, in which these discoveries stopped:
deep obscurity continued to cover the region of the boy's conduct
at school. It had been promptly given me, I have noted, to face
that mystery without a pang. Perhaps even it would be nearer the
truth to say that—without a word—he himself had cleared it up.
He had made the whole charge absurd. My conclusion bloomed
there with the real rose-flush of his innocence: he was only too
fine and fair for the little horrid unclean school-world, and he had
paid a price for it. I reflected acutely that the sense of such individual differences, such superiorities of quality, always, on the part
of the majority—which could include even stupid sordid head-
masters—turns infallibly to the vindictive.

Both the children had a gentleness—it was their only fault, and
it never made Miles a muff [2]—that kept them (how shall I express it?) almost impersonal and certainly quite unpunishable. They
were like those cherubs of the anecdote who had—morally at any
rate—nothing to whack! [3] I remember feeling with Miles in especial
as if he had had, as it were, nothing to call even an infinitesimal
history. We expect of a small child scant enough "antecedents,"
but there was in this beautiful little boy something extraordinarily
sensitive, yet extraordinarily happy, that, more than in any creature
of his age I have seen, struck me as beginning anew each day. He
had never for a second suffered. I took this as a direct disproof
of his having really been chastised. If he had been wicked he
would have "caught" it, and I should have caught it by the rebound
—I should have found the trace, should have felt the wound and
the dishonour. I could reconstitute nothing at all, and he was therefore an angel. He never spoke of his school, never mentioned a

2. **English children's slang for "sissy".**   3. **The ethereal nature of angels has long
been the basis for countless anecdotes.**

comrade or a master; and I, for my part, was quite too much disgusted to allude to them. Of course I was under the spell, and the wonderful part is that, even at the time, I perfectly knew I was. But I gave myself up to it; it was an antidote to any pain, and I had more pains than one. I was in receipt in these days of disturbing letters from home, where things were not going well. But with this joy of my children what things in the world mattered? That was the question I used to put to my scrappy retirements. I was dazzled by their loveliness.

There was a Sunday—to get on—when it rained with such force and for so many hours that there could be no procession to church; in consequence of which, as the day declined, I had arranged with Mrs. Grose that, should the evening show improvement, we would attend together the late service. The rain happily stopped, and I prepared for our walk, which, through the park and by the good road to the village, would be a matter of twenty minutes. Coming downstairs to meet my colleague in the hall, I remembered a pair of gloves that had required three stitches and that had received them—with a publicity perhaps not edifying—while I sat with the children at their tea, served on Sundays, by exception, in that cold clean temple of mahogany and brass, the "grown-up" dining-room. The gloves had been dropped there, and I turned in to recover them. The day was grey enough, but the afternoon light still lingered, and it enabled me, on crossing the threshold, not only to recognise, on a chair near the wide window, then closed, the articles I wanted, but to become aware of a person on the other side of the window and looking straight in. One step into the room had sufficed; my vision was instantaneous; it was all there. The person looking straight in was the person who had already appeared to me. He appeared thus again with I won't say greater distinctness, for that was impossible, but with a nearness that represented a forward stride in our intercourse and made me, as I met him, catch my breath and turn cold. He was the same—he was the same, and seen, this time, as he had been seen before, from the waist up, the window, though the dining-room was on the ground floor, not going down to the terrace on which he stood. His face was close to the glass, yet the effect of this better view was, strangely, just to show me how intense the former had been. He remained but a few seconds—long enough to convince me he also saw and recognised; but it was as if I had been looking at him for years and had known him always. Something, however, happened this time that had not happened before; his stare into my face, through the glass and across the room, was as deep and hard as then, but it quitted me for a moment during which I could still watch it, see it fix successively several other things. On the spot there came to me the added shock of a certitude that it was not for me he had come.

He had come for some one else.

The flash of this knowledge—for it was knowledge in the midst of dread—produced in me the most extraordinary effect, starting, as I stood there, a sudden vibration of duty and courage. I say courage because I was beyond all doubt already far gone. I bounded straight out of the door again, reached that of the house, got in an instant upon the drive and, passing along the terrace as fast as I could rush, turned a corner and came full in sight. But it was in sight of nothing now—my visitor had vanished. I stopped, almost dropped, with the real relief of this; but I took in the whole scene—I gave him time to reappear. I call it time, but how long was it? I can't speak to the purpose to-day of the duration of these things. That kind of measure must have left me: they could n't have lasted as they actually appeared to me to last. The terrace and the whole place, the lawn and the garden beyond it, all I could see of the park, were empty with a great emptiness. There were shrubberies and big trees, but I remember the clear assurance I felt that none of them concealed him. He was there or was not there: not there if I did n't see him. I got hold of this; then, instinctively, instead of returning as I had come, went to the window. It was confusedly present to me that I ought to place myself where he had stood. I did so; I applied my face to the pane and looked, as he had looked, into the room. As if, at this moment, to show me exactly what his range had been, Mrs. Grose, as I had done for himself just before, came in from the hall. With this I had the full image of a repetition of what had already occurred. She saw me as I had seen my own visitant; she pulled up short as I had done; I gave her something of the shock that I had received. She turned white, and this made me ask myself if I had blanched as much. She stared, in short, and retreated just on *my* lines, and I knew she had then passed out and come round to me and that I should presently meet her. I remained where I was, and while I waited I thought of more things than one. But there 's only one I take space to mention. I wondered why *she* should be scared.

V

Oh she let me know as soon as, round the corner of the house, she loomed again into view. "What in the name of goodness is the matter—?" She was now flushed and out of breath.

I said nothing till she came quite near. "With me?" I must have made a wonderful face. "Do I show it?"

"You 're as white as a sheet. You look awful."

I considered; I could meet on this, without scruple, any degree of innocence. My need to respect the bloom of Mrs. Grose's had dropped, without a rustle, from my shoulders, and if I wavered for the instant it was not with what I kept back. I put out my hand to her and she took it; I held her hard a little, liking to feel her close to me. There was a kind of support in the shy heave of her surprise. "You came for me for church, of course, but I can't go."

"Has anything happened?"

"Yes. You must know now. Did I look very queer?"

"Through this window? Dreadful!"

"Well," I said, "I've been frightened." Mrs. Grose's eyes expressed plainly that *she* had no wish to be, yet also that she knew too well her place not to be ready to share with me any marked inconvenience. Oh it was quite settled that she *must* share! "Just what you saw from the dining-room a minute ago was the effect of that. What *I* saw—just before—was much worse."

Her hand tightened. "What was it?"

"An extraordinary man. Looking in."

"What extraordinary man?"

"I have n't the least idea."

Mrs. Grose gazed round us in vain. "Then where is he gone?"

"I know still less."

"Have you see him before?"

"Yes—once. On the old tower."

She could only look at me harder. "Do you mean he 's a stranger?"

"Oh very much!"

"Yet you did n't tell me?"

"No—for reasons. But now that you 've guessed—"

Mrs. Grose's round eyes encountered this charge. "Ah I have n't guessed!" she said very simply. "How can I if *you* don't imagine?"

"I don't in the very least."

"You've seen him nowhere but on the tower?"

"And on this spot just now."

Mrs. Grose looked round again. "What was he doing on the tower?"

"Only standing there and looking down at me."

She thought a minute. "Was he a gentleman?"

I found I had no need to think. "No." She gazed in deeper wonder. "No."

"Then nobody about the place? Nobody from the village?"

"Nobody—nobody. I did n't tell you, but I made sure."

She breathed a vague relief: this was, oddly, so much to the good. It only went indeed a little way. "But if he is n't a gentleman—"

"What *is* he? He's a horror."

"A horror?"

"He 's—God help me if I know *what* he is!"

Mrs. Grose looked round once more; she fixed her eyes on the duskier distance and then, pulling herself together, turned to me with full inconsequence. "It 's time we should be at church."

"Oh I 'm not fit for church!"

"Won't it do you good?"

"It won't do *them*—!" I nodded at the house.

"The children?"

"I can't leave them now."

"You 're afraid—"

I spoke boldly "I 'm afraid of *him*."

Mrs. Grose's large face showed me, at this, for the first time, the far-away faint glimmer of a consciousness more acute: I somehow made out in it the delayed dawn of an idea I myself had not given her and that was as yet quite obscure to me. It comes back to me that I thought instantly of this as something I could get from her; and I felt it to be connected with the desire she presently showed to know more. "When was it—on the tower?"

"About the middle of the month. At this same hour."

"Almost at dark," said Mrs. Grose.

"Oh no, not nearly. I saw him as I see you."

"Then how did he get in?"

"And how did he get out?" I laughed. "I had no opportunity to ask him! This evening, you see," I pursued, "he has not been able to get in."

"He only peeps?"

"I hope it will be confined to that!" She had now let go my hand; she turned away a little. I waited an instant; then I brought out: "Go to church. Goodbye. I must watch."

Slowly she faced me again. "Do you fear for them?"

We met in another long look. "Don't *you*?" Instead of answering she came nearer to the window and, for a minute, applied her face to the glass. "You see how he could see," I meanwhile went on.

She did n't move. "How long was he here?"

"Till I came out. I came to meet him."

Mrs. Grose at last turned round, and there was still more in her face. "I could n't have come out."

"Neither could I!" I laughed again. "But I did come. I 've my duty."

"So have I mine," she replied; after which she added: "What 's he like?"

"I 've been dying to tell you. But he 's like nobody."

"Nobody?" she echoed.

"He has no hat." Then seeing in her face that she already, in this, with a deeper dismay, found a touch of picture, I quickly added stroke to stroke. "He has red hair, very red, close-curling, and a pale face, long in shape, with straight good features and little rather queer whiskers that are as red as his hair. His eyebrows are somehow darker; they look particularly arched and as if they might move a good deal. His eyes are sharp, strange—awfully; but I only know clearly that they 're rather small and very fixed. His mouth 's wide, and his lips are thin, except for his little whiskers he 's quite clean-shaven. He gives me a sort of sense of looking like an actor."

"An actor!" It was impossible to resemble one less, at least, than Mrs. Grose at that moment.

"I 've never seen one, but so I suppose them. He 's tall, active, erect," I continued, "but never—no, never!—a gentleman."

My companion's face had blanched as I went on; her round eyes started and her mild mouth gaped. "A gentleman?" she gasped, confounded, stupefied: "a gentleman *he?*"

"You know him then?"

She visibly tried to hold herself. "But he *is* handsome?"

I saw the way to help her. "Remarkably!"

"And dressed—?"

"In somebody's clothes. They 're smart, but they 're not his own."

She broke into a breathless affirmative groan. "They 're the master's!"

I caught it up. "You *do* know him?"

She faltered but a second. "Quint!" she cried.

"Quint?"

"Peter Quint—his own man, his valet, when he was here!"

"When the master was?"

Gaping still, but meeting me, she pieced it all together. "He never wore his hat, but he did wear—well, there were waistcoats missed! They were both here—last year. Then the master went, and Quint was alone."

I followed, but halting a little. "Alone?"

"Alone with *us.*" Then as from a deeper depth, "In charge," she added.

"And what became of him?"

She hung fire so long that I was still more mystified. "He went too," she brought out at last.

"Went where?"

Her expression, at this, became extraordinary. "God knows where! He died."

"Died?" I almost shrieked.

She seemed fairly to square herself, plant herself more firmly to express the wonder of it. "Yes. Mr. Quint's dead." [4]

4. Fourth weekly installment ended here.

VI

It took of course more than that particular passage to place us together in presence of what we had now to live with as we could, my dreadful liability to impressions of the order so vividly exemplified, and my companion's knowledge henceforth—a knowledge half consternation and half compassion—of that liability. There had been this evening, after the revelation that left me for an hour so prostrate—there had been for either of us no attendance on any service but a little service of tears and vows, of prayers and promises, a climax to the series of mutual challenges and pledges that had straightway ensued on our retreating together to the schoolroom and shutting ourselves up there to have everything out. The result of our having everything out was simply to reduce our situation to the last rigour of its elements. She herself had seen nothing, not the shadow of a shadow, and nobody in the house but the governess was in the governess's plight; yet she accepted without directly impugning my sanity the truth as I gave it to her, and ended by showing me on this ground an awestricken tenderness, a deference to my more than questionable privilege, of which the very breath has remained with me as that of the sweetest of human charities.

What was settled between us accordingly that night was that we thought we might bear things together; and I was not even sure that in spite of her exemption it was she who had the best of the burden. I knew at this hour, I think, as well as I knew later, what I was capable of meeting to shelter my pupils; but it took me some time to be wholly sure of what my honest comrade was prepared for to keep terms with so stiff an agreement. I was queer company enough—quite as queer as the company I received; but as I trace over what we went through I see how much common ground we must have found in the one idea that, by good fortune, *could* steady us. It was the idea, the second movement, that led me straight out, as I may say, of the inner chamber of my dread. I could take the air in the court, at least, and there Mrs. Grose could join me. Perfectly can I recall now the particular way strength came to me before we separated for the night. We had gone over and over every feature of what I had seen.

"He was looking for some one else, you say—some one who was not you?"

"He was looking for little Miles." A portentous clearness now possessed me. "*That's* whom he was looking for."

"But how do you know?"

"I know, I know, I know!" My exaltation grew. "And *you* know, my dear!"

She did n't deny this, but I required, I felt, not even so much telling as that. She took it up again in a moment. "What if *he* should see him?"

"Little Miles? That's what he wants!"

She looked immensely scared again. "The child?"

"Heaven forbid! The man. He wants to appear to *them*." That he might was an awful conception, and yet somehow I could keep it at bay; which moreover, as we lingered there, was what I succeeded in practically proving. I had an absolute certainty that I should see again what I had already seen, but something within me said that by offering myself bravely as the sole subject of such experience, by accepting, by inviting, by surmounting it all, I should serve as an expiatory victim and guard the tranquillity of the rest of the household. The children in special I should thus fence about and absolutely save. I recall one of the last things I said that night to Mrs. Grose.

"It does strike me that my pupils have never mentioned—!"

She looked at me hard as I musingly pulled up. "His having been here and the time they were with him?"

"The time they were with him, and his name, his presence, his history, in any way. They 've never alluded to it."

"Oh the little lady does n't remember. She never heard or knew."

"The circumstances of his death?" I thought with some intensity. "Perhaps not. But Miles would remember—Miles would know."

"Ah don't try him!" broke from Mrs. Grose.

I returned her the look she had given me. "Don't be afraid." I continued to think. "It *is* rather odd."

"That he has never spoken of him?"

"Never by the least reference. And you tell me they were 'great friends.'"

"Oh it was n't *him!*" Mrs. Grose with emphasis declared. "It was Quint's own fancy. To play with him, I mean—to spoil him." She paused a moment; then she added: "Quint was much too free."

This gave me, straight from my vision of his face—*such* a face! —a sudden sickness of disgust. "Too free with *my* boy?"

"Too free with every one!"

I forbore for the moment to analyse this description further than by the reflexion that a part of it applied to several of the members of the household, of the half-dozen maids and men who were still of our small colony. But there was everything, for our apprehension, in the lucky fact that no discomfortable legend, no perturbation of scullions, had ever, within any one's memory, attached to the kind old place. It had neither bad name nor ill fame, and

Mrs. Grose, most apparently, only desired to cling to me and to quake in silence. I even put her, the very last thing of all, to the test. It was when, at midnight, she had her hand on the schoolroom door to take leave. "I *have it* from you then—for it 's of great importance—that he was definitely and admittedly bad?"

"Oh not admittedly. *I* knew it—but the master did n't."

"And you never told him?"

"Well, he did n't like tale-bearing—he hated complaints. He was terribly short with anything of that kind, and if people were all right to *him*—"

"He would n't be bothered with more?" This squared well enough with my impression of him: he was not a trouble-loving gentleman, nor so very particular perhaps about some of the company he himself kept. All the same, I pressed my informant. "I promise you *I* would have told!"

She felt my discrimination. "I dare say I was wrong. But really I was afraid."

"Afraid of what?"

"Of things that man could do. Quint was so clever—he was so deep."

I took this in still more than I probably showed. "You were n't afraid of anything else? Not of his effect—?"

"His effect?" she repeated with a face of anguish and waiting while I faltered.

"On innocent little precious lives. They were in your charge."

"No, they were n't in mine!" she roundly and distressfully returned. "The master believed in him and placed him here because he was supposed not to be quite in health and the country air so good for him. So he had everything to say. Yes"—she let me have it—"even about *them*."

"Them—that creature?" I had to smother a kind of howl. "And you could bear it?"

"No. I could n't—and I can't now!" And the poor woman burst into tears.

A rigid control, from the next day, was, as I have said, to follow them; yet how often and how passionately, for a week, we came back together to the subject! Much as we had discussed it that Sunday night, I was, in the immediate later hours in especial—for it may be imagined whether I slept—still haunted with the shadow of something she had not told me. I myself had kept back nothing, but there was a word Mrs. Grose had kept back. I was sure moreover by morning that this was not from a failure of frankness, but because on every side there were fears. It seems to me indeed, in raking it all over, that by the time the morrow's sun was high I had restlessly read into the facts before us almost all the meaning they were to receive from subsequent and more cruel occurrences. What they gave me above all was just the sinister figure of the living man—the dead one would keep a while!—and of the months he had continuously passed at Bly, which, added up, made a formidable stretch. The limit of this evil time had arrived only when, on the dawn of a winter's morning, Peter Quint was found, by a labourer going to early work, stone dead on the road from the village: a catastrophe explained—superficially at least—by a visible wound to his head; such a wound as might have been produced (and as, on the final evidence, *had* been) by a fatal slip, in the dark and after leaving the public-house, on the steepish icy slope, a wrong path altogether, at the bottom of which he lay. The icy slope, the turn mistaken at night and in liquor, accounted for much —practically, in the end and after the inquest and boundless chatter, for everything; but there had been matters in his life, strange passages and perils, secret disorders, vices more than suspected, that would have accounted for a good deal more.

I scarce know how to put my story into words that shall be a credible picture of my state of mind; but I was in these days literally able to find a joy in the extraordinary flight of heroism the occasion demanded of me. I now saw that I had been asked for a service admirable and difficult; and there would be a greatness in letting it be seen—oh in the right quarter!—that I could succeed where many another girl might have failed. It was an immense help to me—I confess I rather applaud myself as I look back!—that I saw my response so strongly and so simply. I was there to protect and defend the little creatures in the world the most bereaved and the most loveable, the appeal of whose helplessness had suddenly become only too explicit, a deep constant ache of one's own engaged affection. We were cut off, really, together; we were united in our danger. They had nothing but me, and I—well, I had *them*. It was in short a magnificent chance. This chance presented itself to me in an image richly material. I was a screen—I was to stand before them. The more I saw the less they would. I began to watch them in a stifled suspense, a disguised tension, that might well, had it continued too long, have turned to something like madness. What saved me, as I now see, was that it turned to another matter altogether. It did n't last as suspense—it was superseded by horrible proofs. Proofs, I say, yes—from the moment I really took hold.

This moment dated from an afternoon hour that I happened to spend in the grounds with the younger of my pupils alone. We had left Miles indoors, on the red cushion of a deep window-seat; he had wished to finish a book, and I had been glad to encourage a purpose so laudable in a young man whose only defect was a certain ingenuity of restlessness. His sister, on the contrary, had been alert to come out, and I strolled with her half an hour, seeking the shade, for the sun was still high and the day exceptionally warm. I was aware afresh with her, as we went, of how, like her brother, she contrived—it was the charming thing in both children—to let me alone without appearing to drop me and to accompany me without appearing to oppress. They were never importunate and yet never listless. My attention to them all really went to seeing them amuse themselves immensely without me: this was a spectacle they seemed actively to prepare and that employed me as an active admirer. I walked in a world of their invention—they had no occasion whatever to draw upon mine; so that my time was taken only with being for them some remarkable person or thing that the game of the moment required and that was merely, thanks to my superior, my exalted stamp, a happy and highly distinguished sinecure. I forget what I was on the present occasion; I only remember that I was something very important and very quiet and that Flora was playing very hard. We were on the edge of the lake, and, as we had lately begun geography, the lake was the Sea of Azof.[5]

Suddenly, amid these elements, I became aware that on the other side of the Sea of Azof we had an interested spectator. The way this knowledge gathered in me was the strangest thing in the world—the strangest, that is, except the very much stranger in which it quickly merged itself. I had sat down with a piece of work—for I was something or other that could sit—on the old stone bench which overlooked the pond; and in this position I began to take in with certitude and yet without direct vision the presence, a good way off, of a third person. The old trees, the thick shrubbery, made a great and pleasant shade, but it was all suffused with the brightness of the hot still hour. There was no ambiguity in anything; none whatever at least in the conviction I from one moment to another found myself forming as to what I should see straight before me and across the lake as a consequence of raising my eyes. They were attached at this juncture to the stitching in which I was engaged, and I can feel once more the spasm of my effort not to move them till I should so have steadied myself as to be able to make up my mind what to do. There was an alien object in view—a figure whose right of presence I instantly and passionately questioned. I recollect counting over perfectly the possibilities, reminding myself that nothing was more natural for instance than the appearance of one of the men about the place, or even of a messenger, a postman or a tradesman's boy, from the village. That reminder had as little effect on my practical certitude as I was conscious—still even without looking—of its having upon

5. A long, narrow, shallow, windy inland sea, connecting with the Black Sea.

the character and attitude of our visitor. Nothing was more natural than that these things should be the other things they absolutely were not.

Of the positive identity of the apparition I would assure myself as soon as the small clock of my courage should have ticked out the right second; meanwhile, with an effort that was already sharp enough, I transferred my eyes straight to little Flora, who, at the moment, was about ten yards away. My heart had stood still for an instant with the wonder and terror of the question whether she too would see; and I held my breath while I waited for what a cry from her, what some sudden innocent sign either of interest or of alarm, would tell me. I waited, but nothing came; then in the first place—and there is something more dire in this, I feel, than in anything I have to relate—I was determined by a sense that within a minute all spontaneous sounds from her had dropped; and in the second by the circumstance that also within the minute she had, in her play, turned her back to the water. This was her attitude when I at last looked at her—looked with the confirmed conviction that we were still, together, under direct personal notice. She had picked up a small flat piece of wood which happened to have in it a little hole that had evidently suggested to her the idea of sticking in another fragment that might figure as a mast and make the thing a boat. This second morsel, as I watched her, she was very markedly and intently attempting to tighten in its place. My apprehension of what she was doing sustained me so that after some seconds I felt I was ready for more. Then I again shifted my eyes—I faced what I had to face.

VII

I got hold of Mrs. Grose as soon after this as I could; and I can give no intelligible account of how I fought out the interval. Yet I still hear myself cry as I fairly threw myself into her arms: "They *know*—it's too monstrous: they know, they know!"

"And what on earth—?" I felt her incredulity as she held me.

"Why all that *we* know—and heaven knows what more besides!" Then as she released me I made it out to her, made it out perhaps only now with full coherency even to myself. "Two hours ago, in the garden"—I could scarce articulate—"Flora *saw!*"

Mrs. Grose took it as she might have taken a blow in the stomach. "She has told you?" she panted.

"Not a word—that's the horror. She kept it to herself! The child of eight, *that* child!" Unutterable still for me was the stupefaction of it.

Mrs. Grose of course could only gape the wider. "Then how do you know?"

"I was there—I saw with my eyes: saw she was perfectly aware."

"Do you mean aware of *him?*"

"No—of *her.*" I was conscious as I spoke that I looked prodigious things, for I got the slow reflexion of them in my companion's face. "Another person—this time; but a figure of quite as unmistakeable horror and evil: a woman in black, pale and dreadful —with such an air also, and such a face!—on the other side of the lake. I was there with the child—quiet for the hour; and in the midst of it she came."

"Came how—from where?"

"From where they come from! She just appeared and stood there —but not so near."

"And without coming nearer?"

"Oh for the effect and the feeling she might have been as close as you!"

My friend, with an odd impulse, fell back a step. "Was she some one you 've never seen?"

"Never. But some one the child has. Some one *you* have." Then to show how I had thought it all out: "My predecessor—the one who died."

"Miss Jessel?"

"Miss Jessel. You don't believe me?" I pressed.

She turned right and left in her distress. "How can you be sure?"

This drew from me, in the state of my nerves, a flash of impatience. "Then ask Flora—*she 's* sure!" But I had no sooner spoken than I caught myself up. "No, for God's sake *don't!* She'll say she is n't—she 'll lie!"

Mrs. Grose was not too bewildered instinctively to protest. "Ah how *can* you?"

"Because I 'm clear. Flora does n't want me to know."

"It 's only then to spare you."

"No, no—there are depths, depths! The more I go over it the more I see in it, and the more I see in it the more I fear. I don't know what I *don't* see, what I *don't* fear!"

Mrs. Grose tried to keep up with me. "You mean you 're afraid of seeing her again?"

"Oh no; that 's nothing—now!" Then I explained. "It's of *not* seeing her."

But my companion only looked wan. "I don't understand."

"Why, it 's that the child may keep it up—and that the child assuredly *will*—without my knowing it."

At the image of this possibility Mrs. Grose for a moment collapsed, yet presently to pull herself together again as from the positive force of the sense of what, should we yield an inch, there would really be to give way to. "Dear, dear—we must keep our heads! And after all, if she does n't mind it—!" She even tried a grim joke. "Perhaps she likes it!"

"Like *such* things—a scrap of an infant!"

"Is n't it just a proof of her blest innocence?" my friend bravely enquired.

She brought me, for the instant, almost round. "Oh we must clutch at *that*—we must cling to it! If it is n't a proof of what you say, it 's a proof of—God knows what! For the woman 's a horror of horrors."

Mrs. Grose, at this, fixed her eyes a minute on the ground; then at last raising them, "Tell me how you know," she said.

"Then you admit it 's what she was?" I cried.

"Tell me how you know," my friend simply repeated.

"Know? By seeing her! By the way she looked."

"At you, do you mean—so wickedly?"

"Dear me, no—I could have borne that. She gave me never a glance. She only fixed the child."

Mrs. Grose tried to see it. "Fixed her?"

"Ah with such awful eyes!"

She stared at mine as if they might really have resembled them. "Do you mean of dislike?"

"God help us, no. Of something much worse."

"Worse than dislike?"—this left her indeed at a loss.

"With a determination—indescribable. With a kind of fury of intention."

I made her turn pale. "Intention?"

"To get hold of her." Mrs. Grose—her eyes just lingering on mine—gave a shudder and walked to the window; and while she stood there looking out I completed my statement. "*That 's* what Flora knows."

After a little she turned round. "The person was in black, you say?"

"In mourning—rather poor, almost shabby. But—yes—with extraordinary beauty." I now recognised to what I had at last, stroke by stroke, brought the victim of my confidence, for she quite visibly weighed this. "Oh handsome—very, very," I insisted; "wonderfully handsome. But infamous."

She slowly came back to me. "Miss Jessel—*was* infamous." She once more took my hand in both her own, holding it as tight as if to fortify me against the increase of alarm I might draw from this disclosure. "They were both infamous," she finally said.

So for a little we faced it once more together; and I found absolutely a degree of help in seeing it now so straight. "I appreciate," I said, "the great decency of your not having hitherto spoken; but the time has certainly come to give me the whole thing." She appeared to assent to this, but still only in silence; seeing which I went on: "I must have it now. Of what did she die? Come, there was something between them."

"There was everything."

"In spite of the difference—?"

"Oh of their rank, their condition"—she brought it woefully out. "*She* was a lady."

I turned it over; I again saw. "Yes—she was a lady."

"And he so dreadfully below," said Mrs. Grose.

I felt that I doubtless need n't press too hard, in such company, on the place of a servant in the scale; but there was nothing to prevent an acceptance of my companion's own measure of my predecessor's abasement. There was a way to deal with that, and I dealt; the more readily for my full vision—on the evidence—of our employer's late clever good-looking "own" man; impudent, assured, spoiled, depraved. "The fellow was a hound."

Mrs. Grose considered as if it were perhaps a little a case for a sense of shades. "I 've never seen one like him. He did what he wished."

"With *her?*"

"With them all."

It was as if now in my friend's own eyes Miss Jessel had again appeared. I seemed at any rate for an instant to trace their evocation of her as distinctly as I had seen her by the pond; and I brought out with decision: "It must have been also what *she* wished!"

Mrs. Grose's face signified that it had been indeed, but she said at the same time: "Poor woman—she paid for it!"

"Then you do know what she died of?" I asked.

"No—I know nothing. I wanted not to know; I was glad enough I did n't; and I thanked heaven she was well out of this!"

"Yet you had then your idea—"

"Of her real reason for leaving? Oh yes—as to that. She could n't have stayed. Fancy it here—for a governess! And afterwards I imagined—and I still imagine. And what I imagine is dreadful."

"Not so dreadful as what *I* do," I replied; on which I must have shown her—as I was indeed but too conscious—a front of miserable defeat. It brought out again all her compassion for me, and at the renewed touch of her kindness my power to resist broke down. I burst, as I had the other time made her burst, into tears; she took me to her motherly breast, where my lamentation overflowed. "I don't do it!" I sobbed in despair; "I don't save or shield them! It's far worse than I dreamed. They 're lost" [6]

6. Fifth weekly installment and "Part Second" ended here.

VIII

What I had said to Mrs. Grose was true enough: there were in the matter I had put before her depths and possibilities that I lacked resolution to sound; so that when we met once more in the wonder of it we were of a common mind about the duty of resistance to extravagant fancies. We were to keep our heads if we should keep nothing else—difficult indeed as that might be in the face of all that, in our prodigious experience, seemed least to be questioned. Late that night, while the house slept, we had another talk in my room; when she went all the way with me as to its being beyond doubt that I had seen exactly what I had seen. I found that to keep her thoroughly in the grip of this I had only to ask her how, if I had "made it up," I came to be able to give, of each of the persons appearing to me, a picture disclosing, to the last detail, their special marks—a portrait on the exhibition of which she had instantly recognised and named them. She wished, of course —small blame to her!—to sink the whole subject; and I was quick to assure her that my own interest in it had now violently taken the form of a search for the way to escape from it. I closed with her cordially on the article of the likelihood that with recurrence —for recurrence we took for granted—I should get used to my danger; distinctly professing that my personal exposure had suddenly become the least of my discomforts. It was my new suspicion that was intolerable; and yet even to this complication the later hours of the day had brought a little ease.

On leaving her, after my first outbreak, I had of course returned to my pupils, associating the right remedy for my dismay with that sense of their charm which I had already recognised as a resource I could positively cultivate and which had never failed me yet. I had simply, in other words, plunged afresh into Flora's special society and there become aware—it was almost a luxury!—that she could put her little conscious hand straight upon the spot that ached. She had looked at me in sweet speculation and then had accused me to my face of having "cried." I had supposed the ugly signs of it brushed away; but I could literally—for the time at all events—rejoice, under this fathomless charity, that they had not entirely disappeared. To gaze into the depths of blue of the child's eyes and pronounce their loveliness a trick of premature cunning was to be guilty of a cynicism in preference to which I naturally preferred to abjure my judgement and, so far as might be, my agitation. I could n't abjure for merely wanting to, but I could repeat to Mrs. Grose—as I did there, over and over, in the small hours—that with our small friends' voices in the air, their pressure on one's heart and their fragrant faces against one's cheek, everything fell to the ground but their incapacity and their beauty. It was a pity that, somehow, to settle this once for all, I had equally to re-enumerate the signs of subtlety that, in the afternoon, by the lake, had made a miracle of my show of self-possession. It was a pity to be obliged to re-investigate the certitude of the moment itself and repeat how it had come to me as a revelation that the inconceivable communion I then surprised must have been for both parties a matter of habit. It was a pity I should have had to quaver out again the reasons for my not having, in my delusion, so much as questioned that the little girl saw our visitant even as I actually saw Mrs. Grose herself, and that she wanted, by just so much as she did thus see, to make me suppose she did n't, and at the same time, without showing anything, arrive at a guess as to whether I myself did! It was a pity I needed to recapitulate the portentous little activities by which she sought to divert my attention—the perceptible increase of movement, the greater intensity of play, the singing, the gabbling of nonsense and the invitation to romp.

Yet if I had not indulged, to prove there was nothing in it, in this review, I should have missed the two or three dim elements of comfort that still remained to me. I should n't for instance have been able to asseverate to my friend that I was certain—which was so much to the good—that *I* at least had not betrayed myself. I should n't have been prompted, by stress of need, by desperation of mind—I scarce know what to call it—to invoke such further aid to intelligence as might spring from pushing my colleague fairly to the wall. She had told me, bit by bit, under pressure, a great deal; but a small shifty spot on the wrong side of it all still sometimes brushed my brow like the wing of a bat; and I remember how on this occasion—for the sleeping house and the concentration alike of our danger and our watch seemed to help—I felt the importance of giving the last jerk to the curtain. "I don't believe anything so horrible," I recollect saying; "no, let us put it definitely, my dear, that I don't. But if I did, you know, there 's a thing I should require now, just without sparing you the least bit more—oh not a scrap, come!—to get out of you. What was it you had in mind when, in our distress, before Miles came back, over the letter from his school, you said, under my insistence, that you did n't pretend for him he had n't literally *ever* been 'bad'? He has *not*, truly, 'ever,' in these weeks that I myself have lived with him and so closely watched him; he has been an imperturbable little prodigy of delightful loveable goodness. Therefore you might perfectly have made the claim for him if you had not, as it happened, seen an exception to take. What was your exception, and to what passage in your personal observation of him did you refer?"

It was a straight question enough, but levity was not our note, and in any case I had before the grey dawn admonished us to separate got my answer. What my friend had had in mind proved immensely to the purpose. It was neither more nor less than the particular fact that for a period of several months Quint and the boy had been perpetually together. It was indeed the very appropriate item of evidence of her having ventured to criticise the propriety, to hint at the incongruity, of so close an alliance, and even to go so far on the subject as a frank overture to Miss Jessel would take her. Miss Jessel had, with a very high manner about it, requested her to mind her business, and the good woman had on this directly approached little Miles. What she had said to him, since I pressed, was that *she* liked to see young gentlemen not forget their station.

I pressed again, of course, the closer for that. "You reminded him that Quint was only a base menial?"

"As you might say! And it was his answer, for one thing, that was bad."

"And for another thing?" I waited. "He repeated your words to Quint?"

"No, not that. It's just what he *would n't!*" she could still impress on me. "I was sure, at any rate," she added, "that he did n't. But he denied certain occasions."

"What occasions?"

"When they had been about together quite as if Quint were his tutor—and a very grand one—and Miss Jessel only for the little lady. When he had gone off with the fellow, I mean, and spent hours with him."

"He then prevaricated about it—he said he had n't?" Her assent was clear enough to cause me to add in a moment: "I see. He lied."

"Oh!" Mrs. Grose mumbled. This was a suggestion that it did n't matter; which indeed she backed up by a further remark. "You see, after all, Miss Jessel did n't mind. She did n't forbid him."

I considered. "Did he put that to you as a justification?"

At this she dropped again. "No, he never spoke of it."

"Never mentioned her in connexion with Quint?"

She saw, visibly flushing, where I was coming out. "Well, he did n't show anything. He denied," she repeated; "he denied."

Lord, how I pressed her now! "So that you could see he knew what was between the two wretches?"

"I don't know—I don't know!" the poor woman wailed.

"You do know, you dear thing," I replied; "only you have n't my dreadful boldness of mind, and you keep back, out of timidity and modesty and delicacy, even the impression that in the past, when you had, without my aid, to flounder about in silence, most of all made you miserable. But I shall get it out of you yet! There was something in the boy that suggested to you," I continued, "his covering and concealing their relation."

"Oh he could n't prevent—"

"Your learning the truth? I dare say! But, heavens," I fell, with vehemence, a-thinking, "what it shows that they must, to that extent, have succeeded in making of him!"

"Ah nothing that 's not nice *now!*" Mrs. Grose lugubriously pleaded.

"I don't wonder you looked queer," I persisted, "when I mentioned to you the letter from his school!"

"I doubt if I looked as queer as you!" she retorted with homely force. "And if he was so bad then as that comes to, how is he such an angel now?"

"Yes indeed—and if he was a fiend at school! How, how, how? Well," I said in my torment, "you must put it to me again, though I shall not be able to tell you for some days. Only put it to me again!" I cried in a way that made my friend stare. "There are directions in which I must n't for the present let myself go." Meanwhile I returned to her first example—the one to which she had just previously referred—of the boy's happy capacity for an occasional slip. "If Quint—on your remonstrance at the time you speak of—was a base menial, one of the things Miles said to you, I find myself guessing, was that you were another." Again her admission was so adequate that I continued: "And you forgave him that?"

"Would n't *you?*"

"Oh yes!" And we exchanged there, in the stillness, a sound of the oddest amusement. Then I went on: "At all events, while he was with the man—"

"Miss Flora was with the woman. It suited them all!"

It suited me too, I felt, only too well; by which I mean that it suited exactly the particular deadly view I was in the very act of forbidding myself to entertain. But I so far succeeded in checking the expression of this view that I will throw, just here, no further light on it than may be offered by the mention of my final observation to Mrs. Grose. "His having lied and been impudent are, I confess, less engaging specimens than I had hoped to have from you of the outbreak in him of the little natural man. Still," I mused, "they must do, for they make me feel more than ever that I must watch."

It made me blush, the next minute, to see in my friend's face how much more unreservedly she had forgiven him than her anecdote struck me as pointing out to my own tenderness any way to do. This was marked when, at the schoolroom door, she quitted me. "Surely you don't accuse *him*—"

"Of carrying on an intercourse that he conceals from me? Ah remember that, until further evidence, I now accuse nobody." Then before shutting her out to go by another passage to her own place, "I must just wait," I wound up.

IX

I waited and waited, and the days took as they elapsed something from my consternation. A very few of them, in fact, passing, in constant sight of my pupils, without a fresh incident, sufficed to give to grievous fancies and even to odious memories a kind of brush of the sponge. I have spoken of the surrender to their extraordinary childish grace as a thing I could actively promote in myself, and it may be imagined if I neglected now to apply at this source for whatever balm it would yield. Stranger than I can express certainly, was the effort to struggle against my new lights. It would doubtless have been a greater tension still, however, had it not been so frequently successful. I used to wonder how my little charges could help guessing that I thought strange things about them; and the circumstance that these things only made them more interesting was not by itself a direct aid to keeping them in the dark. I trembled lest they should see that they *were* so immensely more interesting. Putting things at the worst, at all events, as in meditation I so often did, any clouding of their innocence could only be—blameless and fore-doomed as they were—a reason the more for taking risks. There were moments when I knew myself to catch them up by an irresistible impulse and press them to my heart. As soon as I had done so I used to wonder—"What will they think of that? Does n't it betray too much?" It would have been easy to get into a sad wild tangle about how much I might betray; but the real account, I feel, of the hours of peace I could still enjoy was that the immediate charm of my companions was a beguilement still effective even under the shadow of the possibility that it was studied. For if it occurred to me that I might occasionally excite suspicion by the little outbreaks of my sharper passion for them, so too I remember asking if I might n't see a queerness in the traceable increase of their own demonstrations.

They were at this period extravagantly and preternaturally fond of me; which, after all, I could reflect, was no more than a graceful response in children perpetually bowed down over and hugged. The homage of which they were so lavish succeeded in truth for my nerves quite as well as if I never appeared to myself, as I may say, literally to catch them at a purpose in it. They had never, I think, wanted to do so many things for their poor protectress; I mean— though they got their lessons better and better, which was naturally what would please her most—in the way of diverting, entertaining, surprising her; reading her passages, telling her stories, acting her charades, pouncing out at her, in disguises, as animals and historical characters, and above all astonishing her by the "pieces" they had secretly got by heart and could interminably recite. I should never get to the bottom—were I to let myself go even now—of the prodigious private commentary, all under still more private correction, with which I in these days overscored their full hours. They had shown me from the first a facility for everything, a general faculty which, taking a fresh start, achieved remarkable flights. They got their little tasks as if they loved them; they indulged, from the mere exuberance of the gift, in the most unimposed little miracles of memory. They not only popped out at me as tigers and as Romans, but as Shakespeareans, astronomers and navigators. This was so singularly the case that it had presumably much to do with the fact as to which, at the present day, I am at a loss for a different explanation: I allude to my unnatural composure on the subject of another school for Miles. What I remember is that I was content for the time not to open the question, and that contentment must have sprung from the sense of his perpetually striking show of cleverness. He was too clever for a bad governess, for a parson's daughter, to spoil; and the strangest if not the brightest thread in the pensive embroidery I just spoke of was the impression I might have got, if I had dared to work it out, that he was under some influence operating in his small intellectual life as a tremendous incitement.

If it was easy to reflect, however, that such a boy could postpone school, it was at least as marked that for such a boy to have been "kicked out" by a school-master was a mystification without end. Let me add that in their company now—and I was careful almost never to be out of it—I could follow no scent very far. We lived in a cloud of music and affection and success and private theatricals. The musical sense in each of the children was of the quickest, but the elder in especial had a marvellous knack of catching and repeating. The schoolroom piano broke into all gruesome fancies; and when that failed there were confabulations in corners, with a sequel of one of them going out in the highest spirits in order to "come in" as something new. I had had brothers myself, and it was no revelation to me that little girls could be slavish idolaters of little boys. What surpassed everything was that there was a little boy in the world who could have for the inferior age, sex and intelligence so fine a consideration. They were extraordinarily at one, and to say that they never either quarrelled or complained is to make the note of praise coarse for their quality of sweetness. Sometimes perhaps indeed (when I dropped into coarseness) I came across traces of little understandings between them by which one of them should keep me occupied while the other slipped away. There is a naïf side, I suppose, in all diplomacy; but if my pupils practised upon me it was surely with the minimum of grossness. It was all in the other quarter that, after a lull, the grossness broke out.

I find that I really hang back; but I must take my horrid plunge. In going on with the record of what was hideous at Bly I not only challenge the most liberal faith—for which I little care; but (and this is another matter) I renew what I myself suffered, I again push my dreadful way through it to the end. There came suddenly an hour after which, as I look back, the business seems to me to have been all pure suffering; but I have at least reached the heart of it, and the straightest road out is doubtless to advance. One evening— with nothing to lead up or prepare it—I felt the cold touch of the impression that had breathed on me the night of my arrival and which, much lighter then as I have mentioned, I should probably have made little of in memory had my subsequent sojourn been less agitated. I had not gone to bed; I sat reading by a couple of candles. There was a roomful of old books at Bly—last-century fiction some of it, which, to the extent of a distinctly deprecated renown, but never to so much as that of a stray specimen, had reached the sequestered home and appealed to the unavowed curiosity of my youth. I remember that the book I had in my hand was Fielding's "Amelia";[7] also that I was wholly awake. I recall further both a general conviction that it was horribly late and a particular objection to looking at my watch. I figure finally that the white curtain draping, in the fashion of those days, the head of Flora's little bed, shrouded, as I had assured myself long before, the perfection of childish rest. I recollect in short that though I was deeply interested in my author I found myself, at the turn of a page and with his spell all scattered, looking straight up from him and hard at the door of my room. There was a moment during which I listened, reminded of the faint sense I had had, the first night, of there being something undefinably astir in the house, and noted the soft breath of the open casement just move the half-drawn blind. Then, with all the marks of a deliberation that must have seemed magnificent had there been any one to admire it, I laid down my book, rose to my feet and, taking a candle, went straight out of the room and, from the passage, on which my light made little impression, noiselessly closed and locked the door.

I can say now neither what determined nor what guided me, but I went straight along the lobby, holding my candle high, till I came within sight of the tall window that presided over the great turn of the staircase. At this point I precipitately found myself aware of three things. They were practically simultaneous, yet they had flashes of succession. My candle, under a bold flourish, went out,

7. *Amelia* (1751) by Henry Fielding (1707–54), a novel about an all-good, long-suffering heroine.

and I perceived, by the uncovered window, that the yielding dusk of earliest morning rendered it unnecessary. Without it, the next instant, I knew that there was a figure on the stair. I speak of sequences, but I require no lapse of seconds to stiffen myself for a third encounter with Quint. The apparition had reached the landing halfway up and was therefore on the spot nearest the window, where, at sight of me, it stopped short and fixed me exactly as it had fixed me from the tower and from the garden. He knew me as well as I knew him; and so, in the cold faint twilight, with a glimmer in the high glass and another on the polish of the oak stair below, we faced each other in our common intensity. He was absolutely, on this occasion, a living detestable dangerous presence. But that was not the wonder of wonders; I reserve this distinction for quite another circumstance: the circumstance that dread had unmistakeably quitted me and that there was nothing in me unable to meet and measure him.

I had plenty of anguish after that extraordinary moment, but I had, thank God, no terror. And he knew I had n't—I found myself at the end of an instant magnificently aware of this. I felt, in a fierce rigour of confidence, that if I stood my ground a minute I should cease—for the time at least—to have him to reckon with; and during the minute, accordingly, the thing was as human and hideous as a real interview: hideous just because it *was* human, as human as to have met alone, in the small hours, in a sleeping house, some enemy, some adventurer, some criminal. It was the dead silence of our long gaze at such close quarters that gave the whole horror, huge as it was, its only note of the unnatural. If I had met a murderer in such a place and at such an hour we still at least would have spoken. Something would have passed, in life, between us; if nothing had passed one of us would have moved. The moment was so prolonged that it would have taken but little more to make me doubt if even *I* were in life. I can't express what followed it save by saying that the silence itself—which was indeed in a manner an attestation of my strength—became the element into which I saw the figure disappear; in which I definitely saw it turn, as I might have seen the low wretch to which it had once belonged turn on receipt of an order, and pass, with my eyes on the villainous back that no hunch could have more disfigured, straight down the staircase and into the darkness in which the next bend was lost.[8]

X

I remained a while at the top of the stair, but with the effect presently of understanding that when my visitor had gone, he had gone; then I returned to my room. The foremost thing I saw there

8. Sixth weekly installment ended here.

by the light of the candle I had left burning was that Flora's little
bed was empty; and on this I caught my breath with all the terror
that, five minutes before, I had been able to resist. I dashed at the
place in which I had left her lying and over which—for the small
silk counterpane and the sheets were disarranged—the white curtains
had been deceivingly pulled forward; then my step, to my unutterable relief, produced an answering sound: I noticed an agitation of
the window-blind, and the child, ducking down, emerged rosily from
the other side of it. She stood there in so much of her candour and
so little of her night-gown, with her pink bare feet and the golden
glow of her curls. She looked intensely grave, and I had never had
such a sense of losing an advantage acquired (the thrill of which
had just been so prodigious) as on my consciousness that she
addressed me with a reproach—"You naughty: where *have* you
been?" Instead of challenging her own irregularity I found myself
arraigned and explaining. She herself explained, for that matter,
with the loveliest eagerest simplicity. She had known suddenly, as
she lay there, that I was out of the room, and had jumped up to
see what had become of me. I had dropped, with the joy of her reappearance, back into my chair—feeling then, and then only, a
little faint; and she had pattered straight over to me, thrown herself
upon my knee, given herself to be held with the flame of the candle
full in the wonderful little face that was still flushed with sleep. I
remember closing my eyes an instant, yieldingly, consciously, as
before the excess of something beautiful that shone out of the blue
of her own. "You were looking for me out of the window?" I said.
"You thought I might be walking in the grounds?"

"Well, you know, I thought some one was"—she never blanched
as she smiled out that at me.

Oh how I looked at her now! "And did you see any one?"

"Ah *no!*" she returned almost (with the full privilege of childish
inconsequence) resentfully, though with a long sweetness in her
little drawl of the negative.

At that moment, in the state of my nerves, I absolutely believed
she lied; and if I once more closed my eyes it was before the dazzle
of the three or four possible ways in which I might take this up.
One of these for a moment tempted me with such singular force
that, to resist it, I must have gripped my little girl with a spasm
that, wonderfully, she submitted to without a cry or a sign of fright.
Why not break out at her on the spot and have it all over?—give it
to her straight in her lovely little lighted face? "You see, you see,
you *know* that you do and that you already quite suspect I believe
it; therefore why not frankly confess it to me, so that we may at
least live with it together and learn perhaps, in the strangeness of
our fate, where we are and what it means?" This solicitation

dropped, alas, as it came: if I could immediately have succumbed to it I might have spared myself—well, you'll see what. Instead of succumbing I sprang again to my feet, looked at her bed and took a helpless middle way. "Why did you pull the curtain over the place to make me think you were still there?"

Flora luminously considered; after which, with her little divine smile: "Because I don't like to frighten you!"

"But if I had, by your idea, gone out—?"

She absolutely declined to be puzzled; she turned her eyes to the flame of the candle as if the question were as irrelevant, or at any rate as impersonal, as Mrs. Marcet [9] or nine-times-nine. "Oh but you know," she quite adequately answered, "that you might come back, you dear, and that you *have!*" And after a little, when she had got into bed, I had, a long time, by almost sitting on her for the retention of her hand, to show how I recognised the pertinence of my return.

You may imagine the general complexion, from that moment, of my nights. I repeatedly sat up till I did n't know when; I selected moments when my room-mate unmistakeably slept, and, stealing out, took noiseless turns in the passage. I even pushed as far as to where I had last met Quint. But I never met him there again, and I may as well say at once that I on no other occasion saw him in the house. I just missed, on the staircase, nevertheless, a different adventure. Looking down it from the top I once recognised the presence of a woman seated on one of the lower steps with her back presented to me, her body half-bowed and her head, in an attitude of woe, in her hands. I had been there but an instant, however, when she vanished without looking round at me. I knew, for all that, exactly what dreadful face she had to show; and I wondered whether, if instead of being above I had been below, I should have had the same nerve for going up that I had lately shown Quint. Well, there continued to be plenty of call for nerve. On the eleventh night after my latest encounter with that gentleman—they were all numbered now—I had an alarm that perilously skirted it and that indeed, from the particular quality of its unexpectedness, proved quite my sharpest shock. It was precisely the first night during this series that, weary with vigils, I had conceived I might again without laxity lay myself down at my old hour. I slept immediately and, as I afterwards knew, till about one o'clock; but when I woke it was to sit straight up, as completely roused as if a hand had shaken me. I had left a light burning, but it was now out, and I felt an instant certainty that Flora had extinguished it. This brought me to my feet and straight, in the darkness, to her bed, which I found she had left. A glance at

9. Jane Marcet (1769–1858) was the author of elementary children's texts and popularized accounts of the social and natural sciences.

the window enlightened me further, and the striking of a match completed the picture.

The child had again got up—this time blowing out the taper, and had again, for some purpose of observation or response, squeezed in behind the blind and was peering out into the night. That she now saw—as she had not, I had satisfied myself, the previous time— was proved to me by the fact that she was disturbed neither by my re-illumination nor by the haste I made to get into slippers and into a wrap. Hidden, protected, absorbed, she evidently rested on the sill—the casement opened forward—and gave herself up. There was a great still moon to help her, and this fact had counted in my quick decision. She was face to face with the apparition we had met at the lake, and could now communicate with it as she had not then been able to do. What I, on my side, had to care for was, without disturbing her, to reach, from the corridor, some other window turned to the same quarter. I got to the door without her hearing me; I got out of it, closed it and listened, from the other side, for some sound from her. While I stood in the passage I had my eyes on her brother's door, which was but ten steps off and which, indescribably, produced in me a renewal of the strange impulse that I lately spoke of as my temptation. What if I should go straight in and march to *his* window?—what if, by risking to his boyish bewilderment a revelation of my motive, I should throw across the rest of the mystery the long halter of my boldness?

This thought held me sufficiently to make me cross to his threshold and pause again. I preternaturally listened; I figured to myself what might portentously be; I wondered if his bed were also empty and he also secretly at watch. It was a deep soundless minute, at the end of which my impulse failed. He was quiet; he might be innocent; the risk was hideous; I turned away. There was a figure in the grounds—a figure prowling for a sight, the visitor with whom Flora was engaged; but it was n't the visitor most concerned with my boy. I hesitated afresh, but on other grounds and only a few seconds; then I had made my choice. There were empty rooms enough at Bly, and it was only a question of choosing the right one. The right one suddenly presented itself to me as the lower one— though high above the gardens—in the solid corner of the house 'that I have spoken of as the old tower. This was a large square chamber, arranged with some state as a bedroom, the extravagant size of which made it so inconvenient that it had not for years, though kept by Mrs. Grose in exemplary order, been occupied. I had often admired it and I knew my way about in it; I had only, after just faltering at the first chill gloom of its disuse, to pass across it and unbolt in all quietness one of the shutters. Achieving this transit I uncovered the glass without a sound and, applying my face to the pane, was able, the darkness without being much less than within, to see that I commanded the right direction. Then I saw something more. The moon made the night extraordinarily penetrable and showed me on the lawn a person, diminished by distance, who stood there motionless as if fascinated, looking up to where I had appeared—looking, that is, not so much straight at me as at something that was apparently above me. There was clearly another person above me—there was a person on the tower; but the presence on the lawn was not in the least what I had conceived and had confidently hurried to meet. The presence on the lawn—I felt sick as I made it out—was poor little Miles himself.

XI

It was not till late next day that I spoke to Mrs. Grose; the rigour with which I kept my pupils in sight making it often difficult to meet her privately: the more as we each felt the importance of not provoking—on the part of the servants quite as much as on that of the children—any suspicion of a secret flurry or of a discussion of mysteries. I drew a great security in this particular from her mere smooth aspect. There was nothing in her fresh face to pass on to others the least of my horrible confidences. She believed me, I was sure, absolutely: if she had n't I don't know what would have become of me, for I could n't have borne the strain alone. But she was a magnificent monument to the blessing of a want of imagination, and if she could see in our little charges nothing but their beauty and amiability, their happiness and cleverness, she had no direct communication with the sources of my trouble. If they had been at all visibly blighted or battered she would doubtless have grown, on tracing it back, haggard enough to match them; as matters stood, however, I could feel her, when she surveyed them with her large white arms folded and the habit of serenity in all her look, thank the Lord's mercy that if they were ruined the pieces would still serve. Flights of fancy gave place, in her mind, to a steady fireside glow, and I had already begun to perceive how, with the development of the conviction that—as time went on without a public accident—our young things could, after all, look out for themselves, she addressed her greatest solicitude to the sad case presented by their deputy-guardian. That, for myself, was a sound simplification: I could engage that, to the world, my face should tell no tales, but it would have been, in the conditions, an immense added worry to find myself anxious about hers.

At the hour I now speak of she had joined me, under pressure, on the terrace, where, with the lapse of the season, the afternoon sun was now agreeable; and we sat there together while before us and at a distance, yet within call if we wished, the children strolled to and fro in one of their most manageable moods. They moved slowly, in unison, below us, over the lawn, the boy, as they went, reading aloud from a story-book and passing his arm round his sister to keep her quite in touch. Mrs. Grose watched them with positive placidity; then I caught the suppressed intellectual creak with which she conscientiously turned to take from me a view of the back of the tapestry. I had made her a receptacle of lurid things, but there was an odd recognition of my superiority—my accomplishments and my function—in her patience under my pain. She offered her mind to my disclosures as, had I wished to mix a witch's broth and propose it with assurance, she would have held out a large clean saucepan. This had become thoroughly her attitude by the time that, in my recital of the events of the night, I reached the point of what Miles had said to me when, after seeing him, at such a monstrous hour, almost on the very spot where he happened now to be, I had gone down to bring him in; choosing then, at the window, with a concentrated need of not alarming the house, rather that method than any noisier process. I had left her meanwhile in little doubt of my small hope of representing with success even to her actual sympathy my sense of the real splendour of the little inspiration with which, after I had got him into the house, the boy met my final articulate challenge. As soon as I appeared in the moonlight on the terrace he had come to me as straight as possible; on which I had taken his hand without a word and led him, through the dark spaces, up the staircase where Quint had so hungrily hovered for him, along the lobby where I had listened and trembled, and so to his forsaken room.

Not a sound, on the way, had passed between us, and I had wondered—oh *how* I had wondered!—if he were groping about in his dreadful little mind for something plausible and not too grotesque. It would tax his invention certainly, and I felt, this time, over his real embarrassment, a curious thrill of triumph. It was a sharp trap for any game hitherto successful. He could play no longer at perfect propriety, nor could he pretend to it; so how the deuce would he get out of the scrape? There beat in me indeed, with the passionate throb of this question, an equal dumb appeal as to how the deuce *I* should. I was confronted at last, as never yet, with all the risk attached even now to sounding my own horrid note. I remember in fact that as we pushed into his little chamber, where the bed had not been slept in at all and the window, uncovered to the moonlight, made the place so clear that there was no need of striking a match—I remember how I suddenly dropped, sank upon the edge of the bed from the force of the idea that he must know how he really, as they say, "had" me. He could do what he liked, with all his cleverness to help him, so long as I should continue to defer to the old tradition of the criminality of those caretakers of the young who minister to superstitions and fears. He "had" me indeed, and in a cleft stick; for who would ever absolve me, who would consent that I should go unhung, if, by the faintest tremor of an overture, I were the first to introduce into our perfect intercourse an element so dire? No, no: it was useless to attempt to convey to Mrs. Grose, just as it is scarcely less so to attempt to suggest here, how, during our short stiff brush there in the dark, he fairly shook me with admiration. I was of course thoroughly kind and merciful; never, never yet had I placed on his small shoulders hands of such tenderness as those with which, while I rested against the bed, I held him there well under fire. I had no alternative but, in form at least, to put it to him.

"You must tell me now—and all the truth. What did you go out for? What were you doing there?"

I can still see his wonderful smile, the whites of his beautiful eyes and the uncovering of his clear teeth, shine to me in the dusk. "If I tell you why, will you understand?" My heart, at this, leaped into my mouth. *Would* he tell me why? I found no sound on my lips to press it, and I was aware of answering only with a vague repeated grimacing nod. He was gentleness itself, and while I wagged my head at him he stood there more than ever a little fairy prince. It was his brightness indeed that gave me a respite. Would it be so great if he were really going to tell me? "Well," he said at last, "just exactly in order that you should do this."

"Do what?"

"Think me—for a change—*bad!*" I shall never forget the sweetness and gaiety with which he brought out the word, nor how, on top of it, he bent forward and kissed me. It was practically the end of everything. I met his kiss and I had to make, while I folded him for a minute in my arms, the most stupendous effort not to cry. He had given exactly the account of himself that permitted least my going behind it, and it was only with the effect of confirming my acceptance of it that, as I presently glanced about the room, I could say—

"Then you did n't undress at all?"

He fairly glittered in the gloom. "Not at all. I sat up and read."

"And when did you go down?"

"At midnight. When I'm bad I *am* bad!"

"I see, I see—it's charming. But how could you be sure I should know it?"

"Oh I arranged that with Flora." His answers rang out with a readiness! "She was to get up and look out."

"Which is what she did do." It was I who fell into the trap!

"So she disturbed you, and, to see what she was looking at, you also looked—you saw."

"While you," I concurred, "caught your death in the night air!"

He literally bloomed so from this exploit that he could afford radiantly to assent. "How otherwise should I have been bad enough?" he asked. Then, after another embrace, the incident and our interview closed on my recognition of all the reserves of goodness that, for his joke, he had been able to draw upon.

XII

The particular impression I had received proved in the morning light, I repeat, not quite successfully presentable to Mrs. Grose, though I re-enforced it with the mention of still another remark that he had made before we separated. "It all lies in half a dozen words," I said to her, "words that really settle the matter. 'Think, you know, what I *might* do!' He threw that off to show me how good he is. He knows down to the ground what he 'might do.' That's what he gave them a taste of at school."

"Lord, you do change!" cried my friend.

"I don't change—I simply make it out. The four, depend upon it, perpetually meet. If on either of these last nights you had been with either child you'd clearly have understood. The more I've watched and waited the more I've felt that if there were nothing else to make it sure it would be made so by the systematic silence of each. *Never*, by a slip of the tongue, have they so much as alluded to either of their old friends, any more than Miles has alluded to his expulsion. Oh yes, we may sit here and look at them, and they may show off to us there to their fill; but even while they pretend to be lost in their fairy-tale they're steeped in their vision of the dead restored to them. He's not reading to her," I declared; "they're talking of *them*—they're talking horrors! I go on, I know, as if I were crazy; and it's a wonder I'm not. What I've seen would have made *you* so; but it has only made me more lucid, made me get hold of still other things."

My lucidity must have seemed awful, but the charming creatures who were victims of it, passing and repassing in their interlocked sweetness, gave my colleague something to hold on by; and I felt how tight she held as, without stirring in the breath of my passion, she covered them still with her eyes. "Of what other things have you got hold?"

"Why of the very things that have delighted, fascinated and yet, at bottom, as I now so strangely see, mystified and troubled me. Their more than earthly beauty, their absolutely unnatural goodness. It's a game," I went on; "It's a policy and a fraud!"

"On the part of little darlings—?"

"As yet mere lovely babies? Yes, mad as that seems!" The very act of bringing it out really helped me to trace it—follow it all up and piece it all together. "They have n't been good—they 've only been absent. It has been easy to live with them because they 're simply leading a life of their own. They 're not mine—they 're not ours. They 're his and they 're hers!"

"Quint's and that woman's?"

"Quint's and that woman's. They want to get to them."

Oh how, at this, poor Mrs. Grose appeared to study them! "But for what?"

"For the love of all the evil that, in those dreadful days, the pair put into them. And to ply them with that evil still, to keep up the work of demons, is what brings the others back."

"Laws!" said my friend under her breath. The exclamation was homely, but it revealed a real acceptance of my further proof of what, in the bad time—for there had been a worse even than this! —must have occurred. There could have been no such justification for me as the plain assent of her experience to whatever depth of depravity I found credible in our brace of scoundrels. It was in obvious submission of memory that she brought out after a moment: "They *were* rascals! But what can they now do?" she pursued.

"Do?" I echoed so loud that Miles and Flora, as they passed at their distance, paused an instant in their walk and looked at us. "Don't they do enough?" I demanded in a lower tone, while the children, having smiled and nodded and kissed hands to us, resumed their exhibition. We were held by it a minute; then I answered: "They can destroy them!" At this my companion did turn, but the appeal she launched was a silent one, the effect of which was to make me more explicit. "They don't know as yet quite how—but they 're trying hard. They 're seen only across, as it were, and beyond —in strange places and on high places, the top of towers, the roof of houses, the outside of windows, the further edge of pools; but there 's a deep design, on either side, to shorten the distance and overcome the obstacle: so the success of the tempters is only a question of time. They 've only to keep to their suggestions of danger."

"For the children to come?"

"And perish in the attempt!" Mrs. Grose slowly got up, and I scrupulously added: "Unless, of course, we can prevent!"

Standing there before me while I kept my seat she visibly turned things over. "Their uncle must do the preventing. He must take them away."

"And who 's to make him?"

She had been scanning the distance, but she now dropped on me a foolish face. "You, Miss."

"By writing to him that his house is poisoned and his little nephew and niece mad?"

"But if they *are*, Miss?"

"And if I am myself, you mean? That 's charming news to be sent him by a person enjoying his confidence and whose prime undertaking was to give him no worry."

Mrs. Grose considered, following the children again. "Yes, he do hate worry. That was the great reason—"

"Why those fiends took him in so long? No doubt, though his indifference must have been awful. As I 'm not a fiend, at any rate, I should n't take him in."

My companion, after an instant and for all answer, sat down again and grasped my arm. "Make him at any rate come to you."

I stared. "To *me?*" I had a sudden fear of what she might do. " 'Him'?"

"He ought to *be* here—he ought to help."

I quickly rose and I think I must have shown her a queerer face than ever yet. "You see me asking him for a visit?" No, with her eyes on my face she evidently could n't. Instead of it even—as a woman reads another—she could see what I myself saw: his derision, his amusement, his contempt for the breakdown of my resignation at being left alone and for the fine machinery I had set in motion to attract his attention to my slighted charms. She did n't know—no one knew—how proud I had been to serve him and to stick to our terms; yet she none the less took the measure, I think, of the warning I now gave her. "If you should so lose your head as to appeal to him for me—"

She was really frightened. "Yes, Miss?"

"I would leave, on the spot, both him and you." [1]

XIII

It was all very well to join them, but speaking to them proved quite as much as ever an effort beyond my strength—offered, in close quarters, difficulties as insurmountable as before. This situation continued a month, and with new aggravations and particular notes, the note above all, sharper and sharper, of the small ironic consciousness on the part of my pupils. It was not, I am as sure to-day as I was sure then, my mere infernal imagination: it was absolutely traceable that they were aware of my predicament and that this strange relation made, in a manner, for a long time, the air in which we moved. I don't mean that they had their tongues in their cheeks or did anything vulgar, for that was not one of their dangers: I do mean, on the other hand, that the element of the unnamed and untouched became, between us, greater than any other, and that so much avoidance could n't have been made successful without a

1. Seventh weekly installment and "Part Third" approximately ended here (see Textual Notes).

great deal of tacit arrangement. It was as if, at moments, we were perpetually coming into sight of subjects before which we must stop short, turning suddenly out of alleys that we perceived to be blind, closing with a little bang that made us look at each other— for, like all bangs, it was something louder than we had intended —the doors we had indiscreetly opened. All roads lead to Rome, and there were times when it might have struck us that almost every branch of study or subject of conversation skirted forbidden ground. Forbidden ground was the question of the return of the dead in general and of whatever, in especial, might survive, for memory, of the friends little children had lost. There were days when I could have sworn that one of them had, with a small invisible nudge, said to the other: "She thinks she'll do it this time—but she *won't!*" To "do it" would have been to indulge for instance—and for once in a way—in some direct reference to the lady who had prepared them for my discipline. They had a delightful endless appetite for passages in my own history to which I had again and again treated them; they were in possession of everything that had ever happened to me, had had, with every circumstance, the story of my smallest adventures and of those of my brothers and sisters and of the cat and the dog at home, as well as many particulars of the whimsical bent of my father, of the furniture and arrangement of our house and of the conversation of the old women of our village. There were things enough, taking one with another, to chatter about, if one went very fast and knew by instinct when to go round. They pulled with an art of their own the strings of my invention and my memory; and nothing else perhaps, when I thought of such occasions afterwards, gave me so the suspicion of being watched from under cover. It was in any case over *my* life, *my* past and *my* friends alone that we could take anything like our ease; a state of affairs that led them sometimes without the least pertinence to break out into sociable reminders. I was invited—with no visible connexion—to repeat afresh Goody Gosling's celebrated *mot* [2] or to confirm the details already supplied as to the cleverness of the vicarage pony.

It was partly at such junctures as these and partly at quite different ones that, with the turn my matters had now taken, my predicament, as I have called it, grew most sensible. The fact that the days passed for me without another encounter ought, it would have appeared, to have done something toward soothing my nerves. Since the light brush, that second night on the upper landing, of the presence of a woman at the foot of the stair, I had seen nothing, whether in or out of the house, that one had better not have seen. There was many a corner round which I expected to come upon

2. The allusion here has never been explained; does James mean a favorite Mother Goose rhyme?

Quint, and many a situation that, in a merely sinister way, would have favoured the appearance of Miss Jessel. The summer had turned, the summer had gone; the autumn had dropped upon Bly and had blown out half our lights. The place, with its grey sky and withered garlands, its bared spaces and scattered dead leaves, was like a theatre after the performance—all strewn with crumpled playbills. There were exactly states of the air, conditions of sound and of stillness, unspeakable impressions of the *kind* of ministering moment, that brought back to me, long enough to catch it, the feeling of the medium in which, that June evening out of doors, I had had my first sight of Quint, and in which too, at those other instants, I had, after seeing him through the window, looked for him in vain in the circle of shrubbery. I recognised the signs, the portents—I recognised the moment, the spot. But they remained unaccompanied and empty, and I continued unmolested; if unmolested one could call a young woman whose sensibility had, in the most extraordinary fashion, not declined but deepened. I had said in my talk with Mrs. Grose on that horrid scene of Flora's by the lake—and had perplexed her by so saying—that it would from that moment distress me much more to lose my power than to keep it. I had then expressed what was vividly in my mind: the truth that, whether the children really saw or not—since, that is, it was not yet definitely proved—I greatly preferred, as a safeguard, the fulness of my own exposure. I was ready to know the very worst that was to be known. What I had then had an ugly glimpse of was that my eyes might be sealed just while theirs were most opened. Well, my eyes *were* sealed, it appeared, at present—a consummation for which it seemed blasphemous not to thank God. There was, alas, a difficulty about that: I would have thanked him with all my soul had I not had in a proportionate measure this conviction of the secret of my pupils.

How can I retrace to-day the strange steps of my obsession? There were times of our being together when I would have been ready to swear that, literally, in my presence, but with my direct sense of it closed, they had visitors who were known and were welcome. Then it was that, had I not been deterred by the very chance that such an injury might prove greater than the injury to be averted, my exaltation would have broken out. "They 're here, they 're here, you little wretches," I would have cried, "and you can't deny it now!" The little wretches denied it with all the added volume of their sociability and their tenderness, just in the crystal depths of which—like the flash of a fish in a stream—the mockery of their advantage peeped up. The shock had in truth sunk into me still deeper than I knew on the night when, looking out either for Quint or for Miss Jessel under the stars, I had seen there the boy over whose rest I watched and who had immediately brought in with him—had straightway there turned on me—the lovely upward look with which, from the battlements above us, the hideous apparition of Quint had played. If it was a question of a scare my discovery on this occasion had scared me more than any other, and it was essentially in the scared state that I drew my actual conclusions. They harassed me so that sometimes, at odd moments, I shut myself up audibly to rehearse—it was at once a fantastic relief and a renewed despair—the manner in which I might come to the point. I approached it from one side and the other while, in my room, I flung myself about, but I always broke down in the monstrous utterance of names. As they died away on my lips I said to myself that I should indeed help them to represent something infamous if by pronouncing them I should violate as rare a little case of instinctive delicacy as any schoolroom probably had ever known. When I said to myself: "*They* have the manners to be silent, and you, trusted as you are, the baseness to speak!" I felt myself crimson and covered my face with my hands. After these secret scenes I chattered more than ever, going on volubly enough till one of our prodigious palpable hushes occurred—I can call them nothing else—the strange dizzy lift or swim (I try for terms!) into a stillness, a pause of all life, that had nothing to do with the more or less noise we at the moment might be engaged in making and that I could hear through any intensified mirth or quickened recitation or louder strum of the piano. Then it was that the others, the outsiders, were there. Though they were not angels they "passed," as the French say, causing me, while they stayed, to tremble with the fear of their addressing to their younger victims some yet more infernal message or more vivid image than they had thought good enough for myself.

What it was least possible to get rid of was the cruel idea that, whatever I had seen, Miles and Flora saw *more*—things terrible and unguessable and that sprang from dreadful passages of intercourse in the past. Such things naturally left on the surface, for the time, a chill that we vociferously denied we felt; and we had all three, with repetition, got into such splendid training that we went, each time, to mark the close of the incident, almost automatically through the very same movements. It was striking of the children at all events to kiss me inveterately with a wild irrelevance and never to fail—one or the other—of the precious question that had helped us through many a peril. "When do you think he *will* come? Don't you think we *ought* to write?"—there was nothing like that enquiry, we found by experience, for carrying off an awkwardness. "He" of course was their uncle in Harley Street; and we lived in much profusion of theory that he might at any moment arrive to mingle in our circle. It was impossible to have given less encouragement than he had administered to such a doctrine, but if we had not had the doctrine to fall back upon we should have deprived each other of some of our finest exhibitions. He never wrote to them—that may have been selfish, but it was a part of the flattery of his trust of myself; for the way in which a man pays his highest tribute to a woman is apt to be but by the more festal celebration of one of the sacred laws of his comfort. So I held that I carried out the spirit of the pledge given not to appeal to him when I let our young friends understand that their own letters were but charming literary exercises. They were too beautiful to be posted; I kept them myself; I have them all to this hour. This was a rule indeed which only added to the satiric effect of my being plied with the supposition that he might at any moment be among us. It was exactly as if our young friends knew how almost more awkward than anything else that might be for me. There appears to me moreover as I look back no note in all this more extraordinary than the mere fact that, in spite of my tension and of their triumph, I never lost patience with them. Adorable they must in truth have been, I now feel, since I did n't in these days hate them! Would exasperation, however, if relief had longer been postponed, finally have betrayed me? It little matters, for relief arrived. I call it relief though it was only the relief that a snap brings to a strain or the burst of a thunderstorm to a day of suffocation. It was at least change, and it came with a rush.

XIV

Walking to church a certain Sunday morning, I had little Miles at my side and his sister, in advance of us and at Mrs. Grose's, well in sight. It was a crisp clear day, the first of its order for some time; the night had brought a touch of frost and the autumn air, bright and sharp, made the church-bells almost gay. It was an odd accident of thought that I should have happened at such a moment to be particularly and very gratefully struck with the obedience of my little charges. Why did they never resent my inexorable, my perpetual society? Something or other had brought nearer home to me that I had all but pinned the boy to my shawl, and that in the way our companions were marshalled before me I might have appeared to provide against some danger of rebellion. I was like a gaoler with an eye to possible surprises and escapes. But all this belonged—I mean their magnificent little surrender—just to the special array of the facts that were most abysmal. Turned out for Sunday by his uncle's tailor, who had had a free hand and a notion of pretty waistcoats and of his grand little air, Miles's whole title to independence, the rights of his sex and situation, were so stamped upon him that if he had suddenly struck for freedom I should have had nothing to say. I was by the strangest of chances wondering how I should meet him when the revolution unmistakeably occurred. I call it a revolution because I now see how, with the word he spoke, the curtain rose on the last act of my dreadful drama and the catastrophe was precipitated. "Look here, my dear, you know," he charmingly said, "when in the world, please, am I going back to school?"

Transcribed here the speech sounds harmless enough, particularly as uttered in the sweet, high, casual pipe with which, at all interlocutors, but above all at his eternal governess, he threw off intonations as if he were tossing roses. There was something in them that always made one "catch," and I caught at any rate now so effectually that I stopped as short as if one of the trees of the park had fallen across the road. There was something new, on the spot, between us, and he was perfectly aware I recognised it, though to enable me to do so he had no need to look a whit less candid and charming than usual. I could feel in him how he already, from my at first finding nothing to reply, perceived the advantage he had gained. I was so slow to find anything that he had plenty of time, after a minute, to continue with his suggestive but inconclusive smile: "You know, my dear, that for a fellow to be with a lady *always*—!" His "my dear" was constantly on his lips for me, and nothing could have expressed more the exact shade of the sentiment with which I desired to inspire my pupils than its fond familiarity. It was so respectfully easy.

But oh how I felt that at present I must pick my own phrases! I remember that, to gain time, I tried to laugh, and I seemed to see in the beautiful face with which he watched me how ugly and queer I looked. "And always with the same lady?" I returned.

He neither blenched nor winked. The whole thing was virtually out between us. "Ah of course she 's a jolly 'perfect' lady; but after all I 'm a fellow, don't you see? who 's—well, getting on."

I lingered there with him an instant ever so kindly. "Yes, you 're getting on." Oh but I felt helpless!

I have kept to this day the heartbreaking little idea of how he seemed to know that and to play with it. "And you can't say I 've not been awfully good, can you?"

I laid my hand on his shoulder, for though I felt how much better it would have been to walk on I was not yet quite able. "No, I can't say that, Miles."

"Except just that one night, you know—!"

"That one night?" I could n't look as straight as he.

"Why when I went down—went out of the house."

"Oh yes. But I forget what you did it for."

"You forget?"—he spoke with the sweet extravagance of childish reproach. "Why it was just to show you I could!"

"Oh yes—you could."

"And I can again."

I felt I might perhaps after all succeed in keeping my wits about me. "Certainly. But you won't."

"No, not *that* again. It was nothing."

"It was nothing," I said. "But we must go on."

He resumed our walk with me, passing his hand into my arm. "Then when *am* I going back?"

I wore, in turning it over, my most responsible air. "Were you very happy at school?"

He just considered. "Oh I 'm happy enough anywhere!"

"Well then," I quavered, "if you 're just as happy here—!"

"Ah but that is n't everything! Of course *you* know a lot—"

"But you hint that you know almost as much?" I risked as he paused.

"Not half I want to!" Miles honestly professed. "But it is n't so much that."

"What is it then?"

"Well—I want to see more life."

"I see; I see." We had arrived within sight of the church and of various persons, including several of the household of Bly, on their way to it and clustered about the door to see us go in. I quickened our step; I wanted to get there before the question between us opened up much further; I reflected hungrily that he would have for more than an hour to be silent; and I thought with envy of the comparative dusk of the pew and of the almost spiritual help of the hassock on which I might bend my knees. I seemed literally to be running a race with some confusion to which he was about to reduce me, but I felt he had got in first when, before we had even entered the churchyard, he threw out—

"I want my own sort!"

It literally made me bound forward. "There are n't many of your own sort, Miles!" I laughed. "Unless perhaps dear little Flora!"

"You really compare me to a baby girl?"

This found me singularly weak. "Don't you then *love* our sweet Flora?"

"If I did n't—and you too; if I did n't—!" he repeated as if retreating for a jump, yet leaving his thought so unfinished that, after we had come into the gate, another stop, which he imposed on me by the pressure of his arm, had become inevitable. Mrs. Grose and Flora had passed into the church, the other worshippers had followed and we were, for the minute, alone among the old thick graves. We had paused, on the path from the gate, by a low oblong table-like tomb.

"Yes, if you did n't—?"

He looked, while I waited, about at the graves. "Well, you know what!" But he did n't move, and he presently produced something that made me drop straight down on the stone slab as if suddenly to rest. "Does my uncle think what *you* think?"

I markedly rested. "How do you know what I think?"

"Ah well, of course I don't; for it strikes me you never tell me. But I mean does *he* know?"

"Know what, Miles?"

"Why the way I 'm going on."

I recognised quickly enough that I could make, to this enquiry, no answer that would n't involve something of a sacrifice of my employer. Yet it struck me that we were all, at Bly, sufficiently sacrificed to make that venial. "I don't think your uncle much cares."

Miles, on this, stood looking at me. "Then don't you think he can be made to?"

"In what way?"

"Why by his coming down."

"But who 'll get him to come down?"

"*I* will!" the boy said with extraordinary brightness and emphasis. He gave me another look charged with that expression and then marched off alone into church.

XV

The business was practically settled from the moment I never followed him. It was a pitiful surrender to agitation, but my being aware of this had somehow no power to restore me. I only sat there on my tomb and read into what our young friend had said to me the fulness of its meaning; by the time I had grasped the whole of which, I had also embraced, for absence, the pretext that I was ashamed to offer my pupils and the rest of the congregation such an example of delay. What I said to myself above all was that Miles had got something out of me and that the gage of it for him would be just this awkward collapse. He had got out of me that there was something I was much afraid of, and that he should probably be able to make use of my fear to gain, for his own purpose, more freedom. My fear was of having to deal with the intolerable question of the grounds of his dismissal from school, since that was really but the question of the horrors gathered behind. That his uncle should arrive to treat with me of these things was a solution that, strictly speaking, I ought now to have desired to bring on; but I could so little face the ugliness and the pain of it that I simply procrastinated and lived from hand to mouth. The boy, to my deep discomposure, was immensely in the right, was in a position to say to me: "Either you clear up with my guardian the mystery of this interruption of my studies, or you cease to expect me to lead with you a life that 's so unnatural for a boy." What was so unnatural for the particular boy I was concerned with was this sudden revelation of a consciousness and a plan.

That was what really overcame me, what prevented my going in. I walked round the church, hesitating, hovering; I reflected that I had already, with him, hurt myself beyond repair. Therefore I could patch up nothing and it was too extreme an effort to squeeze beside him into the pew: he would be so much more sure than ever to pass his arm into mine and make me sit there for an hour in close mute contact with his commentary on our talk. For the first minute since his arrival I wanted to get away from him. As I paused beneath the high east window and listened to the sounds of worship I was taken with an impulse that might master me, I felt, and completely, should I give it the least encouragement. I might easily put an end to my ordeal by getting away altogether. Here was my chance; there was no one to stop me; I could give the whole thing up—turn my back and bolt. It was only a question of hurrying again, for a few preparations, to the house which the attendance at church of so many of the servants would practically have left unoccupied. No one, in short, could blame me if I should just drive desperately off. What was it to get away if I should get away only till dinner? That would be in a couple of hours, at the end of which—I had the acute prevision—my little pupils would play at innocent wonder about my non-appearance in their train.

"What *did* you do, you naughty bad thing? Why in the world, to worry us so—and take our thoughts off too, don't you know? —did you desert us at the very door?" I could n't meet such questions nor, as they asked them, their false little lovely eyes; yet it was all so exactly what I should have to meet that, as the prospect grew sharp to me, I at last let myself go.

I got, so far as the immediate moment was concerned, away; I came straight out of the churchyard and, thinking hard, retraced my steps through the park. It seemed to me that by the time I reached the house I had made up my mind to cynical flight. The Sunday stillness both of the approaches and of the interior, in which I met no one, fairly stirred me with a sense of opportunity. Were I to get off quickly this way I should get off without a scene, without a word. My quickness would have to be remarkable, however, and the question of a conveyance was the great one to settle. Tormented, in the hall, with difficulties and obstacles, I remember sinking down at the foot of the staircase—suddenly collapsing there on the lowest step and then, with a revulsion, recalling that it was exactly where, more than a month before, in the darkness of night and just so bowed with evil things, I had seen the spectre of the most horrible of women. At this I was able to straighten myself; I went the rest of the way up; I made, in my turmoil, for the schoolroom, where there were objects belonging to me that I should have to take. But I opened the door to find again, in a flash, my eyes unsealed. In the presence of what I saw I reeled straight back upon resistance.

Seated at my own table in the clear noonday light I saw a person whom, without my previous experience, I should have taken at the first blush for some housemaid who might have stayed at home to look after the place and who, availing herself of rare relief from observation and of the schoolroom table and my pens, ink and paper, had applied herself to the considerable effort of a letter to her sweetheart. There was an effort in the way that, while her arms rested on the table, her hands, with evident weariness, supported her head; but at the moment I took this in I had already become aware that, in spite of my entrance, her attitude strangely persisted. Then it was—with the very act of its announcing itself— that her identity flared up in a change of posture. She rose, not as if she had heard me, but with an indescribable grand melancholy of indifference and detachment, and, within a dozen feet of me, stood there as my vile predecessor. Dishonoured and tragic, she was all before me; but even as I fixed and, for memory, secured it, the awful image passed away. Dark as midnight in her black dress, her haggard beauty and her unutterable woe, she had looked at me long enough to appear to say that her right to sit at my table was as good as mine to sit at hers. While these instants lasted indeed I had the extraordinary chill of a feeling that it was I who was the intruder. It was as a wild protest against it that, actually addressing her—"You terrible miserable woman!"—I heard myself break into a sound that, by the open door, rang through the long passage and the empty house. She looked at me as if she heard me, but I had recovered myself and cleared the air. There was nothing in the room the next minute but the sunshine and the sense that I must stay.[3]

XVI

I had so perfectly expected the return of the others to be marked by a demonstration that I was freshly upset at having to find them merely dumb and discreet about my desertion. Instead of gaily denouncing and caressing me they made no allusion to my having failed them, and I was left, for the time, on perceiving that she too said nothing, to study Mrs. Grose's odd face. I did this to such purpose that I made sure they had in some way bribed her to silence; a silence that, however, I would engage to break down

3. Eighth weekly installment ended here.

on the first private opportunity. This opportunity came before tea: I secured five minutes with her in the housekeeper's room, where, in the twilight, amid a smell of lately-baked bread, but with the place all swept and garnished, I found her sitting in pained placidity before the fire. So I see her still, so I see her best: facing the flame from her straight chair in the dusky shining room, a large clean picture of the "put away"—of drawers closed and locked and rest without a remedy.

"Oh yes, they asked me to say nothing; and to please them— so long as they were there—of course I promised. But what had happened to you?"

"I only went with you for the walk," I said. "I had then to come back to meet a friend."

She showed her surprise. "A friend—*you*?"

"Oh yes, I 've a couple!" I laughed. "But did the children give you a reason?"

"For not alluding to your leaving us? Yes; they said you 'd like it better. *Do* you like it better?"

My face had made her rueful. "No, I like it worse!" But after an instant I added: "Did they say why I should like it better?"

"No; Master Miles only said 'We must do nothing but what she likes!' "

"I wish indeed he would! And what did Flora say?"

"Miss Flora was too sweet. She said 'Oh of course, of course!' —and I said the same."

I thought a moment. "You were too sweet too—I can hear you all. But none the less, between Miles and me, it 's now all out."

"All out?" My companion stared. "But what, Miss?"

"Everything. It doesn't matter. I 've made up my mind. I came home, my dear," I went on, "for a talk with Miss Jessel."

I had by this time formed the habit of having Mrs. Grose literally well in hand in advance of my sounding that note; so that even now, as she bravely blinked under the signal of my word, I could keep her comparatively firm. "A talk! Do you mean she spoke?"

"It came to that. I found her, on my return, in the schoolroom."

"And what did she say?" I can hear the good woman still, and the candour of her stupefaction.

"That she suffers the torments—!"

It was this, of a truth, that made her, as she filled out my picture, gape. "Do you mean," she faltered "—of the lost?"

"Of the lost. Of the damned. And that 's why, to share them—" I faltered myself with the horror of it.

But my companion, with less imagination, kept me up. "To share them—?"

"She wants Flora." Mrs. Grose might, as I gave it to her, fairly have fallen away from me had I not been prepared. I still held her there, to show I was. "As I 've told you, however, it does n't matter."

"Because you 've made up your mind? But to what?"

"To everything."

"And what do you call 'everything'?"

"Why to sending for their uncle."

"Oh Miss, in pity do," my friend broke out.

"Ah but I will, I *will*! I see it 's the only way. What 's 'out,' as I told you, with Miles is that if he thinks I 'm afraid to—and has ideas of what he gains by that—he shall see he 's mistaken. Yes, yes; his uncle shall have it here from me on the spot (and before the boy himself if necessary) that if I 'm to be reproached with having done nothing again about more school—"

"Yes, Miss—" my companion pressed me.

"Well, there 's that awful reason."

There were now clearly so many of these for my poor colleague that she was excusable for being vague. "But—a—which?"

"Why the letter from his old place."

"You 'll show it to the master?"

"I ought to have done so on the instant."

"Oh no!" said Mrs. Grose with decision.

"I 'll put it before him," I went on inexorably, "that I can't undertake to work the question on behalf of a child who has been expelled—"

"For we 've never in the least known what!" Mrs. Grose declared.

"For wickedness. For what else—when he 's so clever and beautiful and perfect? Is he stupid? Is he untidy? Is he infirm? Is he ill-natured? He 's exquisite—so it can be only *that*; and that would open up the whole thing. After all," I said, "it 's their uncle's fault. If he left here such people—!"

"He did n't really in the least know them. The fault 's mine." She had turned quite pale.

"Well, you shan't suffer," I answered.

"The children shan't!" she emphatically returned.

I was silent a while; we looked at each other. "Then what am I to tell him?"

"You need n't tell him anything. *I* 'll tell him."

I measured this. "Do you mean you 'll write—?" Remembering she could n't, I caught myself up. "How do you communicate?"

"I tell the bailiff. *He* writes."

"And should you like him to write our story?"

My question had a sarcastic force that I had not fully intended, and it made her after a moment inconsequently break down. The tears were again in her eyes. "Ah Miss, *you* write!"

"Well—to-night," I at last returned; and on this we separated.

XVII

I went so far, in the evening, as to make a beginning. The weather had changed back, a great wind was abroad, and beneath the lamp, in my room, with Flora at peace beside me, I sat for a long time before a blank sheet of paper and listened to the lash of the rain and the batter of the gusts. Finally I went out, taking a candle; I crossed the passage and listened a minute at Miles's door. What, under my endless obsession, I had been impelled to listen for was some betrayal of his not being at rest, and I presently caught one, but not in the form I had expected. His voice tinkled out. "I say, you there—come in." It was gaiety in the gloom!

I went in with my light and found him in bed, very wide awake but very much at his ease. "Well, what are *you* up to?" he asked with a grace of sociability in which it occurred to me that Mrs. Grose, had she been present, might have looked in vain for proof that anything was "out."

I stood over him with my candle. "How did you know I was there?"

"Why of course I heard you. Did you fancy you made no noise? You 're like a troop of cavalry!" he beautifully laughed.

"Then you were n't asleep?"

"Not much! I lie awake and think."

I had put my candle, designedly, a short way off, and then, as he held out his friendly old hand to me, had sat down on the edge of his bed. "What is it," I asked, "that you think of?"

"What in the world, my dear, but *you?*"

"Ah the pride I take in your appreciation does n't insist on that! I had so far rather you slept."

"Well, I think also, you know, of this queer business of ours."

I marked the coolness of his firm little hand. "Of what queer business, Miles?"

"Why the way you bring me up. And all the rest!"

I fairly held my breath a minute, and even from my glimmering taper there was light enough to show how he smiled up at me from his pillow. "What do you mean by all the rest?"

"Oh you know, you know!"

I could say nothing for a minute, though I felt as I held his hand and our eyes continued to meet that my silence had all the air of admitting his charge and that nothing in the whole world of reality was perhaps at that moment so fabulous as our actual relation. "Certainly you shall go back to school," I said, "if it be

that that troubles you. But not to the old place—we must find
another, a better. How could I know it did trouble you, this
question, when you never told me so, never spoke of it at all?"
His clear listening face, framed in its smooth whiteness, made him
for the minute as appealing as some wistful patient in a children's
hospital; and I would have given, as the resemblance came to me,
all I possessed on earth really to be the nurse or the sister of
charity who might have helped to cure him. Well, even as it was
I perhaps might help! "Do you know you've never said a word
to me about your school—I mean the old one; never mentioned it
in any way?"

He seemed to wonder; he smiled with the same loveliness. But
he clearly gained time; he waited, he called for guidance. "Have
n't I?" It was n't for *me* to help him—it was for the thing I
had met!

Something in his tone and the expression of his face, as I got
this from him, set my heart aching with such a pang as it had
never yet known; so unutterably touching was it to see his little
brain puzzled and his little resources taxed to play, under the spell
laid on him, a part of innocence and consistency. "No, never—
from the hour you came back. You 've never mentioned to me one
of your masters, one of your comrades, nor the least little thing
that ever happened to you at school. Never, little Miles—no never
—have you given me an inkling of anything that *may* have happened there. Therefore you can fancy how much I 'm in the dark.
Until you came out, that way, this morning, you had since the
first hour I saw you scarce even made a reference to anything in
your previous life. You seemed so perfectly to accept the present."
It was extraordinary how my absolute conviction of his secret
precocity—or whatever I might call the poison of an influence that
I dared but half-phrase—made him, in spite of the faint breath of
his inward trouble, appear as accessible as an older person, forced
me to treat him as an intelligent equal. "I thought you wanted to
go on as you are."

It struck me that at this he just faintly coloured. He gave, at any
rate, like a convalescent slightly fatigued, a languid shake of his
head. "I don't—I don't. I want to get away."

"You 're tired of Bly?"

"Oh no, I like Bly."

"Well then—?"

"Oh *you* know what a boy wants!"

I felt I did n't know so well as Miles, and I took temporary
refuge. "You want to go to your uncle?"

Again, at this, with his sweet ironic face, he made a movement
on the pillow. "Ah you can't get off with that!"

I was silent a little, and it was I now, I think, who changed colour. "My dear, I don't want to get off!"

"You can't even if you do. You can't, you can't!"—he lay beautifully staring. "My uncle must come down and you must completely settle things."

"If we do," I returned with some spirit, "you may be sure it will be to take you quite away."

"Well, don't you understand that that's exactly what I'm working for? You'll have to *tell* him—about the way you've let it all drop: you'll have to tell him a tremendous lot!"

The exultation with which he uttered this helped me somehow for the instant to meet him rather more. "And how much will *you*, Miles, have to tell him? There are things he'll ask you!"

He turned it over. "Very likely. But what things?"

"The things you've never told me. To make up his mind what to do with you. He can't send you back—"

"I don't want to go back!" he broke in. "I want a new field."

He said it with admirable serenity, with positive unimpeachable gaiety; and doubtless it was that very note that most evoked for me the poignancy, the unnatural childish tragedy, of his probable reappearance at the end of three months with all this bravado and still more dishonour. It overwhelmed me now that I should never be able to bear that, and it made me let myself go. I threw myself upon him and in the tenderness of my pity I embraced him. "Dear little Miles, dear little Miles—!"

My face was close to his, and he let me kiss him, simply taking it with indulgent good humour. "Well, old lady?"

"Is there nothing—nothing at all that you want to tell me?"

He turned off a little, facing round toward the wall and holding up his hand to look at as one had seen sick children look. "I've told you—I told you this morning."

Oh I was sorry for him! "That you just want me not to worry you?"

He looked round at me now as if in recognition of my understanding him; then ever so gently, "To let me alone," he replied.

There was even a strange little dignity in it, something that made me release him, yet, when I had slowly risen, linger beside him. God knows *I* never wished to harass him, but I felt that merely, at this, to turn my back on him was to abandon or, to put it more truly, lose him. "I've just begun a letter to your uncle," I said.

"Well then, finish it!"

I waited a minute. "What happened before?"

He gazed up at me again. "Before what?"

"Before you came back. And before you went away."

For some time he was silent, but he continued to meet my eyes. "What happened?"

It made me, the sound of the words, in which it seemed to me I caught for the very first time a small faint quaver of consenting consciousness—it made me drop on my knees beside the bed and seize once more the chance of possessing him. "Dear little Miles, dear little Miles, if you *knew* how I want to help you! It 's only that, it 's nothing but that, and I 'd rather die than give you a pain or do you a wrong—I 'd rather die than hurt a hair of you. Dear little Miles"—oh I brought it out now even if I *should* go too far—"I just want you to help me to save you!" But I knew in a moment after this that I had gone too far. The answer to my appeal was instantaneous, but it came in the form of an extraordinary blast and chill, a gust of frozen air and a shake of the room as great as if, in the wild wind, the casement had crashed in. The boy gave a loud high shriek which, lost in the rest of the shock of sound, might have seemed, indistinctly, though I was so close to him, a note either of jubilation or of terror. I jumped to my feet again and was conscious of darkness. So for a moment we remained, while I stared about me and saw the drawn curtains unstirred and the window still tight. "Why the candle 's out!" I then cried.

"It was I who blew it, dear!" said Miles.

XVIII

The next day, after lessons, Mrs. Grose found a moment to say to me quietly: "Have you written, Miss?"

"Yes—I've written." But I did n't add—for the hour—that my letter, sealed and directed, was still in my pocket. There would be time enough to send it before the messenger should go to the village. Meanwhile there had been on the part of my pupils no more brilliant, more exemplary morning. It was exactly as if they had both had at heart to gloss over any recent little friction. They performed the dizziest feats of arithmetic, soaring quite out of *my* feeble range, and perpetrated, in higher spirits than ever, geographical and historical jokes. It was conspicuous of course in Miles in particular that he appeared to wish to show how easily he could let me down. This child, to my memory, really lives in a setting of beauty and misery that no words can translate; there was a distinction all his own in every impulse he revealed; never was a small natural creature, to the uninformed eye all frankness and freedom, a more ingenious, a more extraordinary little gentleman. I had perpetually to guard against the wonder of contemplation into which my initiated view betrayed me; to check the irrelevant gaze and discouraged sigh in which I constantly both attacked and renounced the enigma of what such a little gentleman could have done that deserved a penalty. Say that, by the dark prodigy I knew, the imagination of all evil *had* been opened up to him: all the justice within me ached for the proof that it could ever have flowered into an act.

He had never at any rate been such a little gentleman as when, after our early dinner on this dreadful day, he came round to me and asked if I should n't like him for half an hour to play to me. David playing to Saul could never have shown a finer sense of the occasion.[4] It was literally a charming exhibition of tact, of magnanimity, and quite tantamount to his saying outright: "The true knights we love to read about never push an advantage too far. I know what you mean now: you mean that—to be let alone yourself and not followed up—you 'll cease to worry and spy upon me, won't keep me so close to you, will let me go and come. Well, I 'come,' you see—but I don't go! There 'll be plenty of time for that. I do really delight in your society and I only want to show you that I contended for a principle." It may be imagined whether I resisted this appeal or failed to accompany him again, hand in hand, to the schoolroom. He sat down at the old piano and played as he had never played; and if there are those who think he had better have been kicking a football I can only say that I wholly agree with them. For at the end of a time that under his influence I had quite ceased to measure I started up with a strange sense of having literally slept at my post. It was after luncheon, and by the schoolroom fire, and yet I had n't really in the least slept; I had only done something much worse—I had forgotten. Where all this time was Flora? When I put the question to Miles he played on a minute before answering, and then could only say: "Why, my dear, how do *I* know?"—breaking moreover into a happy laugh which immediately after, as if it were a vocal accompaniment, he prolonged into incoherent extravagant song.

I went straight to my room, but his sister was not there; then, before going downstairs, I looked into several others. As she was nowhere about she would surely be with Mrs. Grose, whom in the comfort of that theory I accordingly proceeded in quest of. I found her where I had found her the evening before, but she met my quick challenge with blank scared ignorance. She had only supposed that, after the repast, I had carried off both the children; as to which she was quite in her right, for it was the very first time I had allowed the little girl out of my sight without some special provision. Of course now indeed she might be with the maids, so that the immediate thing was to look for her without an air of

4. I Samuel, xvi.14–23.

alarm. This we promptly arranged between us; but when, ten minutes later and in pursuance of our arrangement, we met in the hall, it was only to report on either side that after guarded enquiries we had altogether failed to trace her. For a minute there, apart from observation, we exchanged mute alarms, and I could feel with what high interest my friend returned me all those I had from the first given her.

"She 'll be above," she presently said—"in one of the rooms you have n't searched."

"No; she 's at a distance." I had made up my mind. "She has gone out."

Mrs. Grose stared. "Without a hat?"

I naturally also looked volumes. "Is n't that woman always without one?"

"She 's with *her?*"

"She 's with *her!*" I declared. "We must find them."

My hand was on my friend's arm, but she failed for the moment, confronted with such an account of the matter, to respond to my pressure. She communed, on the contrary, where she stood, with her uneasiness. "And where 's Master Miles?"

"Oh *he 's* with Quint. They 'll be in the schoolroom."

"Lord, Miss!" My view, I was myself aware—and therefore I suppose my tone—had never yet reached so calm an assurance.

"The trick 's played," I went on; "they 've successfully worked their plan. He found the most divine little way to keep me quiet while she went off."

" 'Divine'?" Mrs. Grose bewilderedly echoed.

"Infernal then!" I almost cheerfully rejoined. "He has provided for himself as well. But come!"

She had helplessly gloomed at the upper regions. "You leave him—?"

"So long with Quint? Yes—I don't mind that now."

She always ended at these moments by getting possession of my hand, and in this manner she could at present still stay me. But after gasping an instant at my sudden resignation, "Because of your letter?" she eagerly brought out.

I quickly, by way of answer, felt for my letter, drew it forth, held it up, and then, freeing myself, went and laid it on the great hall-table. "Luke will take it," I said as I came back. I reached the house-door and opened it; I was already on the steps.

My companion still demurred: the storm of the night and the early morning had dropped, but the afternoon was damp and grey. I came down to the drive while she stood in the doorway. "You go with nothing on?"

"What do I care when the child has nothing? I can't wait to dress," I cried, "and if you must do so I leave you. Try meanwhile yourself upstairs."

"With *them?*" Oh on this the poor woman promptly joined me! [5]

XIX

We went straight to the lake, as it was called at Bly, and I dare say rightly called, though it may have been a sheet of water less remarkable than my untravelled eyes supposed it. My acquaintance with sheets of water was small, and the pool of Bly, at all events on the few occasions of my consenting, under the protection of my pupils, to affront its surface in the old flat-bottomed boat moored there for our use, had impressed me both with its extent and its agitation. The usual place of embarkation was half a mile from the house, but I had an intimate conviction that, wherever Flora might be, she was not near home. She had not given me the slip for any small adventure, and, since the day of the very great one that I had shared with her by the pond, I had been aware, in our walks, of the quarter to which she most inclined. This was why I had now given to Mrs. Grose's steps so marked a direction —a direction making her, when she perceived it, oppose a resistance that showed me she was freshly mystified. "You 're going to the water, Miss?—you think she's *in*—?"

"She may be, though the depth is, I believe, nowhere very great. But what I judge most likely is that she 's on the spot from which, the other day, we saw together what I told you."

"When she pretended not to see—?"

"With that astounding self-possession! I 've always been sure she wanted to go back alone. And now her brother has managed it for her."

Mrs. Grose still stood where she had stopped. "You suppose they really *talk* of them?"

I could meet this with an assurance! "They say things that, if we heard them, would simply appal us."

"And if she *is* there—?"

"Yes?"

"Then Miss Jessel is?"

"Beyond a doubt. You shall see."

"Oh thank you!" my friend cried, planted so firm that, taking it in, I went straight on without her. By the time I reached the pool, however, she was close behind me, and I knew that, whatever, to her apprehension, might befall me, the exposure of sticking to me struck her as her least danger. She exhaled a moan of relief

5. Ninth weekly installment and "Part Fourth" ended here.

as we at last came in sight of the greater part of the water without
a sight of the child. There was no trace of Flora on that nearer
side of the bank where my observation of her had been most
startling, and none on the opposite edge, where, save for a margin
of some twenty yards, a thick copse came down to the pond. This
expanse, oblong in shape, was so narrow compared to its length
that, with its ends out of view, it might have been taken for a
scant river. We looked at the empty stretch, and then I felt the
suggestion in my friend's eyes. I knew what she meant and I replied with a negative headshake.

"No, no; wait! She has taken the boat."

My companion stared at the vacant mooring-place and then
again across the lake. "Then where is it?"

"Our not seeing it is the strongest of proofs. She has used it
to go over, and then has managed to hide it."

"All alone—that child?"

"She 's not alone, and at such times she 's not a child: she 's an
old, old woman." I scanned all the visible shore while Mrs. Grose
took again, into the queer element I offered her, one of her plunges
of submission; then I pointed out that the boat might perfectly
be in a small refuge formed by one of the recesses of the pool,
an indentation masked, for the hither side, by a projection of the
bank and by a clump of trees growing close to the water.

"But if the boat 's there, where on earth 's *she?*" my colleague
anxiously asked.

"That's exactly what we must learn." And I started to walk
further.

"By going all the way round?"

"Certainly, far as it is. It will take us but ten minutes, yet it 's
far enough to have made the child prefer not to walk. She went
straight over."

"Laws!" cried my friend again: the chain of my logic was ever
too strong for her. It dragged her at my heels even now, and when
we had got halfway round—a devious tiresome process, on ground
much broken and by a path choked with overgrowth—I paused to
give her breath. I sustained her with a grateful arm, assuring her
that she might hugely help me; and this started us afresh, so that
in the course of but few minutes more we reached a point from
which we found the boat to be where I had supposed it. It had
been intentionally left as much as possible out of sight and was
tied to one of the stakes of a fence that came, just there, down to
the brink and that had been an assistance to disembarking. I recognised, as I looked at the pair of short thick oars, quite safely
drawn up, the prodigious character of the feat for a little girl; but
I had by this time lived too long among wonders and had panted

to too many livelier measures. There was a gate in the fence, through which we passed, and that brought us after a trifling interval more into the open. Then "There she is!" we both exclaimed at once.

Flora, a short way off, stood before us on the grass and smiled as if her performance had now become complete. The next thing she did, however, was to stoop straight down and pluck—quite as if it were all she was there for—a big ugly spray of withered fern. I at once felt sure she had just come out of the copse. She waited for us, not herself taking a step, and I was conscious of the rare solemnity with which we presently approached her. She smiled and smiled, and we met; but it was all done in a silence by this time flagrantly ominous. Mrs. Grose was the first to break the spell: she threw herself on her knees and, drawing the child to her breast, clasped in a long embrace the little tender yielding body. While this dumb convulsion lasted I could only watch it—which I did the more intently when I saw Flora's face peep at me over our companion's shoulder. It was serious now—the flicker had left it; but it strengthened the pang with which I at that moment envied Mrs. Grose the simplicity of *her* relation. Still, all this while, nothing more passed between us save that Flora had let her foolish fern again drop to the ground. What she and I had virtually said to each other was that pretexts were useless now. When Mrs. Grose finally got up she kept the child's hand, so that the two were still before me; and the singular reticence of our communion was even more marked in the frank look she addressed me. "I 'll be hanged," it said, "if I *'ll* speak!"

It was Flora who, gazing all over me in candid wonder, was the first. She was struck with our bareheaded aspect. "Why where are your things?"

"Where yours are, my dear!" I promptly returned.

She had already got back her gaiety and appeared to take this as an answer quite sufficient. "And where 's Miles?" she went on.

There was something in the small valour of it that quite finished me: these three words from her were, in a flash like the glitter of a drawn blade, the jostle of the cup that my hand for weeks and weeks had held high and full to the brim and that now, even before speaking, I felt overflow in a deluge. "I 'll tell you if you 'll tell *me*—" I heard myself say, then heard the tremor in which it broke.

"Well, what?"

Mrs. Grose's suspense blazed at me, but it was too late now, and I brought the thing out handsomely. "Where, my pet, is Miss Jessel?"

XX

Just as in the churchyard with Miles, the whole thing was upon us. Much as I had made of the fact that this name had never once, between us, been sounded, the quick smitten glare with which the child's face now received it fairly likened my breach of the silence to the smash of a pane of glass. It added to the interposing cry, as if to stay the blow, that Mrs. Grose at the same instant uttered over my violence—the shriek of a creature scared, or rather wounded, which, in turn, within a few seconds, was completed by a gasp of my own. I seized my colleague's arm. "She 's there, she 's there!"

Miss Jessel stood before us on the opposite bank exactly as she had stood the other time, and I remember, strangely, as the first feeling now produced in me, my thrill of joy at having brought on a proof. She was there, so I was justified; she was there, so I was neither cruel nor mad. She was there for poor scared Mrs. Grose, but she was there most for Flora; and no moment of my monstrous time was perhaps so extraordinary as that in which I consciously threw out to her—with the sense that, pale and ravenous demon as she was, she would catch and understand it—an inarticulate message of gratitude. She rose erect on the spot my friend and I had lately quitted, and there was n't in all the long reach of her desire an inch of her evil that fell short. This first vividness of vision and emotion were things of a few seconds, during which Mrs. Grose's dazed blink across to where I pointed struck me as showing that she too at last saw, just as it carried my own eyes precipitately to the child. The revelation then of the manner in which Flora was affected startled me in truth far more than it would have done to find her also merely agitated, for direct dismay was of course not what I had expected. Prepared and on her guard as our pursuit had actually made her, she would repress every betrayal; and I was therefore at once shaken by my first glimpse of the particular one for which I had not allowed. To see her, without a convulsion of her small pink face, not even feign to glance in the direction of the prodigy I announced, but only, instead of that, turn at *me* an expression of hard still gravity, an expression absolutely new and unprecedented and that appeared to read and accuse and judge me—this was a stroke that somehow converted the little girl herself into a figure portentous. I gaped at her coolness even though my certitude of her thoroughly seeing was never greater than at that instant, and then, in the immediate need to defend myself, I called her passionately to witness. "She 's there, you little unhappy thing—there, there, *there*, and you know it as well as you know me!" I had said shortly before to Mrs. Grose that she was not at these times a child, but an old, old woman, and my description of her could n't have been more strikingly confirmed than in the way in which, for all notice of this, she simply showed me, without an expressional concession or admission, a countenance of deeper and deeper, of indeed suddenly quite fixed reprobation. I was by this time—if I can put the whole thing at all together—more appalled at what I may properly call her manner than at anything else, though it was quite simultaneously that I became aware of having Mrs. Grose also, and very formidably, to reckon with. My elder companion, the next moment, at any rate, blotted out everything but her own flushed face and her loud shocked protest, a burst of high disapproval. "What a dreadful turn, to be sure, Miss! Where on earth do you see anything?"

I could only grasp her more quickly yet, for even while she spoke the hideous plain presence stood undimmed and undaunted. It had already lasted a minute, and it lasted while I continued, seizing my colleague, quite thrusting her at it and presenting her to it, to insist with my pointing hand. "You don't see her exactly as *we* see?—you mean to say you don't now—*now*? She 's as big as a blazing fire! Only look, dearest woman, *look*—!" She looked, just as I did, and gave me, with her deep groan of negation, repulsion, compassion—the mixture with her pity of her relief at her exemption—a sense, touching to me even then, that she would have backed me up if she had been able. I might well have needed that, for with this hard blow of the proof that her eyes were hopelessly sealed I felt my own situation horribly crumble, I felt—I *saw*—my livid predecessor press, from her position, on my defeat, and I took the measure, more than all, of what I should have from this instant to deal with in the astounding little attitude of Flora. Into this attitude Mrs. Grose immediately and violently entered, breaking, even while there pierced through my sense of ruin a prodigious private triumph, into breathless reassurance.

"She is n't there, little lady, and nobody 's there—and you never see nothing, my sweet! How can poor Miss Jessel—when poor Miss Jessel 's dead and buried? *We* know, don't we love?"—and she appealed, blundering in, to the child. "It 's all a mere mistake and a worry and a joke—and we 'll go home as fast as we can!"

Our companion, on this, had responded with a strange quick primness of propriety, and they were again, with Mrs. Grose on her feet, united, as it were, in shocked opposition to me. Flora continued to fix me with her small mask of disaffection, and even at that minute I prayed God to forgive me for seeming to see that, as she stood there holding tight to our friend's dress, her incomparable childish beauty had suddenly failed, had quite vanished. I 've said it already—she was literally, she was hideously hard; she had turned common and almost ugly. "I don't know what you mean. I see nobody. I see nothing. I never *have*. I think you 're cruel. I don't like you!" Then, after this deliverance, which might have been that of a vulgarly pert little girl in the street, she hugged Mrs. Grose more closely and buried in her skirts the dreadful little face. In this position she launched an almost furious wail. "Take me away, take me away—oh take me away from *her!*"

"From *me?*" I panted.

"From you—from you!" she cried.

Even Mrs. Grose looked across at me dismayed; while I had nothing to do but communicate again with the figure that, on the opposite bank, without a movement, as rigidly still as if catching, beyond the interval, our voices, was as vividly there for my disaster as it was not there for my service. The wretched child had spoken exactly as if she had got from some outside source each of her stabbing little words, and I could therefore, in the full despair of all I had to accept, but sadly shake my head at her. "If I had ever doubted all my doubt would at present have gone. I 've been living with the miserable truth, and now it has only too much closed round me. Of course I 've lost you: I 've interfered, and you 've seen, under *her* dictation"—with which I faced, over the pool again, our infernal witness—"the easy and perfect way to meet it. I 've done my best, but I 've lost you. Good-bye." For Mrs. Grose I had an imperative, an almost frantic "Go, go!" before which, in infinite distress, but mutely possessed of the little girl and clearly convinced, in spite of her blindness, that something awful had occurred and some collapse engulfed us, she retreated, by the way we had come, as fast as she could move.

Of what first happened when I was left alone I had no subsequent memory. I only knew that at the end of, I suppose, a quarter of an hour, an odorous dampness and roughness, chilling and piercing my trouble, had made me understand that I must have thrown myself, on my face, to the ground and given way to a wildness of grief. I must have lain there long and cried and wailed, for when I raised my head the day was almost done. I got up and looked a moment, through the twilight, at the grey pool and its blank haunted edge, and then I took, back to the house, my dreary and difficult course. When I reached the gate in the fence the boat, to my surprise, was gone, so that I had a fresh reflexion to make on Flora's extraordinary command of the situation. She passed that night, by the most tacit and, I should add, were not the word so grotesque a false note, the happiest of arrangements, with Mrs. Grose. I saw neither of them on my return, but on the other hand I saw, as by an ambiguous compensation, a great deal of Miles. I saw—I can use no other phrase—so much of him that

it fairly measured more than it had ever measured. No evening
I had passed at Bly was to have had the portentous quality of this
one; in spite of which—and in spite also of the deeper depths of
consternation that had opened beneath my feet—there was literally, in the ebbing actual, an extraordinarily sweet sadness. On
reaching the house I had never so much as looked for the boy;
I had simply gone straight to my room to change what I was wearing and to take in, at a glance, much material testimony to Flora's
rupture. Her little belongings had all been removed. When later,
by the schoolroom fire, I was served with tea by the usual maid,
I indulged, on the article of my other pupil, in no enquiry whatever. He had his freedom now—he might have it to the end! Well,
he did have it; and it consisted—in part at least—of his coming
in at about eight o'clock and sitting down with me in silence.
On the removal of the tea-things I had blown out the candles and
drawn my chair closer: I was conscious of a mortal coldness and
felt as if I should never again be warm. So when he appeared I was
sitting in the glow with my thoughts. He paused a moment by the
door as if to look at me; then—as if to share them—came to the
other side of the hearth and sank into a chair. We sat there in
absolute stillness; yet he wanted, I felt, to be with me.[6]

XXI

Before a new day, in my room, had fully broken, my eyes opened
to Mrs. Grose, who had come to my bedside with worse news.
Flora was so markedly feverish that an illness was perhaps at hand;
she had passed a night of extreme unrest, a night agitated above
all by fears that had for their subject not in the least her former
but wholly her present governess. It was not against the possible
re-entrance of Miss Jessel on the scene that she protested—it was
conspicuously and passionately against mine. I was at once on my
feet, and with an immense deal to ask; the more that my friend
had discernibly now girded her loins to meet me afresh. This I felt
as soon as I had put to her the question of her sense of the child's
sincerity as against my own. "She persists in denying to you that
she saw, or has ever seen, anything?"

My visitor's trouble truly was great. "Ah Miss, it is n't a matter
on which I can push her! Yet it is n't either, I must say, as if
I much needed to. It has made her, every inch of her, quite old."

"Oh I see her perfectly from here. She resents, for all the world
like some high little personage, the imputation on her truthfulness
and, as it were, her respectability. 'Miss Jessel indeed—*she!*' Ah
she 's 'respectable,' the chit! The impression she gave me there
yesterday was, I assure you, the very strangest of all: it was quite

6. Tenth weekly installment ended here.

beyond any of the others. I *did* put my foot in it! She 'll never speak to me again."

Hideous and obscure as it all was, it held Mrs. Grose briefly silent; then she granted my point with a frankness which, I made sure, had more behind it. "I think indeed, Miss, she never will. She do have a grand manner about it!"

"And that manner"—I summed it up—"is practically what 's the matter with her now."

Oh that manner, I could see in my visitor's face, and not a little else besides! "She asks me every three minutes if I think you 're coming in."

"I see—I see." I too, on my side, had so much more than worked it out. "Has she said to you since yesterday—except to repudiate her familiarity with anything so dreadful—a single other word about Miss Jessel?"

"Not one, Miss. And of course, you know," my friend added, "I took it from her by the lake that just then and there at least there *was* nobody."

"Rather! And naturally you take it from her still."

"I don't contradict her. What else can I do?"

"Nothing in the world! You 've the cleverest little person to deal with. They 've made them—their two friends, I mean—still cleverer even than nature did; for it was wondrous material to play on! Flora has now her grievance, and she'll work it to the end."

"Yes, Miss; but to *what* end?"

"Why that of dealing with me to her uncle. She 'll make me out to him the lowest creature—!"

I winced at the fair show of the scene in Mrs. Grose's face; she looked for a minute as if she sharply saw them together. "And him who thinks so well of you!"

"He has an odd way—it comes over me now," I laughed, "—of proving it! But that does n't matter. What Flora wants of course is to get rid of me."

My companion bravely concurred. "Never again to so much as look at you."

"So that what you 've come to me now for," I asked, "is to speed me on my way?" Before she had time to reply, however, I had her in check. "I 've a better idea—the result of my reflexions. My going *would* seem the right thing, and on Sunday I was terribly near it. Yet that won't do. It 's *you* who must go. You must take Flora."

My visitor, at this, did speculate. "But where in the world—?"

"Away from here. Away from *them*. Away, even most of all, now, from me. Straight to her uncle."

"Only to tell on you—?"

"No, not 'only'! To leave me, in addition, with my remedy."
She was still vague. "And what *is* your remedy?"

"Your loyalty, to begin with. And then Miles's."

She looked at me hard. "Do you think he—?"

"Won't, if he has the chance, turn on me? Yes, I venture still
to think it. At all events I want to try. Get off with his sister as
soon as possible and leave me with him alone." I was amazed,
myself, at the spirit I had still in reserve, and therefore perhaps
a trifle the more disconcerted at the way in which, in spite of this
fine example of it, she hesitated. "There 's one thing, of course,"
I went on: "they must n't, before she goes, see each other for
three seconds." Then it came over me that, in spite of Flora's
presumable sequestration from the instant of her return from the
pool, it might already be too late. "Do you mean," I anxiously
asked, "that they *have* met?"

At this she quite flushed. "Ah, Miss, I 'm not such a fool as that!
If I 've been obliged to leave her three or four times, it has been
each time with one of the maids, and at present, though she 's alone,
she 's locked in safe. And yet—and yet!" There were too many
things.

"And yet what?"

"Well, are you so sure of the little gentleman?"

"I 'm not sure of anything but *you*. But I have, since last evening,
a new hope. I think he wants to give me an opening. I do believe
that—poor little exquisite wretch!—he wants to speak. Last evening, in the firelight and the silence, he sat with me for two hours
as if it were just coming."

Mrs. Grose looked hard through the window at the grey gathering day. "And did it come?"

"No, though I waited and waited I confess it did n't, and it was
without a breach of the silence, or so much as a faint allusion to
his sister's condition and absence, that we at last kissed for good-
night. All the same," I continued, "I can't, if her uncle sees her,
consent to his seeing her brother without my having given the
boy—and most of all because things have got so bad—a little more
time."

My friend appeared on this ground more reluctant than I could
quite understand. "What do you mean by more time?"

"Well, a day or two—really to bring it out. He 'll then be on
my side—of which you see the importance. If nothin comes I
shall only fail, and you at the worst have helped me by doing on
your arrival in town whatever you may have found possible." So
I put it before her, but she continued for a little so lost in other
reasons that I came again to her aid. "Unless indeed," I wound
up, "you really want *not* to go."

I could see it, in her face, at last clear itself: she put out her hand to me as a pledge. "I 'll go—I 'll go. I 'll go this morning."

I wanted to be very just. "If you *should* wish still to wait I 'd engage she should n't see me."

"No, no: it 's the place itself. She must leave it." She held me a moment with heavy eyes, then brought out the rest. "Your idea 's the right one. I myself, Miss—"

"Well?"

"I can't stay."

The look she gave me with it made me jump at possibilities. "You mean that, since yesterday, you *have* seen—?"

She shook her head with dignity. "I 've *heard*—!"

"Heard?"

"From that child—horrors! There!" she sighed with tragic relief. "On my honour, Miss, she says things—!" But at this evocation she broke down; she dropped with a sudden cry upon my sofa and, as I had seen her do before, gave way to all the anguish of it.

It was quite in another manner that I for my part let myself go. "Oh thank God!"

She sprang up again at this, drying her eyes with a groan. " 'Thank God'?"

"It so justifies me!"

"It does that, Miss!"

I could n't have desired more emphasis, but I just waited "She 's so horrible?"

I saw my colleague scarce knew how to put it. "Really shocking."

"And about me?"

"About you, Miss—since you must have it. It 's beyond everything, for a young lady; and I can't think wherever she must have picked up—"

"The appalling language she applies to me? I can then!" I broke in with a laugh that was doubtless significant enough.

It only in truth left my friend still more grave. "Well, perhaps I ought to also—since I 've heard some of it before! Yet I can't bear it," the poor woman went on while with the same movement she glanced, on my dressing-table, at the face of my watch. "But I must go back."

I kept her, however. "Ah if you can't bear it—!"

"How can I stop [7] with her, you mean? Why just *for* that: to get her away. Far from this," she pursued, "far from *them*—"

"She may be different? she may be free?" I seized her almost with joy. "Then in spite of yesterday you *believe*—"

"In such doings?" Her simple description of them required, in the light of her expression, to be carried no further, and she gave

7. Stay.

me the whole thing as she had never done. "I believe."

Yes, it was a joy, and we were still shoulder to shoulder: if I might continue sure of that I should care but little what else happened. My support in the presence of disaster would be the same as it had been in my early need of confidence, and if my friend would answer for my honesty I would answer for all the rest. On the point of taking leave of her, none the less, I was to some extent embarrassed. "There 's one thing of course—it occurs to me —to remember. My letter giving the alarm will have reached town before you."

I now felt still more how she had been beating about the bush and how weary at last it had made her. "Your letter won't have got there. Your letter never went."

"What then became of it?"

"Goodness knows! Master Miles—"

"Do you mean *he* took it?" I gasped.

She hung fire, but she overcame her reluctance. "I mean that I saw yesterday, when I came back with Miss Flora, that it was n't where you had put it. Later in the evening I had the chance to question Luke, and he declared that he had neither noticed nor touched it." We could only exchange, on this, one of our deeper mutual soundings, and it was Mrs. Grose who first brought up the plumb with an almost elate "You see!"

"Yes, I see that if Miles took it instead he probably will have read it and destroyed it."

"And don't you see anything else?"

I faced her a moment with a sad smile. "It strikes me that by this time your eyes are open even wider than mine."

They proved to be so indeed, but she could still almost blush to show it. "I make out now what he must have done at school." And she gave, in her simple sharpness, an almost droll disillusioned nod. "He stole!"

I turned it over—I tried to be more judicial. "Well—perhaps."

She looked as if she found me unexpectedly calm. "He stole *letters!*"

She could n't know my reasons for a calmness after all pretty shallow; so I showed them off as I might. "I hope then it was to more purpose than in this case! The note, at all events, that I put on the table yesterday," I pursued, "will have given him so scant an advantage—for it contained only the bare demand for an interview—that he 's already much ashamed of having gone so far for so little, and that what he had on his mind last evening was precisely the need of confession." I seemed to myself for the instant to have mastered it, to see it all. "Leave us, leave us"—I was already, at the door, hurrying her off. "I 'll get it out of him. He 'll meet me. He 'll confess. If he confesses he 's saved. And if he 's saved—"

"Then *you* are?" The dear woman kissed me on this, and I took her farewell. "I 'll save you without him!" she cried as she went.

XXII

Yet it was when she had got off—and I missed her on the spot— that the great pinch really came. If I had counted on what it would give me to find myself alone with Miles I quickly recognised that it would give me at least a measure. No hour of my stay in fact was so assailed with apprehensions as that of my coming down to learn that the carriage containing Mrs. Grose and my younger pupil had already rolled out of the gates. Now I *was*, I said to myself, face to face with the elements, and for much of the rest of the day, while I fought my weakness, I could consider that I had been supremely rash. It was a tighter place still than I had yet turned round in; all the more that, for the first time, I could see in the aspect of others a confused reflexion of the crisis. What had happened naturally caused them all to stare; there was too little of the explained, throw out whatever we might, in the suddenness of my colleague's act. The maids and the men looked blank; the effect of which on my nerves was an aggravation until I saw the necessity of making it a positive aid. It was in short by just clutching the helm that I avoided total wreck; and I dare say that, to bear up at all, I became that morning very grand and very dry. I welcomed the consciousness that I was charged with much to do, and I caused it to be known as well that, left thus to myself, I was quite remarkably firm. I wandered with that manner, for the next hour or two, all over the place and looked, I have no doubt, as if I were ready for any onset. So, for the benefit of whom it might concern, I paraded with a sick heart.

The person it appeared least to concern proved to be, till dinner, little Miles himself. My perambulations had given me meanwhile no glimpse of him, but they had tended to make more public the change taking place in our relation as a consequence of his having at the piano, the day before, kept me, in Flora's interest, so beguiled and befooled. The stamp of publicity had of course been fully given by her confinement and departure, and the change itself was now ushered in by our non-observance of the regular custom of the schoolroom. He had already disappeared when, on my way down, I pushed open his door, and I learned below that he had breakfasted—in the presence of a couple of the maids—with Mrs. Grose and his sister. He had then gone out, as he said, for a stroll; than which nothing, I reflected, could better have expressed his frank view of the abrupt transformation of my office. What he would now permit this office to consist of was yet to be settled: there was at the least a queer relief—I mean for myself in especial —in the renouncement of one pretension. If so much had sprung to the surface I scarce put it too strongly in saying that what had perhaps sprung highest was the absurdity of our prolonging the fiction that I had anything more to teach him. It sufficiently stuck out that, by tacit little tricks in which even more than myself he carried out the care for my dignity, I had had to appeal to him to let me off straining to meet him on the ground of his true capacity. He had at any rate his freedom now; I was never to touch it again: as I had amply shown, moreover, when, on his joining me in the schoolroom the previous night, I uttered, in reference to the interval just concluded, neither challenge nor hint. I had too much, from this moment, my other ideas. Yet when he at last arrived the difficulty of applying them, the accumulations of my problem, were brought straight home to me by the beautiful little presence on which what had occurred had as yet, for the eye, dropped neitiher stain nor shadow.

To mark, for the house, the high state I cultivated I decreed that my meals with the boy should be served, as we called it, down-stairs; so that I had been awaiting him in the ponderous pomp of the room outside the window of which I had had from Mrs. Grose, that first scared Sunday, my flash of something it would scarce have done to call light. Here at present I felt afresh—for I had felt it again and again—how my equilibrium depended on the suc-cess of my rigid will, the will to shut my eyes as tight as possible to the truth that what I had to deal with was, revoltingly, against nature. I could only get on at all by taking "nature" into my con-fidence and my account, by treating my monstrous ordeal as a push in a direction unusual, of course, and unpleasant, but demanding after all, for a fair front, only another turn of the screw of ordinary human ·virtue. No attempt, none the less, could well require more tact than just this attempt to supply, one's self, *all* the nature. How could I put even a little of that article into a suppression of reference to what had occurred? How on the other hand could I make a reference without a new plunge into the hideous obscure? Well, a sort of answer, after a time, had come to me, and it was so far confirmed as that I was met, incontestably, by the quickened vision of what was rare in my little companion. It was indeed as if he had found even now—as he had so often found at lessons —still some other delicate way to ease me off. Was n't there light in the fact which, as we shared our solitude, broke out with a specious glitter it had never yet quite worn?—the fact that (op-portunity aiding, precious opportunity which had now come) it would be preposterous, with a child so endowed, to forego the help one might wrest from absolute intelligence? What had his intelligence been given him for but to save him? Might n't one, to reach his mind, risk the stretch of a stiff arm across his character? It was as if, when we were face to face in the dining-room, he had literally shown me the way. The roast mutton was on the table and I had dispensed with attendance. Miles, before he sat down, stood a moment with his hands in his pockets and looked at the joint, on which he seemed on the point of passing some humorous judgement. But what he presently produced was: "I say, my dear, is she really very awfully ill?"

"Little Flora? Not so bad but that she 'll presently be better. London will set her up. Bly had ceased to agree with her. Come here and take your mutton."

He alertly obeyed me, carried the plate carefully to his seat and, when he was established, went on. "Did Bly disagree with her so terribly all at once?"

"Not so suddenly as you might think. One had seen it coming on."

"Then why did n't you get her off before?"

"Before what?"

"Before she became too ill to travel."

I found myself prompt. "She 's *not too* ill to travel; she only might have become so if she had stayed. This was just the moment to seize. The journey will dissipate the influence"—oh I was grand! —"and carry it off."

"I see, I see"—Miles, for that matter, was grand too. He settled to his repast with the charming little "table manner" that, from the day of his arrival, had relieved me of all grossness of admonition. Whatever he had been expelled from school for, it was n't for ugly feeding. He was irreproachable, as always, today; but was unmistakably more conscious. He was discernibly trying to take for granted more things than he found, without assistance, quite easy; and he dropped into peaceful silence while he felt his situation. Our meal was of the briefest—mine a vain pretence, and I had the things immediately removed. While this was done Miles stood again with his hands in his little pockets and his back to me—stood and looked out of the wide window through which, that other day, I had seen what pulled me up. We continued silent while the maid was with us—as silent, it whimsically occurred to me, as some young couple who, on their wedding-journey, at the inn, feel shy in the presence of the waiter. He turned round only when the waiter had left us. "Well—so we 're alone!" [8]

8. Eleventh weekly installment ended here.

XXIII

"Oh more or less." I imagine my smile was pale. "Not absolutely. We should n't like that!" I went on.

"No—I suppose we should n't. Of course we 've the others."

"We 've the others—we 've indeed the others," I concurred.

"Yet even though we have them," he returned, still with his hands in his pockets and planted there in front of me, "they don't much count, do they?"

I made the best of it, but I felt wan. "It depends on what you call 'much'!"

"Yes"—with all accommodation—"everything depends!" On this, however, he faced to the window again and presently reached it with his vague restless cogitating step. He remained there a while with his forehead against the glass, in contemplation of the stupid shrubs I knew and the dull things of November. I had always my hypocrisy of "work," behind which I now gained the sofa. Steadying myself with it there as I had repeatedly done at those moments of torment that I have described as the moments of my knowing the children to be given to something from which I was barred, I sufficiently obeyed my habit of being prepared for the worst. But an extraordinary impression dropped on me as I extracted a meaning from the boy's embarrassed back—none other than the impression that I was not barred now. This inference grew in a few minutes to sharp intensity and seemed bound up with the direct perception that it was positively *he* who was. The frames and squares of the great window were a kind of image, for him, of a kind of failure. I felt that I saw him, in any case, shut in or shut out. He was admirable but not comfortable: I took it in with a throb of hope. Was n't he looking through the haunted pane for something he could n't see?—and was n't it the first time in the whole business that he had known such a lapse? The first, the very first: I found it a splendid portent. It made him anxious, though he watched himself; he had been anxious all day and, even while in his usual sweet little manner he sat at table, had needed all his small strange genius to give it a gloss. When he at last turned round to meet me it was almost as if this genius had succumbed. "Well, I think I 'm glad Bly agrees with *me!*"

"You 'd certainly seem to have seen, these twenty-four hours, a good deal more of it than some time before. I hope," I went on bravely, "that you 've been enjoying yourself."

"Oh yes, I 've been ever so far; all round about—miles and miles away. I 've never been so free."

He had really a manner of his own, and I could only try to keep up with him. "Well, do you like it?"

He stood there smiling; then at last he put into two words—
"Do *you?*"—more discrimination than I had ever heard two words
contain. Before I had time to deal with that, however, he continued as if with the sense that this was an impertinence to be
softened. "Nothing could be more charming than the way you
take it, for of course, if we 're alone together now it 's you that are
alone most. But I hope," he threw in, "you don't particularly
mind!"

"Having to do with you?" I asked. "My dear child, how can
I help minding? Though I 've renounced all claim to your company—you 're so beyond me—I at least greatly enjoy it. What else
should I stay on for?"

He looked at me more directly, and the expression of his face,
graver now, struck me as the most beautiful I had ever found in it.
"You stay on just for *that?*"

"Certainly. I stay on as your friend and from the tremendous
interest I take in you till something can be done for you that may
be more worth your while. That need n't surprise you." My voice
trembled so that I felt it impossible to suppress the shake. "Don't
you remember how I told you, when I came and sat on your bed
the night of the storm, that there was nothing in the world I would
n't do for you?"

"Yes, yes!" He, on his side, more and more visibly nervous,
had a tone to master; but he was so much more successful than I
that, laughing out through his gravity, he could pretend we were
pleasantly jesting."Only that, I think, was to get me to do something for *you!*"

"It was partly to get you to do something," I conceded. "But,
you know, you did n't do it."

"Oh yes," he said with the brightest superficial eagerness, "you
wanted me to tell you something."

"That 's it. Out, straight out. What you have on your mind,
you know."

"Ah then is *that* what you 've stayed over for?"

He spoke with a gaiety through which I could still catch the
finest little quiver of resentful passion; but I can't begin to express
the effect upon me of an implication of surrender even so faint.
It was as if what I had yearned for had come at last only to astonish
me. "Well, yes—I may as well make a clean breast of it. It was
precisely for that."

He waited so long that I supposed it for the purpose of repudiat-
ing the assumption on which my action had been founded; but
what he finally said was: "Do you mean now—here?"

"There could n't be a better place or time." He looked round
him uneasily, and I had the rare—oh the queer!—impression of

the very first symptom I had seen in him of the approach of immediate fear. It was as if he were suddenly afraid of me—which struck me indeed as perhaps the best thing to make him. Yet in the very pang of the effort I felt it vain to try sternness, and I heard myself the next instant so gentle as to be almost grotesque. "You want so to go out again?"

"Awfully!" He smiled at me heroically, and the touching little bravery of it was enhanced by his actually flushing with pain. He had picked up his hat, which he had brought in, and stood twirling it in a way that gave me, even as I was just nearly reaching port, a perverse horror of what I was doing. To do it in *any* way was an act of violence, for what did it consist of but the obtrusion of the idea of grossness and guilt on a small helpless creature who had been for me a revelation of the possibilities of beautiful inter-course? Was n't it base to create for a being so exquisite a mere alien awkwardness? I suppose I now read into our situation a clearness it could n't have had at the time, for I seem to see our poor eyes already lighted with some spark of a prevision of the anguish that was to come. So we circled about with terrors and scruples, fighters not daring to close. But it was for each other we feared! That kept us a little longer suspended and unbruised. "I 'll tell you everything," Miles said—"I mean I 'll tell you anything you like. You 'll stay on with me, and we shall both be all right, and I *will* tell you—I *will*. But not now."

"Why not now?"

My insistence turned him from me and kept him once more at his window in a silence during which, between us, you might have heard a pin drop. Then he was before me again with the air of a person for whom, outside, some one who had frankly to be reckoned with was waiting. "I have to see Luke."

I had not yet reduced him to quite so vulgar a lie, and I felt proportionately ashamed. But, horrible as it was, his lies made up my truth. I achieved thoughtfully a few loops of my knitting. "Well then go to Luke, and I 'll wait for what you promise. Only in return for that satisfy, before you leave me, one very much smaller request."

He looked as if he felt he had succeeded enough to be able still a little to bargain. "Very much smaller—?"

"Yes, a mere fraction of the whole. Tell me"—oh my work preoccupied me, and I was off-hand!—"if, yesterday afternoon, from the table in the hall, you took, you know, my letter."

XXIV

My grasp of how he received this suffered for a minute from something that I can describe only as a fierce split of my attention—a stroke that at first, as I sprang straight up, reduced me to the mere blind movement of getting hold of him, drawing him close and, while I just fell for support against the nearest piece of furniture, instinctively keeping him with his back to the window. The appearance was full upon us that I had already had to deal with here: Peter Quint had come into view like a sentinel before a prison. The next thing I saw was that, from outside, he had reached the window, and then I knew that, close to the glass and glaring in through it, he offered once more to the room his white face of damnation. It represents but grossly what took place within me at the sight to say that on the second my decision was made; yet I believe that no woman so overwhelmed ever in so short a time recovered her command of the *act*. It came to me in the very horror of the immediate presence that the act would be, seeing and facing what I saw and faced, to keep the boy himself unaware. The inspiration—I can call it by no other name—was that I felt how voluntarily, how transcendently, I *might*. It was like fighting with a demon for a human soul, and when I had fairly so appraised it I saw how the human soul—held out, in the tremor of my hands, at arms' length—had a perfect dew of sweat on a lovely childish forehead. The face that was close to mine was as white as the face against the glass, and out of it presently came a sound, not low nor weak, but as if from much further away, that I drank like a waft of fragrance.

"Yes—I took it."

At this, with a moan of joy, I enfolded, I drew him close; and while I held him to my breast, where I could feel in the sudden fever of his little body the tremendous pulse of his little heart, I kept my eyes on the thing at the window and saw it move and shift its posture. I have likened it to a sentinel, but its slow wheel, for a moment, was rather the prowl of a baffled beast. My present quickened courage, however, was such that, not too much to let it through, I had to shade, as it were, my flame. Meanwhile the glare of the face was again at the window, the scoundrel fixed as if to watch and wait. It was the very confidence that I might now defy him, as well as the positive certitude, by this time, of the child's unconsciousness, that made me go on. "What did you take it for?"

"To see what you said about me."

"You opened the letter?"

"I opened it."

My eyes were now, as I held him off a little again, on Miles's own face, in which the collapse of mockery showed me how complete was the ravage of uneasiness. What was prodigious was that at last, by my success, his sense was sealed and his communication stopped: he knew that he was in presence, but knew not of what, and knew still less that I also was and that I did know. And what did this strain of trouble matter when my eyes went back to the window only to see that the air was clear again and—by my personal triumph—the influence quenched? There was nothing there. I felt that the cause was mine and that I should surely get *all*. "And you found nothing!"—I let my elation out.

He gave the most mournful, thoughtful little headshake. "Nothing."

"Nothing, nothing!" I almost shouted in my joy.

"Nothing, nothing," he sadly repeated.

I kissed his forehead; it was drenched. "So what have you done with it?"

"I 've burnt it."

"Burnt it?" It was now or never. "Is that what you did at school?"

Oh what this brought up! "At school?"

"Did you take letters?—or other things?"

"Other things?" He appeared now to be thinking of something far off and that reached him only through the pressure of his anxiety. Yet it did reach him. "Did I *steal?*"

I felt myself redden to the roots of my hair as well as wonder if it were more strange to put to a gentleman such a question or to see him take it with allowances that gave the very distance of his fall in the world. "Was it for that you might n't go back?"

The only thing he felt was rather a dreary little surprise. "Did you know I might n't go back?"

"I know everything."

He gave me at this the longest and strangest look. "Everything?"

"Everything. Therefore *did* you—?" But I could n't say it again. Miles could, very simply. "No. I did n't steal."

My face must have shown him I believed him utterly; yet my hands—but it was for pure tenderness—shook him as if to ask him why, if it was all for nothing, he had condemned me to months of torment. "What then did you do?"

He looked in vague pain all round the top of the room and drew his breath, two or three times over, as if with difficulty. He might have been standing at the bottom of the sea and raising his eyes to some faint green twilight. "Well—I said things."

"Only that?"

"They thought it was enough!"

"To turn you out for?"

Never, truly, had a person "turned out" shown so little to explain it as this little person! He appeared to weigh my question, but in a manner quite detached and almost helpless. "Well, I suppose I ought n't."

"But to whom did you say them?"

He evidently tried to remember, but it dropped—he had lost it.

"I don't know!"

He almost smiled at me in the desolation of his surrender, which was indeed practically, by this time, so complete that I ought to have left it there. But I was infatuated—I was blind with victory, though even then the very effect that was to have brought him so much nearer was already that of added separation. "Was it to every one?" I asked.

"No; it was only to—" But he gave a sick little headshake. "I don't remember their names."

"Were they then so many?"

"No—only a few. Those I liked."

Those he liked? I seemed to float not into clearness, but into a darker obscure, and within a minute there had come to me out of my very pity the appalling alarm of his being perhaps innocent. It was for the instant confounding and bottomless, for if he *were* innocent what then on earth was I? Paralysed, while it lasted, by the mere brush of the question, I let him go a little, so that, with a deep-drawn sigh, he turned away from me again; which, as he faced toward the clear window, I suffered, feeling that I had nothing now there to keep him from. "And did they repeat what you said?" I went on after a moment.

He was soon at some distance from me, still breathing hard and again with the air, though now without anger for it, of being confined against his will. Once more, as he had done before, he looked up at the dim day as if, of what had hitherto sustained him, nothing was left but an unspeakable anxiety. "Oh yes," he nevertheless replied—"they must have repeated them. To those *they* liked," he added.

There was somehow less of it than I had expected; but I turned it over. "And these things came round—?"

"To the masters? Oh yes!" he answered very simply. "But I did n't know they 'd tell."

"The masters? They did n't—they 've never told. That 's why I ask you."

He turned to me again his little beautiful fevered face. "Yes, it was too bad."

"Too bad?"

"What I suppose I sometimes said. To write home."

I can't name the exquisite pathos of the contradiction given to such a speech by such a speaker; I only know that the next instant I heard myself throw off with homely force: "Stuff and nonsense!" But the next after that I must have sounded stern enough. "What *were* these things?"

My sternness was all for his judge, his executioner; yet it made him avert himself again, and that movement made *me*, with a single bound and an irrepressible cry, spring straight upon him.

For there again, against the glass, as if to blight his confession and stay his answer, was the hideous author of our woe—the white face of damnation. I felt a sick swim at the drop of my victory and all the return of my battle, so that the wildness of my veritable leap only served as a great betrayal. I saw him, from the midst of my act, meet it with a divination, and on the perception that even now he only guessed, and that the window was still to his own eyes free, I let the impulse flame up to convert the climax of his dismay into the very proof of his liberation. "No more, no more, no more!" I shrieked to my visitant as I tried to press him against me.

"Is she *here?*" Miles panted as he caught with his sealed eyes the direction of my words. Then as his strange "she" staggered me and, with a gasp, I echoed it, "Miss Jessel, Miss Jessel!" he with sudden fury gave me back.

I seized, stupefied, his supposition—some sequel to what we had done to Flora, but this made me only want to show him that it was better still than that. "It 's not Miss Jessel! But it 's at the window—straight before us. It 's *there*—the coward horror, there for the last time!"

At this, after a second in which his head made the movement of a baffled dog's on a scent and then gave a frantic little shake for air and light, he was at me in a white rage, bewildered, glaring vainly over the place and missing wholly, though it now, to my sense, filled the room like the taste of poison, the wide overwhelming presence. "It 's *he?*"

I was so determined to have all my proof that I flashed into ice to challenge him. "Whom do you mean by 'he'?"

"Peter Quint—you devil!" His face gave again, round the room, its convulsed supplication. "*Where?*"

They are in my ears still, his supreme surrender of the name and his tribute to my devotion. "What does he matter now, my own? —what will he *ever* matter? *I* have you," I launched at the beast, "but he has lost you for ever!" Then for the demonstration of my work, "There, *there!*" I said to Miles.

But he had already jerked straight round, stared, glared again, and seen but the quiet day. With the stroke of the loss I was so proud of he uttered the cry of a creature hurled over an abyss, and the grasp with which I recovered him might have been that of catching him in his fall. I caught him, yes, I held him—it may be imagined with what a passion; but at the end of a minute I began to feel what it truly was that I held. We were alone with the quiet day, and his little heart, dispossessed, had stopped.[9]

9. Last weekly installment and "Part Fifth" ended here.

The Text

Textual History

During Henry James's life, *The Turn of the Screw* was published in five authorized forms: as a serial in *Collier's Weekly* early in 1898, as the first of two tales in separate English and American books in October, 1898, as the second of four tales in a volume of the New York Edition in 1908 (see Textual Notes, below), and as the first volume of *The Uniform Tales of Henry James* published by Martin Secker in London, April, 1915, but on the "distinct understanding, please, that he conform *literatim* and punctuation to [the New York Edition] text. It is vital that he adhere to that authentic punctuation—to the last comma or rather, more essentially, no-comma." [1] Collation indicates that Secker did adhere, for the few variants are clearly accidental. As a result this last volume will not be considered here or in the Textual Notes which follow.

James's composition of the tale fell between two major publications— *What Maisie Knew*, which was serialized in *The Chap Book* from January 15 to August 1, 1897, and *In the Cage*, which was begun early in 1898 after James moved from London to Lamb House in Rye, and which appeared in August. After finishing *Maisie* (there is evidence that he was still at work on it during the summer), he wrote the short *John Delavoy*, which was printed in November, 1897, in America (but was not published until 1898), thus leaving the fall of 1897 open for work on *The Turn of the Screw*.

October and November are the logical months because as late as September 25, James wrote to A. C. Benson without mentioning the tale, yet in the spring of 1898 he wrote Benson (see below, pp. 108–109) that the "germ" of the narrative was based on a story told to James by Benson's father (see Notebook entry of January, 1895, below, pp. 106–107) and that he had written the tale in the fall of 1897.[2] If James had started the story in September he surely would have acknowledged the source in the first letter. By October 28, 1897, however, when James contracted with Blackwood's to write his *William Whetmore Story and His Friends* he said that he was too busy to undertake it at present. The only other James items of this time are a very few short notes and essays; thus, in all prob-

1. Unpublished letter, Henry James to his agent J. B. Pinker, September 11, 1914, in the Yale University Library. Quoted by Leon Edel and Dan H. Laurence, *A Bibliography of Henry James* (London: Rupert Hart-Davis, second edition, revised, 1961), p. 155. (The editor is indebted to this volume for many of the facts which follow.)

2. In December, 1897, James mentioned that fall had been lingering since mid-October, and in December, 1898, he said that for the past several years summer had been extending itself right through September.

ability he was then at work on *The Turn of the Screw*.

By the end of November he had finished, for on December 1 he wrote to his sister-in-law (see letter to Alice James, p. 107) that he had not answered her last letter because for a "long time" he had been hard at work on "my little book" which " I *have*, at last, finished." Even though he went on to say that he was ready to start another book, this present reference must be to *The Turn of the Screw*; the editors at *Collier's* had to have time to plan and set the illustrated serial version, and James took time amid his preparations for his move to the country after Christmas to revise a typescript of the serial version as the basis for separate book publication by Heinemann in England. On January 27, 1898, the first installment of the serial appeared in America, and an edition of *The Turn of the Screw* was deposited in the British Museum for purposes of copyright in England, but was, in fact, never published. The plates for pages 3-169 of this edition which contain the entire tale were used, however, in the first English edition of *The Two Magics*, the only difference being that the words "THE END" were removed from page 169 when another story, *Covering End*, was added in the spring of 1898 to complete the book. Because of the finished nature of this January deposit copy,[3] and because James made no changes in the text of *The Turn of the Screw* before the October publication of *The Two Magics*, his preparation of the story for Heinemann (and Macmillan, see below) must have been completed in December.

No one can ever say with any assurance why and when James ever wrote a story. As his Notebooks show, he mulled over "germs" or ideas for various periods of time, long and short, some coming into fruition, singly or variously grafted, and some remaining dormant. In this case, the Backgrounds and Sources section shows that James had always been interested in the ghost-story and that in January 1895, in the aftermath of his retreat from the theater and return to fiction, he recorded the "germ" of *The Turn of the Screw*, but there are no indications that he played with the idea in any way before the fall of 1897, at which time, as S. P. Rosenbaum points out in a note written especially for this edition (see below, pp. 254–259), James was approached for a story by Robert Collier who had left college in June to join his father on *Collier's Weekly*. On the one hand, Collier wanted to raise the tone of this popular magazine and sought out Henry James who was beginning to be thought of as a writer of more importance than merely "the author of *Daisy Miller*"; on the other hand, James knew the level of the audience of *Collier's* (he had been negotiating the year before with Clement King Shorter to do a "thrilling" love-story for the popular *London Illustrated News* [see Cargill, footnote 8, below p. 164]) and could well have turned to his Notebook for a sensational

3. Because the description of this edition by Edel and Laurence (see note 1, above) does not agree with the deposit copy which I examined, perhaps a fuller description of this copy is in order: pp. ii + 169 + 7 [blank]; contents: [i-ii], half-title: The Turn of the Screw, verso blank; [1–2], title page all in black: The Turn of / The Screw / By Henry James / [acorn design, as on title page of *The Two Magics*] / London: William Heinemann / *All rights reserved* MDCCCXCVIII, verso blank; [3] – 169, corrected pages; [170–176], all blank.

idea, here the ghost-story told to him by Archbishop Benson.

No manuscript of the story exists, for by 1897 James was regularly dictating to a typist, this time to a Scotsman (see below, p. 178), and few publishers then bothered to keep typescript "copy." Nevertheless, the consistency of American spelling in the first three editions affords sufficient evidence to allow the assertion that all three are based primarily on the same typescript, the one which he sent to Collier. When he mailed it off, James retained a copy which he revised slightly for his book publishers, then had identical copies made, for the first English and American editions differ only with regard to a few commas and in hyphenation practice even though they were set separately (transatlantic distribution was expressly forbidden). Thus, technically, we have three editions in 1898, but only two versions. Then, because the New York Edition has behind it probably a corrected copy of the English edition (hyphenation affords the only evidence), the same typescript may be said to lie behind all three of the major versions. Nowhere along the line did James rewrite or recast whole passages or chapters.

Even though there is a consistency of thrust running through the three versions (all texts follow the same chapter divisions), there are clear differences among the three. The periodical version, in addition to being divided into a frame and twenty-four chapters, has twelve installments and five "Parts." In the *Two Magics* version, these parts are removed, small inconsistencies are cleared up, an early naming of Miss Jessel is suppressed, the ending of one chapter is deleted, the atmosphere of suspense is heightened, Flora's age is raised, and more focus is placed on the governess. But the major revisions appear in the 1908 New York version. Here James seemed intent on shifting the center of attention away from the details of action observed by the governess to the reactions felt by the governess. By removing commas (see the letter quoted above) he came closer to approximating the stream of her consciousness (see the essay by Leon Edel below, pp. 228–234). By increasing the use of the possessive pronoun "my" and by replacing verbs of perception and thought with those of feeling and intuition (see book by Cranfill and Clark, below in Bibliography), James draws us intimately into the course of her narrative. The effect is more vital and vivid than that created by either of the earlier versions. For both textual and aesthetic reasons, the text of the New York Edition was chosen as the copy text of the present Norton Critical Edition.

Textual Notes

The following records mostly various major changes which James made in wording, but some variant spelling and punctuation have been recorded in order to support conclusions given above in the note on Textual History. Words in boldface give the reading of the Norton-New York Edition text for which variants from earlier editions are given. Ellipses are used in readings of any length taken from the present text. The numbers preceding an entry give the page and line numbers of the Norton text from which the reading is taken. Variant readings are given in regular type below a bold-face entry, and each separate reading is preceded by an italicized capital letter identifying the text. The letters and the texts for which they stand are as follows:

P the periodical text published in twelve installments in *Collier's Weekly*, from vol. XX, no. 17 (January 27, 1898) to vol. XXI, no. 2 (April 16, 1898).

E the first English edition published by William Heinemann in *The Two Magics: The Turn of the Screw* [and] *Covering End*, October 5, 1898.

A the first American edition published by The Macmillan Company, *The Two Magics*, in October, 1898 (probably also on the 5th).

N *The Novels and Tales of Henry James*, New York Edition, vol. XII (*The Aspern Papers; The Turn of the Screw; The Liar; The Two Faces*), published in New York by Charles Scribner's Sons and issued in London by Macmillan and Company in 1908.

The texts following an entry are given in the chronological order of their revision. Texts not referred to in a given entry—and not noted earlier as lacking the passage in question—agree with the New York Edition reading. Editorial comment on variants is given in italic type, and emendations in the New Edition have been marked with an asterisk. Occasionally words common to variant readings have been added at the beginning or end of an entry to help identify the variant.

1.1 The story
P between the title and the first line
PART FIRST
1.4 note it as
P remark that it was
E A say that it was
1.12 shocked
P E A shaken
1.23 been concerned with
P E A involved
1.26 two children
P E A they
1.29 this converser
P E A his interlocutor
2.37 summer. I
N omits the period which all texts have
4.15 night of the fourth
P night—it was almost the whole!—of the fourth
4.39 figured
P E A conceived
5.1 his
P E A their
5.29 quite
P both
5.41 "Pardon
P E A "Excuse
6.34 The whole thing took indeed more nights than one, but on the first occasion the same lady
P Then the same lady
6.40 author's hand
P first installment ends here
7.2 all my doubts bristle
P E A myself doubtful
7.10 took a flight
P E A encountered a reprieve

7.28-29 affected me on the spot as a creature too charming not to make it a great fortune
P E A appeared to me on the spot a creature so charming as to make it a great fortune
7.31 hadn't made more of a point to me of this.
P E A had not told me more of her.
7.37 wonderful appeal
P E A extraordinary charm
7.42-43 that of her being so inordinately
P E A the clear circumstance of her being so
7.43 felt
P E A perceived
8.39 it was already conveyed between us, too grossly
Omitted from P E and A
9.15-18 I forthwith wanted * * * Mrs. Grose assented
P E A I expressed that the proper, as well as the pleasant and friendly thing would be therefore that on the arrival of the public conveyance I should be in waiting for him with his little sister; an idea in which Mrs. Grose concurred
no comma after proper in E and A
9.29 Regular lessons, in this agitation, certainly suffered some wrong;
P E A Lessons, in this agitation, certainly suffered some delay;
9.43-44 to my present older and more informed eyes it would show a very reduced importance.
P E A to my older and more informed

eyes it would now appear sufficiently contracted.

10.15-16 to a change of note
P E A in keen apprehension
11.1 the
P E A my
12.16-17 apprehension of ridicule.
P danger of absurdity.
12.20 she was also young and pretty—
P Oh, Miss Jessel—that was her name —was also young and pretty;
13.17 my work."
P second installment ends here
14.34 weeks
P a considerable time,
15.5-6 fenced about and ordered and arranged,
P inclosed and protected
E A enclosed and protected,
15.25 yielded.
P E A responded.
17.23 it was intense to me that
P E A I had the sharpest sense that, *comma only in P*
17.25 crenellations
P E A crenelations
17.27 I knew.
P third installment and first part end here
17.28 It was not
P between the running title and the roman numeral PART SECOND
18.36 monstrous.
P E A gross.
19.2-4 through nothing could I so like it [*my work*] as through feeling that to throw myself into it was to throw myself out of trouble.
P nothing so made me like it as precisely to feel that I could throw myself into it in trouble.
E A through nothing could I so like it as through feeling that I could throw myself into it in trouble.
19.33 nothing to call even an infinitesimal
P E A no
19.34 scant enough "antecedents,"
P no long one,
E A a scant one
19.41-42 trace, should have felt the wound and the dishonour.
P E A trace.
19.42 could reconstitute
P E A found
21.12 to-day
A today
24.43 express the wonder of it. "Yes. Mr. Quint's dead."
P articulate the wonder of it. "Yes. Yes. Quint is dead."
E A utter the wonder of it. "Yes. Mr. Quint is dead."
24.43 Mr. Quint's dead."
P fourth installment ends here
25.10-11 the schoolroom
P Mrs. Grose's room
25.27 stiff an agreement.
P E A comprising a contact.
26.14-15 the rest of the household.
P E A companions.

26.22 way. They've never alluded to it."
P E A way." *omit the rest*
26.44 scullions,
P the kitchen,
27.3 the schoolroom
P my
27.14 informant.
P E A interlocutress.
28.30 engaged affection.
P E A committed heart.
28.35 tension
P E A excitement
28.39 proofs. Proofs, and say, yes— from the moment I really took hold.
P facts. Facts and say, yes—from the moment I really read them.
28.44-45 a certain ingenuity of
P E A an occasional excess of the
29.20 amid these elements,
P amid these circumstances
E A in these circumstances
29.37-38 an alien object in view—a figure
P a third person in view—a person
30.36 articulate
P produce it
30.40 eight
P six
31.39 understand."
P E A understand you."
32.12 was?"
P was!"
32.41 disclosure.
P admission.
33.22-23 now in my friend's own eyes Miss Jessel had again appeared.
P Miss Jessel had again appeared in my friend's remembering eyes.
33.44 They're lost!"
P fifth installment and second part end here
34.1 What I had said
P between the running title and the roman numeral PART THIRD
34.8-9 had another talk in my room; when
P had, in the schoolroom, another talk, and then she
34.10-11 I found that to keep her thoroughly in the grip of this
P To hold her perfectly in the pinch of this, I found,
E To hold her perfectly in the pinch of that, I found,
A To hold her perfectly in the pinch of that, I found
35.27 but a small shifty spot on the wrong side of
P but the blur of a little dumb spot behind
35.45 straight question enough,
P E A dreadfully austere inquiry,
36.9 high manner about it,
P strange manner,
E A most strange manner,
38.1 her
P my
38.10 balm
Omitted from P

38.21-22 when I knew myself to catch them up by an irresistible impulse and press
P E A when, by an irresistible impulse, I found myself catching them up and pressing
39.11 as Shakespeareans,
P masqueraded with brilliancy as Shakespeareans,
40.3 horrid
Omitted from P E and 1
40.7 dreadful
Omitted from P E and A
41.36 low wretch
P base varlet
41.39 bend was lost.
P sixth installment ends here
43.37 vigils,
P E A watching,
44.11 still moon
P glitter of starlight
45.3 The moon
P Thick stars
45.31-32 Flights of fancy gave place, in her mind, to a steady fireside glow,
P The place of the imagination was taken up by her ample kindness,
45.39 worry
P E A strain
46.40-41 window, uncovered to the moonlight
P windows bare to the constellations,
47.22 fairy
Omitted from P
49.44-45 his house is poisoned and his little nephew and niece mad?"
P I have the honor to inform him that they see the dead come back?"
50.27 him and you."
P continues him and you."
Then what's your remedy?" she asked as I watched the children.
I continued, without answering, to watch them. "I would leave *them*," and went on.
"But what *is* your remedy?" she persisted.
It seemed, after all, to have come to me then and there. "To speak to them." And I joined them.
seventh installment and third part end here.
50.28 It was all
P between the running title and the roman numeral PART FOURTH
51.15 the lady who
P the lady—never once named—who
51.21-22 whimsical bent
P eccentric habits
E A eccentric nature
51.34 pony
P jackdaw.
53.5-6 it was essentially in the scared state that I drew my actual conclusions.
P E A it was in the condition of nerves produced by it that I made my actual inductions
57.29 of which, I
All texts omit the comma

59.34 must stay.
P eighth installment ends here
60.7-8 picture of the "put away"— of drawers closed and locked and rest without remedy.
P image of cupboards closed and diligence vaguely baffled.
E A image of the *etc. as in N*
62.3 to-night
A tonight
67.19 where she stood,
P E A on the spot
68.4-5 promptly joined me!
P ninth installment and fourth part end here
68.6 We went
P between the running title and the roman numeral PART FIFTH
69.34 halfway
P E half way
A half-way
70.36-37 words from her were, in a flash . . . blade, the jostle
N lacks the punctuation of P E and A
71.37-39 a figure portentous. I gaped at her coolness even though my certitude of her thoroughly seeing was never greater
P E A the very presence that could make me quail. I quailed even though my certitude that she thoroughly saw was never greater
71.41-42 know it as well as you know
P E A see her as well as you see
72.41 disaffection
P E A reprobation
74.1 fairly measured more than it had ever measured.
P E A was as if it were more than it had ever been.
74.9 Her little belongings had all been removed.
Omitted from P
74.21 with me.
P tenth installment ends here
78.45—79.1 He'll meet me. He'll confess.
Omitted from P
80.14-15 arrived the difficulty
P arrived for our main repast the difficulty
81.3 a stiff arm across
P a rude long arm across
E A an angular arm over
81.29 expelled
P E A driven
81.43 waiter
P maid
81.44 alone!"
P eleventh installment ends here
85.43 success,
P triumph
86.6 little headshake.
P little melancholy headshake.
88.10-11 shrieked to my visitant as I tried to press him against me.
P E A shrieked, as I tried to press him against me, to my visitant
88.35 work,
P triumph,

Backgrounds and Sources

James maintained an interest in the ghost-story throughout his writing career—indeed, one of his last efforts was to try to complete the long unfinished *The Sense of the Past*. He seemed never troubled by the fact that to many this "genre" is by nature inferior, unworthy of serious artistic endeavor, for it provided him with, to use the phrase which he borrowed from Hawthorne, a meeting-place of "the actual and the imaginary." Because these realms *are* fused in the ghost-story, James would have been particularly amused to note that the most often evoked proposition concerning *The Turn of the Screw* is "either the ghosts are *real* or they are *not*."

His own remarks on the tale are scattered among his Notebooks, letters, and the New York Prefaces. To be understood fully, they must be read with James's various audiences in mind: himself, family and friends, acquaintances, or the reading public. Talking to himself, he is always honest, but not always serious, and, as is the case with most intimate conversations, the words carry more powerful connotations to the participants than to the eavesdropper. With his family and close friends he is more coherent but slightly less open; with mere acquaintances or strangers he is polite, polished, and totally guarded. Finally, in the famous New York Prefaces he seems all these things at once. Based on the Notebooks but executed in the interrupted periods of James's mature style they are both honest and dishonest. As a result they never contain the "final word"; rather, as James wrote Howells, "they are, in general, a sort of plea for Criticism, for Discrimination, for Appreciation on other than infantile lines" (*Letters,* II, 99).

That other sources beyond, and sometimes tending to be contradictory to, those named by James have been suggested by scholars is an indication that James might not always have told the whole truth regarding the "germs" of his stories. Such a suggestion is, of course, itself a critical appraisal, and three of the four essays which conclude this section not only propose that James used additional, unnamed sources, but also are filled with critical discussion of *The Turn of the Screw*. In fact, taken together they serve as an introduction to the Essays in Criticism section, for they review the whole history of reactions to the tale, especially the reactions to Edmund Wilson's casual Freudian reactions.

Page references to material included in this Norton Critical Edition have been bracketed and changed to refer to this edition.

James on the Ghost-Story

A Review †

["*Mysteries * * * at Our Own Doors*"]

* * * People talk of novels with a purpose; and from this class of works, both by her patrons and her enemies, Miss Braddon's tales are excluded. But what novel ever betrayed a more resolute purpose than the production of what we may call Miss Braddon's second manner? Her purpose was at any hazard to make a hit, to catch the public ear. It was a difficult task, but audacity could accomplish it. Miss Braddon accordingly resorted to extreme measures, and created the sensation novel. It is to this audacity, this courage of despair, as manifested in her later works, that we have given the name of pluck. In these works it has settled down into a quiet determination not to let her public get ahead of her. A writer who has suddenly leaped into a popularity greatly disproportionate to his merit, can only retain his popularity by observing a strictly respectful attitude to his readers. This has been Miss Braddon's attitude, and she has maintained it with unwearied patience. She has been in her way a disciple as well as a teacher. She has kept up with the subtle innovations to which her art, like all others, is subject, as well as with the equally delicate fluctuations of the public taste. The result has been a very obvious improvement in her style.

She has been preceded in the same path by Mr. Wilkie Collins, whose "Woman in White", with its diaries and letters and its general ponderosity, was a kind of nineteenth century version of "Clarissa Harlowe." ¹ Mind, we say a nineteenth century version. To Mr. Collins belongs the credit of having introduced into fiction those most mysterious of mysteries, the mysteries which are at our own doors. This innovation gave a new impetus to the literature of horrors. It was fatal to the authority of Mrs. Radcliffe and her ever-

† From a review of *Aurora Floyd*, by M. E. Braddon, *The Nation*, I (November 9, 1865), 593 Mary Elizabeth Braddon (1837–1915) became famous with her first sensationalist novel, *Lady Audley's Secret* (1862).
1. Wilkie Collins (1824–89) wrote *Woman in White* in 1860, one of the earliest complicated, lengthy novels of detection. Samuel Richardson (1689–1761) published his seven volume novel *Clarissa Harlowe* over two years, 1747–48. Both novels are presented from shifting points of view.

lasting castle in the Apennines.[2] What are the Apennines to us, or we to the Apennines? Instead of the terrors of "Udolpho", we were treated to the terrors of the cheerful country-house and the busy London lodgings. And there is no doubt that these were infinitely the more terrible. Mrs. Radcliffe's mysteries were romances pure and simple; while those of Mr. Wilkie Collins were stern reality. The supernatural, which Mrs. Radcliffe constantly implies, though she generally saves her conscience, at the eleventh hour, by explaining it away, requires a powerful imagination in order to be as exciting as the natural, as Mr. Collins and Miss Braddon, without any imagination at all, know how to manage it. A good ghost-story, to be half as terrible as a good murder-story, must be connected at a hundred points with the common objects of life. The best ghost-story probably ever written—a tale published some years ago in *Blackwood's Magazine* [3]—was constructed with an admirable understanding of this principle. Half of its force was derived from its prosaic, commonplace, daylight accessories. Less delicately terrible, perhaps, than the vagaries of departed spirits, but to the full as *interesting*, as the modern novel reader understands the word, are the numberless possible forms of human malignity. Crime, indeed, has always been a theme for dramatic poets; but with the old poets its dramatic interest lay in the fact that it compromised the criminal's moral repose. Whence else is the interest of *Orestes* and *Macbeth?* With Mr. Collins and Miss Braddon (our modern Euripides and Shakespeare) the interest of crime is in the fact that it compromises the criminal's personal safety. The play is a tragedy, not in virtue of an avenging diety, but in virtue of a preventive system of law; not through the presence of a company of fairies, but through that of an admirable organization of police detectives. Of course, the nearer the criminal and the detective are brought home to the reader, the more lively his "sensation." They are brought home to the reader by a happy choice of probable circumstances; and it is through their skill in the choice of these circumstances—their thorough-going realism—that Mr. Collins and Miss Braddon have become famous. * * *

We have said that although Mr. Collins anticipated Miss Braddon in the work of devising domestic mysteries adapted to the wants of a sternly prosaic age, she was yet the founder of the sensation novel. Mr. Collins's productions deserve a more respectable name. They are massive and elaborate constructions—monuments of mosaic work, for the proper mastery of which it would seem, at first, that an index and note-book were required. They are not so much works of art as works of science. To read "The Woman in

2. Anne Radcliffe (1764–1823), early writer of horror stories with rationalized conclusions; her most famous, *The Mysteries of Udolpho* (1794).

3. Noted for its horror, mystery stories, especially in the middle decades of the nineteenth century.

White", requires very much the same intellectual effort as to read Motley or Froude.[4] We may say, therefore, that Mr. Collins being to Miss Braddon what Richardson is to Miss Austen,[5] we date the novel of domestic mystery from the former lady, for the same reason that we date the novel of domestic tranquillity from the latter. Miss Braddon began by a skilful combination of bigamy, arson, murder, and insanity. These phenomena are all represented in the deeds of Lady Audley. The novelty lay in the heroine being, not a picturesque Italian of the fourteenth century, but an English gentlewoman of the current year, familiar with the use of the railway and the telegraph. The intense probability of the story is constantly reiterated. Modern England—the England of to-day's newspaper—crops up at every step. * * *

A Notebook Entry †

["*Subject for a Ghost-Story*"]

January 22d [1888]. Subject for a ghost-story.

Imagine a door—either walled-up, or that has been long locked—at which there is an occasional knocking—a knocking which—as the other side of the door is inaccessible—can only be ghostly. The occupant of the house or room, containing the door, has long been familiar with the sound; and, regarding it as ghostly, has ceased to heed it particularly—as the ghostly presence remains on the other side of the door, and never reveals itself in other ways. But this person may be imagined to have some great and constant trouble; and it may be observed by another person, relating the story, that the knocking increases with each fresh manifestation of the trouble. He breaks open the door and the trouble ceases—as if the spirit had desired to be admitted, that it might interpose, redeem and protect.

A Notebook Entry ‡

["*Another Theme of the Same Kind*"]

A young girl, unknown to herself, is followed, constantly, by a figure which other persons see. She is perfectly unconscious of it—but there is a dread that she may cease to be so. The figure is that

---

4. John Lathrop Motley, American (1814–77), and James Anthony Froude, Englishman (1818–94), were both celebrated historians of the grand style.
5. Jane Austen (1775–1817), whose *Pride and Prejudice* (1813) fits James's description.
† From *The Notebooks of Henry James* edited by F. O. Matthiessen and Kenneth B. Murdock; copyright © 1947 by Oxford Press, Inc., p. 9; reprinted by permission of the publisher. See below, Preface to *The Altar of the Dead*, p. 105.
‡ From *The Notebooks of Henry James* edited by F. O. Matthiessen and Kenneth B. Murdock, pp. 9–10; copyright © 1947 by Oxford Press, Inc.; reprinted by permission of the publisher. Entry undated, but follows the previous one.

of a young man—and there is a theory that the day that she falls in love, she may suddenly perceive it. Her mother dies, and the narrator of the story then discovers, by finding an old miniature among her letters and papers, that the figure is that of a young man whom she has jilted in her youth, and who therefore committed suicide. The girl *does* fall in love, and sees the figure. She accepts her lover, and never sees it again!

To G. B. Shaw †

["*The Imagination* * * * *Leads a Life of Its Own*"]

My dear Bernard Shaw   Rye. 20th Jan: 1909.

* * * I do such things because I happen to be a man of imagination and taste, extremely interested in life, and because the imagination, thus, from the moment direction and motive play upon it from all sides, absolutely enjoys and insists on and incurably leads a life of its own, for which just this vivacity itself is its warrant. You surely haven't done all your own so interesting work without learning what it is for the imagination to *play* with an idea—an idea about life—under a happy obsession, for all it is worth. Half the beautiful things that the benefactors of the human species have produced would surely be wiped out if you don't allow this adventurous and speculative imagination its rights. You simplify too much, by the same token, when you limit the field of interest to what you call the scientific—your employment of which term in such a connection even greatly, I confess, confounds and bewilders me. * * *

Believe me your most truely,
Henry James

From a Preface ‡

["*The Question* * * * *of the 'Supernatural'*"]

* * * I fear I can defend such doings but under the plea of my amusement in them—an amusement I of course hoped others might succeed in sharing.[1] But so comes in exactly the principle under

† From *The Selected Letters of Henry James* edited by Leon Edel (Farrar, Straus & Cudahy, Inc., (New York, 1956), pp. 133–134; reprinted by permission of William Morris Agency, Inc. Shaw had suggested that James's play *The Saloon* (from the story "Owen Wingrave," see next item) would be more logical if the hero at the end "killed" the ghost, instead of the way James ordered it.
‡ From the Preface to *The Altar of the*

Dead * * * *and other Tales*, volume XVII, *The Novels and Tales of Henry James*, The New York Edition, pp. xv–xxi, copyright © 1909 by Charles Scribner's Sons; renewal copyright 1937 by Henry James; reprinted by permission of the publisher.
1. James is defending his right to "dramatise," or simply present objectively his stories (as in the letter to Shaw, above).

the wide strong wing of which several such matters are here harvested; things of a type that might move me, had I space, to a pleading eloquence. Such compositions as "The Jolly Corner," printed here not for the first time, but printed elsewhere only as I write and after my quite ceasing to expect it; "The Friends of the Friends," to which I here change the colourless title of "The Way It Came" (1896), "Owen Wingrave" (1893), "Sir Edmund Orme" (1891), "The Real Right Thing" (1900), would obviously never have existed but for that love of "a story as a story" which had from far back beset and beguiled their author. To this passion, the vital flame at the heart of any sincere attempt to lay a scene and launch a drama, he flatters himself he has never been false; and he will indeed have done his duty but little by it if he has failed to let it, whether robustly or quite insidiously, fire his fancy and rule his scheme. He has consistently felt it (the appeal to wonder and terror and curiosity and pity and to the delight of fine recognitions, as well as to the joy, perhaps sharper still, of the mystified state) the very source of wise counsel and the very law of charming effect. He has revelled in the creation of alarm and suspense and surprise and relief, in all the arts that practise, with a scruple for nothing but any lapse of application, on the credulous soul of the candid or, immeasurably better, on the seasoned spirit of the cunning, reader. He has built, rejoicingly, on that blest faculty of wonder just named, in the latent eagerness of which the novelist so finds, throughout, his best warrant that he can but pin his faith and attach his car to it, rest in fine his monstrous weight and his queer case on it, as on a strange passion planted in the heart of man for his benefit, a mysterious provision made for him in the scheme of nature. He has seen this particular sensibility, the need and the love of wondering and the quick response to any pretext for it, as the beginning and the end of his affair—thanks to the innumerable ways in which that chord may vibrate. His prime care has been to master those most congruous with his own faculty, to make it vibrate as finely as possible—or in other words to the production of the interest appealing most (by its kind) to himself. This last is of course the particular clear light by which the genius of representation ever best proceeds —with its beauty of adjustment to any strain of attention whatever. Essentially, meanwhile, excited wonder must have a subject, must face in a direction, must be, increasingly, *about* something. Here comes in then the artist's bias and his range—determined, these things, by his own fond inclination. About what, good man, does he himself most wonder?—for upon that, whatever it may be, he will naturally most abound. Under that star will he gather in what he shall most seek to represent; so that if you follow thus his range of representation you will know how, you will see where, again, good man, he for himself most aptly vibrates.

All of which makes a desired point for the little group of compositions here placed together; the point that, since the question has
ever been before me but of wondering and, with all achievable
adroitness, of causing to wonder, so the whole fairy-tale side of life
has used, for its tug at my sensibility, a cord all its own. When we
want to wonder there's no such good ground for it as the wonderful
—premising indeed always, by an induction as prompt, that this
element can but be at best, to fit its different cases, a thing of
appreciation. What is wonderful in one set of conditions may quite
fail of its spell in another set; and, for that matter, the peril of the
unmeasured strange, in fiction, being the silly, just as its strength,
when it saves itself, is the charming, the wind of interest blows
where it lists, the surrender of attention persists where it can. The
ideal, obviously, on these lines, is the straight fairy-tale, the case
that has purged in the crucible all its *bêtises* [2] while keeping all its
grace. It may seem odd, in a search for the amusing, to try to steer
wide of the silly by hugging close the "supernatural"; but one
man's amusement is at the best (we have surely long had to recognise) another's desolation; and I am prepared with the confession
that the "ghost-story," as we for convenience call it, has ever been
for me the most possible form of the fairy-tale. It enjoys, to my eyes,
this honour by being so much the neatest—neat with that neatness
without which *representation*, and therewith beauty, drops. One's
working of the spell is of course—decently and effectively—but by
the represented thing, and the grace of the more or less closely
represented state is the measure of any success; a truth by the
general smug neglect of which it 's difficult not be struck. To begin
to wonder, over a case, I must begin to believe—to begin to give
out (that is to attend) I must begin to take in, and to enjoy *that*
profit I must begin to see and hear and feel. This would n't seem,
I allow, the general requirement—as appears from the fact that so
many persons profess delight in the picture of marvels and prodigies
which by any, even the easiest, critical measure *is* no picture; in
the recital of wonderful horrific or beatific things that are neither
represented nor, so far as one makes out, seen as representable: a
weakness not invalidating, round about us, the most resounding
appeals to curiosity. The main condition of interest—that of some
appreciable rendering of sought effects—is absent from them; so
that when, as often happens, one is asked how one "likes" such
and such a "story" one can but point responsively to the lack of
material for a judgement.

The apprehension at work, we thus see, would be of certain

2. Absurdities.

projected conditions, and its first need therefore is that these
appearances be constituted in some other and more colourable fashion than by the author's answering for them on his more or less
gentlemanly honour. This is n't enough; *give* me your elements,
treat me your subject, one has to say—I must wait till then to tell
you how I like them. I might "rave" about them all were they
given and treated; but there is no basis of opinion in such matters
without a basis of vision, and no ground for that, in turn, without
some communicated closeness of truth. There are portentous situations, there are prodigies and marvels and miracles as to which this
communication, whether by necessity or by chance, works comparatively straight—works, by our measure, to some convincing consequence; there are others as to which the report, the picture, the
plea, answers no tithe of the questions we would put. Those questions *may* perhaps then, by the very nature of the case, be unanswerable—though often again, no doubt, the felt vice is but in the
quality of the provision made for them: on any showing, my own
instinct, even in the service of great adventures, is all for the best
terms of things; all for ground on which touches and tricks may be
multiplied, the greatest number of questions answered, the greatest
appearance of truth conveyed. With the preference I have noted
for the "neat" evocation—the image, of any sort, with fewest at-
tendant vaguenesses and cheapnesses, fewest loose ends dangling
and fewest features missing, the image kept in fine the most
susceptible of intensity—with this predilection, I say, the safest
arena for the play of moving accidents and mighty mutations and
strange encounters, or whatever odd matters, is the field, as I may
call it, rather of their second than of their first exhibition. By which,
to avoid obscurity, I mean nothing more cryptic than I feel myself
show them best by showing almost exclusively the way they are
felt, by recognising as their main interest some impression strongly
made by them and intensely received. We but too probably break
down, I have ever reasoned, when we attempt the prodigy, the
appeal to mystification, in itself; with its "objective" side too emphasised the report (it is ten to one) will practically run thin. We
want it clear, goodness knows, but we also want it thick, and we
get the thickness in the human consciousness that entertains and
records, that amplifies and interprets it. That indeed, when the
question is (to repeat) of the "supernatural," constitutes the only
thickness we do get; here prodigies, when they come straight, come
with an effect imperilled; they keep all their character, on the other
hand, by looming through some other history—the indispensable
history of somebody's *normal* relation to something. It 's in such
connexions as these that they most interest, for what we are then
mainly concerned with is their imputed and borrowed dignity.

Intrinsic values they have none—as we feel for instance in such a matter as the would-be portentous climax of Edgar Poe's "Arthur Gordon Pym," where the indispensable history is absent, where the phenomena evoked, the moving accidents, coming straight, as I say, are immediate and flat, and the attempt is all at the horrific in itself. The result is that, to my sense, the climax fails—fails because it stops short, and stops short for want of connexions. There *are* no connexions; not only, I mean, in the sense of further statement, but of our own further relation to the elements, which hang in the void: whereby we see the effect lost, the imaginative effort wasted.

I dare say, to conclude, that whenever, in quest, as I have noted, of the amusing, I have invoked the horrific, I have invoked it, in such air as that of "The Turn of the Screw," that of "The Jolly Corner," that of "The Friends of the Friends," that of "Sir Edmund Orme," that of "The Real Right Thing," in earnest aversion to waste and from the sense that in art economy is always beauty. The apparitions of Peter Quint and Miss Jessel, in the first of the tales just named, the elusive presence nightly "stalked" through the New York house by the poor gentleman in the second, are matters as to which in themsleves, really, the critical challenge (essentially nothing ever but the spirit of fine attention) may take a hundred forms—and a hundred felt or possibly proved infirmities is too great a number. Our friends' respective minds about them, on the other hand, are a different matter—challengeable, and repeatedly, if you like, but never challengeable without some consequent further stiffening of the whole texture. Which proposition involves, I think, a moral. The moving accident, the rare conjunction, whatever it be, does n't make the story—in the sense that the story is our excitement, our amusement, our thrill and our suspense; the human emotion and the human attestation, the clustering human conditions we expect presented, only make it. The extraordinary is most extraordinary in that it happens to you and me, and it 's of value (of value for others) but so far as visibly brought home to us. At any rate, odd though it may sound to pretend that one feels on safer ground in tracing such an adventure as that of the hero of "The Jolly Corner" than in pursuing a bright career among pirates or detectives, I allow that composition to pass as the measure or limit, on my own part, of any achievable comfort in the "adventure-story"; and this not because I may "render"—well, what my poor gentleman attempted and suffered in the New York house—better than I may render detectives or pirates or other splendid desperadoes, though even here too there would be something to say; but because the spirit engaged with the forces of violence interests me most when I can think of it as engaged most deeply, most finely and most "subtly" (precious term!). For then it is that, as with the longest and firmest prongs of consciousness, I grasp and hold the throbbing subject; *there* it is above all that I find the steady light of the picture.

After which attempted demonstration I drop with scant grace perhaps to the admission here of a general vagueness on the article of my different little origins. I have spoken of these in three or four connexions, but ask myself to no purpose, I fear, what put such a matter as "Owen Wingrave" or as "The Friends of the Friends," such a fantasy as "Sir Edmund Orme," into my head.[3] The habitual teller of tales finds these things in old note-books—which however but shifts the burden a step; since how, and under what inspiration, did they first wake up in these rude cradles? One's notes, as all writers remember, sometimes explicitly mention, sometimes indirectly reveal, and sometimes wholly dissimulate, such clues and such obligations. The search for these last indeed, through faded or pencilled pages, is perhaps one of the sweetest of our more pensive pleasures. Then we chance on some idea we *have* afterwards treated; then, greeting it with tenderness, we wonder at the first form of a motive that was to lead us so far and to show, no doubt, to eyes not our own, for so other; then we heave the deep sigh of relief over all that is never, thank goodness, to be done again. * * *

3. The germ of "Sir Edmund Orme" seems to be the journal entry of January 22, 1888, above, p. 99.

James on
The Turn of the Screw

A Notebook Entry †

["*Grose*"]

Names. Hanmer—Meldrum—Synge—Grundle—Adwick—Blanchett—Sansom—Saunt—Highmore—Hannington (or place)—Medley (house)—Myrtle—Saxon—Yule—Chalkley—Grantham—Farange—Grose—Corfe—Lebus—Glasspoole (or place)—Bedfont, Redfont (places?)—Vereker—Gainer—Gayner—Shum—Oswald—Gonville—Mona (girl)—Mark—Floyer—Minton—Panton—Summervale — Chidley — Shirley — Dreever — Trendle — Stannace — Housefield — Longworth — Langsom — Nettlefold — Nettlefield—Beaumorris—Delacoombe—Treston—Mornington—Warmington—Harmer—Oldfield—Horsefield—Eastmead.

A Notebook Entry ‡

["*Note Here the Ghost-Story*"]

Saturday, January 12th, 1895. Note here the ghost-story told me at Addington (evening of Thursday 10th), by the Archbishop of Canterbury: the mere vague, undetailed, faint sketch of it—being all he had been told (very badly and imperfectly), by a lady who had no art of relation, and no clearness: the story of the young children (indefinite number and age) left to the care of servants in an old country-house, through the death, presumably, of parents. The servants, wicked and depraved, corrupt and deprave the children; the children are bad, full of evil, to a sinister degree. The servants *die* (the story vague about the way of it) and their apparitions, figures, return to haunt the house *and* children, to whom they seem to beckon, whom they invite and solicit, from

† From *The Notebooks of Henry James* edited by F. O. Matthiesen and Kenneth B. Murdock; copyright © 1947 by Oxford Press, Inc., p. 178, reprinted by permission of the publisher. An entry placed between those of November 18, 1894 and January 12, 1895. See *Selected Letters* edited by Leon Edel.

pp. 99–100, for James's explanation of such lists.

‡ From *The Notebooks of Henry James* edited by F. O. Matthiesen and Kenneth B. Murdock, pp. 178–179, copyright © 1947 by Oxford Press, Inc.; reprinted by permission of the publisher.

across dangerous places, the deep ditch of a sunk fence, etc.—so that the children may destroy themselves, lose themselves, by responding, by getting into their power. So long as the children are kept from them, they are not lost; but they try and try and try, these evil presences, to get hold of them. It is a question of the children 'coming over to where they are.' It is all obscure and imperfect, the picture, the story, but there is a suggestion of strangely gruesome effect in it. The story to be told—tolerably obviously—by an outside spectator, observer.

To Alice James †
[*"Finished My Little Book"*]

Dictated.

34 De Vere Gardens, W.
1st December, 1897

Dearest Alice,

It's too hideous and horrible, this long time that I have not written you and that your last beautiful letter, placed, for reminder, well within sight, has converted all my emotion on the subject into a constant, chronic blush. The reason has been that I have been driving very hard for another purpose this inestimable aid to expression, and that, as I have a greater loathing than ever for the mere manual act, I haven't, on the one side, seen my way to inflict on you a written letter, or on the other had the virtue to divert, till I should have finished my little book, to another stream any of the valued and expensive industry of my amanuensis. I *have*, at last, finished my little book—that is *a* little book, and so have two or three mornings of breathing-time before I begin another. * * *

Henry James.

To A. C. Benson [1]
[*"Of the Ghostly and Ghastly"*]

34 De Vere Gardens, W.
March 11th, 1898.

My dear Arthur,

I suppose that in the mysterious scheme of providence and fate such an inspiration as your charming note—out of the blue!—of a

† From *The Letters of Henry James*, two volumes, edited by Percy Lubbock; copyright © 1920 by Charles Scribner's Sons; renewal copyright by William James and Margaret James Porter; reprinted by permission of the publisher. I, 263. The remaining letters in this section are also from this volume, pp. 278–280, 290, 296–297, 298–299, 300–301, 351–353, 354–359, and 408–409. Alice was the wife of William James. 1. A. C. Benson (1862–1925), genteel man of letters, son of the just deceased Archbishop of Canterbury.

couple of days ago, is intended somehow to make up to me for the terror with which my earlier—in fact *all* my past—productions inspire me, and for the insurmountable aversion I feel to looking at them again or to considering them in any way. This morbid state of mind is really a blessing in disguise—for it has for happy consequences that such an incident as your letter becomes thereby extravagantly pleasant and gives me a genial glow. All thanks and benedictions—I shake your hand very hard—or *would* do so if I could attribute to you anything so palpable, personal and actual *as* a hand. Yet I shall never write a sequel to the P. *of an* L.[2]—admire my euphonic indefinite article. It's all too faint and far away—too ghostly and ghastly—and I have bloodier things *en tête*.[3] I can do better than that!

But à propos, precisely, of the ghostly and ghastly, I have a little confession to make to you that has been on my conscience these three months and that I hope will excite in your generous breast nothing but tender memories and friendly sympathies.

On one of those two memorable—never to be obliterated—winter nights that I spent at the sweet Addington, your father, in the drawing-room by the fire, where we were talking a little, in the spirit of recreation, of such things, repeated to me the few meagre elements of a small and gruesome spectral story that had been told *him* years before and that he could only give the dimmest account of—partly because he had forgotten details and partly—and much more—because there had *been* no details and no coherency in the tale as he received it, from a person who also but half knew it. The vaguest essence only was there—some dead servants and some children. This essence *struck* me and I made a note of it (of a most scrappy kind) on going home. There the note remained till this autumn, when, struck with it afresh, I wrought it into a fantastic fiction which, first intended to be of the briefest, finally became a thing of some length and is now being "serialised" in an American periodical. It will appear late in the spring (chez Heinemann) in a volume with *one* other story, and then I will send it to you. In the meanwhile please think of the *doing* of the thing on my part as having sprung from that kind old evening at Addington—quite gruesomely as my unbridled imagination caused me to see the inevitable development of the subject. It was all worth mentioning to you. I am very busy and very decently fit and very much yours, always, my dear Arthur,

Henry James.

2. James's *The Portrait of a Lady* 3. In mind.
(1881).

To Paul Bourget [1]

["*A Little Volume Just Published*"]

Dictated

Lamb House, Rye.
19th August, 1898.

Mon cher Ami,

* * * I ordered my year-old "Maisie" the other day to be sent
to you, and I trust she will by this time have safely arrived—in
spite of some ambiguity in the literation of the name of your villa
as, with your letter in my hand, I earnestly meditate upon it. I
have also despatched to Madame Paul myself a little volume just
published [2]—a poor little pot-boiling study of nothing at all, *qui ne
tire pas à conséquence.*[3] It is but a monument to my fatal technical
passion, which prevents my ever giving up anything I have begun.
So that when something that I have supposed to be a subject turns
out on trial really to be none, *je m'y acharne d'autant plus,*[4] for
mere superstition—superstitious fear, I mean, of the consequences
and omens of weakness. The small book in question is really but
an exercise in the art of not appearing to one's self to fail. You
will say it is rather cruel that for such exercises the public also
should have to pay. Well, Madame Paul and you get your *exem-
plaire*[5] for nothing. * * *

Henry James.

To Dr. Waldstein [1]

["*That Wanton Little Tale*"]

Lamb House, Rye.
Oct: 21st, 1898.

Dear Sir,

Forgive my neglect, under great pressure of occupation, of your
so interesting letter of 12th. I have since receiving it had complicated calls on my time. That the *Turn of the Screw* has been
suggestive and significant to you—in any degree—it gives me great
pleasure to hear; and I can only thank you very kindly for the
impulse of sympathy that made you write. I am only afraid, perhaps,

1. Paul Bourget (1852–1935), French
essayist and novelist, whom James first
met in 1884.
2. Probably refers to *In the Cage,*
which James wrote after *The Turn of
the Screw,* but which was published in
August, two months before *The Two
Magics.* Much of what James says here
may well be applied to *The Turn of the
Screw.*
3. Which is really inconsequential.
4. I persist all the more.
5. Copy.
1. Louis Waldstein, M.D. (1853–1915),
author of *The Subconscious Self and
Its Relation to Education and Health,*
London, 1897.

that my conscious intention strikes you as having been larger than I deserve it should be thought. It is the intention so primarily, with me, always, of the artist, the *painter*, that *that* is what I most, myself, feel in it—and the lesson, the idea—ever—conveyed is only the one that deeply lurks in any vision prompted by life. And as regards a presentation of things so fantastic as in that wanton little Tale, I can only rather blush to see real substance read into them—I mean for the generosity of the reader. *But,* of course, where there *is* life, there's truth, and the truth was at the back of my head. The poet is always justified when he is not a humbug; always grateful to the justifying commentator. My bogey-tale dealt with things so hideous that I felt that to save it at all it needed some infusion of beauty or prettiness, and the beauty of the pathetic was the only attainable—was indeed inevitable. But ah, the exposure indeed, the helpless plasticity of childhood that isn't dear or sacred to *some*body! That *was* my little tragedy—over which you show a wisdom for which I thank you again. Believe me, thus, my dear Sir, yours most truly,

Henry James.

To H. G. Wells [1]

[*"The Thing Is Essentially a Pot-Boiler"*]

Lamb House, Rye.
Dec. 9th, 1898.

My dear H. G. Wells,

Your so liberal and graceful letter is to my head like coals of fire—so repeatedly for all these weeks have I had feebly to suffer frustrations in the matter of trundling over the marsh to ask for your news and wish for your continued amendment. The shortening days and the deepening mud have been at the bottom of this affair. I never get out of the house till 3 o'clock, when night is quickly at one's heels. I would have taken a regular day—I mean started in the a.m.—but have been so ridden, myself, by the black care of an unfinished and *running* (galloping, leaping and bounding,) serial that parting with a day has been like parting with a pound of flesh.[2] I am still a neck ahead, however, and *this* week will see me through; I accordingly hope very much to be able to turn up on one of the ensuing days. I will sound a horn, so that you yourself be not absent on the chase. Then I will express more articulately

---

1. H. G. Wells (1866–1946), at this time a friend and neighbor of James. Later they were to fall out, Wells cruelly parodying James's stories like *The Turn of the Screw* in *Boon*, London, 1915. See *Henry James and H. G. Wells: A Record of their Friendship,* *their Debate on the Art of Fiction, and their Quarrel,* edited with an Introduction by Leon Edel and Gordon N. Ray, Urbana, Ill., 1958.
2. *The Awkward Age* began in *Harper's Weekly* on October 1, 1898 and ran through January 7, 1899.

my appreciation of your various signs of critical interest, as well as assure you of my sympathy in your own martyrdom. What will you have? It's all a grind and a bloody battle—as well as a considerable lark, and the difficulty itself is the refuge from the vulgarity. Bless your heart, I think I could easily say worse of the T. of the S., the young woman, the spooks, the style, the everything, than the worst any one else could manage. One knows the most damning things about one's self. Of course I had, about my young woman, to take a very sharp line. The grotesque business I had to make her picture and the childish psychology I had to make her trace and present, were, for me at least, a very difficult job, in which absolute lucidity and logic, a singleness of effect, were imperative. Therefore I had to rule out subjective complications of her own—play of tone etc.; and keep her impersonal save for the most obvious and indispensable little note of neatness, firmness and courage—without which she wouldn't have had her data. But the thing is essentially a pot-boiler and a *jeu d'esprit*.

With the little play,[3] the absolute creature of its conditions, I had simply to make up a deficit and take a small *revanche*.[4] For three moral years had the actress for whom it was written (utterly to try to *fit*) persistently failed to produce it, and I couldn't wholly waste my labour. The B.P.[5] won't read a play with the mere names of the speakers—so I simply paraphrased these and added such indications as might be the equivalent of decent acting—a history and an evolution that seem to me moreover explicatively and sufficiently smeared all over the thing. The moral is of course Don't write one-act plays. But I didn't mean thus to sprawl. I envy your hand your needle-pointed fingers. As you don't say that you're *not* better I prepare myself to be greatly struck with the same, and with kind regards to your wife,

Believe me yours ever,

Henry James

To F. W. H. Myers [1]

[*"The T. of the S. Is a Very Mechanical Matter"*]

Lamb House, Rye.
Dec. 19th, 1898.

My dear Myers,

I don't know what you will think of my unconscionable delay to acknowledge your letter of so many, so very many days ago, nor

---

3. *Covering End,* the second work in *The Two Magics,* was originally a one-act play which James wrote for Ellen Terry. In 1908 James recast the story into a three-act play under the title *The High Bid* which ran successfully.
4. Revenge.

5. British Public.
1. F. W. H. Myers (1843–1901), minor poet and man of letters, one of the founders of the Society of Psychical Research, of which William James was once president.

exactly how I can make vivid to you the nature of my hindrances and excuses. I have, in truth, been (until some few days since) intensely and anxiously busy, finishing, under pressure, a long job that had from almost the first—I mean from long before I had reached the end—begun to be (loathsome name and fact!) "serialized"—so that the printers were at my heels and I had to make a sacrifice of my correspondence *utterly*—to keep the sort of cerebral freshness required for not losing my head or otherwise collapsing. But I won't expatiate. Please believe my silence has been wholly involuntary. And yet, now that I *am* writing I scarce know what to say to you on the subject on which you wrote, especially as I'm afraid I don't quite *understand* the principal question you put to me about "The Turn of the Screw." However, that scantily matters; for in truth I am afraid I have on some former occasions rather awkwardly signified to you that I somehow can't pretend to give any coherent account of my small inventions "after the fact." There they are—the fruit, at best, of a very imperfect ingenuity and with all the imperfections thereof on their heads. The one thing and another that are questionable and ambiguous in them I mostly take to be conditions of their having got themselves pushed through at all. The *T. of the S.* is a very mechanical matter, I honestly think—an inferior, a merely *pictorial*, subject and rather a shameless pot-boiler. The thing that, as I recall it, I most wanted not to fail of doing, under penalty of extreme platitude, was to give the impression of the communication to the children of the most infernal imaginable evil and danger—the condition, on their part, of being as *exposed* as we can humanly conceive children to be. This was my artistic knot to untie, to put any sense of logic into the thing, and if I had known any way of producing *more* the image of their contact and condition I should assuredly have been proportionately eager to resort to it. I evoked the worst I could, and only feel tempted to say, as in French: "Excusez du peu!" [2]

I am living so much down here that I fear I am losing hold of some of my few chances of occasionally seeing you. The charming old humble-minded "quaintness" and quietness of this little brown hilltop city lays a spell upon me. I send you and your wife and all your house all the greetings of the season and am, my dear Myers, yours very constantly,

Henry James.

2. Bear with it.

To W. D. Howells [1]

[*"Another Duplex Book Like the 'Two Magics'"*]

Lamb House, Rye.
29th June, 1900.

My dear Howells,

* * * I brood with mingled elation and depression on your ingenious, your really inspired, suggestion that I shall give you a ghost, and that my ghost shall be "international." I say inspired because, singularly enough, I set to work some months ago at an international ghost, and on just this scale, 50,000 words; entertaining for a little the highest hopes of him. He was to have been wonderful and beautiful; he was to have been called (perhaps too metaphysically) "The Sense of the Past"; and he was to have been supplied to a certain Mr_____ [2] who was then approaching me —had then approached me. . . . The outstretched arm, however, alas, was drawn in again, or lopped off, or otherwise paralysed and negatived, and I was left with my little project—intrinsically, I hasten to add, and most damnably difficult—on my hands. * * *

I'm not even sure that the international ghost is what will most bear being worried out—though, again, in another particular, the circumstances, combining with your coincident thought, seemed pointed by the finger of providence. What _____ wanted was two Tales—both tales of "terror" and making another duplex book like the "Two Magics." Accordingly I had had (dreadful deed!) to puzzle out more or less a second, a different piece of impudence of the same general type. But I had only, when the project collapsed, caught hold of the tip of the tail of this other monster—whom I now mention because his tail seemed to show him as necessarily still more interesting than No. 1. If I can at all recapture *him*, or anything like him, I will do my best to sit down to him and "mount" him with due neatness. In short, I will do what I can. If I can't be terrible, I shall nevertheless still try to be international The difficulties are that it's difficult to be terrible save in the short piece and international save in the long. But trust me. [3] * * *

Henry James.

1. William Dean Howells (1837–1920), James's life-long friend, had written asking for a ghost-story for the *Atlantic Monthly*.
2. Some representative from Doubleday, see below, p. 115.
3. James never did finish *The Sense of the Past*, although he returned to it

in the last years of his life. Even though he and Howells agreed in August to drop the project, James's interest in the "international" theme led directly to his masterpiece, *The Ambassadors* (1903). Indeed, in this and in the following selections, one can sense James moving away from the ghost-story.

A Notebook Entry †

["*Something As Simple As* The Turn of the Screw"]

Lamb House, August 9th, 1900.

I've a great desire to see if I can worry out, as I've worried out before, some possible *alternative* to the 50,000 words story as to which I've been corresponding with Howells, and as to which I've again attacked—been attacking—*The Sense of the Past.* I fumble, I yearn, *je tâtonne*,[1] a good deal for an alternative to *that* idea, which proves in execution so damnably difficult and so complex. I don't mind, God knows, the mere difficulty, however damnable; but it's fatal to find one's self in for a subject that one can't possibly treat, or hope, or begin, to treat, in the space, and that can only betray one, as regards that, after one is expensively launched. The ideal is something as simple as *The Turn of the Screw,* only different and less grossly and merely apparitional. I was rather taken with Howells's suggestion of an 'international ghost'—I kindle, I vibrate, respond to suggestion, imaginatively, so almost unfortunately, so generously and precipitately, easily. The formula, for so short a thing, rather caught me up—the more that, as the thing *has* to be but the 50,000, the important, the serious, the sincere things I have in my head are all too ample for it. And then there was the remarkable coincidence of my having begun *The Sense of the Past,* of its being really 'international,' which seemed in a small way the finger of providence. But I'm afraid the finger of providence is pointing me astray.

* * * I *had* a vague sense, last autumn when I was so deludedly figuring out *The S. of the P.* for 'Doubleday,' that, as a no. 2 thing (in 'Terror') for the same volume, there dwelt a possibility in something expressive of the peculiarly acute Modern, the current polyglot, the American-experience-abroad line. I saw something; it glimmered on me; but I didn't in my then uncertainty, follow it up. *Is* there anything to follow up? *Vedremo bene.*[2] I want something *simpler* than *The S. of the P.,* but I don't want anything, if may be, of less dignity, as it were. *The S. of the P.* rests on an idea—and it's only the idea that can give me the situation. *The Advertiser* [3] is an idea—a beautiful one, if one could happily fantasticate it. Perhaps one *can*—I must see, I must, precisely, sound that little depth. Remember this is the kind of sacred process in which ½ *a dozen*

---

† From *The Notebooks of Henry James,* edited by F. O. Matthiesen and Kenneth B. Murdock, pp. 298–300; copyright © 1947 by Oxford Press, Inc.; reprinted by permission of the publisher.
1. I grope.
2. Well, we'll wait and see.
3. This was the name which James gave in his notebooks to a story-line which he toyed with, but never incorporated into a tale or novel.

days, a WEEK, of depth, of stillness, are but all too well spent. THAT kind of control of one's nerves, command of one's coolness, is the real economy. The *fantasticated* is, for this job, my probable formula, and I know what I mean by it as differentiated from the type, the squeezed sponge, of *The T. of the S.* 'Terror' *peut bien en être*,[4] and all the effective *malaise*,[5] above all, the case demands. Ah, things swim before me, *caro mio*, and I only need to sit tight, to keep my place and fix my eyes, to see them float past me in the current into which I can cast my little net and make my little haul. Hasn't one got hold of, doesn't one make out, rather, something in the general glimmer of the notion of what the quasi-grotesque Europeo-American situation, in the way the gruesome, may, *pushed to the full and right expression of its grotesqueness*, has to give? That general formula haunts me, and as a *morality* as well as a terror, an idea as well as a ghost. Here truly *is* the tip of a tail to catch, a trail, a scent, a latent light to follow up. * * *

To W. D. Howells

["*A Little 'Tale of Terror'* "]

Lamb House, Rye,
August 9, 1900

My dear Howells,

* * * Lending myself as much as possible to your suggestion of a little "tale of terror" that should be also international, I took straight up again the idea I spoke to you of having already, some months ago, tackled and, for various reasons, laid aside. I have been attacking it again with intensity and on the basis of a simplification that would make it easier, and have done for it, thus, 110 pages of type. The upshot of this, alas, however, is that though this second start is, if I—or if *you*—like, magnificent, it seriously confronts me with the element of *length*; showing me, I fear, but too vividly, that, do what I will for compression, I shall not be able to squeeze my subject into 50,000 words. It will make, even if it doesn't, for difficulty, still beat me, 70,000 or 80,000—dreadful to say; and that faces me as an excessive addition to the ingredient of "risk" we speak of. On the other hand I am not sure that I can hope to substitute for this particular affair *another* affair of "terror" which will be expressible in the 50,000; and that for an especial reason. This reason is that, above all when one has done the thing, already, as I have rather repeatedly, it is not easy to concoct a "ghost" of any freshness. The want of ease is extremely marked, moreover, if the thing is to be done on a certain scale of length. One might still

---

4. Could be part of it.   5. Impending sense of disaster.

toss off a spook or two more if it were a question only of the "short-story" dimension; but prolongation and extension constitute a strain which the mere apparitional—discounted, also, as by my past dealings with it—doesn't do enough to mitigate. * * *

My one chance is yet, I admit, to try to attack the same (the subject) from still another quarter, at still another angle, that I make out as a possible one and which may keep it squeezeable and short. If this experiment fails, I fear I shall have to "chuck" the supernatural and the high fantastic. I have just finished, as it happens, a fine flight (of eighty thousand words) into the high fantastic, which has rather depleted me, or at any rate affected me as discharging my obligations in that quarter. But I believe I mentioned to you in my last "The Sacred Fount"—this has been "sold" to Methuen here, and by this time, probably, to somebody else in the U.S.[1]—but, alas, not to be serialized (as to which indeed it is inapt)—as to the title of which kindly preserve silence. The *vraie vérité*, the fundamental truth lurking behind all the rest, is furthermore, no doubt, that preoccupied with half a dozen things of the altogether human order now fermenting in my brain, I don't care for "terror" (terror, that is, without "pity") so much as I otherwise might. This would seem to make it simple for me to say to you: "Hang it, if I can't pull off my Monster on *any* terms, I'll just do for you a neat little *human*—and not the less international —fifty-thousander consummately addressed to your more cheerful department; do for you, in other words, an admirable short novel of manners, thrilling too in its degree, but definitely ignoring the bugaboo."

Henry James.

To W. D. Howells

["*A Story of the '8 to 10 Thousand Words'*"]

Lamb House, Rye.
December 11th, 1902.

My dear Howells,
* * * I am melted at your reading *en famille* The Sacred Fount, which you will, I fear, have found chaff in the mouth and which is one of several things of mine, in these last years, that have paid the penalty of having been conceived only as the "short story" that (alone, apparently) I could hope to work off somewhere (which I mainly failed of,) and then *grew* by a rank force of its own into something of which the idea had, modestly, never been to be a book. That is essentially the case with the S. F., planned, like The Spoils of Poynton, What Maisie Knew, The Turn of

1. To Charles Scribner's Sons, their first James novel.

the Screw, and various others, as a story of the "8 to 10 thousand words"!! and then having accepted its bookish necessity or destiny in consequence of becoming already, at the start, 20,000, accepted it ruefully and blushingly, moreover, since, *given the tenuity of the idea*, the larger quantity of treatment hadn't been aimed at. I remember how I would have "chucked" *The Sacred Fount* at the 15th thousand word, if in the first place I could have afforded to "waste" 15,000, and if in the second I were not always ridden by a superstitious terror of not finishing, for finishing's and for the precedent's sake, what I have begun. I am a fair coward about *dropping*, and the book in question, I fear, is, more than anything else, a monument to that superstition. When, if it meets my eye, I say to myself, "You know you might not have finished it," I make the remark not in natural reproach, but, I confess, in craven relief. * * *

Yours always and ever,
Henry James.

The New York Preface †

["*An Exercise of the Imagination*"]

* * * That particular challenge [1] at least "The Turn of the Screw" does n't incur; and this perfectly independent and irresponsible little fiction rejoices, beyond any rival on a like ground, in a conscious provision of prompt retort to the sharpest question that may be addressed to it. For it has the small strength—if I should n't say rather the unattackable ease—of a perfect homogeneity, of being, to the very last grain of its virtue, all of a kind; the very kind, as happens, least apt to be baited by earnest criticism, the only sort of criticism of which account need be taken. To have handled again this so full-blown flower of high fancy is to be led back by it to easy and happy recognitions. Let the first of these be that of the starting-point itself—the sense, all charming again, of the circle, one winter afternoon, round the hall-fire of a grave old country-house where (for all the world as if to resolve itself promptly and obligingly into convertible, into "literary" stuff) the talk turned, on I forget what homely pretext, to apparitions and night-fears, to the marked and sad drop in the general supply, and still more in the general quality, of such commodities. The good, the really effective and heart-shaking ghost-stories (roughly so to term them) appeared all to

† From the Preface to *The Aspern Papers; The Turn of the Screw; The Liar; the Two Faces*, volume XII, *The Novels and Tales of Henry James*, The New York Edition, pp. xiv–xxii; copyright © 1908 by Charles Scribner's Sons; renewal copyright 1937 by Henry James; reprinted by permission of the publisher.

1. James concluded his remarks on *The Aspern Papers* by claiming that if he had had the time and opportunity he "could have perfectly 'worked out' Jeffrey Aspern."

have been told, and neither new crop nor new type in any quarter awaited us. The new type indeed, the mere modern "psychical" case, washed clean of all queerness as by exposure to a flowing laboratory tap, and equipped with credentials vouching for this—the new type clearly promised little, for the more it was respectably certified the less it seemed of a nature to rouse the dear old sacred terror. Thus it was, I remember, that amid our lament for a beautiful lost form, our distinguished host expressed the wish that he might but have recovered for us one of the scantest of fragments of this form at its best. He had never forgotten the impression made on him as a young man by the withheld glimpse, as it were, of a dreadful matter that had been reported years before, and with as few particulars, to a lady with whom he had youthfully talked. The story would have been thrilling could she but have found herself in better possession of it, dealing as it did with a couple of small children in an out-of-the-way place, to whom the spirits of certain "bad" servants, dead in the employ of the house, were believed to have appeared with the design of "getting hold" of them. This was all, but there had been more, which my friend's old converser had lost the thread of: she could only assure him of the wonder of the allegations as she had anciently heard them made. He himself could give us but this shadow of a shadow—my own appreciation of which, I need scarcely say, was exactly wrapped up in that thinness. On the surface there was n't much, but another grain, none the less, would have spoiled the precious pinch addressed to its end as neatly as some modicum extracted from an old silver snuff-box and held between finger and thumb. I was to remember the haunted children and the prowling servile spirits as a "value," of the disquieting sort, in all conscience sufficient; so that when, after an interval, I was asked for something seasonable by the promoters of a periodical dealing in the time-honoured Christmas-tide toy, I bethought myself at once of the vividest little note for sinister romance that I had ever jotted down.

Such was the private source of "The Turn of the Screw"; and I wondered, I confess, why so fine a germ, gleaming there in the wayside dust of life, had never been deftly picked up. The thing had for me the immense merit of allowing the imagination absolute freedom of hand, of inviting it to act on a perfectly clear field, with no "outside" control involved, no pattern of the usual or the true or the terrible "pleasant" (save always of course the high pleasantry of one's very form) to consort with. This makes in fact the charm of my second reference, that I find here a perfect example of an exercise of the imagination unassisted, unassociated—playing the game, making the score, in the phrase of our sporting day, off its own bat. To what degree the game was worth playing I

need n't attempt to say: the exercise I have noted strikes me now,
I confess, as the interesting thing, the imaginative faculty acting
with the *whole* of the case on its hands. The exhibition involved
is in other words a fairy-tale pure and simple—save indeed as to its
springing not from an artless and measureless, but from a conscious
and cultivated credulity. Yet the fairy-tale belongs mainly to either
of two classes, the short and sharp and single, charged more or less
with the compactness of anecdote (as to which let the familiars of
our childhood, Cinderella and Blue-Beard and Hop o' my Thumb
and Little Red Riding Hood and many of the gems of the Brothers
Grimm directly testify), or else the long and loose, the copious, the
various, the endless, where, dramatically speaking, roundness is
quite sacrificed—sacrificed to fulness, sacrificed to exuberance, if
one will: witness at hazard almost any one of the Arabian Nights.
The charm of all these things for the distracted modern mind is in
the clear field of experience, as I call it, over which we are thus
led to roam; an annexed but independent world in which nothing
is right save as we rightly imagine it. We have to do *that*, and we
do it happily for the short spurt and in the smaller piece, achieving
so perhaps beauty and lucidity; we flounder, we lose breath, on
the other hand—that is we fail, not of continuity, but of an agreeable unity, of the "roundness" in which beauty and lucidity largely
reside—when we go in, as they say, for great lengths and breadths.
And this, oddly enough, not because "keeping it up" is n't abundantly within the compass of the imagination appealed to in certain
conditions, but because the finer interest depends just on *how* it
is kept up.

Nothing is so easy as improvisation, the running on and on of
invention; it is sadly compromised, however, from the moment
its stream breaks bounds and gets into flood. Then the waters may
spread indeed, gathering houses and herds and crops and cities into
their arms and wrenching off, for our amusement, the whole face
of the land—only violating by the same stroke our sense of the
course and the channel, which is our sense of the uses of a
stream and the virtue of a story. Improvisation, as in the Arabian
Nights, may keep on terms with encountered objects by sweeping
them in and floating them on its breast; but the great effect it so
loses—that of keeping on terms with itself. This is ever, I intimate,
the hard thing for the fairy-tale; but by just so much as it struck me
as hard did it in "The Turn of the Screw" affect me as irresistibly
prescribed. To improvise with extreme freedom and yet at the
same time without the possibility of ravage, without the hint of a
flood; to keep the stream, in a word, on something like ideal terms
with itself; that was here my definite business. The thing was to
aim at absolute singleness, clearness and roundness, and yet to

depend on an imagination working freely, working (call it) with extravagance; by which law it would n't be thinkable except as free and would n't be amusing except as controlled. The merit of the tale, as it stands, is accordingly, I judge, that it has struggled successfully with its dangers. It is an excursion into chaos while remaining, like Blue-Beard and Cinderella, but an anecdote—though an anecdote amplified and highly emphasised and returning upon itself; as, for that matter, Cinderella and Blue-Beard return. I need scarcely add after this that it is a piece of ingenuity pure and simple, of cold artistic calculation, an *amusette* [2] to catch those not easily caught (the "fun" of the capture of the merely witless being ever but small), the jaded, the disillusioned, the fastidious. Otherwise expressed, the study is of a conceived "tone," the tone of suspected and felt trouble, of an inordinate and incalculable sore—the tone of tragic, yet of exquisite, mystification. To knead the subject of my young friend's, the supposititious narrator's, mystification thick, and yet strain the expression of it so clear and fine that beauty would result: no side of the matter so revives for me as that endeavour. Indeed if the artistic value of such an experiment be measured by the intellectual echoes it may again, long after, set in motion, the case would make in favour of this little firm fantasy—which I seem to see draw behind it today a train of associations. I ought doubtless to blush for thus confessing them so numerous that I can but pick among them for reference. I recall for instance a reproach made me by a reader capable evidently, for the time, of some attention, but not quite capable of enough, who complained that I had n't sufficiently "characterised" my young woman engaged in her labyrinth; had n't endowed her with signs and marks, features and humours, had n't in a word invited her to deal with her own mystery as well as with that of Peter Quint, Miss Jessel and the hapless children. I remember well, whatever the absurdity of its now coming back to me, my reply to that criticism—under which one's artistic, one's ironic heart shook for the instant almost to breaking. "You indulge in that stricture at your ease, and I don't mind confiding to you that—strange as it may appear!—one has to choose ever so delicately among one's difficulties, attaching one's self to the greatest, bearing hard on those and intelligently neglecting the others. If one attempts to tackle them all one is certain to deal completely with none; whereas the effectual dealing with a few casts a blest golden haze under cover of which, like wanton mocking goddesses in clouds, the others find prudent to retire. It was 'déjà très-joli,' [3] in 'The Turn of the Screw,' please believe, the general proposition of our young woman's keeping crystalline her record

2. A piece of child's play.   3. Nicely established.

of so many intense anomalies and obscurities—by which I don't of course mean her explanation of them, a different matter; and I saw no way, I feebly grant (fighting, at the best too, periodically, for every grudged inch of my space) to exhibit her in relations other than those; one of which, precisely, would have been her relation to her own nature. We have surely as much of her own nature as we can swallow in watching it reflect her anxieties and inductions. It constitutes no little of a character indeed, in such conditions, for a young person, as she says, 'privately bred,' that she is able to make her particular credible statement of such strange matters. She has 'authority,' which is a good deal to have given her, and I could n't have arrived at so much had I clumsily tried for more."

For which truth I claim part of the charm latent on occasion in the extracted reasons of beautiful things—putting for the beautiful always, in a work of art, the close, the curious, the deep. Let me place above all, however, under the protection of that presence the side by which this fiction appeals most to consideration: its choice of its way of meeting its gravest difficulty. There were difficulties not so grave: I had for instance simply to renounce all attempt to keep the kind and degree of impression I wished to produce on terms with the to-day so copious psychical record of cases of apparitions. Different signs and circumstances, in the reports, mark these cases; different things are done—though on the whole very little appears to be—by the persons appearing; the point is, however, that some things are never done at all: this negative quantity is large—certain reserves and proprieties and immobilities consistently impose themselves. Recorded and attested "ghosts" are in other words as little expressive, as little dramatic, above all as little continuous and conscious and responsive, as is consistent with their taking the trouble—and an immense trouble they find it, we gather —to appear at all. Wonderful and interesting therefore at a given moment, they are inconceivable figures in an *action*—and "The Turn of the Screw" was an action, desperately, or it was nothing. I had to decide in fine between having my apparitions correct and having my story "good"—that is producing my impression of the dreadful, my designed horror. Good ghosts, speaking by book, make poor subjects, and it was clear that from the first my hovering prowling blighting presences, my pair of abnormal agents, would have to depart altogether from the rules. They would be agents in fact; there would be laid on them the dire duty of causing the situation to reek with an air of Evil. Their desire and their ability to do so, visibly measuring meanwhile their effect, together with their observed and described success—this was exactly my central idea; so that, briefly, I cast my lot with pure romance, the appearances conforming to the true type being so little romantic.

This is to say, I recognise again, that Peter Quint and Miss Jessel are not "ghosts" at all, as we now know the ghost, but goblins, elves, imps, demons as loosely constructed as those of the old trials for witchcraft; if not, more pleasingly, fairies of the legendary order, wooing their victims forth to see them dance under the moon. Not indeed that I suggest their reducibility to any form of the pleasing pure and simple; they please at the best but through having helped me to express my subject all directly and intensely. Here it was—in the use made of them—that I felt a high degree of art really required; and here it is that, on reading the tale over, I find my precautions justified. The essence of the matter was the villainy of motive in the evoked predatory creatures; so that the result would be ignoble—by which I mean would be trivial—were this element of evil but feebly or inanely suggested. Thus arose on behalf of my idea the lively interest of a possible suggestion and process of *adumbration*; the question of how best to convey that sense of the depths of the sinister without which my fable would so woefully limp. Portentous evil—how was I to save that, as an intention on the part of my demon-spirits, from the drop, the comparative vulgarity, inevitably attending, throughout the whole range of possible brief illustration, the offered example, the imputed vice, the cited act, the limited deplorable presentable instance? To bring the bad dead back to life for a second round of badness is to warrant them as indeed prodigious, and to become hence as shy of specifications as of a waiting anti-climax. One had seen, in fiction, some grand form of wrong-doing, or better still of wrong-being, imputed, seen it promised and announced as by the hot breath of the Pit—and then, all lamentably, shrink to the compass of some particular brutality, some particular immorality, some particular infamy portrayed: with the result, alas, of the demonstration's falling sadly short. If *my* bad things, for "The Turn of the Screw," I felt, should succumb to this danger, if they should n't seem sufficiently bad, there would be nothing for me but to hang an artistic head lower than I had ever known occasion to do.

The view of that discomfort and the fear of that dishonour, it accordingly must have been, that struck the proper light for my right, though by no means easy, short cut. What, in the last analysis, had I to give the sense of? Of their being, the haunting pair, capable, as the phrase is, of everything—that is of exerting, in respect to the children, the very worst action small victims so conditioned might be conceived as subject to. What would *be* then, on reflexion, this utmost conceivability?—a question to which the answer all admirably came. There is for such a case no eligible *absolute* of the wrong; it remains relative to fifty other elements, a matter of appreciation, speculation, imagination—these things moreover quite exactly in the light of the spectator's, the critic's, the reader's experience. Only make the reader's general vision of evil intense enough, I said to myself—and that already is a charming job—and his own experience, his own imagination, his own sympathy (with the children) and horror (of their false friends) will supply him quite sufficiently with all the particulars. Make him *think* the evil, make him think it for himself, and you are released from weak specifications. This ingenuity I took pains—as indeed great pains were required—to apply; and with a success apparently beyond my liveliest hope. Droll enough at the same time, I must add, some of the evidence—even when most convincing—of this success. How can I feel my calculation to have failed, my wrought suggestion not to have worked, that is, on my being assailed, as has befallen me, with the charge of a monstrous emphasis, the charge of all indecently expatiating? There is not only from beginning to end of the matter not an inch of expatiation, but my values are positively all blanks save so far as an excited horror, a promoted pity, a created expertness—on which punctual effects of strong causes no writer can ever fail to plume himself—proceed to read into them more or less fantastic figures. Of high interest to the author meanwhile—and by the same stroke a theme for the moralist —the artless resentful reaction of the entertained person who has abounded in the sense of the situation. He visits his abundance, morally, on the artist—who has but clung to an ideal of faultlessness. Such indeed, for this latter, are some of the observations by which the prolonged strain of that clinging may be enlivened! * * *

Other Suggested Sources

ROBERT LEE WOLFF

The Genesis of "The Turn of the Screw" †

"The Turn of the Screw" has been perhaps the most widely read and discussed of the stories of Henry James. Critics as diverse as Heywood Broun and William Lyon Phelps, to mention only two, have testified to their appreciation of its apparent horrors; they and others accept as genuine the ghosts who haunt the children.[1] Edna Kenton, on the other hand, pointing out the obtuseness of these readers, caught, as she puts it, in James's trap, has suggested a second set of horrors behind the first:[2]

> The children hounded by the prowling ghosts—this is the hard and shining surface story of *The Turn of the Screw*; or, to put it more accurately, it is the traditional and accepted interpretation of the story as it has come down through a quarter of a century of readers' reactions resulting from "a cold artistic calculation" on the part of its highly entertained author . . . no reader has more to go on than the young governess' word . . . it is she— always she herself—who sees the lurking shapes and heralds them to her little world.[3]

This is the view taken by the artist Charles Demuth, whose four illustrations for the story appear with Miss Kenton's article;[4] the

† From *American Literature*, XIII (March 1941), 1–8. Reprinted by permission of the author and Duke University Press.
1. Broun in his Introduction to the Modern Library Edition (New York, 1930); Phelps in *Howells, James, Bryant, and Other Essays* (New York, 1924), pp. 143 ff. All page references to "The Turn of the Screw," are to *The Novels and Tales of Henry James* (New York, 1908), XII, 147 ff.
2. "Henry James to the Ruminant Reader: The Turn of the Screw," *The Arts*, VI, 245-255 (Nov., 1924).
3. Ibid., [p. 210.]
4. The illustrations appear on pp. 247, 249, 250, and 253 of the above-cited number of *The Arts*. They are also to be found reproduced in *Charles Demuth*, ed. A. E. Gallatin (New York, 1927), unpaged; and, according to *The Index of Twentieth Century Artists* (1935), II, 149, in William Murrell, *Charles Demuth*, "American Artists Series," Whitney Museum of Art" (New York, 1931), pp. 41, 43. [Actually Demuth painted five illustration, the first being entitled: "At a House in Harley Street" (shows a suave young gentleman standing above the seated governess, holding her hands and obviously imploring her to take the position). See Andrew Carnduff Ritchie, *Charles Demuth* (The Museum of Modern Art: New York, 1950). Editor.]

scenes in the story which he has chosen to reproduce, the tortured forms and expressions, are proof positive that he regards the governess, who sees the ghosts and tells the story, as a neurotic, suffering from sex repression.[5] Edmund Wilson has examined this view of the story even more closely; he analyzes the narrative step by step.[6] Going beyond Miss Kenton's suggestion that the governess alone sees the ghosts, Wilson finds several matters of Freudian significance, including the governess's final passion for the little boy, which leads her, in the end, to frighten him to death.[7] He concludes that the story "is simply a variation on one of James's familiar themes: the frustrated Anglo-Saxon spinster." [8] This second set of psychological horrors beneath the already terrible surface of the story goes a long way toward justifying Douglas, James's fictional narrator, the possessor of the governess's manuscript, who is made to say of the story, before he reads it to his audience: "It's beyond anything. Nothing at all that I know touches it. . . . For dreadful-dreadfulness! . . . For general uncanny ugliness and horror and pain." [9]

All this discussion considered, then, it is surprising that we know so little about the genesis of "The Turn of the Screw." James himself, in his Preface, tell us only this:

> . . . the starting point itself—the sense all charming again, of the circle, one winter afternoon, round the hall-fire of a grave old country-house, where (for all the world as if to resolve itself promptly and obligingly into "literary stuff") the talk turned, on

5. The following are the titles of Demuth's pictures: "I can see . . . the way . . . his hand . . . passed from one crenelation to the next." (The governess's expression of rapture in this picture is masterly.) "They moved slowly, in unison, below us, over the lawn, the boy, as they went, reading aloud from a story-book, and passing his arm round his sister to keep her quite in touch." "She had picked up a small flat piece of wood, which happened to have in it a little hole that had evidently suggested to her the idea of sticking in another fragment that might figure as a mast and make the thing a boat." "Did I steal?" (This last, of course, shows part of the dreadful final interview between the governess and little Miles.) Demuth has deliberately chosen four scenes with ambiguous meanings and hidden sexual significance.
6. "The Ambiguity of Henry James," in Wilson's *The Triple Thinkers* (New York, 1938), pp. 122ff.
7. Wilson mentions, of course, the two pieces of wood (above, n. 5), "the fact that the male apparition first appears on a tower and the female apparition

on a lake" (*ibid.*, p. 125), the governess's complex loves, first for her employer and then for the little boy, and her unwillingness to trouble her employer over the matter of the apparitions for fear that he would think she had attempted to attract his attention to her own "slighted charms." Wilson does not, however, mention specifically many other phenomena and expressions susceptible of a Freudian interpretation, for example: "Flora whom . . . I had established in the schoolroom with a sheet of white paper, a pencil, and a copy of nice 'round O's' now presented herself at the open door" [p. 11]. The story is full of candles which are blown out; the ghosts are seen in corridors and on staircases, and through windows; when Miles and the governess are left alone at dinner they are "silent while the maid was with us—as silent, it whimsically occurred to me, as some young couple who, on their wedding journey, at the inn, feel shy in the presence of the waiter" [p. 81].
8. *The Triple Thinkers*, pp. 131–132.
9. "The Turn of the Screw," [pp. 1–2].

I forget what homely pretext, to apparitions and night-fears, to the marked and sad drop in the general supply, and still more in the general quality of such commodities. . . . Thus it was, I remember, that amid our lament for a beautiful lost form, our distinguished host expressed the wish that he might have recovered for us one of the scantest of fragments of this form at its best. He had never forgotten the impression, made upon him as a young man, by the withheld glimpse, as it were, of a dreadful matter that had been reported years before, and with as few particulars, to a lady with whom he had youthfully talked. The story would have been thrilling, could she but have found herself in better possession of it, dealing as it did with a couple of small children in an out-of-the-way place, to whom the spirits of certain "bad" servants, dead in the employ of the house, were believed to have appeared with the design of "getting hold" of them. This was all, but there had been more, which my friend's old converser had lost the thread of: she could only assure him of the wonder of the allegations as she had anciently heard them made. He himself could give us but the shadow of a shadow. . . . On the surface there wasn't much, but another grain, none the less, would have spoiled the precious pinch. . . . I was to remember the haunted children and the prowling servile spirits as a "value" of the disquieting sort. . . . Such was the private source of "The Turn of the Screw." [1]

The "distinguished host" of this preface was the Archbishop of Canterbury, Edward White Benson, father of A. C. Benson and of E. F. Benson, both distinguished authors and friends of Henry James. The "grave old country-house" was Addington, at Croydon, near London, country seat of the Archbishop. On March 11, 1898, just before "The Turn of the Screw" was to be published, James wrote to A. C. Benson, whose father, the Archbishop, had died in 1896:

. . . on one of those two memorable—never to be obliterated—winter nights that I spent at the sweet Addington, your father, in the drawing room by the fire . . . repeated to me the few meagre elements of a small and gruesome spectral story that had been told *him* years before. . . . The vaguest essence only was there—some dead servants and some children. This essence *struck* me and I made a note of it (of a most scrappy kind) on going home. There the note remained till this autumn, when, struck with it fresh, I wrought it into a fantastic fiction which, first intended to be of the briefest, finally became a thing of some length, and is now being "serialized" in an American periodical. [2]

1. Preface to "The Turn of the Screw," [pp. 118–119].
2. *Collier's Weekly*, where it ran from Feb. 5 to April 16, 1898. [Actually the first installment appeared in the January 27 number. Editor.]

It will appear late in the spring (chez Heinemann) in a volume with *one* other story, and then I will send it to you.[3]

The Benson sons have fortunately been enormously articulate about their family life,[4] and one is not disappointed when one examines their works for reference to this auspicious evening at Addington, when, James says, the Archbishop of Canterbury sowed the seeds for "The Turn of the Screw." A. C. Benson, in the chapter on James in his *Memories and Friends*,[5] tells us a little more about this occasion:

> Again, he came to us at Addington on the day after the collapse of one of his plays. . . . He and my father, on that occasion, found much to say to each other. Indeed it was not long after that date that he presented me with his *Two Magics*,[6] saying that I should at once guess the reason for the gift. I read the book, but could not divine the connection. He then told me that it was on that visit that my father had told him a story which was the germ of that most tragical and even appalling story *The Turn of the Screw*. My father took a certain interest in psychical matters, but we have never been able to recollect any story that he ever told which could have provided a hint for so grim a subject.

Writing years later, A. C. Benson had probably forgotten James's letter to him before the book itself appeared. What he remembered was his own surprise at finding the germ of the story attributed to his father, who had, of course, died by the time the story was written.

We are incidentally now able to fix the date of this visit of James to Addington. Only two of James's plays were actually produced, *The American* and *Guy Domville*; and of these two only *Guy Domville* can be said to have had a "collapse." In fact, James was much upset by an incident on the opening night, January 5, 1895, and the play ran only a month.[7] It is, then, reasonable to

3. *The Letters of Henry James*, ed. Percy Lubbock (New York, 1920), I [pp. 108–109]. The volume was *The Two Magics*, which contained "The Turn of the Screw" and "Covering End."

4. A. C. Benson, *Life of Edward White Benson, Sometime Archbishop of Canterbury*, (2 vols.; London, 1899). There is no mention in this book of the evening at Addington, but Benson records the fact that his father liked Henry James's early novels, and once quoted from *Roderick Hudson* in a sermon (I, 601). Also *The Trefoil* (New York, 1924), about the life of the Benson family before 1882, when their

father became Archbishop, and *Diary of A. C. Benson*, ed. Percy Lubbock (New York, 1926), and memoirs of his youngest brother, Hugh. E. F. Benson has written *Our Family Affairs, 1867–96* (London, 1920). In all of these, there are interesting references to Henry James, none of which is especially relevant here.

5. New York, 1924, pp. 216–217.

6. See above, n. 3.

7. *Letters*, I, 146–147. See also Edmund Gosse, *Aspects and Impressions* (London, 1922), pp. 33–34; and Elizabeth Robins, *Theatre and Friendship* (London, 1924), pp. 166 ff.

assume that the visit to Addington took place in January, 1895, perhaps on the sixth, the day after James "had been exposed, apparently by a misunderstanding, to the hostility of the grosser part of the audience." [8] A date early in 1895 is confirmed by another letter from James to A. C. Benson, dated February 24, 1895, in which he says: "Remembrance for me, is, thank heaven, a great romance; and I have already the most gently-gilded image of my evening and morning at the wide fair Addington." [9]

The feeling of uncertainty, produced by A. C. Benson, as to just what his father did tell James on this January night in 1895 is increased when one turns to E. F. Benson's delightful book *As We Were: A Victorian Peep Show:* [1]

> One evening, while he was staying with us at Addington, he and my father lingered, talking together after tea, while we all drifted away to our various occupations, and though we heard no mention of the contents of that conversation at the time, there came of it an odd and interesting sequel. For, years later, Henry James wrote to my brother, on the eve of the publication of the volume containing *The Turn of the Screw*, to the effect that the story had been told him on that occasion by my father. It is among the grimmest stories of the world. . . . But the odd thing is that to all of us the story was absolutely new, and neither my mother, nor my brother nor I had the faintest recollection of any tale of my father's which resembled it. The contents of the family story-box are usually fairly well known to the members of the circle, and it seems very improbable that we should all have forgotten so arresting a tale if it was ever told us. The whole incident is difficult to unravel, but Henry James was quite definite that my father told him this story, though in outline only. . . . It is possible, of course, that my father merely gave him the barest hint for the story. . . .

Difficult to unravel, indeed, is this failure of Archbishop Benson's whole family to remember anything about the story attributed to him after his death by Henry James. Thus it has become difficult to accept at face value James's account of the genesis of the story; but, even if we do so, we are given merely "the shadow of a shadow," as James himself says: merely the *theme* of wicked ghostly servants and victimized children.

It is now time to call the reader's attention to the striking picture, herewith reproduced. Entitled "The Haunted House" and

8. *Letters*, I, 147. [See also the notebook entry of January 12, 1895, above, p. 106. When this article was written *The Notebooks of Henry James* had not been published. Editor.]

9. Henry James, *Letters to A. C. Benson and Auguste Monod*, ed. E. F. Benson (London, n. d.), p. 5.
1. London, 1930, p. 278.

drawn by T. Griffiths,[2] it depicts two children, a boy and a girl, looking in terror across a lake at a house with a tower. From one window of the house there shines a ghostly light, which is reflected in the water; the children are standing under a great tree, and the shrubbery around the lake is very thick. It is needless to point out that there are many of these scenic elements in "The Turn of the Screw," although of course in the story the children never are together on the far side of the lake. Haunted house with tower, lake, frightened little boy and girl—how attractive it would be to prove that Henry James saw this picture before he wrote "The Turn of the Screw," and that to its vivid pictorial impression he was able, perhaps subconsciously, to add whatever nucleus of anecdote had been supplied by Archbishop Benson.

Fortunately the proof is simple. The picture appears in the special Christmas number for 1891 of *Black and White*,[3] a weekly illustrated London review. It does not illustrate any story; it is simply included as an artistic effort, to please the reader of the magazine, according to a custom followed by many illustrated magazines of the period, notably this one. In the same number there appears for the first time Henry James's story "Sir Edmund Orme." [4] Thus it is impossible to imagine that James did not see this number of *Black and White* [5]—in fact, it will be proved beyond a doubt that he did—and so the probability that he also saw this picture is estab-

2. About T. Griffiths I have been able to find very little information. Listed in Ulrich Thieme and Felix Becker, *Allgemeines Lexikon der Bildenden Künstler* (Leipzig, 1922), XV, 29, as Tom Griffiths, he is said to have come from Leeds, and to have exhibited regularly in the Royal Academy showings from 1871 to 1904. The London exhibitions in which he showed pictures are listed in Algernon Graves, *Dictionary of Artists Who Have Contributed to the Principal London Exhibitions from 1760–1893* (London, 1895), p. 118; and the titles of his Academy pictures are listed in the same author's *The Royal Academy Exhibitors 1709–1904* (London, 1905), III, 325. In 1879, for example, his picture was called "*Dark and more dark the shades of evening grow*," Wordsworth. The annual programs of the Academy name his pictures, but never reproduce them. [The picture is reproduced between pages six and seven of Wolff's original article. Editor.]
3. II., 39.
4. *Ibid.*, pp. 8–15. Complete files of *Black and White* are to be found in the United States only in the Library of Congress and the Yale University Library. Volume II, with this special Christmas number presumably included,

is also in the Public Library in Seattle, Washington (*Union List of Serials in the Libraries of the United States and Canada*, ed. Winifred Gregory, New York, 1927, p. 245).

Although the editor's name is never mentioned in the pages of *Black and White* itself, he was James Nicoll Dunn, who had already been connected with the *Dundee Adventurer*, *The Scotsman*, the *National Observer*, and the *Pall Mall Gazette*, and who later edited the *Morning Post* and the *Manchester Courier* (T. H. S. Escott, *Masters of English Journalism*, London, 1911, pp. 302–303).
5. *Black and White* was published weekly in London from Feb. 6, 1891, to Jan. 13, 1913, when it was merged with the *Sphere*. Besides "Sir Edmund Orme," James also contributed, in its first year, "Brooksmith," which appeared in the number for May 2, pp. 417–422. Among other contributors during this first year were Robert Louis Stevenson ("The Bottle Imp" and "The South Seas"), Rudyard Kipling ("Brugglesmith" and "Children of the Zodiac"), Thomas Hardy ("To Please His Wife"), J. M. Barrie ("Is It a Man?"), and Bret Harte (several contributions).

lished as extremely strong. If he saw it, it almost surely served him as a source for the setting of "The Turn of the Screw."

That he forgot entirely about this picture, at least in his conscious mind, is very probable, but that his subconscious mind may very well have remembered it, is indicated by no fewer than three suggestive passages in his writings. In a letter to F. W. H. Myers, dated December 19, 1898, James says: "The *T. of the S.* is a very mechanical matter, I honestly think—an inferior, a merely *pictorial*, subject and rather a shameless pot-boiler. . . ." [6] (Italics are James's own.) In a letter to Dr. Louis Waldstein, dated October 21, 1898, he says: "That *The Turn of the Screw* has been suggestive and significant to you . . . it gives me pleasure to hear. . . . I am only afraid, perhaps, that my conscious intention strikes you as having been larger than I deserve it should be thought. It is the intention so primarily, with me, always, of the artist, of the *painter*, that *that* is what I most myself, felt in it. . . ." [7] (Again the italics are James's own.) Thus twice in letters, he stresses and underlines the notion that "The Turn of the Screw" is essentially, somehow, related to painting and pictures. Perhaps this point should not be labored too far, since, as is well known, James regarded his later style as essentially "pictorial," and frequently, in referring to his own works, uses this word or some equivalent. "The Turn of the Screw," however, is one of the earliest examples of his later style, and James's own emphasis upon painting in connection with it may be worth noting.

The third passage is to be found in his own Preface to Volume XVII (1909) of his *Collected Works*, which includes "Sir Edmund Orme": "Moved to say that of *Sir Edmund Orme* I remember absolutely nothing, I yet pull myself up ruefully to retrace the presumption that this morsel must first have appeared, with a large picture, in a weekly newspaper and, as then struck me, in the smallest of all possible print. . . ." [8] This, in point of fact, is exactly the way in which "Sir Edmund Orme" did appear in *Black and White*. This lapse of memory also enabled James to forget the other picture he had seen, at the time of the appearance of "Sir Edmund Orme," a picture, which together with Archbishop Benson's anecdote, had served as the chief source of "The Turn of the Screw." At any rate, we now know beyond all doubt that at least he had seen the number of *Black and White* in which "The Haunted House" appeared.

Professor Lowes has given, in *The Road to Xanadu*, a masterly

6. *Letters*, ed. Lubbock [p. 112].
7. *Ibid.*, [p. 110].
8. P. xxiii. Cf. Le Roy Phillips, *A Bibliography of the Works of Henry James* (New York, 1930), p. 39. Incidentally, the date and the place of the first appearance of "Sir Edmund Orme" have here been established, and the gap in Phillips's bibliography has been filled.

demonstration of the ways in which the creative imagination works. He shows over and over again how widely disparate elements of Coleridge's reading and experience separately "sank below the level of Coleridge's conscious mental processes and disappeared," [9] only later to be drawn up again, now fused by the shaping imagination into artistic unity. The chapter from which this quotation is drawn is called "The Deep Well," a title, curiously enough, taken from Henry James's description of his own creative processes. About the original suggestion of the plot for *The American*, James says: "I . . . dropped it for the time into the deep well of unconscious cerebration not without the hope, doubtless, that it might eventually emerge from that reservoir. . . ." [1]

It seems entirely probable, then, that at Christmas time, 1891, Henry James saw Tom Griffiths's picture called "The Haunted House," the memory of which disappeared into the well; that in January, 1895, he heard a fragment of a story from Archbishop Benson, the memory of which likewise disappeared into the well; and that, early in 1898, the idea of the picture and the idea of the anecdote emerged from the reservoir, fused by the shaping imagination, the anecdote having supplied the ideas for the plot, and the picture those for the setting of "The Turn of the Screw."

FRANCIS X. ROELLINGER

Psychical Research and "The Turn of the Screw" †

Readers of his letters and Prefaces will recall that Henry James ascribed the germinal idea of "The Turn of the Screw" to an anecdote told him by Edward White Benson, a fragment of a tale "dealing . . . with a couple of small children in an out-of-the-way place, to whom the spirits of certain 'bad' servants, dead in the employ of the house, were believed to have appeared with the design of 'getting hold' of them." [1] Benson's death two years before the story was written precluded the chance of confirmation, but his sons have questioned the accuracy of the ascription. "My father took a certain interest in psychical matters," wrote A. C. Benson,

---

9. *The Road to Xanadu* (Boston and New York, 1927), p. 60.
1. *Ibid.*, p. 56 and p. 480 n. 54.
† From *American Literature*, XX (January, 1949), 401–412. Reprinted by permission of the author and Duke University Press.
1. Preface to *The Novels and Tales of Henry James*, the New York Edition (New York, 1907–1917), XII, [p.

119]. All subsequent references to "The Turn of the Screw" and to its Preface are to this edition. The "distinguished host" referred to in this Preface is identified in a letter from James to A. C. Benson, March 11, 1898. See *The Letters of Henry James*, ed. Percy Lubbock (New York, 1920), [pp. 108–109].

"but we have never been able to recollect any story which could have provided a hint for so grim a tale." [2] E. F. Benson was also present during James's visit to Addington, his father's house, in January, 1895, the occasion on which the Archbishop is supposed to have related the anecdote. "But the odd thing," he remarks, "is that to all of us it ["The Turn of the Screw"] was absolutely new, and neither my mother, nor my brother nor I had the faintest recollection of any tale of my father's which resembled it." [3] A recent investigator, Robert Lee Wolff, concludes that this testimony makes it "difficult to accept at face value James's account of the genesis of the story." [4] Mr. Wolff finds a partial solution to the puzzle in a new source, a picture entitled "The Haunted House," published in the same number of an illustrated London review that contained one of James's earlier ghost stories. After adducing proof that James saw this picture, Mr. Wolff points out striking similarities between the details of the picture and of the story. He does not, however, entirely disallow James's version of the origin; he merely suggests that the picture might have been involved in the development of the story: "To its vivid pictorial impression [James] was able, perhaps subconsciously, to add whatever nucleus of anecdote had been supplied by Archbishop Benson." [5]

Since the appearance of Mr. Wolff's essay, new evidence has come to light in the recently published *Notebooks of Henry James*. An entry dated "Saturday, January 12th, 1895" supports the later testimony of the letters and Preface, and gives the most accurate account we have had thus far of the extent of James's indebtedness to Benson's anecdote:

Note here the ghost-story told me at Addington (evening of Thursday 10th), by the Archbishop of Canterbury: the mere vague, undetailed, faint sketch of it—being all he had been told (very badly and imperfectly), by a lady who had no art of relation, and no clearness: the story of the young children (indefinite number and age) left to the care of servants in an old country-house, through the death, presumably, of parents. The servants, wicked and depraved, corrupt and deprave the children; the children are bad, full of evil, to a sinister degree. The servants *die* (the story vague about the way of it) and their apparitions, figures, return to haunt the house *and* children, to whom they seem to beckon, whom they invite and solicit, from across dangerous places, the deep ditch of a sunk fence, etc.—so that the children may destroy themselves, lose themselves, by responding, by getting into their power. So long as the children are kept from them, they are not lost; but they try and try and try, these evil

2. "Henry James," *Cornhill Magazine*, n.s. XL, 512 (April, 1916).
3. *As We Were: A Victorian Peep Show* (London, 1930), p. 278.
4. "The Genesis of 'The Turn of the Screw,' " *American Literature*, XIII (March, 1941), [p. 129].
5. *Ibid.*, [p. 130].

presences, to get hold of them. It is a question of the children 'coming over to where they are.' It is all obscure and imperfect, the picture, the story, but there is a suggestion of strangely gruesome effect in it. The story to be told—tolerably obviously—by an outside spectator, observer.[6]

It is possible that in two days the active and fertile imagination of Henry James had already begun a transformation of the Archbishop's anecdote that was eventually to make the story unrecognizable to his sons, but it is unlikely that memory should have failed, in so short a time, to assign the anecdote to its proper source.

Although this note removes all doubt regarding the source of the original idea for the story, it does not invalidate Mr. Wolff's suggestion that James might have drawn details from other sources, for the note is, as James remarks, "the mere vague, undetailed, faint sketch" of a ghost story, and "The Turn of the Screw" was not written until more than two years later. One possible and very likely source of inspiration, first mentioned many years ago by the late Dorothy Scarborough, has apparently escaped serious notice. In support of her contention that the publications of the Society for Psychical Research were a fountainhead for writers of ghost stories at the turn of the century, Miss Scarborough asserted that "Henry James based his ghost story, 'The Turn of the Screw,' on an incident reported to the Psychical Society [sic], of a spectral old woman corrupting the mind of a child."[7] No authority is given for this interesting assertion, which, in the light of evidence that has appeared since Miss Scarborough wrote, now seems erroneous. If James did not "base" his story on the published reports of the Society, they might nevertheless have been a logical source of suggestions for the development of Benson's anecdote. For many reasons, the omission of an investigation of this possibility is remarkable. James's interest in psychical phenomena is well known to his readers, and is the subject of frequent mention in the recollections of his friends. Although he was not a member of the Society, founded in 1882, several friends were active in its affairs, two of them—F. W. H. Myers and Edmund Gurney—being founders. William James was a corresponding member from 1884 to 1889, vice president from 1890 to 1893, and president from 1894 to 1896. A report on the proceedings of a general meeting of the Society on October 31, 1890, states that "the paper by Professor

6. *The Notebooks of Henry James,* ed. F. O. Matthiessen and Kenneth B. Murdock (New York, 1947), [pp. 106–107].
7. *The Supernatural Element in Modern English Fiction* (New York, 1917), p. 204. Before I came upon this remark in Miss Scarborough's book, Mr. John Bronson Friend, of Shelburne, Massachusetts, had called my attention to the possibility of a relation between the reports of the Society and James's story. I am heavily indebted to Mr. Friend for provocation and for many valuable suggestions for this essay.

William James . . . on 'Observations of Certain Phenomena of Trance' was read by his brother, Henry James." [8] William James directed the American section of the "Census of Hallucinations" conducted by the Society from 1889 to 1894.[9] The findings of the Census were made known not only through its own publications, but through reprints and summaries in magazines, in texts such as William James's *Principles of Psychology*, and in such collections as Frank E. Podmore's *Studies in Psychical Research*, and Andrew Lang's *Book of Dreams and Ghosts*, all of which appeared shortly before "The Turn of the Screw" was written.[1]

That James had read and studied the reports of the Society is evident from the Preface, in which he refers frequently to the "new" ghost, "the mere modern 'psychical' case," and to the "today so copious psychical record of cases of apparitions." [2] He leaves no doubt of his familiarity with the typical patterns of the reports:

> Different signs and circumstances . . . mark these cases; different things are done—though on the whole very little appears to be—by the persons appearing; the point is, however, that some things are never done at all: this negative quantity is large—certain reserves and properties and immobilities consistently impose themselves. Recorded and attested "ghosts" are in other words as little expressive, as little dramatic, above all as little continuous and conscious and responsive, as is consistent with their taking the trouble—and immense trouble they find it, we gather—to appear at all.[3]

If James emphasizes the artistic limitations of the "recorded and attested" ghosts, it is chiefly to make clear to the reader his reasons for ignoring these limitations in the construction of his own phantoms. "I had to decide," he says, "between having my apparitions correct and having my story 'good.' " [4] The Preface was written many years after the story was first published, and James might well have been replying to a criticism that he had failed to adhere to scientific accounts of the nature of apparitions and hallucinations. With his characteristic air of deprecation he stresses the point that he had no intention of making his apparitions "correct," and dwells

8. "Proceedings of the General Meeting," *Proceedings of the Society for Psychical Research*, VI, 660 (1889–1890). This publication is hereinafter referred to as P.S.P.R.
9. The "Census" was conducted by collecting answers to a widely distributed questionnaire. There were 410 collectors (members of the Society and their friends), 17,000 informants, most of whom were "educated persons." Further assistance in the inquiry was obtained "by a special appeal to psychologists made by Professor Sidgwick in *Mind,* and through articles by him and other members of the Committee published in various more popular periodicals (*Nineteentth Century, New Review, Murray's Magazine, Review of Reviews*)." See "Report on the Census of Hallucinations," P.S.P.R., X, 25–422 (1894).
1. According to the letter to A. C. Benson cited above, the story was written in the fall of 1897.
2. Preface, [pp. 119, 122].
3. *Ibid.,* [p. 122].
4. *Ibid.,* [p. 122].

upon the differences rather than the similarities between his ghosts and those of the reports. This disclaimer would have been unnecessary, had he used the familiar ghost of popular fiction. For James and his contemporary readers, steeped in the lore of psychical research, the significant point about his ghosts was that they were departures from the usually inartistic and meaningless apparitions of scientific investigation. For readers today who approach the story with preconceptions still largely derived from the familiar phantoms of Gothic fiction, it is important to realize that the ghosts of "The Turn of the Screw" are conceived to a surprising extent in terms of the cases reported to the Society. From the point of view of this emphasis the story becomes an interesting *tour de force*, an attempt to re-create what James refers to as "a beautiful lost form," and to rouse, as he puts it, "the dear old sacred horror" without departing any more than artistically necessary from the then current knowledge of psychical phenomena.

The contrast between the "old" and the "new" ghost is cited in the reports:

> In the magazine ghost stories . . . the ghost is a fearsome being, dressed in a sweeping sheet and shroud, carrying a lighted candle, and speaking in dreadful words from fleshless lips. It enters at the stroke of midnight, through the sliding panel, just by the bloodstain on the floor. . . . Or it may be only a clanking of chains, a tread as of armed men heard whilst the candles burn blue and the dogs howl.[5]

In the majority of cases reported to the Society, the ghost does not appear at any known fixed time of day or year. It is usually seen distinctly "in all kinds of light, from broad daylight to the faint light of dawn." It is described in detail, and appears "in such clothes as are now, or have recently been, worn by living persons." It is seen "on looking round, as a human being might be," or it seems "to come in at the door." It rarely makes noises: "to hear its footsteps, for instance, seems to be unusual." Sudden death, "often either murder or suicide, appears to be connected with the cause of the apparition" in many cases. Percipients are not limited by sex, age, or profession. If several persons are together when the ghost appears, "it will sometimes be seen by all and sometimes not, and failure to see it is not always merely the result of not directing attention to it." [6]

The ghosts of "The Turn of the Screw" conform precisely to the second of these generic types. They do not appear at any fixed time of day or year. They are so distinctly seen that the governess

5. "Report of the Committee on Haunted Houses," *P.S.P.R.*, II, 139 (1884).

6. *P.S.P.R.*, II, 139 (1884); III, 144, 145 (1885).

is able to give a detailed description of both to the housekeeper, who recognizes them at once. Six of the eight apparitions occur in daylight. Quint appears in the cast-off clothes of his master, and Miss Jessel in a black dress. The governess usually comes upon them suddenly and unexpectedly, on coming into view of the house, on entering a room or turning down a stair. They are silent, they never speak, they only look. The cause of death is not definitely stated in either case, but circumstances lend themselves to the interpretation that Quint was murdered and that Miss Jessel committed suicide. A remarkable feature of the story, stressed in the prologue, is that the percipients are children; although rare in fiction, it is common in the reports, ten such cases appearing in the first three volumes. On one occasion the governess directs the attention of Mrs. Grose to the apparition of Miss Jessel, but the housekeeper is unable to see it. In short, James eschews the incredible ghosts of sensational fiction for the more plausible and so-called "veridical" apparitions of the reports. He even employs, to good effect and despite his strenuous disclaimer, the mysterious absence of any apparent object or intelligent mystery until the governess begins to develop her theory that they have come "to get hold" of the children. But neither the governess nor the reader is ever positive of the correctness of this theory. "To knead the subject of my young friend's . . . mystification thick" is one of the chief artistic problems cited by James in the Preface. He protests that the motive of the ghosts is not specified, that his values "are positively all blanks," and that his strategy is to make the reader "think" the evil for himself.[7] At the end of the story, the governess's explanation is still only her theory, but the reader is hard pressed for a better one.[8]

7. Preface, [pp. 121–124].
8. Edmund Wilson has suggested what he considers to be a better one. In an essay entitled "The Ambiguity of Henry James," Mr. Wilson develops the theory, first suggested by Edna Kenton, that "the young governess who tells the story is a neurotic case of sex-repression, and the ghosts are not ghosts at all, but merely the hallucinations of the governess" (*Hound & Horn*, VII, 385, April–May, 1934). An extended version of this essay appears in *The Triple Thinkers* (New York, 1938), pp. 122–164. More recently, Mr. Wilson has retracted somewhat: "There are, however, points in the story which are difficult to explain on this theory, and it is probable that James . . . was unconscious of having raised something more frightening than the ghosts he had contemplated." See "Books," *New Yorker*, XX, 69 (May 27, 1944). The passage from the notebooks quoted above makes it clear that James intended the ghosts to be more frightening than the governess. For able refutations of the Freudian theory, see A. J. A. Waldock, "Mr. Edmund Wilson and 'The Turn of the Screw,'" *Modern Language Notes*, LXII, 331–334 (May, 1947), and R. B. Heilman, "The Freudian Reading of '*The Turn of the Screw*,'" *Modern Language Notes*, LXII, 433–445 (Nov., 1947.) Professor Heilman presents unanswerable internal and external evidence to show that "the Freudian reading of Henry James's *The Turn of the Screw* does violence not only to the story but also to the Preface." His conclusion is that "a great deal of unnecessary mystery has been made of the apparent ambiguity of the story. Actually, most of it is a by-product of James's method: his indirection; his refusal, in his fear of anticlimax to define the evil; his rigid adherence to point of view for a reassuring comment on those uncomfortable characters, the apparitions" (*loc. cit.*, pp. 433, 441).

But not all of the reports are of pointless apparitions. At least one, which would seem to be the case cited by Miss Scarborough, contains a possible suggestion for the governess's theory. It concerns a "haunted house" in London, and it begins with the testimony of a woman interviewed by Edmund Gurney and described by him as a "sensible and clear-headed person." She relates her experiences in the house as "a little girl, with a sister and brother younger than myself." "I remember well," she writes, "an old lady who proved the greatest trouble we children had, first because she was a mystery, and secondly because she got us into trouble with our father." The old lady appeared one day while the witness and her brother were playing a favorite game. Chairs were arranged to represent a carriage in which they sat, covering their heads with a tablecloth for a roof:

> One of us took to riding outside our carriage on purpose to watch the strange old lady. For she always *looked* a great deal—or seemed to our youthful eyes to do so—and we all thought she would do something horrid to us the first time she caught us under the table-cloth. We even kept a large ruler close to us on purpose to throw at her if she touched us.

Whenever they asked the servants about the old lady they received evasive replies. Finally they "talked about her to each other, but did not mention her in public." [9]

Several aspects of this case parallel the story: the account by a "sensible and clear-headed person," one who, as James says in the Preface, has "authority"; the appearance of the ghost to children, not of "indefinite number" as in Benson's anecdote, but specifically to a boy and a girl; their secrecy about the ghost in the presence of adults; their impression that the ghost always "looked" a great deal, which is precisely what the ghosts of the story do so terribly; and most striking of all, their idea that she might "do something horrid" to them if she "touched" them, an idea not inconsistent with the apparitions of Quint and Miss Jessel.

There are pertinent resemblances of detail in another case, which begins with an account written by a governess employed in a house in Ireland. In the notes on the evidence, Mrs. Henry Sidgwick remarks that this governess "kept a diary for many years," in which she carefully recorded the strange events described in her report:

> On the 18th of April, 1867, about 7.40 P. M., I was going to my room, which I at that time shared with one of my pupils, when just as I reached the top of the stairs I plainly saw the figure of a female dressed in black, with a large white collar or kerchief, very dark hair, and pale face. . . . She moved slowly and went into the room, the door of which was open. I thought it was Marie, the French maid . . . but the next moment I saw that the

9. Mrs. Henry Sidgwick, "Notes on the Evidence, Collected by the Society, for Phantasms of the Dead," P.S.P.R., III, 126, 127 (1885).

figure was too tall and walked better. I then fancied it was some visitor who had arrived unexpectedly . . . and had gone into the wrong bedroom.

Late one evening in September the governess was "siting in the schoolroom" when the same figure appeared and "seemed to go up one step of the stairs." On this occasion the witness felt rather nervous "from thinking it was someone who had no business in the house, or that someone was playing me a trick." Two daughters of the house, under the governess's care at the time, testified that they also saw the ghost, one "while sitting in the schoolroom rather late," the other when, returning from a walk one day at noon, she went to the window and "looked through the glass and saw a lady standing at the bottom of the stairs." [1]

This case presents several important details that appear in the story, particulars not given in Benson's anecdote. The woman in the anecdote is vaguely described as having had the story from someone else: no governess is mentioned. James concludes his note by saying that his own story should be told "by an outside spectator, observer." The governess who writes her own account of her experiences is a change from, or addition to, the original idea, a change or addition parallel with this case. Other parallels are the pale-faced woman in black; the appearance of this woman to the children; and certain details of scene, such as the schoolroom, the stairs, the peering through a window. Miss Jessel is described as "a woman in black, pale and dreadful." She too appears in a schoolroom and at the foot of a stairs. Quint is also seen on the stairs and appears twice at windows. On one occasion the governess peers through a window, frightening the housekeeper who just happens to be entering the room. Especially striking is the percipient's impression that the apparition is an actual person, the maid or an unexpected visitor, just as James's governess, coming upon Miss Jessel in the schoolroom, sees a figure that "I should have taken at the first blush for some housemaid"; and on the first appearance of Quint, wonders whether "some unscrupulous traveler . . . had made his way in unobserved"; and considers the possibility of "there having been in the house . . . a person of whom I was in ignorance"; and does not feel sure until three days later that she "had not been practiced upon by the servants nor made the object of any 'game.'" [2]

A third case involving a similar figure of a woman "tall, dark, and pale, dressed in black," also seen so distinctly that the witness "did not suppose but that she was some stranger got into the place," presents an incident that recalls the situations of two of the most vivid scenes in the story. The percipient is again a woman in charge of a child "of about five or six":

1. *Ibid.*, pp. 119, 120, 121, 122.   2. "The Turn of the Screw," [pp. 59, 16, 17, 18].

She was amusing herself with some toys, and I was reading,
when she stopped and looked intently at the partition just above
the cupboard. It was painted a plain color; there was no picture,
or light or shadow where she was looking. I asked the child what
she was looking at. "At the face," she replied. "Never mind,"
I said, "go on with your play," and so she did, but very soon
stopped again. She came up to me, and looking at the same
place, she said, "Oh, the face." "Someone looking out of window
[*sic*]," I said inconsequently, as the window was behind us. "Oh
no," she said, "it wants you, Miss Alice, it wants you." I saw
nothing, but picked up the child, and took refuge in the nursery.[3]

The incident is reminiscent of the scene in which the governess is
seated on a bench near a small lake, occupied with a piece of work
while Flora plays on the shore. The governess hears the child stop
in her play, and without raising her head, senses that they are
being watched by a third person. When she looks up, the child
has turned her back to the apparition on the far side of the lake
and has begun to play with a piece of wood to give the impression,
so the governess surmises, that she is not aware of the ghost. In
another scene the governess is quizzing Miles when suddenly the
face of Quint leers through a window behind him. She shrieks in
horror and grasps the boy in her arms. Terrified, he looks about
the room, trying to see what she sees, and then falls lifeless in her
grasp, apparently frightened to death. In both report and story
there is the idea that the ghost is "after" someone, although the
report reverses the situations in the story, the child thinking that
"the face" has come for the governess.

Such are the reports that present the most remarkable parallels
with "The Turn of the Screw." A few minor but interesting details
from other cases are worthy of mention. The identification of the
ghost in one of these conforms to the way in which the ghosts are
identified by the governess, who describes both in such vivid detail
that the housekeeper immediately recognizes them. In the report
in question there is a similar recognition scene in which the percipient, also without previous knowledge of the dead person or the
ghost, describes the apparition to a servant who exclaims, "That
was her, miss!"[4] In another unusual case, the witness testifies to
having experienced "an icy wind and a feeling of being 'watched,'"
two details that recall the incident of "an extraordinary blast and
chill, a gust of frozen air," and the governess's awareness, "without
direct vision," of Miss Jessel across the lake.[5]

The *Proceedings* also contains theoretical discussions of the nature of apparitions that would have interested Henry James. Ed-

3. Sidgwick, *op. cit.*, p. 124.
4. Edmund Gurney and F. W. H.
Myers, "On Apparitions Occurring
Soon After Death," P.S.P.R., V, 446
(1889).
5. Cf. Sidgwick, op. cit., p. 115, and

[pp. 65] and [29] of "The Turn of
the Screw" in the edition cited. Andrew
Lang cites this case in *The Book of
Dreams and Ghosts* (London, 1897),
p. 196.

mund Gurney tried to account for the ghost by postulating "the survival of a mere image, impressed, we cannot guess how, on we cannot guess what, by that person's physical organism, and perceptible at times to those endowed with some cognate form of sensitiveness." [6] The notion of a "cognate form of sensitiveness" would have appealed to James, for the phrase is an apt description of a quality with which he endows his characters. The mysterious effects upon each other of the *personae* of *The Sacred Fount*, for example, appear to be based on just such an assumption of cognate forms of sensitiveness and insensitiveness. One might say of the governess that her fine affection for the children and keen awareness of their helpless plasticity endow her with a sensitiveness that enables her to perceive the terrible evil that threatens them. The governess and the ghosts might be said to have cognate forms of sensitiveness because they have in common unique though opposed interests in the children. Not to endow the housekeeper, who fails to see the ghosts, is characteristic of James. According to Myers, an apparition might be "a manifestation of persistent personal energy,—or an indication that some kind of force is being exercised after death which is in some way connected with a person previously known on earth." [7] This theory also fits the story perfectly, the ghosts being nothing if not a manifestation of such "persistent personal energy" or "force" connected in an evil way with their relation to the children before death.

Although prototypes of Miss Jessel are abundant in the reports, no psychical Quint appears, but his absence is somewhat compensated for by the unexpected emergence of a real one. A correspondent quoted by Myers in one of his articles on "Phantasms of the Dead" signs his testimony with the name of "Wilson Quint." [8] If James found the appropriate name for his spectral valet in the signature of this innocent correspondent—and we know that he took extraordinary pains over the selection and invention of appropriate names for his characters, searching the columns of the *Times*, weighing the suggestiveness of their sounds, considering their juxtaposition on the page—how he must have rejoiced at the discovery of this monosyllable which, taken with "Peter," makes his evil valet one of the most unforgettably named of James's characters. [9]

Although these striking parallels do not prove conclusively that James drew upon the reports, they do show that he constructed his apparitions much more in terms of the "mere modern 'psychical' case" than perhaps he himself realized or was willing to admit.

6. Quoted by F. W. H. Myers, "On Recognized Apparitions Occurring More Than a Year after Death," P.S.P.R., VI, 15 (1889).
7. *Ibid.*, p. 15.
8. *"On Indications of Continued Terrene Knowledge on the Part of Phantasms of the Dead,"* P.S.P.R., VIII, 206 (1892).
9. For James's interest in names, see the list of names entered at frequent intervals in the notebooks, his letter to a correspondent who protested his use of a family name, and the comment by the editors in *The Notebooks of Henry James*, pp. 8, 63.

Ideas regarding psychical phenomena were much in the air throughout the eighties and nineties; it was no accident that among Archbishop Benson's guests on that January night "the talk turned . . .
to apparitions and night-fears." The reports are not mentioned in
the notebooks, but the remarks in the Preface are ample evidence
that James had taken careful note of them. One wonders how
Benson's case escaped the Census of Hallucinations: it would not
have been surprising to find it there, for the name of "Mrs. Benson,
Lambeth Palace," appears on the lists of associates and members
of the Society from 1883 to 1896.

Shortly after the publication of "The Turn of the Screw," F. W.
H. Myers wrote to James, apparently asking him several questions
about the story, and James belatedly replied:

> I scarce know what to say to you on the subject on which you
> wrote, especially as I'm afraid I don't quite *understand* the prin-
> cipal question you put to me about "The Turn of the Screw."
> However, that scantily matters; for in truth I am afraid I have
> on some former occasions rather awkwardly signified to you that
> I somehow can't pretend to give any coherent account of my
> small inventions "after the fact." [1]

The reply is obviously evasive, for the entry in the notebooks and
the discussion in the Preface are very coherent accounts of this
particular invention, both before and after the fact. It would be
interesting to know what "principal question" this authority on
psychical research addressed to the creator of the ghosts of "The
Turn of the Screw."

MIRIAM ALLOTT

Mrs. Gaskell's "The Old Nurse's Story": A Link Between "Wuthering Heights" and "The Turn of the Screw" †

In 1850 Mrs. Gaskell received from Charlotte Brontë a copy of
Wuthering Heights (see Charlotte Brontë's letter to Mr. Williams,
1 January, 1851). Two years later her supernatural tale, "The Old
Nurse's Story," appeared in the 1852 Christmas number of Dickens's periodical, *Household Words*, as a contribution to the chain
story, "A Round of Stories by the Christmas Fire". Mrs. Gaskell
was a born story-teller, never more obviously so than when she let

1. *Letters,* [p. 112].
† From *Notes and Queries,* VIII, new
series (March, 1961), 101–102. Reprinted by permission of Oxford University Press.

herself go in creating a Gothic atmosphere of thrills and chills. It seems fairly certain that in this case she took a hint from *Wuthering Heights*, which she refers to in connexion with Charlotte's "wild tales of the ungovernable families" near Haworth —"*Wuthering Heights* even seemed tame comparatively", she remarks.[1]

It seems equally certain that Mrs. Gaskell's story in turn "inoculated" Henry James.[2] His own story of possession, *The Turn of the Screw*, has important elements in common with it.[3]

The story related by the "old nurse", Hester, tells how as a young girl in charge of the little orphan Rosamund, she comes to live in an old house in the Cumberland Fells and is gradually made aware of supernatural presences haunting the place and threatening the child, to whom she is deeply attached. From an old organ, "broken and destroyed" but played upon by the phantom hands of "the old lord" (the former head of the house), music "rose above the great gusts of wind, and wailed and triumphed just like a living creature". Another phantom, a female child with a "dark wound on its right shoulder", appears to Rosamund on a cold moonlit night, beckons to her through the window and draws her up on to the Fells, where a lady "weeping and crying" but "proud and grand" lulls her to rest in her arms. Rosamund is afterwards found half frozen under a holly tree, with only her own footmarks visible in the snow. Later Hester herself sees the ghostly child, thinly clad in the bitter dusk and "crying and beating against the window-panes, as if she wanted to be let in", though no sound is made by her "little battering hands". Rosamund struggles frantically in Hester's restraining grasp and thereafter, even at her prayers (the idea of exorcism is implied), keeps saying, "I hear my little girl plaining and crying very sad—Oh! let her in, or she will die". The climax comes on a night of violent moaning wind. Rosamund hears the phantom child crying still more loudly. In a surge of violence, doors break open and all three phantoms appear. During a moment of nightmare vision the inhabitants of the house see these figures re-enact their old drama of passion, jealousy and revenge. Throughout Hester holds on to Rosamund, fighting an exhausting final battle for her salvation. Unlike Miles in *The Turn of the Screw*, Rosamund survives the moment of dispossession.

The most immediately noticeable resemblance to *Wuthering Heights* lies in the figure of the phantom child, exiled, wounded,

1. See Elizabeth Haldane, *Mrs. Gaskell and her Friends* (1930), pp. 143–4.
2. For James's opinion of Mrs. Gaskell see his review of *Wives and Daughters*, reprinted in *Notes and Reviews* (1921), and *William Wetmore Story and His Friends* (1903), I, 352 ff.

3. The central idea for the story, as is well known, came from the then Archbishop of Canterbury (see *The Notebooks of Henry James*, [p. 106], but James's working out of the idea recalls "The Old Nurse's Story".

and crying to be "let in". In *Wuthering Heights*, Chapter III, Lockwood, lying in the first Catherine's oak-panelled bed, falls into a fitful sleep disturbed by a fir-branch tapping the window "as the blast wailed by". In his dream he smashes the glass to reach the branch, his fingers close on the fingers of "a little ice-cold hand", he hears the dead Catherine's voice sobbing "let me in—let me in . . ." and sees "obscurely, a child's face looking through the window". In terror, he pulls the child's wrist on to the broken pane and rubs it to and fro till the blood runs down. Still the child wails, "let me in!"

From this recurring group of elements in *Wuthering Heights*[4] —fir-tree and tapping branch, ice-cold wind, sensations of pain, feelings of exile, savagery and awe—Mrs. Gaskell's imagination makes its own selection. The branch tapping in the wind is recalled by her description of the trees round the house, "so close that in some places their branches dragged against the walls when the wind blew". Pain and savagery are associated with the "dark mark" on her phantom child's shoulder, which is caused by a blow from the crutch of "the old lord" (the child's grandfather). The prevailing atmosphere of the novel is recreated in the wildness of the setting, the wailing of the wind and the emphasis on the cycle of the seasons—in this case from autumn deep into winter—and on storm and snow. Above all there is the powerful and violent atmosphere of the supernatural. Lastly, the story enacted by the three phantoms reflects the "ungovernable" passions found in *Wuthering Heights*.

There is a striking similarity between the governess's struggle for Miles in *The Turn of the Screw* and Hester's for Rosamund's in "The Old Nurse's Story". In the final chapter of *The Turn of the Screw*, with Peter Quint's "white face of damnation" at the window, the governess grasps the boy and holds on to him to the end. "It was like fighting with a demon for a human soul", she says. In "The Old Nurse's Story", Hester holds on to Rosamund as the phantoms appear. Rosamund calls Hester "wicked" for detaining her, as Miles calls his governess "you devil" for her power over him and Quint. Hester goes on,

> I held her tight with all my strength; with a set will I held her. If I had died, my hands would have grasped her still . . . my darling, who had got down to the ground, and whom I, upon my knees now, was holding with both arms clasped round her neck . . .

Meanwhile the child cries, ". . . they are drawing me . . . I feel them—I feel them. I must go!" Eventually she finds release, not in death but in a swoon. The thwarted phantoms retreat.

4. See my article, *"Wuthering Heights:*   in *Criticism,* viii (1958), 27–47.
The Rejection of Heathcliff?", *Essays*

There are other similarities in the prowling of the phantoms outside the house in the moonlight, and in the fact that one of them is a ravaged female figure, a "lady", passionate in life and now doomed and wretched. Finally, *The Turn of the Screw*, like Mrs. Gaskell's story, is supposed to be a Christmas entertainment. Its introduction also recalls that in supernatural stories of this "festive" kind, the appearance of a ghost to a child "gives the effect of another turn of the screw". Captivated by this effect James goes further: two children give "two turns", he says, and unfolds the tale of Miles and Flora.

OSCAR CARGILL

The Turn of the Screw and Alice James †

I

The tenderest of men, Henry James could hardly have used the illness of his sister Alice as the basis of a story while she lived, or later, without elaborately disguising it—particularly since that illness, though not concealed, was only guardedly revealed as mental.[1] But the heroism of Alice, fully as much as his experience and special knowledge of hysteria, must have strongly tempted him to exploit the extraordinary dramatic possibilities of her disease long

† [From *PMLA*, LXXVIII (June, 1963), 238–249. Printed by permission of the author and the Modern Langauge Association.]
Invited in 1956 to contribute to that outstanding undergraduate quarterly, *The Chicago Review*, and having the previous winter noted the parallels between *The Turn of the Screw* and "The Case of Miss Lucy R.," I wrote the sketch "Henry James as Freudian Pioneer," *C.R.*, X (Summer 1956), 13–29. When Gerald Willen asked my permission to reprint this sketch in his *A Casebook on Henry James's "The Turn of the Screw"* (New York, 1960), pp. 223–238, I wished greatly to revise the sketch but I yielded my wishes when he indicated this would hold up his publication. I had previously recognized that I must repudiate the sketch (which I now do) and provide a more adequate statement. These points are not made in *C.R.*: that (1) W. J. knew the Freud-Breuer book the year after its publication and was sufficiently impressed to talk about it; (2) the Prologue is essential to the story—the climax, in fact, and the governess has been altered from villainess to heroine; (3) the special significance of the narrators Griffin and Douglas, with Douglas as lover; (4) analysis of the governess' "trauma," an explanation of why Miles was actually dismissed from school, and new causes for the governess' state; (5) the important Saul-David allusion; (6) the reader's alternatives in interpretation suggested by the setting of *Jane Eyre* against *The Mysteries of Udolpho;* (7) Fielding's *Amelia* introduced as an illuminating source; (8) the suggestion that the story might have been written for Clement Shorter; and (9) there are more extensive parallels between the *Journal of Alice James* and *The Turn of the Screw*. Earlier forms of this essay were presented at the first Fales lecture, New York Univ., and at colloquia at Brown and Duke Universities.

1. F. O. Matthiessen, "Alice," *The James Family* (New York, 1948), pp. 272–285.

before he composed *The Turn of the Screw*.[2] Delicacy, propriety, affection instantly inhibited the development of so rich a "germ," but it remained planted in James's ingenious and subtle mind until he could bring the derivative narrative forth so altered that his closest intimates would not suspect its source or connections. The product is one of the greatest horror stories of all time.[3]

Until Edmund Wilson designated *The Turn of the Screw* a study in psychopathology,[4] only three persons had the temerity to guess that it was something more than a ghost story—a view which still has the preponderance of support today.[5] The three attracted no attention, but Wilson stirred up an indignant and vociferous opposition which literally "threw the book at him"—the book, however, being James's own comments on his story which could be read as leading away from Wilson's interpretation. It apparently did not occur to any of Wilson's critics that James might have an adequate motive for disguising his purpose in the tale; neither they nor Wilson referred to Alice James, though her tragic story provides an explanation for the "ambiguity" of both the commentary and the tale itself. James's "strategy" consisted in overlaying his real story with another which might, with plausibility, be construed as a ghost story. The limitations of that "strategy" are, however, that it temporarily confounds the acute and perceptive and, like life, rewards the obtuse and conventional. Thanks to it, *The Turn of the Screw* continues to be misread as "a pure ghost story."[6]

For a proper reading some of the difficulties that James himself interposed must be skirted or eliminated. The chief of these seems to be James's indication that the primary source of his inspiration was the fragment of a ghost story given him by a friend. A circle of intimates, one winter afternoon, round the hall fire of an old country house, lamenting the disappearance of the old-fashioned

2. I do not challenge the accepted view of the time of composition of *The Turn of the Screw* as after 12 Jan. 1895 (see note [1, p. 148]), but the *idea* for the story may have been in gestation a long time. The richness and variety of sources suggest this. James made his first *major* study of a neurotic in 1886 in *The Bostonians*.

3. "For sheer measureless evil and horror there are very few tales in world literature that can compare with *The Turn of the Screw*." *The Great Short Novels,* ed. Phillip Rahv (New York, 1944), p. 623.

4. "The Ambiguity of Henry James," *Hound & Horn,* VII (Apr.–May 1934), 385–406.

5. See Bibliography, "Henry James Number," *Modern Fiction Studies,* III (Spring 1957), 94. Omit Cargill, Edel, Kenton, Wilson.

6. Leon Edel, who reprinted *The Turn* of the Screw in *The Ghostly Tales of Henry James* (New Brunswick, N. J., 1948), pp. 425–550, finds no anomaly in approaching the story as "a ghostly tale, pure and simple," examining the governess "as a deeply fascinating psychological case," and finding the tale "a projection of H. J.'s own haunted state." In "Hugh Walpole and Henry James: The Fantasy of the 'Killer and the Slain'," *American Imago,* VIII (Dec. 1951), 3–21, however, he supplies an extreme Freudian reading to the relation of the governess and Miles, but in his introduction to Harold C. Goddard's "A Pre-Freudian Reading of *The Turn of the Screw*," *Nineteenth-Century .Fiction,* XII (June 1957), [pp. 181–209], he is more positive that "James wrote a ghost story . . . [but] offered sufficient data to permit the diagnosis that she [the governess] is mentally disturbed."

ghost story, were comforted by their host with "one of the scantest fragments of this form at its best," got from a lady when he was young:

> The story would have been thrilling could she have found herself in better possession of it, dealing as it did with a couple of small children in an out-of-the-way place, to whom the spirits of certain bad servants, dead in the employ of the house, were believed to have appeared with the design of "getting hold" of them. This was all, but there had been more, which my old friend's converser had lost the thread of: she could only assure him of the wonder of the allegations as she had anciently heard them made.[7]

When James's letters were published in 1920, the novelist's recollection of this "germ" for his tale was apparently supported by a letter to Arthur Christopher Benson, dated 11 March 1898, after the story had begun to appear in *Collier's Weekly*,[8] in which the host is stated to have been the latter's distinguished father, the Archbishop, and the time and place "one of those two memorable—never to be obliterated—winter nights that I spent at the sweet Addington . . . in the drawing room by the fire." The "essence" of the anecdote struck James and he went home and made a note of it "of the most scrappy kind." [9] With the publication of James's *Notebooks* (1947) his "scrappy" memorandum came to light:

> *Saturday, January 12th, 1895.* Note here the ghost-story told me at Addington (evening of Thursday 10th), by the Archbishop of Canterbury: the mere vague, undetailed faint sketch of it—being all that he had been told (very badly and imperfectly), by a lady who had no art of relation, and no clearness: the story of the young children (indefinite number and age) left to the care of the servants in an old country house, through the death, presumably, of the parents. The servants, wicked and depraved, corrupt and deprave the children; the children are bad, full of evil, to a sinister degree. The servants *die* (the story vague about the way of it) and their apparitions, figures, return to haunt the house *and* children, to whom they seem to beckon, whom they invite and solicit, from across dangerous places, the deep ditch of a sunk fence, etc.—so that the children may destroy themselves, by responding, by getting into their power. So long as the children are kept from them, they are not lost; but they try and try and try, these evil presences, to get hold of them. It is a question

7. *The Art of the Novel: Critical Prefaces by Henry James*, ed. Richard P. Blackmur (New York, 1934), pp. 169–170. [From the New York Preface. Editor.]

8. XX (27 Jan.–2 Apr. 1898); XXI (9–16 Apr.). Leon Edel and Dan H. Laurence, *A Bibliography of Henry James* (London, 1957), p. 331, D494.

9. *The Letters of Henry James* (2 vols., New York, 1920), [pp. 108–109].

of the children "coming over to where they are." It is all obscure and imperfect, the picture, the story, but there is a suggestion of a strangely gruesome effect in it. The story to be told—tolerably obviously—by an outside spectator, observer.[1]

Yet this double verification of the source of his tale is undermined as absolute by the complete double failure of A. C. Benson and his brother to recall that their father ever told such a story. In fact, they are unusually emphatic in their separate denials that the tale was in their father's repertoire.[2] This contradiction is extraordinary, but it is still more extraordinary that James tries immediately, in fact almost insistently, to establish his indebtedness to the Archbishop, for it was not his habit thus to acknowledge his sources. May he not have had a special reason for it in this instance?

Leaving this question unanswered for the moment and temporarily admitting that the Archbishop's narrative may have been in some degree a source, let us concentrate our attention on the most important element that the anecdote leaves out—the narrator of the tale. James's memorandum merely indicates that he once felt that the narrator should be "an outside spectator," an objective observer. This objective narrator he has supplied in the "I"-reporter of the Prologue to the tale, but in addition the Prologue contains *three* other narrators—an extraordinary circumstance, surely, in the work of a writer famous for economy of means. The first of this triumvirate of story tellers is a man named Griffin who has finished his yarn just before the Prologue opens. It was a tale of "an appearance, of a dreadful kind, to a little boy sleeping in a room with his mother and waking her not to dissipate his dread and soothe him to sleep again, but to encounter also, herself, before she had succeeded in doing so, the same sight that had shaken him."[3] A griffin, of course, is a fanciful beast, and we have every reason to believe that Griffin has told a supernatural story with a genuine apparition in it, an apparition which frightens a child and its parent. Only one of Griffin's auditors challenges this interpretation; this is Douglas, the second narrator, who is to produce the written narrative of the governess and the two terrified children. Douglas is obviously named after that noble Scot in Henry IV, Part I, famous for his candor, so faithful in a bad cause, unmasking two

1. *The Notebooks,* [pp. 106–107].
2. "My father took a certain interest in psychical matters, but we have never been able to recollect any story that he ever told which could have provided a hint for so grim a story." A. C. Benson, *Memories and Friends* (New York, 1924), pp. 216–217. "But the odd thing is that to all of us the story was absolutely new, and neither my mother, nor my brother, nor I had the faintest recollection of any tale of my father's which resembled it." E. F. Benson, *As We Were: A Victorian Peep Show* (London, 1930), p. 278. See also Robert Lee Wolff, "The Genesis of 'The Turn of the Screw'," *American Literature,* XIII (March 1941), [p. 129].
3. "The Turn of the Screw," *The Two Magics* (New York, 1898), pp. 3–4. All subsequent references in my essay are to this text.

pretenders before he discovers the King, that after his capture he is set free by Prince Hal.[4] Foil to Griffin, Douglas demurs, "I quite agree—in regard to Griffin's ghost, *or whatever it was*—that its appearing first to the little boy . . . adds a particular touch" (p. 4, my italics). That phrase, *"or whatever it was,"* betrays Douglas' skepticism in regard to supernatural appearances and all but pledges —does it not?—that the tale which he produces, while it will "for sheer terror" surpass everything, will *not* deal with apparitions. Douglas is not a true narrator, but the reader of, and minor commentator on, a long autobiographical document entrusted to him some twenty years ago by his younger sister's governess, who is the last and chief narrator of *The Turn of the Screw*. Douglas vouches with such fervor for the good character of the governess that his friends properly suspect him of having been deeply in love with her. A suggestion that she may have reciprocated his emotion lies in the fact that, in the face of death, she turned over to him her personal account of a harrowing experience (pp. 6–9) which led to the death of one of her charges, for which in some degree she may have been held responsible. May not the relation of these two, of Douglas and the governess, somewhat neglected by the critics, be important for a full understanding of *The Turn of the Screw?*

The fact that they have lacked Douglas' faith in the governess and have been struck by her facility for involvement (she falls in love with her handsome employer on sight [p. 14]) has led a few critics to inquire into her role and into the meaning of her narrative. The first to do this was the anonymous reviewer in the *Critic*, who, shortly after the story appeared in book form, observed, "the heroine . . . has nothing in the least substantial upon which to base her deep and startling cognitions. She perceives what is beyond perception, and the reader who begins by questioning whether she is supposed to be sane ends by accepting her conclusions and thrill-

---

4. *The Living Shakespeare,* ed. Oscar Campbell (New York, 1949), pp. 396, 404, 405, 406–407, 409, especially IV. i.1–5:

> *Hot :* Well said, my noble Scot: if speaking truth
> In this fine age were not thought flattery,
> Such attribution should the Douglas have,
> As not a soldier of this season's stamp
> Should go so general current through the world.

The thought of using Douglas as foil to Griffin probably occurred to James as he dictated the story to his unemotional amanuensis McAlpine: ". . . this iron Scot betrayed not the slightest shade of feeling. I dictated to him sentences that I thought would make him leap from his chair; he shorthanded them as though they had been geometry; and whenever I paused to see him collapse, he would inquire in a dry voice: 'What next?' " William Lyon Phelps, *The Advance of the English Novel* (New York, 1916) pp. 324–325. Edel, *The Ghostly Tales,* p. 426, says that McAlpine could not manage shorthand; curiously Phelps, in repeating the anecdote told him on 23 May 1911, when H. J. visited New Haven, corrects this detail in *Autobiography With Letters* (New York, 1939), p. 551.

ing over the horrors they involve." [5] In 1919 Professor Henry A. Beers casually observed in an essay on Hawthorne: "Recall the ghosts in Henry James's *The Turn of the Screw*—just a suspicion of evil presences. The true interpretation of that story I have sometimes thought to be, that the woman who saw the phantoms was mad." [6]

Five years later, Miss Edna Kenton, noting that James had described the tale as "a piece of ingenuity, pure and simple, of cold artistic calculation, an *amusette* to catch those not easily caught," [7] indicated that she thought *The Turn of the Screw* to be a kind of hoax story to test the attentiveness of his readers, the lazy apprehending it only as a ghost story, the more attentive getting a deeper richness. It is the Kenton thesis that the ghosts *and the children*, the pictorial isolation, are "only the exquisite dramatizations of her [the governess'] little personal mystery, figures for the ebb and flow of the troubled thought within her mind, acting out her story." [8]

Tacitly avoiding Miss Kenton's hoax thesis but fully acknowledging the generic power of her suggestion in regard to the character of the governess, Edmund Wilson in a now famous and always challenging article, "The Ambiguity of Henry James," in the Henry James issue of *Hound & Horn*, contended that the key to *The Turn of the Screw* lies in the fact that "the governess who is made to tell the story is a neurotic case of sex repression, and that the ghosts are not real ghosts but hallucinations of the governess." In 1938 and again in 1948 Wilson, as a result of his own reading and reflection, revised his case, but stuck with conviction to his major premise, the neuroticism of the governess. She is still the fluttered, anxious girl out of a Hampshire vicarage who in her first interview becomes infatuated with her employer, and after confused thinking about him at Bly, discovers her first apparition, the figure of a man on a tower. With her help the figure, after a second appearance, is identified by the housekeeper, Mrs. Grose, as that of the master's handsome valet Peter Quint (now dead), who had appropriated the master's clothes and used "to play with the little boy [Miles] . . . to spoil him." By the shore of a lake where she is watching the little girl Flora at play, the governess sees another apparition, that of Miss Jessel her predecessor, who allegedly had had an affair with the valet. Suspecting the children as privy to this relationship,

5. XXXIII (Dec. 1898), [174]. The book was set up and electrotyped in September 1898. Edel and Laurence, p. 114, surmise the publication date to have been 13 Oct.
6. *Four Americans* (New Haven, 1919), p. 44.
7. *The Art of the Novel*, p. 172.

8. "Henry James to the Ruminant Reader: The Turn of the Screw," *The Arts*, VI (Nov. 1924), [p. 210]. I have not included Professor Goddard's interpretation in my enumeration because of its late publication. Goddard deserves credit, however, for his dissent to the usual interpretation.

she is confirmed in her notion that they have been previously corrupted by these evil servants who have come back to get them. The game of protection which she plays is, however, according to Wilson's further analysis, one in which she transfers her own terror, and *more*, to the children, thwarts the boy's desire to re-enter school or to write to his uncle, fixes upon him an unnatural fervid affection, and finally alienates the housekeeper before she literally frightens her young male charge to death.

Like Miss Kenton, Wilson insists that nobody but the governess sees the ghosts. "She believes that the children see them, but there is never any proof that they do. The housekeeper insists that she does not see them; it is apparently the governess who frightens her." At only one point was Wilson's interpretation labored; he could not adequately explain how Mrs. Grose was able to identify the male apparition from the description given by the governess (who had never met the deceased valet) after her second encounter.[9] The critics of the Wilson thesis—and they were an insistent score—bore down so heavily on this weakness that in 1948 Wilson capitulated, adding a separate note of retraction to his essay: "It is quite plain that James's conscious intention . . . was to write a *bona fide* ghost story; . . . not merely is the governess self-deceived but . . . James is self-deceived about her." [1]

II

That James could be so completely deceived about the motivation of any one of his characters is a thesis very hard to accept in view of his marvelous understanding of human psychology; hence a reasonable doubt bids us review the whole difficulty again. The identification of Peter Quint by the housekeeper is at present the seemingly insurmountable thing, and here we must note that the governess herself indicates to Mrs. Grose, when the latter wavers in accepting the young woman's version of the extraordinary events, that it is *the unimpeachable proof* that she has *not* invented the apparitions: "To hold her [Mrs. Grose] perfectly . . . I found I had only to ask her how, if I had 'made it up,' I came to be able to give, of each of the persons appearing to me, a picture disclosing, to the last detail, their special marks—a portrait on exhibition of which she had instantly recognized and named them" (pp. 80–81). If we persist in thinking this a crushing demonstration that the apparitions are supernatural, are we not more gullible than Mrs. Grose, who at least became suspicious enough, toward the end of the tale, to separate little Flora from the governess and thus save her life?

9. *The Triple Thinkers* (New York, 1948), pp. 88, 88–94, 90, 90–91. I cite the *revised* essay out of justice to Mr. Wilson, but compare pp. 385, 385–389, 387, 387–388, in the original. 1. *The Triple Thinkers*, pp. 123–124. Addendum, dated "1948." But see note [4, p. 153].

Mrs. Grose and we are the victims of a palpable deception, the trick of a demonstrable, pathological liar, a pitiful but dangerous person, with an unhinged fancy. We cannot examine all of the minute details of the governess' tendency (to the close reader they are multitudinous), but we can glance at one or two of the larger demonstrations of her complete unreliability. At the climax of the tale the governess promises to write a letter to her employer telling the state of things at Bly (p. 148); this letter is stolen by little Miles (pp. 187–188); who opens it to discover, as he confesses and as she reiterates, that it contains "nothing" (pp. 203–207). Again, in the sixteenth chapter, the governess reports to Mrs. Grose a conversation which she asserts she has just had with the "ghost" of Miss Jessel in which the latter admitted she is "of the lost" and "of the damned" and that she "wants Flora" (p. 145). But we have just witnessed through the governess' eyes the whole of that encounter and the only words uttered were by the governess,— " 'You terrible, miserable woman!' . . . *There was nothing in the room the next minute but the sunshine* [italics, mine] . . ." (pp. 140–142). And finally, let us look at the first appearance of the apparition of Miss Jessel, the former governess. The present governess is seated before a little lake and Flora is at play in front of her; she suddenly becomes aware "without direct vision" of "the presence, at a distance of a third person." Lifting her eyes from her sewing, the governess perceives a specter across the lake, but little Flora, busy at fitting one piece of wood into another to form a boat, is "*back to* the water" [italics mine] and obviously does not see the visitant (pp. 69–71). Yet when the governess reports the episode to Mrs. Grose, she states a flat untruth, "Flora *saw!*" Upon the housekeeper's expressing some doubt about the episode, the governess breaks out with, "Then ask Flora—*she's* sure!" But she instantly apprehends the danger from this and adds, in consternation, "No, for God's sake, *don't!* . . . she'll lie!" (pp. 72–74). If this is a ghost story, are not the governess' lies inexplicable? Must we not trust her completely to accept the presences as ghosts and not hallucinations? [2]

With some knowledge now of the governess' state, we may look at the mystery of the identification of Peter Quint. After her *second* encounter with the male apparition, the governess produces some minute details about his appearance: he was hatless, wore smart clothes (not his own), had curly red hair and little whiskers. He might have been an actor, but he was never a gentleman. Mrs. Grose (who, the governess sees, has already recognized the man)

2. If the governess is an unreliable witness, those who believe her *in any degree* are faced with the dilemma of picking what is true and false in her narrative.

asks if he were handsome. "'Remarkably!' . . . She had faltered but a second. 'Quint!' she cried . . . 'Peter Quint, his valet, when he was here!'" (pp. 56–58). Mrs. Grose has come out with the identification that the governess *expected.*

When the governess came to Bly, she knew only, on the word of her employer, that her predecessor, Miss Jessel, "was a most respectable person" (p. 13). On her second day at Bly she is conducted about the place by little Flora, who shows it to her "room by room, *secret by secret,* displaying a *disposition to tell me so many more things than she was asked* [italics mine]" (pp. 23, 24). This innocent trait in little Flora must be kept in mind. Two days later the governess picks up from the housekeeper the fact that there had been a man around who had an eye for "young pretty" women, like Miss Jessel and the present governess. This sets her excitable mind at work, and, after she has had her first hallucination, from the prattle of her youngest charge, from her own seemingly artless prompting of the children, and finally from a trip of inquiry to the village, as John Silver has shown,[3] she constructs the detailed description which she supplies to Mrs. Grose in reporting the second visitation. This is Silver's proof (the housekeeper speaks first):

"Was he a gentleman?"
I found I had no need to think. "No." . . .
"Then nobody about the place? *Nobody from the village?*"
"Nobody—nobody. *I didn't tell you, but I made sure.*"[4]

It is important to note also that the governess exhibits during her adventure at Bly a mind singularly susceptible to evil suggestion. The letter informing her that Miles has been dismissed from school gives no reason; since he had been admitted on trial, being younger than any of his fellows (p. 12), the normal assumption would be that it hadn't worked out. But the governess jumps to the preposterous conclusion in regard to the child (he's only ten!) "he's an injury to others." A little later, on no evidence whatsoever, she thinks of "the little, horrid, unclean school-world" that Miles had left (pp. 26, 46). Similarly, there is absolutely no reason for supposing the former governess and valet corrupt; the master gives Miss Jessel a good character and Quint had been his personal man-servant (pp. 13–58). It is Mrs. Grose, out of a petty jealousy common to domestic servants, who, at the prompting of the governess, embroiders the tale about a relation between the pair; it is the governess who gobbles up every morsel of this and invents the

3. "A Note on the Freudian Reading of 'The Turn of the Screw'," *American Literature,* XXIX (May 1957), 207–211.
4. Italics supplied by Silver. Mr. Silver's proof has persuaded Edmund Wilson to make an addendum, dated "1959," to his article in which he shifts back to "James knew exactly what he was doing . . . and intended the governess to be suffering from delusions." *A Casebook,* p. 153.

theme of their evil designs upon the children.[5] That she carries her insinuations to the children themselves (despite what she says to the contrary) is indicated by Mrs. Grose's declaration, after she had taken over Flora, that she has heard "horrors" from the child (p. 185). How can those who believe that this is a ghost story justify her impulse, when she perceives Miles is afraid of her, to make him really fear? Miles betrays that she has suggested an evil relationship between him and Quint, for when in the last scene she calls his direct attention to her specter (Miles "glaring vainly over the place and missing wholly"), the boy guesses at what she means him to see and names her a fiend: "Peter Quint—you devil!" (pp. 188–189, 200–205, 212).

Fiend she is, but a sick young woman, too. It is a triumph of James's art that he can give so much pathological information about the governess without damaging her credibility for many readers. He shows her apprehensive about going to Bly (she has four sleepless nights during the transition [pp. 7, 10–11]), yet her susceptibility to masculine charm is such that she pushes aside her fears to go as a result of her effortless conquest by the master (pp. 15, 34); to the end of her tale her sudden infatuation is the mainspring of her action—she seeks to wring an admission from the tortured boy in order to clear herself with his uncle (p. 201). She sequesters the children's letters because "they were too beautiful to be posted; I kept them myself; I have them to this hour" (p. 128). She will not write herself about events at Bly because she fears that the master will look upon her letter as a device "to attract his attention to my slighted charms" (p. 119). From the beginning to the end she reiterates that she is highly disturbed, excited, and in a nervous state. She is, in addition, "in receipt these days of disturbing letters from home, where things are not going well" (p. 47). There is a broad hint that her trouble is hereditary—she speaks of "the eccentric nature of my father" (p. 122). She exults in her superiority to Mrs. Grose and in the way in which she can influence that ignorant woman: "I had made her the receptacle of lurid things, but there was an odd recognition of my superiority. . . . She offered her mind to my disclosures as, had I wished to mix a witch's broth and proposed it with assurance, she would have held out a large clean saucepan" (p. 109). With disarming candor, the governess summarizes herself, "I was queer company enough—quite as queer as the company I received"—meaning the spectral visitors (p. 60). James with marvelous irony, perhaps the best example in his fiction, has the mad young woman run around the house to a window where she has just seen a visitant and peer in herself—to frighten

5. Pp. 28–31, 42, 58, 62–67. Probably she picked up a good deal of misinformation in the village, too, where Mrs. Grose may have sown the seeds.

Mrs. Grose half out of her wits; then the novelist caps it with the governess' observation, "I wondered why *she* should be scared" (pp. 48–51). Does James not give the whole game away when, after one frightening episode, he has the little boy quiet the governess by playing the piano, and she thinks, "David playing to Saul could never have shown a finer sense of the occasion"?[6] Saul was possessed of an evil spirit when the youth was sent for, and "David took an harp, and played with his hand; so Saul was refreshed, and was well, and the evil spirit departed from him" (I Samuel, xvi. 14–23).

III

One thing is clear, if James got his anecdote from Archbishop Benson, he did not mean us to take it as the *only* source of his story. He specifically labels it "the private source." Might there not have been public sources, i.e., things in print, available to everyone? Has it been properly noticed that James confesses to *many* "intellectual echoes" in recalling the creation of the tale? He adds further, "To knead the subject of my young friend's, the supposititious narrator's mystification thick . . . I seem to see draw behind it today a train of associations . . . so numerous I can but pick among them for reference."[7] Not all of these possibilities can be investigated here, but one of them can hardly be neglected —the direct influence of Sigmund Freud.

6. P. 158. The importance of this allusion was brought to my attention by Professor William M. Gibson. I do not believe James found it first in the Bible though he must have checked the text. It is more likely that he got it from Charlotte Brontë's *Jane Eyre* (Everyman ed., London, 1908), p. 442: "If Saul could have had you for his David, the evil spirit would have been exorcised without the aid of the harp." I have noted also that the unusual "sunk fence" of the Archbishop's anecdote appears in *Jane Eyre*, p. 94. Such fences are more common in Yorkshire than in Kent.

7. *The Art of the Novel*, pp. 170, 173. Leon Edel notes parallels to *Jane Eyre*, mentioned by the governess, but not by title, at the beginning of her narrative (p. 42): "the Jane Eyre who came to a lonely house, had a housekeeper for company and an orphan as her charge, and who fell in love with her employer." *The Ghostly Tales*, p. 431. In this connection we should note, I think, the way in which the governess, "rooted, . . . shaken," refers to *Jane Eyre*: "Was there a secret at Bly—a mystery of Udolpho or an insane, an unmentionable relative kept in an unsuspected confinement?" James is posing, is he not, the dilemma which confronts the reader as well as the governess—he must choose between a supernatural explanation, such as confronts the reader of *The Mysteries of Udolpho* or a natural one such as is given him in *Jane Eyre:* a mad woman?

Edel, very importantly to my mind, suggests a source for the specter on the tower from a description by James in the *Nation* (25 July 1872) of Haddon Hall, which he had reached, past "rook-haunted elms" along "a meadow path by the Wye," rhyming with Bly: "The twilight deepened, the ragged battlements and the low broad oriels glanced duskily from the foliage, the rooks wheeled and clamoured in the glowing sky; and if there had been a ghost on the premises I certainly ought to have seen it. In fact I did see it, as we see ghosts nowadays" (p. 433).

Robert Lee Wolff in "The Genesis of 'The Turn of the Screw'," *American Literature*, XIII (Mar. 1941), [pp. 125–132], calls attention to the fact in the Christmas number of *Black and White*, which contained James's tale "Sir Edmund Orme," "there is a drawing depicting two children, a boy and a girl, looking in terror across a lake at a house with a tower." This is possibly the suggestion for "the sea of Azof" (p. 69).

Wilson's provocative paper should have led the author or others to the writings of Freud for a source for *The Turn of the Screw*. While most critics would concede that an author of genius could in his characterizations anticipate a later scientific elucidation of behavior, none has held that James in his study of the governess combined the perceptions of genius with some actual technical knowledge. The date of the story, 1898, seems too early,[8] save for the remote possibility that there might be something relevant in that early publication of Doctors Breuer and Freud—*Studien über Hysterie*—in 1895. But indeed here *is* included a case of the greatest relevancy, one which supplies more important elements than Archbishop Benson's anecdote, "The Case of Miss Lucy R." [9]

A victim of "chronic purulent rhinitis," Lucy R. came to Freud late in 1891 for a treatment that lasted nine weeks and resulted in a complete cure. Lucy R. was the governess of two children, the daughters of a factory superintendent living in the suburbs of Vienna. She was "an English lady of rather delicate constitution" who was suffering from "depression and lassitude" as well as being "tormented by the subjective sensations of smell," especially the smell of burned pastry. Freud's inquiry led to the discovery that this odor was associated with an actual culinary disaster which had occurred two days prior to her birthday when Lucy R. was teaching her charges to cook in the schoolroom. A letter had arrived from her mother in Glasgow which the children had seized and kept from her (to retain for her birthday) and during the friendly scuffle the cooking had been forgotten. Struck by the fact that the governess' illness had been produced by so small an event, Freud pressed further to discover that she was thinking of returning to her mother, who, he developed, stood in no need of her. The governess then confessed that the house had become "unbearable" to her. "The housekeeper, the cook, and the French maid seemed to be under the impression that I was too proud for my position. They united in intriguing against me and told the grandfather of the children all sorts of things about me." She complained to the grandfather and the father; not receiving, however, quite the support she expected, she offered her resignation, but was persuaded by the father to remain. It was in this period of crisis that the schoolroom accident occurred.

Though Freud had now an adequate "analysis of the subjective sensation of smell," he still was not satisfied, and he made a bold suggestion to the governess in order to study its effect:

8. ". . . Freudian psychology was something Henry James could not have been consciously dealing with." N. Bryllion Fagin, "Another Reading of *The Turn of the Screw*," *MLN*, LXVI (Mar. 1941), p. 198. Fagin appears to have been the first to suggest that the tale is an "allegory of good and evil."

9. Sigmund Freud, *Selected Papers on Hysteria and Other Psychoneuroses*, tr. A. A. Brill, 3rd ed. (Washington, D. C., 1920), pp. 14–30. In another case, that of "Mrs. Emmy von N.," a boy is frightened to death.

I told her I did not believe all these things [exceptional "attachment for the children and sensitiveness towards other persons of the household"] were simply due to her affection for the children, but that I thought she was rather in love with the master, perhaps unwittingly, that she really nurtured the hope of taking the place of the [dead] mother, and it was for that reason that she became so sensitive to the servants. . . . She feared lest they would scoff at her. She answered in her laconic manner: "Yes, I believe it is so."—"But if you knew you were in love with the master, why did you not tell me so?"—"But I did not know it, or rather I did not wish to know it. I wished to crowd it out of my mind."

The governess was not ashamed because she loved the man, she told Freud; she feared ridicule if her feelings were discovered, for he was rich, of a prominent family, and her employer. After this admission she readily gave a complete account of her infatuation: *Her love had sprung out of a single intimate interview with the master.* "He became milder and much more cordial than usual, he told her how much he counted on her in the bringing up of his children, and looked at her rather peculiarly. It was at this moment that she began to love him, and gladly occupied herself with the pleasing hopes she conceived during that conversation. However, this was not followed by anything else, and despite her waiting and persevering, no other heart-to-heart talk following, she decided to crowd it out of her mind."

The governess' confession led to a strange symbolic substitution in her subjective sense of smell—that of the aroma of a cigar; Freud determined by analysis to remove this new memory symbol and thus get at the real root of the neurosis. A visitor, an elderly accountant, after dinner when the men were smoking, had kissed the children and thrown the father into a rage. This recalled an earlier scene in which a lady visitor had also kissed both children on the lips; the father had barely controlled himself until she was gone and then had berated the unfortunate governess. "He said that he held her responsible for this kissing . . . that if it ever happened again, he would trust the education of his children to someone else. This occurred while she believed herself loved and waited for a repetition of that serious and friendly talk. This episode shattered all her hopes." Miss Lucy R. having thus completely disburdened her memory, her rhinitis and neurosis were cured and her sense of smell was restored.

There is one over-all resemblance between "The Case of Miss Lucy R." and the story of the governess of Bly: they are both presented as reports or case histories, within a frame, for unlike most of James's stories, *The Turn of the Screw* is a tale with an elaborate portico. As we have seen, a man named Douglas produces a document which is the governess' story. It is Douglas who tells us that the governess began her adventure by falling in love in the single interview that she had with her future employer— as did Lucy R. This instant infatuation, decidedly not typical of James's stories, may be taken as a sign of susceptibility or abnormality. The employer is rich and handsome and of an old Essex family, he is the uncle of orphaned children—not two girls, but a niece and a nephew—whom he has neither the experience nor the patience to minister to personally. Like Miss Lucy's master, this new master gives the governess a sense of commission and trust in the interview, a factor in her infatuation (pp. 10–15).

And as for the governess' "case"—the story within the story of *The Turn of the Screw*—that has special points of resemblance also with "The Case of Miss Lucy R." The valet and the former governess may be seen as trying to possess little Miles and Flora in their protectress' disturbed fancy as did the kissing male and female visitors the children of the Vienna manufacturer—hint enough for James to differentiate the sexless "bad servants" of Archbishop Benson's anecdote. In the episode of the children's retaining Miss Lucy's letter at a crucial time may well be the germ of the whole elaborate business with letters in *The Turn of the Screw*: the governess retains a letter from Miles's school saying his return is not desired, she prevents Mrs. Grose from engaging to get a letter written to the master describing conditions at Bly, and the empty letter which she herself prepares and which is stolen and destroyed by Miles.

In Miss Lucy's fear that others would discern her feelings is the governess' dread that Miles will reveal them to his uncle and a hint of the suspicion with which the other servants at Bly regard her (pp. 190–191) after Mrs. Grose departs with the ill little Flora for London—thereby saving the child's mind, if not her life (pp. 180, 195). On the other hand, the governess early reveals her love for the master to Mrs. Grose with the same candor that had surprised Freud in Lucy R. (p. 21). Whether James was influenced by Freud's analysis of Lucy's difficulties with her sense of smell or not, his governess has a peculiarly keen organ—she notes the smell of lately baked bread in the housekeeper's room (p. 143), the "fragrance and purity about the children" (pp. 32, 82), and even the talk of little Miles, just before his death, comes to her "like a waft of fragrance" (p. 205). The impatience of the children's uncle (which the governess seems to dread throughout her adventure) derives from the impetuosity of the Vienna manufacturer as certainly as the governess' characterization as a rural parson's daughter comes from the Glasgow mother of Miss Lucy, a suggestion redolent of Presbyterianism.

Most important of all, James's governess experiences what Freud defines as a traumatic experience—similar to the rebuke of Miss Lucy—shortly after coming to Bly. After accepting the post with both trepidation and hope, she passes two sleepless nights in London, is possessed by anxiety on her way down to Bly, is unable to sleep the first night there, and then has a "second [really a fourth] sleepless night." While she is in this exhausted condition, she receives from her employer an unopened letter which announces Miles's dismissal from school. But the unopened letter reveals to her not merely her employer's indifference to the orphans in her care but to herself. Like the reproof given to Lucy R., it shatters her hope of some sort of intimacy with her employer, and the shock of that experience produces from her the senseless charges against little Miles (pp. 24–26). Finally, we are given the broadest possible hint that the governess is ill, for her all important interview takes place in "Harley Street" (pp. 10, 17)—the conventional "physicians' row" of London. Thus, like T. S. Eliot, James has provided us with a sort of "objective correlative" for reading the story.

Seemingly the most difficult evaluation of the governess to accept is that supplied by Douglas (p. 6), who produces her case and who reports later, when he knew her, "She was a most charming person . . . ," and reiterates, "She was the most agreeable woman I have ever known in her position; she would have been worthy of any whatever." It is further obvious that he had been in love with her when she was his sister's governess (pp. 6–9)—without knowing of her illness which had obviously passed.[1] Indeed, she is so attractive as Henry James presents her—the courageous protectress in her own mind to the children whom she betrays—that the majority of critics are unwilling to suspect any wrong of her. But she herself had realized the danger of a recurrence of her madness, and when Douglas had urged marriage upon her and she had repeatedly refused, she had resolved upon writing out the history of her aberration in order that *he* might understand.[2] Is not this the most plausible explanation to account for his possession of the

---

1. William James, *The Principles of Psychology* (2 vols., New York, 1890), II, 30, writes of "sporadic cases of hallucination, visiting people only once in a lifetime (which seem to be far the most frequent type . . .)."

2. The faithfulness of her account makes simple and factual many of H. J.'s own comments on the story which otherwise are cryptic. Consider, for example, how the implication of the following is changed, if James is thinking of the heroine's later attitude toward herself in her writing of her tale: ". . . I had to rule out subjective complications of her own—play of tone etc.; and keep her impersonal save for the most obvious and indis-

pensable little note of neatness, firmness and courage—without which she wouldn't have had her data." *Henry James and H. G. Wells*, ed. Leon Edel and Gordon Ray (London, 1958) p. 56. Discussing "mirrors" in the Preface to *The Princess Casamassima*, James invites the reader to compare the governess with Isabel Archer, whose imagination is "positively the deepest depth of her imbroglio." And he adds, "These persons all, so far as their other passions permit, intense perceivers all, of their respective predicaments." *The Art of the Novel*, pp. 70–71. What does the governess not perceive *vis-à-vis* Douglas?

narrative? She did not want him to think her merely capriciously cruel. This explanation has the merit, at least, of giving to *The Turn of the Screw* its final artistic unity, for when it is made, what we have called the "portico" or "Prologue" to the tale becomes its climax and the governess is translated into the heroine whom everyone apparently wants her to be.

IV

Despite this interpretation of *The Turn of the Screw*, some may claim that, though "The Case of Miss Lucy R." was available, it would hardly have come to James's knowledge.[3] This brings us to the tragic story of Alice James, as revealed in her *Journal*.[4] This woman, of whom the novelist was so fond, lucid and brilliant most of the time, was subject to "violent turns of hysteria," the first attacks occurring in 1867 or 1868 (or earlier), when she was nearing twenty. She writes of her struggle to conquer these "turns":

> As I used to sit immovable, reading in the library, with waves of violent inclination suddenly invading my muscles, taking some one of their varied forms, such as throwing myself out the window or knocking off the head of the benignant Pater, as he sat, with his silver locks, writing at his table; it used to seem to me that the only difference between me and the insane was that I had all the horrors and suffering of insanity, but the duties of doctor, nurse, and strait jacket imposed on me too.[5]

One of her worst attacks came in the "hideous summer of 1876 when I went down to the deep sea and its waters closed over me and I knew neither hope nor peace." "Her malady is a kind of which little is known," her mother reports sadly, and from family letters we learn that "Alice is in New York undergoing motorpathy with Dr. Taylor" or "is being treated electrically by Dr. Neftel." The Monro treatment is tried and abandoned. After the death of her mother ("Alice is unaccountably upheld after this blow," her brother Robertson writes) and that of her father, she went to England to be where her brother Henry could care for her. Lon-

3. The objection of Alexander E. Jones, in "Point of View in *The Turn of the Screw*," *PMLA*, LXXIV (Mar. 1959), 112–122, that, if James were familiar with Lucy R.'s case, he would have adopted also Freud's theorizing about it, seems to demand that James turn scientist as well as remain artist. I hold that James used "The Case of Miss Lucy R." as if it were a purely literary source without drawing on the theoretical material. Nevertheless, without being too minutely accurate scientifically, James does supply all that Freud demanded in a case of "conver-sion hysteria." The unopened letter forwarded by her employer, when his kindly treatment of her earlier led her to look for a personal communication with what expectations her infatuated innocence might attach to it, constitutes the "painful idea" repressed into the subconscious to work itself out in the inventions and hallucinations of the governess.
4. *Alice James: Her Brothers, Her Journal*, ed. Anna Robeson Burr (New York, 1934). Also F. O. Matthiessen, *The James Family*, pp. 272–285.
5. A. J. . . . *Her Journal*, pp. 181–182.

don came to be regarded as too taxing, and she was located with a companion, Kate Loring, in Bournemouth, and then, when she was "much less well," in Leamington. During her English illnesses she was attended by various distinguished alienists; but in December 1891 she was subjected, at the suggestion of William James, to the "therapeutic possibilities" of hypnotism as a device to relieve "all hideous nervous distresses" and pain, which morphine could not.[6]

This treatment of hysteria had been utilized by the great French doctor J.-M. Charcot. In 1882 William James had studied with Charcot[7] and the following year Alphonse Daudet, Henry's friend, had dedicated a novel, *L'Evangeliste*, to Charcot.[8] Henry had used the novel for suggestions for *The Bostonians*, his neurotic Olive Chancellor apparently being derived from Daudet's neurotic Mme Autheman, and both in turn from the studies of Charcot.[9] Hence there is no reason to suppose that Henry James was not as well acquainted with Charcot's therapy as was his brother William. And is it not reasonable to suppose that, when the methods of the Frenchman were succeeded by those of Breuer and Freud,[1] Henry James became acquainted with those as well? If he did not come to read *Studien über Hysterie* because of his continuing interest in his sister's case (she had died of cancer and other complications on 6 March 1892), it is possible that F. W. H. Myers, who had written the first notice of the book in English,[2] may have brought it to his attention. But is it not easier to suppose, in view of their common interest in the nervous illness of their deceased sister, that William James may have called *Studien über Hysterie* to the attention of Henry sometime between 1895 and 1898? In one of his Lowell lectures in 1896 William had declared, "In the relief of certain hysterias by handling the buried idea, whether as in Freud or Janet, we see a portent of the possible usefulness of these discoveries. The awful becomes relatively trivial."[3] In his second lecture on "Conversion" in the Gifford lectures of 1901-02 at

6. A. J. . . . *Her Journal*, pp. 56, 75–82, 244–245.
7. Ralph Barton Perry, *The Thought and Character of William James* (Briefer Version, New York, 1935), p. 181, n. 3.
8. (Paris, 1883). "A l'éloquent et savant Professeur J.-M. Charcot, Medecin de la Salpétrière, Je dédie cette *Observation*."—A.D.
9. See my *The Novels of Henry James* (New York, 1961), pp. 127–129.
1. "Introduction," *The Basic Writings of Sigmund Freud*, ed. Dr. A. A. Brill (New York, 1938), pp. 5–10.
2. *Proceedings of the Society for Psychical Research*, IX, 12–15. A. J. . . .

Her Journal, pp. 197, 249. Myers was also a long-time friend, and associate of William James. Perry, pp. 157, 169, 175, 177, 204–205, 261, 364. Henry's delayed and evasive reply to a letter from Myers suggests that the latter came close to guessing the intent in *The Turn of the Screw. The Letters of Henry James*, ed. Percy Lubbock (2 vols., New York, 1920), [p. 112].
3. Matthiessen, p. 226, n. 1. William James's description of Freud's treatment of hysteria would have to be regarded as imprecise if challenged by the criteria of Alexander E. Jones. See n. [3, p. 160].

Edinburgh, William praised "the wonderful explorations by . . . Janet, Breuer, Freud, . . . and others of the subliminal consciousness of patients with hysteria." While it is true that William came to suspect Freud, almost a decade later, as "a man obsessed with fixed ideas," in the time prior to his brother's composition of *The Turn of the Screw* it would seem that he was most favorably disposed toward the Vienna psychiatrist.[4]

But prior to any knowledge of *Studien über Hysterie* was Henry James's personal acquaintance, of course, with the illness of his sister and with the delusions and fantasies of that illness.[5] "Henry, the Patient, I should call him," Alice had paid him tribute in her *Journal.* "I have given him endless care and anxiety, but notwithstanding this and the fantastic nature of my troubles, I have never seen an impatient look on his face. . . . He comes at my slightest sign, and 'hangs on' to whatever organ may be in eruption, and gives me calm and solace by assuring me my nerves are his nerves, and my stomach his stomach." [6] When William suggested hypnosis as a measure to relieve pain in Alice's last illness, Henry assented to the treatment though the practitioner, Dr. Charles Lloyd Tuckey, was the pioneer in England.[7] About a year after Alice's death, the novelist wrote of Doctor Hugh in "The Middle Years," "This young friend, for a representative of the new psychology, was himself easily hypnotised, and if he became abnormally communicative it was only a sign of his real subjection." [8] When Alice's *Journal* came into Henry's hands, he was "immensely impressed with the thing as a revelation of a moral . . . picture. It is heroic in its individuality, its independence—its face-

4. *The Varieties of Religious Experience* (Mod. Lib., New York, n.d.), p. 230. *Not* in the Index, pp. 519–526. William began planning these lectures as early as 1896, though they were not put into finished written form until 1900." Perry, p. 255. Jay B. Hubbell calls my attention to the fact that H. J. read "everything" that W. J. wrote. See letter, H. J. to W. J., 23 Nov. 1905. The hypochondria of William James is well known, also his tendency to discuss illnesses with everybody. See R. B. Perry, "Morbid Traits," *Thought and Character of William James: Briefer Version* (New York, 1948), pp. 359–369. This increases the possibility of his having discussed Alice's case and Freud-Breuer with H. J.

5. "She [Madame de Mauves] was not striving to balance her sorrow with some strongly flavored joy; for the present, she was trying to live with it peaceably, reputably, and without scandal,—turning the key on it occasionally, as you would on a companion liable to attacks of insanity." *Madame de Mauves, The Great Short Novels of Henry James*, ed. Philip Rahv (New York, 1944), p. 27. This story was published in the Galaxy, XVII (Feb.–Mar. 1874.), 216–233, 354–374.

6. P. 150. 25 Mar. 1890. She also records that Henry had "absolutely a physical repulsion from all personal disorder. 'Tis a sad fate, though, that he should have fastened to him a being like me." p. 218. 12 Apr. 1891.

7. C. L. Tuckey, *Psycho-therapeutics; or Treatment by Hypnotism and Suggestion* (London, 1889). This book had gone into its third edition before Alice's death. In "Henry James as Freudian Pioneer," p. 26, I mistakenly assumed that Dr. Hack Tuke, Alice's alienist from Bethlehem Hospital, was the practitioner who employed hypnosis.

8. "The Middle Years," *The Short Stories of Henry James*, ed. Clifton Fadiman (New York, 1948), p. 302. This was called to my attention by Frederick L. Gwynn.

to-face with the universe for and by herself." [9] In the fortitude of Alice James facing her destiny James may have got the inspiration for making the governess the heroine of his tale and the confessor of her own terrible burden to her lover. But he noted other things in Alice's *Journal*: her lively curiosity for sexual anecdotes, such as the premarital chastity of her previous doctor, Sir Andrew Clark, and the vices of the Eton boys. When she sets down as fact Kate Loring's *always* coming, at a turn of the stairs, upon a waiter and a chambermaid, in "osculatory relaxations," Henry could have regarded that as a shared fantasy, but it may have suggested to him the relations of Peter Quint and Miss Jessel as imagined by the governess.[1] One of the tiniest hints in Alice's *Journal* may be seen as richly fertile in relation to *The Turn of the Screw*: Alice notes, "I can't read anything suggestive, or that survives, or links itself to experience, for it sets my silly stomach fluttering, and my flimsy head skipping so that I have to stop." [2] The governess had been reading Fielding's *Amelia* with great excitement (it having been denied her at home) at a "horribly late" hour when she becomes aware of "something undefinably astir in the house" (pp. 95–96); she rises, has an hallucination of Quint on the stair, and later sees little Miles on the lawn staring up at—she assumes—Quint on the tower, but really at his sister (pp. 99–106). Now the pertinence of the forbidden book is this: because her husband is frequently cast into prison, the beautiful Amelia, pursued by two ardent would-be seducers through a series of exciting adventures, is the sole protectress of two little children, a boy and a girl, Billy being "a good soldier-like Christian." [3] James put *Amelia* into the governess' hands because she could identify with the heroine: Amelia suffers early in the novel from what "some call a fever on the spirits, some a nervous fever, some the vapours, and some the hysterics," but which her husband pronounces "a sort of complication of all the diseases together, with almost madness added to them." [4] James's own interest in *Amelia* was probably aroused because one of the tenacious seducers was named "Colonel James" whereas the other remains unnamed throughout and is simply referred to as "the noble peer." When Douglas of *The Turn of the Screw* fails to reveal the name of the governess, that might be regarded as the protection a lover might offer, but the failure of Mrs. Grose or anyone else ever to call the governess by name, suggested by Fielding's omission possibly, can only be looked upon as an unconscious revelation of how deeply fixed was James's caution to avoid suspicion that

9. *The Letters*, I, 214–216. H. J. to W. J., 28 May 1894.
1. A. J. . . . *Her Journal*, pp. 246–248, 215, 181.
2. A. J. . . . Her Journal, p. 105. Note that Alice had just been reading

Clarissa Harlowe by Richardson.
3. *Amelia* (3 vols., London, 1871), III, 5–6. Not a prototype of Miles, but a suggestion for the latter's name.
4. I, 136–137.

his narrative had its source in Alice's illness.

James's dependence on his personal knowledge of hysteria and on "The Case of Miss Lucy R." makes it clear that Miss Kenton and Edmund Wilson were profoundly right in their characterization of the governess: there are no "ghosts" in the story—the phantoms are creations of an hysterical mind, they are hallucinations. Miss Kenton and Wilson, however, neglect the befuddled heroism of the girl's role. Just how much of the governess' narrative James meant as fantasy may be difficult to determine: Wilson accepts the children as real and the death of little Miles as a fact; Miss Kenton suggests that even the children—"what they are and what they do— are only exquisite dramatizations of her [the governess'] little personal mystery, figures for the ebb and flow of troubled thought within her mind, acting out her story." [5] If Miss Kenton is right, there is no tragedy in The Turn of the Screw. There is only ill-health. But this interpretation is not consistent with James's declaration to Dr. Louis Waldstein, "But, ah, the exposure indeed, the helpless plasticity that isn't dear or sacred to somebody! That was my little tragedy . . ."; or his confession to F. W. H. Myers, "The thing . . . I most wanted not to fail of doing . . . was to give the impression of the communication to the children of the most infernal imaginable evil and danger—the condition, on their part, of being as exposed as we can humanly conceive children to be." [6]

If there are things in the Preface to the volume containing The Turn of the Screw, or elsewhere, that suggest something short of tragedy for both children and the governess, or are ambiguous or mystifying, they are justifiably so: James had the duty of shielding Alice's memory—which he did in such artless phrases as "my bogey-tale," my "irresponsible little fiction," my "fairy tale pure and simple," [7] behind which he could hide all that he wished to hide. Perhaps even ascribing the main source of the story to Archbishop Benson whose anecdote embodied ghosts was also an effort to disguise the truth in the tale.[8] Should we not wonder, perhaps, that

5. Kenton, [p. 210].
6. The Letters, [pp. 110, 112].
7. The Art of the Novel, pp. 169–171.
8. In The Aspern Papers (1888) and elsewhere James had previously shown his awareness and distaste for the prying curiosity of scholars; may he not have deliberately "planted" Archbishop Benson's anecdote for them? Aside from the very positive assertion of Benson's sons that the anecdote was unfamiliar, the only suspicious thing in the notebook entry is the "sunk fence" and this solely because of its possible literary source (see nn. [6, 7, p. 155].) One sees, however, some con-

nection between The Other House and The Turn of the Screw—both are tales of the murder of a child by a trusted woman. The Other House was written for the Illustrated London News, whose editor, Clement Shorter, had just published his Charlotte Brontë and Her Circle (1896). Since his editor was new to him, what would have been more natural to James than to read the biography and review the novels of the Brontë sisters in order to post himself on Shorter's taste? That he read Jane Eyre is clear; Lionel Stevenson has suggested to me that the narrative method—the shift

James did not more positively emphasize the possibilities of reading the tale as a ghost story, did not further lead the reader astray, save that there must have been a faint hope lodged in his heart that the central motif in his story, the horror of children betrayed by their protectress, an innocent mad woman, who, in her turn, becomes heroic, might in a long time emerge and his transcendent skill as an artist be understood? *The Turn of the Screw* is at once the most horrific and tender tale of the nineteenth century.[9] "There is no excellent beauty," said Lord Bacon, "that hath not some strangeness in the proportion."

from Douglas to the governess—may owe something to the shift from Lockwood to Nelly Dean, who narrates and colors most of the story in *Wuthering Heights*. Lucy Snowe in *Villette* scoffs at the legend of a ghost until she sees one, and although she is told by Dr. John that it is a product of her nerves, she persists in believing in her vision until the ghost, who has worn the habit of a nun, exposes himself by leaving his attire on her bed with a note addressed to her. In some way, surely, the Shorter relationship was generic to the story. In view of his acceptance of *The Other House,* may not James have hoped he would take this story? If the reference to the "sunk fence" came from *Jane Eyre,* the entry is misdated. The conjectures in this note, however, do not affect the main argument above in regard to the governess' hallucinations.

9. Those who have stressed *The Turn of the Screw* as an "allegory of good and evil" or "of the dual nature of man" do, at least, focus our attention on how consistently, by the use of popular theological clichés, which the governess got from her eccentric father, James maintains in the main narrative the provincial point of view of this poor girl. Notice especially her eagerness to extract a "confession" from little Miles. "If he confesses," the governess declares, "he's saved" (p. 189). Note that she regards this as "like fighting with a demon for the human soul" (p. 205). The reality of this struggle the governess so vividly conveys to us that it is natural for us to catch meanings that are not there. Even Mrs. Grose is affected by the girl's language; palliating her, when she leaves with little Flora, Mrs. Grose declares she will return to "save" the governess (p. 189). James's well-known low opinion of allegory and his indifference to theology mitigate against an allegorical interpretation. In regard to the governess' "eccentric father," consider the following on the death of Henry James, Sr.: "He announced that he had entered upon the 'spiritual life' and thereafter refused all food. The doctors spoke of 'softening of the brain,' but all evidence indicates that until his last hours, he was in possession of his faculties . . . In long letters to William . . . Henry said his father's passing had been 'most strange . . . and as full of beauty as it was void of suffering. There was none of what we feared —no paralysis, no dementia, no violence'." Leon Edel, *Henry James: The Middle Years* (Philadelphia. 1962), pp. 57–58.

Essays in Criticism

Unless specified otherwise, numbered footnotes in each of the following essays are by the author of that essay. References in the essays to notebooks, letters, and other essays reprinted in the Norton Critical Edition have been changed to refer to this edition.

Early Reactions:
1898-1923

When *The Two Magics* was published in England and America in 1898 so immediately compelling was *The Turn of the Screw* that reviewers practically ignored the second tale, *Covering End* (formerly a one-act play which James converted in order to fill out the book). Reactions varied: a few readers were repulsed, some were charmed, most were mystified. The following selection makes no attempt to cover all of the early criticism (see the article by Ginsberg, noted below, p. 269, and Foley, in the Bibliography), but does try to show the diversity of opinion which the tale aroused.

THE NEW YORK TIMES

Magic of Evil and Love †

AN EXTRAORDINARY NEW VOLUME FROM HENRY JAMES *

Coming immediately on the heels, as one may say, of his painfully elaborate treatment of an almost worthless subject in a story called "In the Cage," to which sufficient consideration was given last week, this still newer volume by Mr. James is doubly surprising and gratifying. We should not care, certainly, to recommend it offhand as agreeable reading for habitually light-hearted or light-minded persons, though to be sure, the second of the two stories which make up its contents is a perfect example of pure comedy, worthy of Meredith, (as, indeed, is most that James writes in this vein,) buoyantly uplifting, rich in humorous fancy, both exquisite and of seeming spontaneity in its play of wit. * * * This merry yet tender tale signifies, presumably, in the comprehensive title, the magic of love, (or is it the magic of money?) and preceding it, in the longer tale called "The Turn of the Screw," is such a

† From *The New York Times Saturday Review of Books and Art*, III (October 15, 1898), 681–82.
* *The Two Magics: The Turn of the Screw; Covering End.* By Henry James. New York: The Macmillan Company, $1.50.

deliberate, powerful, and horribly successful study of the magic of evil, of the subtle influence over human hearts and minds of the sin with which this world is accursed, as our language has not produced since Stevenson wrote his "Jekyll and Hyde" tale, a work to which this is not akin in any other sense than the one here specified.

Mr. James's story is perhaps as allegorical as Stevenson's, but the allegory is not so clear. We have called it "horribly successful," and the phrase seems to still stand, on second thought, to express the awful, almost overpowering sense of the evil that human nature is subject to derive from it by the sensitive reader. We have no doubt that with such a reader Mr. James will invariably produce exactly the effect he aims at. * * * But the work is not horrible in any grotesque or "realistic" sense. The strongest and most affecting argument against sin we have lately encountered in literature (without forcing any didactic purpose upon the reader) it is nevertheless free from the slightest hint of grossness. Of any precise form of evil Mr. James says very little, and on this head he is never explicit. Yet, while the substance of his story is free from all impurity and the manner is always graceful and scrupulously polite, the very breath of hell seems to pervade some of its chapters, and in the outcome goodness, though depicted as alert and militant, is scarcely triumphant. The most depraved "realist" (using that word in its most popular sense, for, correctly speaking, the artistic method of Mr. James is realism as opposed to idealism) could surely not be more powerful, though he might, in his explicitness, defeat his supposed purpose. Mr. James's present purpose, as we understand it, is amply fulfilled.

In this "Turn of the Screw"—the title, used to express a stronger shade of horror and mental anguish than the ordinary ghost story represents, does not seem quite as apposite as some of Mr. James's titles—he is the seer and the moralist, whether designedly so or not. No eloquent outpouring of a Jeremy Collier [1] or other avowed enemy of specified evils could produce a feeling of greater abhorrence for the object attacked. Yet Mr. James's method, as we have already intimated, is free from all superficial signs of a strongly didactic purpose. He simply tells, with no waste of words, as one who reads carefully soon learns, a story.

Just what that story is it would be unfair to divulge here, but a boy of ten years and a girl of eight figure in it prominently, and these are so lovely in their outward semblance of childlike innocence, so charming in their natural dispositions, and in many ways apart from the one way in which the reader presently comes to view them, so delightfully like the imaginative and inherently sagacious children of cultivated persons, that one recalls Kenneth Grahame's "Golden

1. Collier (1650–1726) was the author of *A Short View of the Immorality and Profaneness of the English Stage* (1698). [Editor.]

Age"[2] and some of the other idylls of childhood as one reads of them. Yet these children are accursed, or all but damned, and are shown to have daily, almost hourly, communication with lost souls, the souls that formerly inhabited the bodies of a vicious governess and her paramour, who, in the flesh, began the degradation of their victims. The awful "imagination of evil" this fair boy and girl must possess, the oldness of the heart and soul in each young body, the terrible precocity which enables them to deceive their "pastors and masters" as to their knowledge of the presence of their ghostly mentors, these set forth with perfect clearness and the sobriety of a matter-of-fact narrative are what serve to produce the thrilling effect.

The allegory is plain or not, according to the reader's aptitude for discovering allegories. We do not insist upon that. But to the contention that this seemingly frail story—with a theme which would surely fail of effect, and might become ridiculous in the hands of almost any one of its author's contemporaries—is one of the most moving and, in its implied moral, most remarkable works of fiction published in many years, we steadfastly cling. No man could have undertaken to write it without feeling powerfully the importance of its subjects, and no man could have carried the task through in whom interest in the theme did not grow as the story grew.

The introduction to this tale is sufficiently conventional, but one decides, in looking back, that it serves better than another would. A Christmas house party, with ghost stories told around the fireplace, develops the "Turn of the Screw" in a tale of a ghost seen first by an innocent child, and this leads to the production of this ghost story read from the faded manuscript (supposedly) of a gentlewoman who had had experience with these possessed children. The style of the manuscript, in spite of the insistence upon the woman's penmanship, is obviously the style of Mr. Henry James. But one appreciates not the less the characteristic touch in the statement that it was read 'with a fine clearness that was like a rendering to the ear of the beauty of the author's hand."

THE OUTLOOK

["The Story * * * Is Distinctly Repulsive"] †

Mr. Henry James has written nothing more characteristic in method and style than "The Turn of the Screw," the first of the two stories which make up his latest volume, *The Two Magics*. This

2. Grahame (1859–1932), author of highly romantic fiction, had published *Golden Age* in 1895. [Editor.]

† From *The Outlook*, LX (October 29, 1898), 537.

story concerns itself with the problem of evil, from which men of Puritan ancestry seem never able entirely to detach themselves. It is a ghost story, psychologically conceived, and illustrating a profound moral law. It is, in fact, an account of the possession of two children by two evil spirits. This statement seems very bald, and will remind the reader of the ordinary clumsy, materialistic ghost story. It is hardly necessary to say that Mr. James's tale has nothing in common with the ordinary ghost story; it is altogether on a higher plane both of conception and art. The story itself is distinctly repulsive. (The Macmillan Company, New York.)

THE BOOKMAN

Mr. James's New Book †

Mr. James is in a queer mood. Nearly all his later stories have been tending to the horrible, have been stories of evil, beneath the surface mostly, and of corruption. His genius is essentially a healthy one, we have always felt, and he has had great respect in times past for the *convenancse*.[1] He does not outrage them now; his manners are perfect, even in his late studies of the putrescence of human existence. "What Maisie Knew" was one of these; but the story was a triumph of beauty in the end. Its theme was that purity and candour and joy could be strong enough in the heart of a young creature to counteract the miasma of the evil amid which she lived, not all unconscious either. His purpose was abundantly fulfilled. The first of the two stories here—the other hardly counts, though it is a readable enough extravaganza—is another study of the same unpleasant kind of fact, but so much more horrible, that it surely marks the climax of this darker mood, out of which Mr. James may emerge with a profounder, or perhaps only a bitterer strain. The situation of Maisie is reversed. The circumstances, the conditions, in "The Turn of the Screw," all make for purity, beauty, and joy; and on the surface these are resplendent. But underneath is a sink of corruption, never uncovered, but darkly, potently hinted. One's heart cries out against the picture of the terrible possibility; for the corrupted are children of tender years. Every inch of the picture seems an outrage in our first heat. Even in colder moments, if we admit the fact of infant depravity, if we own that children are supreme actors, and can bar doors on their elders most effectually, we must deny the continuity and the extent of the corruption as suggested here. Mr. James has used symbolism to help him out

† [From *The Bookman*, XV (November, 1898), 54.] "The Two Magics." By Henry James. 65. (Heinemann.) 1. For propriety. [Editor.]

with his theme; so, at least, we may speak of the two ghosts—one of a rascally valet, the other of an iniquitous governess—the origins of the evil in their lifetime, who haunt the children after their death. Their horrible invitations to evil are joyfully responded to. We have never read a more sickening, a more gratuitously melancholy tale. It has all Mr. James's cleverness, even his grace. The plottings of the good governess and the faithful Mrs. Grose to combat the evil, very gradually discovered, are marvellously real. You cannot help but assist at their interviews, and throb with their anxiety. You are amply convinced of the extraordinary charm of the children, of the fascination they exercise over all with whom they come in contact. The symbolism is clumsy; but only there in the story has Mr. James actually failed. It is not so much from a misunderstanding of child nature that he has plunged into the deep mistake of writing the story at all. Here, as elsewhere in his work, there are unmistakable signs of a close watchfulness and a loving admiration of children of the more distinguished order. A theory has run away with him. It is flimsily built on a few dark facts, so scattered and uncertain that they cannot support a theory at all. He has used his amiable knowledge of child life in its brighter phases to give a brilliant setting to this theory. His marvellous subtlety lends his examination of the situation an air of scientific precision. But the clever result is very cruel and untrue.

JOHN D. BARRY

On Books at Christmas †

* * * Equally involved [as *In the Cage*] is the style of his second autumn book, "The Two Magics," which consists of two long tales, one of which is a very up-to-date and absorbing ghost-story. Henry James, I ought to add by way of caution, is by no means a safe author to give for a Christmas gift.

THE CRITIC

The Recent Work of Henry James ‡

Of late Mr. James produces on his readers the effect of one experimenting, for his own sole joy rather than for their edification,

† From *Ainslee's Magazine*, II (December, 1898), 518.

‡ From *The Critic*, XXXIII, old series (December, 1898), 523-524.

with all kinds of intricate problems, but chiefly with that of mastering and presenting situations so super-subtle as to be practically impalpable.

The two new books of his which are out for the holidays contain striking examples of this kind of literary rarefaction. "In the Cage" is a romance in the thousandth dilution. It contains a ghost of a situation, a shadow of a plot, and there is no other living writer who could produce from such tenuous material such a firm, rounded, finished product. Mr. James is the master juggler of literature, under whose hands a grain of sand expands into a garden-plot full of blossoming roses. * * *

But if "In the Cage" convinces us that Mr. James deals as confidently and realistically with "thoughts before thinking," as a grocer deals with pounds of sugar or bars of soap, what is there left to say about "The Turn of the Screw"? This is the first of the two stories linked together in book-form under the apt title of "The Two Magics," and in it the author pushes the same kind of audacity to more surprising lengths. The heroine of "In the Cage" carries her divinations far enough in all conscience, but at least she has real people and tangible telegrams as a basis for her mental processes. The subject-matter of "The Turn of the Screw" is also made up of feminine intuitions, but the heroine—this time a governess—has nothing in the least substantial upon which to base her deep and startling cognitions. She perceives what is beyond all perception, and the reader who begins by questioning whether she is supposed to be sane ends by accepting her conclusions and thrilling over the horrors they involve.

The story, in brief, concerns itself with the hideous fate of two beautiful and charming children who have been subjected to the baneful and corrupting influence of two evil-intentioned servants. These, dying, are unable to give up their hold upon so much beauty and charm, but while suffering the torments of damnation, come back to haunt the children as influences of horror and evil, with "a fury of intentions" to complete the ruin they have begun. The story is told by the governess, who recounts her slow recognition of the situation and her efforts to shield and save her charges. It is the most monstrous and incredible ghost-story that ever was written. At the same time it grasps the imagination in a vise. The reader is bound to the end by the spell, and if, when the lids of the book are closed, he is not convinced as to the possibility of such horrors, he is at least sure that Mr. James has produced an imaginative masterpiece. * * *

THE INDEPENDENT

["Most Hopelessly Evil Story"] †

* * * "The Turn of the Screw" is the most hopelessly evil story that we have ever read in any literature, ancient or modern. How Mr. James could, or how any man or woman could, choose to make such a study of infernal human debauchery, for it is nothing else, is unaccountable. It is the story of two orphan children, mere infants, whose guardian leaves them in a lonely English country house. The little boy and little girl, at the toddling period of life, when they are but helpless babes, fall under the influence of a governess and her lover who poison the very core of their conscience and character and defile their souls in a way and by means darkly and subtly hinted rather than portrayed by Mr. James. The study, while it exhibits Mr. James's genius in a powerful light, affects the reader with a disgust that is not to be expressed. The feeling after perusal of the horrible story is that one has been assisting in an outrage upon the holiest and sweetest fountain of human innocence, and helping to debauch—at least by helplessly standing by—the pure and trusting nature of children. Human imagination can go no further into infamy, literary art could not be used with more refined subtlety of spiritual defilement.

THE CHAUTAUQUAN

["Psychic Phenomena"] ‡

* * * [In *The Turn of the Screw*] Henry James again displays his skill as a delineator of psychic phenomena. In this particular story the theme is the continued influence on two children of a disreputable governess and her accomplice after their disappearance and the discovery of this influence by another governess who is keenly sensitive to psychic impulses. The intangible is here painted with a skill little short of the supernatural, and in dealing with these subtleties of the mind the author has produced a tale whose suggestivness makes the blood bound through the veins with unusual rapidity.

† From *The Independent*, LI (January 5, 1899), 73.
‡ From "Talk about Books," *The*   *Chautauquan*, XXVIII, old series (March, 1899), 630.

OLIVER ELTON

["Facts, or Delusions"] †

Mr. James has put still more force into *The Turn of the Screw,* one of the hideous stories of our language. Is any limitation placed on the choice of an artist by the mere measure of the pain he inflicts upon the nerves? If not, then the subject is admissible. It is a tale where sinister and spectral powers are shown spoiling and daunting the innocence of the young. There is at first sight something wanton in the ruthless fancy—in the re-invasion of our life by the dead butler Peter Quint and his paramour; in the struggle with these visitants for the souls of the two young and beautiful children, a little boy and a little girl, whom in life they have already influenced; in the doubt, raised and kept hanging, whether, after all, the two ghosts who can choose to which persons they will appear, are facts, or delusions of the young governess who tells the story; and in the final defeat of hope by the boy's death just at the moment when he may perhaps be saved. But on reflection we see that all this is the work of a symbolist, who is also a kind of puritan. The ghosts play their part in the bodily sphere as terrifying *dramatis personae*—neither substance nor shadow; they are *there,* as Gorgon faces at the window; while, spiritually, they figure as the survival of the poison which they had sown while living in the breasts of the innocents. And when this influence reawakens, the earthly forms of the sowers gather visible shape, at once as symbols and as actual combatants. The full effect is won by Mr. James's peculiar gift of speaking in the name of women. The whole visitation comes to us through its play upon the nerves, its stimulus to the courage of the young English lady who, desperate and unaided, vainly shelters the children. The tension is heightened by the distrust with which others regard her story, and the aversion towards her inspired by the ghosts in the children themselves.

† From "The Novels of Mr. Henry James," *Modern Studies* (Edward Arnold: London, 1907), pp. 245–289, 255–256. Reprinted by permission of the publishers.

WALTER DE LA MARE

["Evidence of a Subliminal World"] †

That being hopelessly bad is not being vulgar is one of the minor enlightenments of *The Turn of the Screw*—though the turn itself is of the screw of 'ordinary human virtue'. Mrs. Grose comes as near as any of Mr. James's characters to an inadequate realization; his governess, with her queer little flutters, her impassioned self-dedication, faintly recalls no less delightful a prototype than Jane Eyre. The preparative prologue is, if anything, a trifle forced and disproportionate; and its first sentence, 'I remember the whole beginning as a succession of flights and drops, a little see-saw of the right throbs and the wrong,' has a flourish of the master hand some little distance beyond Jane Eyre. But what story in the whole region of fiction can match its deliberate, intentional, insidious horror, the sense and presence of gloating, atrocious, destructive evil which it conveys, the steady, cumulative intensity of the 'awful hushed cold intercourse' between living and dead, of the blind groping of love amid the debauched innocence of childhood? The very names convey a devilish innuendo. The actual confrontations of Quint and of Miss Jessel (as fine and as rare and as clear in imaginative poise as that between the wretched thief of privacy, loyalty, and tenderness and poor Miss Tita in *The Aspern Papers*), between anguished child and that hideous demon, with 'white face of damnation', are evidence of a subliminal world that centuries of psychical research can only supplement. If there are stories of impulses, actions, crises in life that cannot be written, and stories that should not be written, then *The Turn of the Screw* is a triumph against impossibility and a venture unmistakably on the verge.

† From "The Lesson of the Masters," originally published in the *Times Literary Supplement*, May 13, 1915; reprinted in *Private Views* (Faber: London, 1953), pp. 7–11. Reprinted by permission of The Literary Trustees of Walter de la Mare—The Society of Authors.

WILLIAM LYON PHELPS

[The "Iron Scot" Stenographer] †

* * * I did not dream until the year 1898 that our author could draw a winsome, lovable, charming little boy, who would walk straight into our hearts. That year was a notable year in our writer's career; because it saw the publication of "The Turn of the Screw," which I found then and find again to be the most powerful, the most nerve-shattering ghost story I have ever read. The connoting strength of its author's reticence was never displayed to better advantage; had he spoken plainly, the book might have been barred from the mails; yet it is a great work of art, profoundly ethical, and making to all those who are interested in the moral welfare of boys and girls an appeal simply terrific in its intensity. With none of the conventional machinery of the melodrama, with no background of horrible or threatening scenery, with no hysterical language, this story made my blood chill, my spine curl, and every individual hair to stand on end. When I told the author exactly how I felt while reading it, and thanked him for giving me sensations that I thought no author could give me at my age, he said that he was made happy by my testimony. "For," said he, "I meant to scare the whole world with that story; and you had precisely the emotion that I hoped to arouse in everybody. When I wrote it, I was too ill to hold the pen; I therefore dictated the whole thing to a Scot stenographer. I was glad to try this experiment, for I believed that I should be able to judge of its effect on the whole world by its effect on the man who should hear it first. Judge of my dismay when from first to last page this iron Scot betrayed not the slightest shade of feeling! I dictated to him sentences that I thought would make him leap from his chair; he short-handed them as though they had been geometry, and whenever I paused to see him collapse, he would enquire in a dry voice, 'What next?' "

† From "Henry James," *The Yale Review*, V (July, 1916), 794. Later versions of this anecdote appeared in *Howells, James, Bryant, and Other Essays* (New York, 1924), and in *Autobiography with Letters* (New York, 1939).

VIRGINIA WOOLF

["Henry James's Ghosts"] †

Henry James's ghosts have nothing in common with the violent old ghosts—the blood-stained sea captains, the white horses, the headless ladies of dark lanes and windy commons. They have their origin within us. They are present whenever the significant overflows our powers of expressing it; whenever the ordinary appears ringed by the strange. The baffling things that are left over, the frightening ones that persist—these are the emotions that he takes, embodies, makes consoling and companionable. But how can we be afraid? As the gentleman says when he has seen the ghost of Sir Edmund Orme for the first time: "I am ready to answer for it to all and sundry that ghosts are much less alarming and much more amusing than was commonly supposed." The beautiful urbane spirits are only not of this world because they are too fine for it. They have taken with them across the border their clothes, their manners, their breeding, their band-boxes, and valets and ladies' maids. They remain always a little worldly. We may feel clumsy in their presence, but we cannot feel afraid. What does it matter, then, if we do pick up "The Turn of the Screw" an hour or so before bedtime? After an exquisite entertainment we shall, if the other stories are to be trusted, end with this fine music in our ears, and sleep the sounder.

Perhaps it is the silence that first impresses us. Everything at Bly is so profoundly quiet. The twitter of birds at dawn, the far-away cries of children, faint footsteps in the distance stir it but leave it unbroken. It accumulates; it weighs us down; it makes us strangely apprehensive of noise. At last the house and garden die out beneath it. "I can hear again, as I write, the intense hush in which the sounds of evening dropped. The rooks stopped cawing in the golden sky, and the friendly hour lost for the unspeakable minute all its voice." It is unspeakable. We know that the man who stands on the tower staring down at the governess beneath is evil. Some unutterable obscenity has come to the surface. It tries to get in; it tries to get at something. The exquisite little beings who lie innocently asleep must at all costs be protected. But the horror grows. Is it possible that the little girl, as she turns back from the window,

† From "Henry James's Ghost Stories," *Granite and Rainbow* (The Hogarth Press, London), pp. 65–72; originally published in the *Times Literary Supplement*, December 22, 1921. Copyright © 1958 by Leonard Woolf. Pp. 71–72 reprinted by permission of Leonard Woolf and the publisher.

has seen the woman outside? Has she been with Miss Jessel? Has Quint visited the boy? It is Quint who hangs about us in the dark; who is there in that corner and again there in that. It is Quint who must be reasoned away, and for all our reasoning returns. Can it be that we are afraid? But it is not a man with red hair and a white face whom we fear. We are afraid of something un-named, of something, perhaps, in ourselves. In short, we turn on the light. If by its beams we examine the story in safety, note how masterly the telling is, how each sentence is stretched, each image filled, how the inner world gains from the robustness of the outer, how beauty and obscenity twined together worm their way to the depths—still we must own that something remains unaccounted for. We must admit that Henry James has conquered. That courtly, worldly, sentimental old gentleman can still make us afraid of the dark.

F. L. PATTEE

["The Record of a Clinic"] †

Never did he work from his emotions: always he viewed life objectively, coldly, accurately, recording only what he saw within the area he thought worthy of study. Never after his earlier period could he be swept away by his imagination or his feelings. "The Turn of the Screw," for instance, one of his most telling creations, illustrates perfectly the point. The story when he first heard it had appealed to him strongly on the side of the emotional and the romantic, and by an impulse rare with him he had done his best, as he has told us in one of his letters, to record it in the atmosphere of his original emotions. He had sought with all his art, as he has expressed it, "to give the impression of the communication to the children of the most infernal imaginable evil and danger. . . . I evoked the worst I could." Yet so fundamental was his scientific habit, his recording only that which had come within the range of his material experience, that the story may be read not as a ghost story at all, but as the record of a clinic: the study of the growth of a suggested infernal *cliché* in the brain of the nurse who alone sees the ghosts, of her final dementia which is pressed to a focus that overwhelms in her mind every other idea, and makes of the children her innocent victims. As such it becomes a record unspeakably pathetic. The boy becomes a brave little martyr. It is the triumph of science over romance.

†From *The Development of the American Short Story* (Harper and Brothers: New York, 1923), pp. 206–207. Reprinted by permission of the publishers.

Major Criticism:
1924-1957

Among the following essays "the last shall be first and first shall be last": the Goddard essay was not published until 1957, but was written in the early 1920's; and Leon Edel both begins and ends the section. Edmund Wilson fills the middle. The reason for this overall arrangement is that I am more interested in showing the *drift* of Jamesian criticism than in recording its exact bibliographical details. Even though Goddard's essay was not published until after the author's death the date of its composition is important, for the ideas which Goddard had around 1920 foretold a major shift in the winds of criticism of *The Turn of the Screw*, a shift further signalled by Edna Kenton's essay of 1924 which extolled the cleverness of the Master. By 1934, with the appearance of the special James issue of *Hound & Horn*, the clever, psychological James dominated critical thinking. But Wilson's designation, in that special issue, of the governess as "sex-repressed" and the ghosts as her "hallucinations" touched off a debate that continues even after three decades. As Martina Slaughter shows in her essay, the major objection lodged against Wilson was that he misread the text. So Robert Heilman charges in his essay included here. Heilman's reading of the story is interesting not only as an answer to Wilson and as a swing back to the good young governess trying to ward off evil spirits, but also as an example of the New Criticism that so dominated the literary scene in the late 1940's and early 1950's. Finally, the selection from Leon Edel fittingly closes the section because his chapter on "The Point of View" in *The Psychological Novel* showed how a peace could be arranged between the two camps of critics warring over the "proper" interpretation of *The Turn of the Screw*.

HAROLD C. GODDARD

A Pre-Freudian Reading of *The Turn of the Screw* †

Prefatory Note by Leon Edel: The following essay on Henry James's *The Turn of the Screw* was discovered among the posthumous papers of the late Harold C. Goddard, professor of English

† From *Nineteenth-Century Fiction*, XII (June, 1957), 1–36. Copyright © 1957 by the Regents of the University of California. Reprinted by permission of the editors.

and former head of the department at Swarthmore College. According to Professor Goddard's daughter, Eleanor Goddard Worthen, he read this essay to generations of students, but made no attempt to have it published. It was written, she says, "about 1920 or before," and this is evident from the critics he mentions, no one later than William Lyon Phelps. The manuscript was communicated by her to Edmund Wilson, whose 1934 essay on "The Ambiguity of Henry James" first propounded the hallucination theory of *The Turn of the Screw* with a bow in the direction of an earlier essay by the late Edna Kenton. Mr. Wilson, in turn, sent the Goddard paper to me and we both agreed that even at this late date, when the ink flows so freely around the Jamesian ghostly tale, it should be made available to scholars and critics.

To Professor Goddard must now go the credit of being the first to expound, if not to publish, a hallucination theory of the story. Indeed he went much farther than Mr. Wilson was to go after him—and without the aid of Sigmund Freud. Goddard's essay is a singularly valuable example of textual study. He relied wholly on what James had written, and he gave the tale that attentive reading which the novelist invited when he called his work a "trap for the unwary." Professor Goddard does not seem to have been aware, when he read the tale, that there was a "trap" in it. He is the only reader of *The Turn of the Screw* I have found who not only sought to understand the psychology of the governess but examined that heroine from the viewpoint of the children entrusted to her. No other critic has paid attention to the governess' account of the wild look in her own eyes, the terror in her face. Above all, however, we must be grateful to Professor Goddard's scrupulous analysis of the "identification" scene—the scene in which Mrs. Grose is led, step by step, to pronounce the name of Peter Quint. Even the most confirmed hallucinationists have never done sufficient justice to the ambiguity of this scene.

Before the discovery of this essay, Edna Kenton's "Henry James to the Ruminant Reader" published in *The Arts* in November, 1924, stood as the first to attract attention to the importance of the point of view in the tale: the fact that the story is told entirely through the governess' eyes. Miss Kenton did not suggest in her published essay the idea attributed to her by Edmund Wilson that the governess represented a "neurotic case of sex-repression." This idea was wholly Mr. Wilson's, and earlier seems to have been Ezra Pound's, who called the tale "a Freudian affair." Miss Kenton's article is patently innocent of any such theory, and those critics who have spoken of the "Kenton-Wilson" theory of *The Turn of the Screw* quite obviously had read only Wilson, not Kenton.

With the studies of Goddard, Kenton and Wilson before us, I

would suggest that three points are now clearly established: (1) that Henry James wrote a ghost story, a psychological thriller, intended to arouse a maximum of horror in the minds of his readers; (2) that a critical reading of the story to see how James achieved his horror reveals that he maneuvered the reader into the position of believing the governess' story even though her account contains serious contradictions and a purely speculative theory of her own as to the nature and purpose of the apparitions, which she alone sees; (3) that anyone wishing to treat the governess as a psychological "case" is offered sufficient data to permit the diagnosis that she is mentally disturbed. It is indeed valid to speculate that James, in speaking of a "trap," was alluding not only to the question of the governess' credibility as a witness, but to her actual madness.

There is one particular aspect of Professor Goddard's paper which we must not neglect. I refer to the fact that he was able to relate the story to his own memory of a governess he had when he was a boy. I think this important because it represents the use of the reader's personal experience for which James made so large an allowance—as he confided to his doctor, Sir James Mackenzie, who questioned him about the story, and also as he explained in his preface: that is James's refusal to specify the "horrors" so that the reader might fill them in for himself. Goddard's experience happened to be particularly close to the very elements in the story. There was thus a happy conjunction of personal fact with his "factual" reading.

Profesor Goddard's other works, also published posthumously, include *The Meaning of Shakespeare, Atomic Peace, Blake's Fourfold Vision,* and an article published in *College English* proposing that Hamlet's love letter was a forgery by Polonius.

A good many years ago I came upon *The Turn of the Screw* for the first time. I supposed I already knew what it was to be gripped by a powerful tale. But before I had read twenty pages I realized I had never encountered anything of this sort before. From the first, one of the things that chiefly struck me about James's tale was the way in which it united the thrills one is entitled to expect from a ghost story with the quality of being entirely credible, even by daylight. True, it evoked plenty of mystery, propounded plenty of enigmas, along the way. But the main idea of the thing was perfectly plain. So at any rate I thought. For it never occurred to me that there could be two opinions about that. What was my surprise, then, on taking it up with a group of students, to discover that not one of them interpreted it as I did. My faith in what seemed to me the obvious way of taking the story would have been shaken, had I not, on explaining it, found the majority of my fellow readers ready to prefer it to their own. And this experience was repeated with later groups. Yet, even after several years, it had not occurred to me that what seemed the natural interpretation of the narrative was not the generally accepted one among critics, however little it might be among students. And then one day I ran on a comment of Mr. Chesterton's on the story. He took it precisely as my students had. I began watching out in my reading for allusions to the story. I looked up several references to it. They all agreed. Evidently my view was utterly heretical. Naturally I asked myself more sharply than ever why I should take the tale as a matter of course in a way that did not seem to occur to other readers. Was it perversity on my part, or profundity? And then one day it dawned over me that perhaps it was neither. Perhaps it was the result rather of a remarkable parallelism between a strange passage in my own early experience (of which I will tell at the proper time) and what I conceived to be the situation in *The Turn of the Screw*. However that may be, at every rereading of the story I found myself adhering more firmly than ever to my original idea, and I continued to find that it met with hospitable reception among others. Not that there were no skeptics. Or now and then a strenuous objector.

It was not until long afterward that I happened to read James's own comment on *The Turn of the Screw* in the introduction to the collected edition of his works. A man with an hypothesis runs the risk of finding confirmation for it everywhere. Still, I set down for what it is worth the fact that in this introduction I thought I detected a very clear, but very covert, corroboration of the interpretation I favored, and later still, I got a similar impression, on the publication of James's letters,[1] from passages referring to the story.

I

From the point of view of early critics of the tale [Chesterton, Rebecca West, Carl Van Doren, Stuart P. Sherman, William Lyon Phelps, and others],[2] the story may be summarized, in bare outline, as follows:

An English gentleman, by the death of his brother in India, becomes guardian of a small niece and nephew whom he places in charge of a governess at his country home, Bly. On his departure from Bly, he leaves behind him his valet, a certain Peter Quint, with whom the governess, Miss Jessel, soon grows intimate. The valet is thus thrown in close contact with the children, with the boy in particular, who goes about with him as if he were his tutor. Quint and Miss Jessel are a depraved pair and the children do not escape exposure to their evil. As to the details of the contamination

2. Edel's addition. [Editor.]   1. 1920. [Editor.]

they suffer the author leaves us mercifully in the dark. But it is easy enough to guess its general nature. A point at any rate that is certain is the character of the language that the children pick up from their two protectors: language the use of which, later, was the cause of the boy's mysterious expulsion from school. Prior to this, however, Peter Quint, while drunk, slips on the ice and is killed, and Miss Jessel, whose reason for leaving Bly is broadly hinted, goes away—to die.

The world seems well rid of such a pair. But it turns out otherwise. For it is precisely at this point that the full horror of the situation develops and the infernal character of the tale emerges. Such, it transpires, was the passion of Quint and Miss Jessel to possess the souls of the innocent children that they return to their old haunts *after death*, appearing to their helpless victims and infecting them still further with their evil. Meanwhile, however, a new governess has been procured, who, fortunately for the children, is herself susceptible to visitation from the world beyond, and who, accordingly, does not long remain in the dark as to what is going on. Moved by a love for her little charges and a pity for them as deep as were the opposite emotions of their former companions, she attempts to throw herself as a screen between them and the discarnate fiends who pursue them, hoping that by accepting, as it were, the first shock of the impact she may shield and ultimately save the innocent children. In her protracted and lonely struggle with the agents of evil, she succeeds, but at a fearful price. The children are indeed dispossessed. But the little girl is driven in the process into a delirium which threatens the impairment of her intellect, while the boy expires at the very moment when he is snatched back from the brink of the abyss down which he is slipping.

So taken, the story is susceptible equally of two interpretations. It may be conceived, literally, as an embodiment of the author's belief in survival after death and in the power of spirits, in this case of evil spirits, to visit the living upon earth. Or, if one prefers, it may be taken as an allegory, in manner not unlike *Dr. Jekyll and Mr. Hyde:* the concrete representation of the truth that the evil that men do lives after them, infecting life long after they themselves are gone. Either way, except for the heroism of the second governess, the story is one of almost unmitigated horror. One can understand Mr. Chesterton's doubt as to whether the thing ought ever to have been published.

II

It is possible, however, to question the fidelity of either of these versions to the facts of the story and to ask whether another interpretation is not possible which will redeem the narrative from the charge of ugliness and render even its horror subordinate to its beauty.

Consider the second governess for a moment and the situation in which she finds herself. She is a young woman, only twenty, the daughter of a country parson, who, from his daughter's one allusion to him in her story, is of a psychically unbalanced nature; he may, indeed, even have been insane. We are given a number of oblique glimpses into the young woman's home and early environment. They all point to its stifling narrowness. From the confinement of her provincial home this young and inexperienced woman comes up to London to answer an advertisement for a governess. That in itself constitutes a sufficient crisis in the life of one who, after one glimpse, we do not need to be told is an excessively nervous and emotional person. But to add to the intensity of the situation the young woman falls instantly and passionately in love with the man who has inserted the advertisement. She scarcely admits it even to herself, for in her heart she knows that her love is hopeless, the object of her affection being one socially out of her sphere, a gentleman who can never regard her as anything other than a governess. But even this is not all. In her overwrought condition, the unexplained death of the former governess, her predecessor, was enough to suggest some mysterious danger connected with the position offered, especially in view of the master's strange stipulation: that the incumbent should assume *all* responsibility, even to the point of cutting off all communication with him— never writing, never reporting. Something extraordinary, she was convinced, lurked in the background. She would never have accepted the place if it had not been for her newborn passion: she could not bring herself to disappoint him when he seemed to beg compliance of her as a favor—to say nothing of severing her only link with the man who had so powerfully attracted her.

So she goes down to Bly, this slip of a girl, and finds herself no longer a poor parson's daughter but, quite literally, the head of a considerable country establishment. As if to impart the last ingredient to the witch's broth of her emotions, she is carried away almost to the point of ecstasy by the beauty of the two children, Miles and Flora, who have been confided to her care. All this could supply the material for a nervous breakdown in a girl of no worldly experience and of unstable psychical background. At any rate she instantly becomes the victim of insomnia. The very first night she fancies that she hears a light footstep outside her door and in the far distance the cry of a child. And more serious symptoms soon appear.

But before considering these, think what would be bound to happen even to a more normal mentality in such a situation. When a young person, especially a young woman, falls in love and circumstances forbid the normal growth and confession of the passion, the emotion, dammed up, overflows in a psychical experience, a daydream, or internal drama which the mind creates in lieu of the thwarted realization in the objective world. In romantic natures this takes the form of imagined deeds of extraordinary heroism or self-sacrifice done in behalf of the beloved object. The governess' is precisely such a nature and the fact that she knows her love is futile intensifies the tendency. Her whole being tingles with the craving to perform some act of unexplained courage. To carry out her duties as governess is not enough. They are too humdrum. If only the house would take fire by night, and both children be in peril! Or if one of them would fall into the water! But no such crudely melodramatic opportunities occur. What does occur is something far more indefinite, far more provocative to the imaginative than to the active faculties: the boy, Miles, is dismissed from school for no assigned or assignable reason. Once more, the hint of something evil and extraordinary behind the scenes! It is just the touch of objectivity needed to set off the subconsciousness of the governess into an orgy of myth-making. Another woman of a more practical and common sense turn would have made inquiries, would have followed the thing up, would have been insistent. But it is precisely complication and not explanation that this woman wants —though of course she does not know it. The vague feeling of fear with which the place is invested for her is fertile soil for imaginative invention and an inadvertent hint about Peter Quint dropped by the housekeeper, Mrs. Grose, is just the seed that that soil requires. There is no more significant bit of dialogue in the story. Yet the reader, unless he is alert, is likely to pass it by unmarked. The governess and the housekeeper are exchanging confidences. The former asks:

"What was the lady who was here before?"
"The last governess? She was also young and pretty—almost as young and almost as pretty, Miss, even as you."
"Ah then I hope her youth and her beauty helped her!" I recollect throwing off. "He seems to like us young and pretty!"
"Oh he *did*," Mrs. Grose assented: "it was the way he liked everyone!" She had no sooner spoken indeed than she caught herself up. "I mean that's *his* way—the master's."
I was struck. "But of whom did you speak first?"
She looked blank, but she coloured. "Why, of *him*."
"Of the master?"
"Of who else?"
There was so obviously no one else that the next moment I had lost my impression of her having accidentally said more than she meant.

The consciousness of the governess may have lost its impression, but we do not need to be students of psychology to know that that inveterate playwright and stage manager, the subsconscious, would never permit so valuable a hint to go unutilized.

Mrs. Grose, as her coloring shows and as the governess discerns, is thinking of some one other than the master. Of what man would she naturally think, on the mention of Miss Jessel, if not of Miss Jessel's running mate and partner in evil, Peter Quint? It is a momentary slip, but it is none the less fatal. It supplies the one character missing in the heroic drama that the governess' repressed desire is bent on staging: namely, the villain. The hero of that drama is behind the scenes: the master in Harley Street. The heroine, of course, is the governess herself. The villain, as we have said, is this unknown man who "liked them young and pretty." The first complication in the plot is the mysterious dismissal of the boy from school, suggestive of some dim power of evil shadowing the child. The plot itself remains to be worked out, but it will inevitably turn on some act of heroism or self-sacrifice—both by preference—on the part of the heroine for the benefit of the hero and to the discomfiture of the villain. It is a foregone conclusion, too, that the villain will be in some way connected with the boy's predicament at school. (That he really was is a coincidence.) All this is not conjecture. It is elemental human psychology.

Such is the material and plan upon which the dreaming consciousness of the governess sets to work. But how dream when one is the victim of insomnia? Daydream, then? But ordinary daydreams are not enough for the passionate nature of the governess. So she proceeds to act her drama out, quite after the fashion of a highly imaginative child at play. And the first scene of her dramatic creation is compressed into a few moments when she sees the stranger on the tower of Bly by twilight.

Whence does that apparition come? *Out of the governess's unconfessed love and unformulated fear.* It is clearly her love that first evokes him, for, as she tells us, she was thinking, as she strolled about the grounds that afternoon, how charming it would be suddenly to meet "some one," to have "someone" appear at the turn of a path and stand before her and smile and approve, when suddenly, with the face she longed to see still vividly present to her mind, she stopped short. "What arrested me on the spot," she says, "—and with a shock much greater than any vision had allowed for— was the sense that my imagination had, in a flash, turned real. He did stand there!—but high up, beyond the lawn and at the very top of the tower. . . ." Instantly, however, she perceives her mistake. It is not he. In her heart she knows it cannot be. But if her love is too good to be true, her fears, unfortunately, are only too true. And forthwith those fears seize and transform this creation of her imagination. "It produced in me," the governess declares, "this figure, in the clear twilight, I remember, two distinct gasps of emotion, which were, sharply, the shock of my first and that of my second surprise. My second was a violent perception of the mistake of my first: the man who met my eyes was not the person I had precipitately supposed. There came to me thus a bewilderment of vision of which, after these years, there is no living view that I can hope to give." What has happened? The hint that the housekeeper dropped of an unnamed man in the neighborhood has done its work. Around that hint the imagination of the governess precipitates the specter who is to dominate the rest of the tale. And because he is an object of dread he is no sooner evoked than he becomes the raw material of heroism. It only remains to link him with the children and the "play" will be under way with a rush.

This linking takes place on the Sunday afternoon when the governess, just as she is about to go out to church, becomes suddenly aware of a man gazing in at the dining room window. Instantly there comes over her, as she puts it, the "shock of a certitude that it was not for me he had come. He had come for someone else." "The flash of this knowledge," she continues, "—for it was knowledge in the midst of dread—produced in me the most extraordinary effect, starting, as I stood there, a sudden vibration of duty and courage." The governess feels her sudden vibration of duty and courage as the effect of the apparition, but it would be closer to the truth to call it its cause. Why has the stranger come for the children rather than for her? Because she must not merely be brave; she must be brave for someone's sake. The hero must be brought into the drama. She must save the beings whom he has commissioned her to protect. And that she may have the opportunity to save them they must be menaced: they must have enemies. That is the creative logic of her hallucination.

"Hallucination!" a dozen objectors will cry, unable to hold in any longer. "Why! the very word shows that you have missed the whole point of the story. The creature at the window is no hallucination. It is he himself, Peter Quint, returned from the dead. If not, how was Mrs. Grose able to recognize him—and later Miss Jessel—from the governess's description?"

The objection seems well taken. The point, indeed, is a capital one with the governess herself, who clings to it as unshakable proof that she is not mad; for Mrs. Grose, it appears, though she seems to accept her companion's account of her strange experiences, has moments of backsliding, of toying with the hypothesis that the ghosts are mere creatures of the governess' fancy. Whereupon, says the latter, "I had only to ask her how, if I had 'made it up,' I came to be able to give, of each of the persons appearing to me, a picture disclosing, to the last detail, their special marks—a portrait on the exhibition of which she had instantly recognized and named them." This retort floors Mrs. Grose completely, and she wishes "to sink the whole subject."

But Mrs. Grose is a trustful soul, too easily floored perhaps. If we will look into the matter a bit further than she did, we will perceive that it simply is not true that the governess gave such detailed descriptions of Peter Quint and Miss Jessel that Mrs. Grose instantly recognized their portraits. In the case of Miss Jessel, indeed, such a statement is the very reverse of the truth. The "detailed" description consisted, beyond the colorless fact that the ghost was pale, precisely of the two items that the woman who appeared was extremely beautiful and was dressed in black. But Mrs. Grose had already told the governess explicitly, long before any ghost was thought of, that Miss Jessel was beautiful. Whether she had been accustomed to dress in black we never learn. But that makes little difference, for the fact is that it is *the governess herself and not Mrs. Grose at all who does the identifying:*

> "Was she someone you've never seen?" asked Mrs. Grose.
> "Never," the governess replies. "But some one the child has. Some one *you* have." Then to show how I had thought it all out: "My predecessor—the one who died."
> "Miss Jessel?"
> "Miss Jessel," the governess confirms. "You don't believe me?"

And the ensuing conversation makes it abundantly plain that Mrs. Grose is still far from convinced. This seems a trifle odd in view of the fact that Peter Quint is known to be haunting the place. After having believed in one ghost, it ought not to be hard for Mrs. Grose to believe in another, especially when the human counterparts of the two were as inseparable in life as were the valet and the former governess. Which makes it look as if the housekeeper were perhaps not so certain after all in the case of Quint. Why, then, we ask, did she "identify him"? To which the answer is that she identified him because the suggestion for the identification, just as in the case of Miss Jessel, though much more subtly, comes from the governess herself. The skill with which James manages to throw the reader off the scent in this scene is consummate.

In the first place, the housekeeper herself, as we have had several occasions to remark, has already dropped an unintentional hint of someone in the neighborhood who preys on young and pretty governesses. This man, to be sure, is dead, but the new governess, who did not pay strict enough attention to Mrs. Grose's tenses, does not know it. We have already noted the part that the fear of him played in creating the figure on the tower. When now that figure comes closer and appears at the window, it would be strange indeed if, in turning over in her head all the possibilities, the idea of the unknown man to whom the housekeeper had so vaguely referred did not cross at least the fringe of the governess' consciousness. That it actually did is indicated by her prompt assumption that Mrs. Grose can identify their extraordinary visitor. "But now that you've guessed," are her words.

"Ah I haven't guessed," Mrs. Grose replies. And we are quite willing to agree that at this point she hasn't. But notice what follows:

The governess has assured Mrs. Grose that the intruder is not a gentleman.

"But if he isn't a gentleman—" the housekeeper begins.

"What *is* he?" asks the governess, completing the question and supplying the answer:

> "He's a horror."
> "A horror?"
> "He's—God help me if I know *what* he is!"
> Mrs. Grose looked round once more; she fixed her eyes on the duskier distance and then, pulling herself together, turned to me with full inconsequence. "It's time we should be at church."

What was the thought which was seeking entrance to Mrs. Grose's mind as she gazed at the duskier distance and which was sufficiently unwelcome to make her throw it off with her gesture and quick digression? Was it something that the word "horror" had suggested, something vaguely hinted in the governess's "He's— God help me if I know *what* he is!"—as if their visitant were a creature not altogether mortal? We cannot be sure. But when, immediately afterward, the governess refuses to go to church on the ground that the stranger is a menace to the *children*, there is no longer any question as to the thought that dawns over the housekeeper. *A horror in human form that is a menace to the children!* Is there anything, or anyone, in Mrs. Grose's experience that answers that description? A thousand times yes! Peter Quint. Can there be a shadow of doubt that it is Quint of whom she is thinking when, to use the author's words, her

> large face showed me, at this, for the first time, the far-away faint glimmer of a consciousness more acute: I somehow made out in it the delayed dawn of an idea I myself had not given her and that was as yet quite obscure to me. It comes back to me that I thought instantly of this as something I could get from her; and I felt it to be connected with the desire she presently showed to know more.

So do the governess' fears and repressed desires and the house-keeper's memories and anxieties unconsciously collaborate.

The conversation is resumed and the governess gives, in the most vivid detail, a picture of the man she has seen at the window. Following which, from the governess's challenge, "You *do* know him?" the housekeeper holds back for a second, only to admit, a moment later, that it is Peter Quint and to stagger her companion, in the next breath, by her calm declaration that Quint is dead.

Now with regard to all this the critical question is: Granted that Mrs. Grose's mind was already toying with the idea of Quint, how could she have identified him unless the governess' description tallied with the man? For, unlike Miss Jessel's, she has received no advance hint with regard to Quint's personal appearance, and the description, instead of being brief and generalized, is lengthy and concrete. The objection seems fatal to the view that the apparitions were mere creatures of the governess' imagination. But upon examination this line of argument will be found, I think, to prove too much.

Suppose a missing criminal is described as follows: "A squat, ruddy-cheeked man about thirty years old, weighing nearly two hundred pounds; thick lips and pockmarked face; one front tooth missing, two others with heavy gold fillings; big scar above left cheek bone. Wears shell glasses; had on, when last seen, brown suit, gray hat, pink shirt and tan shoes." Then suppose a man, flushed with excitement, were to rush into police headquarters exclaiming that he had found the murderer. "How do you know?" the chief detective asks. "Why! I saw a man about thirty years old with shell glasses and tan shoes!"

Well, it is only a slight exaggeration to say that Mrs. Grose's "identification" of Peter Quint, in the face of the governess' description, is of exactly this sort. The picture the latter draws of the face at the window, with its red curling hair and peculiar whiskers, is so vivid and striking that Mrs. Grose, if she was listening and if it was indeed a description of Quint, ought not to have hesitated a second. But she did hesitate. It may of course be said that she hesitated not because the description did not fit but because Quint was dead. But if so, why, when she does identify him, does she pick out the least characteristic points in the description? Why, when she does "piece it all together" (what irony in that "all"!), does her identification rest not at all on the red whiskers or the thin mouth, but, of all things, on the two facts that the stranger wore no hat and that his clothes looked as if they belonged to someone else? As if good ghosts always wore hats and bad ones carried their terrestrial pilferings into eternity! That touch about "the missing waistcoats" is precisely at Mrs. Grose's intellectual level, the level, as anyone who has ever had the curiosity to attend one knows, of a fifth-rate spiritualist seance.

The thing is really so absurd that we actually wonder whether Mrs. Grose was listening. Recall the beginning of the dialogue:

> "What's he like?" [asks Mrs. Grose].
> "I've been dying to tell you. But he's like nobody."
> "Nobody?" she echoed.
> "He has no hat." Then seeing in her face that she already, in this, with a deeper dismay, found a touch of picture, I quickly added stroke to stroke.

We see what we expect to see. That Mrs. Grose should so instantaneously find a touch of picture in the colorless item that "he had no hat" is a measure of the high degree of her suggestibility, as good proof as one could want that an image is already hovering in the background of her mind waiting to rush into the foreground at the faintest summons. That, as we have seen, is exactly what the image of Peter Quint is doing. And so, is it at all unlikely that in completing the picture of which the mention of the hat has supplied the first touch, Mrs. Grose pays scant attention to the other, verbal picture that the governess is drawing? The point need not be urged, but at any rate she gives no evidence of having heard, and at the governess' concluding sentence, "He gives me a sort of sense of looking like an actor," her echoed "An actor!" sounds almost as if it were at that point that her wandering attention were called back. That of course is only conjecture. But what is not conjecture, and significant enough, is the fact that the two shaky pegs on which Mrs. Grose hangs her identification come, one at the very beginning, the other at the very end, of a long description the intervening portions of which would have supplied her, any one of them, with solid support. When a man crosses a stream on a rotten wooden bridge in spite of the fact that there is a solid one of stone a rod or two away, you naturally wonder whether he has noticed it.

III

"But why waste so much breath," it will be said, "over what is after all such a purely preliminary part of the story and over such an incidental character as Mrs. Grose. Come to the main events, and to the central characters, the children. What *then* becomes of your theory that Quint and Miss Jessel are just hallucinations? How can they be that, when Miles and Flora see them?"

Before coming to this certainly pertinent objection, I wonder if I may interject the personal experience mentioned at the beginning. It may be that this experience subconsciously accounts for my reading of *The Turn of the Screw*. If its influence is justified, it is worth recounting. If it is unjustified, it should be narrated that the reader may properly discount its effect on my interpretation of the tale. It may be that for me this memory turns into realism what for even the author was only romance.

When I was a boy of seven or eight, and my sister a few years older, we had a servant in the family—a Canadian woman, I think she was—who, I now see on looking back (though no one then suspected it), was insane. Some years later her delusions became marked, her insanity was generally recognized, and she was for a time at least confined in an asylum. Now it happened that this woman, who was of an affectionate nature and loved children, used to tell us stories. I do not know whether they were all of one kind, but I do know that the only ones my memory retained were of dead people who came to visit her in the night. I remember with extraordinary vividness her account of a woman in white who came and stood silent at the foot of her bed. I can still see the strange smile—the insane smile, as I now recognize it to have been —that came over the face of the narrator as she told of this visitant. This woman did not long remain a servant in our family. But suppose she had! Suppose our parents had died, or, for some other reason, we had been placed exclusively in her care. (She was a woman of unimpeachable character and kindliest impulses.) What might have happened to us? What might not! Especially if she had conceived the notion that some of her spiritual visitants were of an infernal character and had come to gain possession of us, the children for whom she was responsible. I tremble to think. And yet no greater alteration than this would have been called for in an instance within the range of my own experience to have duplicated essentially what I conceive to be the situation in *The Turn of the Screw.*

Now the unlikelihood of this situation's occurring is precisely the fact that in real life someone would recognize the insanity and interfere to save the children. This was the difficulty that confronted the author of *The Turn of the Screw,* if we may assume for the moment that I have stated his problem correctly. The extraordinary skill and thoroughness with which he has met it are themselves the proof, it seems to me, that he had that difficulty very consciously in his mind. He overcomes it by fashioning the characters of the master and the housekeeper expressly to fit the situation. The children's uncle, from the first, wishes to wash his hands entirely of their upbringing, to put them unreservedly in the hands of their governess, who is *never*, in any conceivable way, to put up her problems or questions to him in person or by letter. The insistence on this from beginning to end seems needlessly emphatic unless it serves some such purpose as the one indicated.

The physical isolation of the little household in the big estate at Bly is also complete. The governess is in supreme authority; only she and the housekeeper have anything to do with the children —and Mrs. Grose's character is shaped to fit the plot. If she is the incarnation of practical household sense and homely affection, she is utterly devoid of worldly experience and imagination. And she is as superstitious as such a person is likely to be. She can neither read nor write, the latter fact, which is a capital one, being especially insisted on. She knows her place and has a correspondingly exalted opinion of persons of higher rank or education. Hence her willingness, even when she cannot understand, to accept as truth whatever the governess tells her. She loves the children deeply and has suffered terribly for them during the reign of Quint and Miss Jessel. (Her relief on the arrival of Miss Jessel's successor, which the latter notices and misinterprets, is natural.) Here is a character, then, and a situation, ideally fitted to allow of the development of the governess' mania unnoticed. James speaks of the original suggestion for *The Turn of the Screw* as "the vividest little note for sinister romance that I had ever jotted down," expressing wonder at the same time "why so fine a germ, gleaming there in the wayside dust of life, had never been deftly picked up." His note, he says in one of his letters, was "of a most scrappy kind." The form which the idea assumed in his mind as it developed we can only conjecture. My own guess would be that it might, in content at least, have run something like this: *Two children, under circumstances where there is no one to realize the situation, are put, for bringing up, in the care of an insane governess.*

IV

With this hypothesis as a clue, we can trace the art with which James hypnotizes us into forgetting that it is the governess' version of the story to which we are listening, and lures us, as the governess unconsciously lured Mrs. Grose, into accepting her coloring of the facts for the facts themselves.

It is solely on the governess' say-so that we agree to the notion that the two specters have returned in search of the *children*. Again it is on her unsupported word that we accept for fact her statement that, on the occasion in the garden when Miss Jessel first appeared, Flora *saw*. The scene itself, after Miss Jessel's advent, is not presented. (Time enough to present his scenes when James has "suggested" to his readers what they shall see.) What happened is narrated by the governess, who simply announces flatly to Mrs. Grose that, "Two hours ago, in the garden, Flora *saw*." And when Mrs. Grose naturally enough demands, ". . . how do you know?" her only answer is, "I was there—I saw with my eyes," an answer valuable or worthless in direct proportion to the governess' power to see things as they are.

In the case of Miles the method is the same except that James, feeling that he now has a grip on the reader, proceeds more boldly. The scene is not narrated this time; it is presented—but only indirectly. The governess, looking down from a window, catches Miles out at midnight on the lawn. He gazes up, as nearly as she can figure, to a point on the building over her head. Whereupon she promptly draws the inference: "There was clearly another person above me—there was a person on the tower." This, when we stop to think, is even "thinner" than in the case of Flora and Miss Jessel, for this time even the governess does not see, she merely infers. The boy gazes up. "Clearly" there was a man upon the tower. That "clearly" lets the cat out of the bag. It shows, as every tyro in psychology should know, that "clear" is precisely what the thing is not.

These two instances are typical of the governess' mania. She seizes the flimsiest pretexts for finding confirmation of her suspicions. Her theories swell to such immense dimensions that when the poor little facts emerge they are immediately swallowed up. She half admits this herself at the very beginning of the story: "It seems to me indeed, in raking it all over," she says of the night following the appearance of Quint at the dining room window, "that by the time the morrow's sun was high I had restlessly read into the facts before us almost all the meaning they were to receive from subsequent and more cruel occurrences." Scarcely ever was the essence of mania better compressed into a sentence than in her statement: "The more I go over it the more I see in it, and the more I see in it the more I fear. I don't know what I *don't* see, what I *don't* fear!" Or again, where in speaking of the children's lessons and her conversations with them she says:

> All roads lead to Rome, and there were times when it might have struck us that almost every branch of study or subject of conversation skirted forbidden ground. Forbidden ground was the question of the return of the dead in general and of whatever, in special, might survive, for memory, of the friends little children had lost. There were days when I could have sworn that one of them had, with a small invisible nudge, said to the other: "She thinks she'll do it this time—but she won't!" To "do it" would have been to indulge for instance—and for once in a way—in some direct reference to the lady who had prepared them for my discipline.

And from this she goes on to the conviction that the children have fallen into the habit of entertaining Quint and Miss Jessel unknown to her.

"There were times of our being together when I would have been ready to swear that, literally, in my presence, but with my direct sense of it closed, they had visitors who were known and were welcome. Then it was that, had I not been deterred by the very chance that such an injury might prove greater than the injury to be averted, my exaltation would have broken out. "They're here, they're here, you little wretches," I would have cried, "and you can't deny it now!'"

Her proof in these cases, it will be noted, is the fact that she "could have sworn" that it was so.

How completely innocent and natural the children really were through all these earlier passages of the drama anyone will see who will divest himself of the suggestion that the governess has planted in his mind. The pranks they play are utterly harmless, and when she questions the perpetrators, because they are perfectly truthful, they have the readiest and most convincing answers at hand. Why did little Miles get up in the middle of the night and parade out on the lawn? Just as he said, in order that, for once, she might think him *bad*. Why did Flora rise from her bed at the same hour? By agreement with Miles. Why did she gaze out the window? To disturb her governess and make her look too. These answers, true every one, ought to have disarmed the children's inquisitor. But she has her satanic hypothesis, so that the very readiness of their replies convicts instead of acquitting them in her eyes. They are inspired answers, she holds, splendidly but diabolically inspired. They scintillate with a mental power beyond the children's years. "Their more than earthly beauty, their absolute unnatural goodness. It's a game," she cries, "it's a policy and a fraud!"

And the same is true of the children's conversation as of their conduct. Always their remarks are direct and ingenious; always she reads into them an infernal meaning—until, when she says of Miles, ". . . horrible as it was his lies made up my truth," we see that the exact reverse of this is the case: that in reality his truth, and Flora's, made up her lies. If Miles asks about "this queer business of ours," meaning the queer way his education is being attended to, she takes it as referring to the boy's queer intercourse with Quint. If, when she remarks to Miles that they are alone, the latter replies that they still have "the others," obviously referring to the servants, the governess is not content to take his words at their face value but must interpret "the others" as referring to the specters. So candid, so unsophisticated, so prompt are the children's answers that even the governess' insane conviction at times seems shaken. But always—so James contrives it—some convenient bit of *objective* evidence comes in to reassure her: the fearful language that Flora uses in her delirium, the boy's lie about the letter, the clear evidence at the end that he has something on his mind that he longs to confess.

As these last examples suggest, it is necessary to qualify the idea that Miles and Flora are just happy natural children. They are that during the earlier passages of the story. But they do not continue to be. And the change is brought about by no one but the governess herself. Herein lies one of the subtlest aspects of the story.

Fear is like faith: it ultimately creates what at first it only imagined. The governess, at the beginning, imagines that the actions and words of the children are strange and unnatural. In the end they become strange and unnatural for the good and sufficient reason that the children gradually become conscious of the strangeness and unnaturalness of her own attitude toward them. They cannot put it into words: they have never heard of nervousness, still less of insanity. But they sense it and grow afraid, and she accepts the abnormal condition into which their fear of *her* has thrown them as proof of their intercourse with the two specters. Thus do her mania and their fear feed and augment each other, until the situation culminates—in a preliminary way—in two scenes of shuddering terror.

The first of these is the occasion when the governess comes at night to Miles's bedside and tries, without mentioning the dreaded name of Quint, to wring from the child a confession of the infernal intercourse which, she is convinced, he is guilty of holding. Forget, for the moment, the governess' version of the occurrence and think of it as it must have appeared to the child. A little boy of ten, who has for some time felt something creepy and uncanny in the woman who has been placed in charge of him and his sister, lies awake in the dark thinking of her and of the strangeness of it all. He hears steps outside his door. At his call the door opens, and there, candle in hand, is this very woman. She enters and sits beside him on the edge of the bed. For a moment or two she talks naturally, asking him why he is not asleep. He tells her. And then, quite suddenly, he notices in her voice the queer tone he has felt before, and the something in her manner, excited but suppressed, that he does not like. As they go on talking, this excitement grows and grows, until in a final outburst she falls on her knees before him and begs him to let her *save* him! Visualize the scene: the hapless child utterly at a loss to know what the dreadful "something" is from which she would "save" him; the insane woman on her knees almost clasping him in her hysterical embrace. Is it any wonder that the interview terminates in a shriek that bursts from the lips of the terror-stricken boy? Nothing could be more natural. Yet, characteristically, the governess interprets the boy's fright and outcry as convincing proof of the presence of the creature she is seeking to exorcise. Utterly unconscious of the child's fear of *her*, she attributes his agitation to the only other adequate cause she can conceive.

The corresponding scene in the case of Flora occurs the next day by the lake. Once more, think of it from the angle of the child. A little girl, too closely watched and confined by her governess, seizes an opportunity for freedom that presents itself and wanders off for half an hour in the grounds of the estate where she lives. A little later, the governess and the housekeeper, out of breath with searching, come upon her. A half-dozen words have hardly been exchanged when the governess, a tremor in her voice, turns suddenly on the child and demands to know where her former governess is—a woman whom the little girl knows perfectly well is dead and buried. The child's face blanches, the housekeeper utters a cry, in answer to which the governess, pointing across the lake and into vacancy cries out: "She's there, she's there!" The child stares at the demented woman in consternation. The latter repeats: "She's there, you little unhappy thing—there, there, *there*, and you know it as well as you know me!" The little girl holding fast to the housekeeper, is frozen in a convulsion of fear. She recovers herself sufficiently to cry out, "I don't know what you mean. I see nobody. I see nothing. I never *have*," and then, hiding her head in the housekeeper's skirts, she breaks out in a wail, "Take me away, take me away—oh take me away from *her*!"

"From *me*?" the governess cries, as if thunderstruck that it is not from the specter that she asks to be delivered.

"From you—from you!" the child confirms.

Again, is not the scene, when innocently taken, perfectly natural? Yet again the governess is incapable of perceiving that the child is striken with terror not at all at the apparition but at *her* and the effect the apparition has had upon her.

V

"All of which is very clever and might be very convincing," it will be promptly objected, "if it did not calmly leave out of account the paramount fact of the whole narrative, that in the end Miles *does* see and identifies Quint by name. It was this "supreme surrender of the name" that justified and redeemed the governess' devotion. Never, never—it was a point of honor—had the name of Quint crossed her lips in Miles's presence. When, then, it crossed his lips in her presence, it was the long sought proof that from the first he had been holding communication with the spirit of the dead man. That is the very point and climax of the story."

If you think so, you have failed to trace the chain of causation down which the name of Peter Quint vibrates from the brain of the governess to the lips of little Miles.[3] True, it was a point of honor with her not to breathe the name of Quint in the children's presence. But how about the name of Quint's companion? Ought not silence with regard to Miss Jessel's to have been equally sacred? It surely should have been. But there, it will be remembered, the governess' self-control failed her. On that day, by the lake, when, as we have seen, she blurted out to Flora her fatal, "Where, my pet, is Miss Jessel?" only to answer her own question a second later by gazing into what to the two others was vacancy and shrieking, "She's there, she's there!" she fixed forever in the child's mind a bond between her own (that is, the governess') strange "possession" and the name of Miss Jessel.

Flora, as we have remarked, is driven half out of her senses with fright, and while she has never "seen" Miss Jessel previously, nothing is more probable than that she "sees" her now. At the very least, memories of her and of the time the child was in her care figure prominently in the delirium that follows the shock of witnessing the governess' strange affliction. Whatever Flora's feelings toward her former governess originally were, from now on they will be linked inextricably with her fear of her present one. The two are merged in a single complex. How do we know? Because the child, in her delirium, uses shocking language or ideas which she has picked up in the days when Miss Jessel consorted with Peter Quint. To poor Mrs. Grose this is, at last, final proof that the governess is right in suspecting the little girl of diabolical intercourse. To the reader it ought to be proof of nothing of the sort. Nearly everyone remembers the case of the ignorant maidservant of the Hebrew scholar who, on being hypnotized, would overflow in a torrent of extraordinary fluent Hebrew. This gift came very far from proving her learned in Hebrew. Quite as little did the "horrors," to use Mrs. Grose's word, to which Flora gives utterance in her fever prove her a depraved or vicious child. An interesting parallel and variant of the same motive is found in the innocent profanity of Hareton Earnshaw in *Wuthering Heights,* verbally shocking language from the lips of a rarely beautiful character.

The next link in the chain is the fact that Miles sees Flora between the time she is taken ill and the scene of his final interview with the governess. The very brevity of the author's reference to this fact suggests his expectation that the breathless or unwary reader will read right over it without getting its significance. (If it has no significance, why mention it at all?) The governess, fearing that Flora, who has now turned against her, will influence Miles to do the same, warns Mrs. Grose against giving her the opportunity to do so.

3. For I do not think we are entitled to infer that Miles learned anything from the stolen letter.

"There's one thing, of course" [she says]: "they mustn't, before she goes, see each other for three seconds." Then it came over me that, in spite of Flora's presumable sequestration from the instant of her return from the pool, it might already be too late. "Do you mean," I anxiously asked, "that they *have* met?"

At this she quite flushed. "Ah, Miss, I'm not such a fool as that! If I've been obliged to leave her three or four times, it has been each time with one of the maids, and at present, though she's alone, she's locked in safe. And yet—and yet!" There were too many things.

"And yet what?"

Mrs. Grose never really answers this "And yet what?" which, together with her flushing when the governess asks her if the children have met, more than intimates that they already have, especially in view of the assumed complete trustworthiness of "the maids." That they do meet later, at any rate, we know from half a sentence thrown in with seeming inadvertence in the next chapter. Vague as the matter is left, it is clear that the boy had an opportunity to fix in his mind a connection between his sister's illness, her dread of their present governess, and—Miss Jessel. It was an uncomprehended connection to be sure, but its effect on the boy's mind must have been all the more powerful on that account—and the more so at this particular moment because under the stress of the governess' attempt to extort a confession from him his mind was already magnifying his venial fault about the letter into a mortal sin.

When, then, at the end, the governess in the presence of her hallucination shrieks to Peter Quint that he shall possess her boy "No more, no more, no more!" and the child, panting in her insane embrace, realizes that she sees someone at the window, how natural, how inevitable, that he should ask if "she" is "*here*," and to the echoed question of the governess, who this "she" is, should reply, "Miss Jessel, Miss Jessel!" Bear in mind that, all through, it is Miss Jessel, according to the governess, who has been visiting Flora, while it is Quint who has been holding communication with Miles. Why, if the boy has been in the habit of consorting with the spirit of Quint and if he senses now the nearness of a ghostly visitant, why, I say, does he not ask if *he* is here? Surely, then, his "Is *she* here?" is the best possible proof that the idea of a spiritual presence has been suggested not at all by past experiences of a similar sort but precisely by something he has overheard from Flora, or about her, plus what he gets at the moment from the governess.

"I seized, stupified, his supposition," she says at his utterance of Miss Jessel's name, "—some sequel to what we had done to Flora, but this made me only want to show him that it was better still than that." (In one flash that "better" lays bare the governess' possession!) "It's not Miss Jessel!" she goes on. "But it's at the window—straight before us. It's *there*, the coward horror, there for the last time!"

If we could hear her voice when she cries, "It's not Miss Jessel!" I suspect that her intonation of the last two words would show how completely, if unconsciously, she conveyed *to* the boy's mind the very name which her whole justification depended on receiving *from* him. The child's next question, "It's *he?*" is but an ellipsis for "If, then, it is not *she*, you mean it must be the other one of the two who were always together?" But the governess, determined not to be the first to mention the unmentionable name, demands, "Whom do you mean by 'he'?

"Peter Quint—you devil!" is the child's reply in words that duplicate, more briefly and even more tragically, the psychology of the "horrors" uttered by his sister in her delirium. But even now he doe not see, though he accepts the governess' assurance that Peter Quint is there. "*Where?*" he cries. And that last word his lips ever utter, as his eye roams helplessly about the room in a vain endeavor to *see*, gives the ultimate lie to the notion that he does see now or has ever seen. But the governess, deluded to the end, takes it as meaning that at last the horror is exorcised and the child himself dispossessed.

VI

If on your first reading of *The Turn of the Screw* the hypothesis did not occur to you that the governess is insane, run through the story again and you will hardly know which to admire more, James's daring in introducing the cruder physical as distinguished from the subtler psychological symptoms on insanity or his skill in covering them up and seeming to explain them away. The insane woman is telling her own story. She cannot see her own insanity— she can only see its reflection, as it were, in the faces, trace its effect on the acts, of others. And because "the others" are in her case children and an ignorant and superstitious woman, these reflections and effects are to be found in the sphere of their emotions rather than in that of their understandings. They see and feel her insanity, but they cannot comprehend or name it.

The most frequent mark of her disease is her insane *look* which is mirrored for us in the countenances and eyes of the others.

Mrs. Grose first sees this look in something like its fullness when the governess gazes through the window of the dining room after she has seen Peter Quint. So terrible is the sight of her face that Mrs. Grose draws back blanched and stunned, quite as if it were a ghost that she had seen. "Did I look very queer?" the governess asks a moment later when the housekeeper has joined her.

"Through this window?" Mrs. Grose returns. "Dreadful!"

There are a dozen other passages that strike the same note:

"I was conscious as I spoke that I looked prodigious things," says the governess, "for I got the slow reflection of them in my companion's face."

"Ah with such awful eyes!" she exclaims in another passage, referring to the way Miss Jessel fixed her gaze on Flora. Whereupon, she continues, Mrs. Grose "stared at mine as if they might really have resembled them." And a moment later: "Mrs. Grose—her eyes just lingering on mine—gave a shudder and walked to the window."

In a later conversation between the same two: "I don't wonder you looked queer," says the governess, "when I mentioned to you the letter from his school!" "I doubt if I looked as queer as you!" the housekeeper retorts.

"I remember that, to gain time, I tried to laugh," the governess writes of her walk to church with Miles, "and I seemed to see in the beautiful face with which he watched me how ugly and queer I looked."

To which should be added the passage, too long to quote, in which Flora recognizes for the first time the full "queerness" of her governess, the passage that culminates in her agonized cry: "Take me away, take me away—oh take me away from *her!*"

The governess' insane laugh, as well as her insane look, is frequently alluded to. Of this we have just mentioned one example. Of references to her maniacal cries there are several: "I had to smother a kind of howl," she says when Mrs. Grose tells her of Quint's relations with the children. Or again, when she catches Miss Jessel sitting at her table: "I heard myself break into a sound that, by the open door, rang through the long passage and the empty house." What do we say of persons who shriek in empty houses—or who frighten children into similar outbreaks? "The boy gave a loud shriek which, lost in the rest of the shock of sound, might have seemed, indistinctly, though I was so close to him, a note either of jubilation or of terror."

The wonder is not that the children cried out, but that they did not cry out sooner or oftener. "I must have gripped my little girl with a spasm that, wonderfully, she submitted to without a cry or a sign of fright." The implications of that sentence prepare us for the scene in Miles's bedchamber where the governess falls on her knees before the boy for the final scene where she locks him in her insane embrace.

But the psychological symptoms are more interesting than the more obviously physical ones.

The consciousness of the governess that she is skirting the brink of the abyss is especially significant. It reminds us of Lear's: "That way madness lies." Only in her case we have to take her word for it that she never goes over the edge.

"We were to keep our heads," she says, "if we should keep nothing else—difficult indeed as that might be. . . ."

"I began to watch them in a stifled suspense," she remarks of the children, "a disguised tension, that might well, had it continued too long, have turned to something like madness. What saved me, as I now see, was that it turned to another matter altogether." Of the truth of this last assertion the governess presents precisely nothing but her own words as proof. Or, to put it from her own angle, she presents—the apparitions. "She was there," she says of Miss Jessel's appearance by the lake, "so I was justified; she was there, so I was neither cruel nor mad." The irony of summoning a specter as witness that one is not mad is evident enough.

Indeed this style of reasoning does not quite satisfy the governess herself in her more normal intervals. There are moments throughout the tale when a lurking doubt of her own sanity comes to the surface. When, for instance, Mrs. Grose begs her to write to the master and explain their predicament, she turns on her with the question whether she can write him that his little niece and nephew are mad. "But if they *are*, Miss?" says Mrs. Grose. "And if I am myself, you mean?" the governess retorts. And when she is questioning Miles, on the very edge of the final catastrophe, the same paralyzing thought floats for a second into her consciousness: ". . . if he *were* innocent what then on earth was I?" That she never succeeded in utterly banishing this terrible hypothesis is shown by the view of the case she takes long after the events are over and she is writing her account of them. "It was not," she sets it down, "I am as sure to-day as I was sure then, my mere infernal imagination." Clear proof that she was sure at neither time.

There are a dozen other passages, if there were only space to quote them, that show how penetratingly, if unconsciously, the sane remnant of the governess' nature can diagnose her own case and comprehend the character of the two apparitions. "What arrested me on the spot," she says of the figure on the tower, ". . . was the sense that my imagination had, in a flash, turned real." "There were shrubberies and big trees," she says when she is hunting for Quint on the lawn, "but I remember the clear assurance I felt that none of them concealed him. He was there or was not there: not there if I didn't see him." The account of the first appearance of Miss Jessel, too, if read attentively, reveals clearly the psychological origin of the apparition, as does the governess' account of the experience, later, to Mrs. Grose:

"I was there with the child—quiet for the hour; and in the midst of it she came."

"Came how—from where?"

"From where they come from! She just appeared and stood there—but not so near."

"And without coming nearer?"

"Oh for the effect and the feeling she might have been as close as you!"

But perhaps the most interesting and convincing point in this whole connection is the fact that the appearance of the ghosts is timed to correspond not at all with some appropriate or receptive moment in the children's experience but very nicely with some mental crisis in the governess'. In the end their emergence is a signal, as it were, of a further loss of self-control on her part, an advance in her mania. "Where, my pet, is Miss Jessel?" she asks Flora, committing the tragic indiscretion of mentioning the interdicted name. And presto! Miss Jessel appears. "Tell me," she says, pressing Miles cruelly to the wall in their last interview, "if, yesterday afternoon, from the table in the hall, you took, you know, my letter." And instantly Peter Quint comes into view "like a sentinel before a prison." But the last instance of all is the most revealing. With the ruthlessness of an inquisitor she has extorted from Miles the confession that he "said things" at school. It is not enough that he tells her to whom he said them. She must follow it up to the bitter end. "What *were* these things?" she demands unpardonably. Whereupon, "again, against the glass, as if to blight his confesson and stay his answer, was the hideous author of our woe— the white face of damnation." If perfect synchronization is any criterion, surely, with these instances before us, the inference is inescapable that if Peter Quint has come out of the grave to infect or capture anyone, it is the governess and not the child.

VII

There will doubtless be those who can quite agree with all I have said about *The Turn of the Screw* who will nevertheless not thank me for saying it. "Here was the one ghost story left," they will protest, "that carried a genuine mystery in it. And you proceed to rationalize it ruthlessly, to turn it, in James's own words, into a 'mere modern "psychical" case, washed clean of all queerness as by exposure to a flowing laboratory tap.' What a pity!"

But do I rationalize it, ruthlessly or otherwise? Is sanity something easier to probe and get to the bottom of than a crude spiritualism? Are Peter Quint and Miss Jessel a whit less mysterious or less appalling because they are evoked by the governess's imagination? Are they a whit less real? Surely the human brain is as solid a fact as the terrestrial globe, and inhabitants of the former have just as authentic an existence as inhabitants of the latter. Nor do I mean by that to imply, as to some I will seem to have implied all through, that Peter Quint and Miss Jessel exist *only* in the brain of the governess. Perhaps they do and perhaps they don't. Like Hawthorne in similar situations—but with an art that makes even Hawthorne look clumsy—James is wise enough and intellectually humble enough to leave that question open. Nobody knows enough about insanity yet to be dogmatic on such a matter. Whether the insane man creates his hallucinations or whether insanity is precisely the power to perceive objective existences of another order, whether higher or lower, than humanity, no open-minded person can possibly pretend to say, however preponderating in the one direction or the other present evidence may seem to him to be. Whoever prefers to, then, is free to believe that the governess sees the actual spirits of Peter Quint and Miss Jessel. Nothing in the tale, I have tried to show, demands that hypothesis. But nothing on the other hand, absolutely contradicts it. Indeed, there is room between these extremes for a third possibility. Perhaps the governess' brain caught a true image of Peter Quint straight from Mrs. Grose's memory via the ether or some subtler medium of thought transference. The tale in these respects is susceptible of various readings. But for one theory it offers, I hold, not an inch of standing ground: for the idea, namely, that the children *saw*.

This is the crucial point. Everything else is incidental. Believe that the children saw, and the tale is one thing. Believe that they did not see, and it is another—as different as light from darkness. Either way the story is one of the most powerful ever written. But in the former event it is merely dreadful. In the latter it is dreadful, but also beautiful. One way, it is a tale of corrupted childhood. The other, it is a tale of incorruptible childhood. Of the two, can it be doubted which it is? Miles and Flora are touched, it is true, by the evil of Peter Quint and Miss Jessel, but they are not tainted. The evil leaves its mark, if you will, but no trace of stain or smirch. The children remain what they were—incarnations of loveliness and charm. Innocence is armor plate: that is what the story seems to say. And does not life bear out that belief? Otherwise, in what but infamy would the younger generation ever end? Miles and Flora, to be sure, are withered at last in the flame of the governess' passion. But corrupted—never! And the withering of them in the flame is rendered tragic rather than merely horrible by the heroism that they display. The things that children suffer in silence! Because, as here, their heroism generally takes the form of endurance rather than of daring, rarely, if ever, in literature or in life, is justice done to the incredible, the appalling courage of childhood. This story does do justice to it.

But in stressing the courage of the children, we must not pass over the same quality in the governess. That is clear enough however we read the tale. But her courage gets an added value, if we accept her mental condition as abnormal, from the fact of its showing the shallowness of the prevailing notion that insanity inevitably betokens a general breakdown of the higher faculties. It may mean that. But it may not. No small part of the horror and tragedy of our treatment of the insane flows from our failure to realize that mental aberration may go hand in hand with strength and beauty of character. It does in this case. The governess is deluded, but she rises to the sublime in her delusion.

The tale clarifies certain of the causes of insanity also. The hereditary seed of the disease in this instance is hinted at in the one reference to the young woman's father. And her environment was precisely the right one for its germination. The reaction upon a sensitive and romantic nature of the narrowness of English middle class life in the last century; that, from the social angle, is the theme of the story. The sudden change of scene, the sudden immense responsibility placed on unaccustomed shoulders, the shock of sudden unrequited affection—all these together—were too much. The brain gives way. And what follows is a masterly tracing of the effects of repressed love and thwarted maternal affection. The whole story might be reviewed with profit under this psychoanalytic aspect. But when it was done, less would probably have been conveyed than James packs into a single simile. He throws it out, with seeming nonchalance, during the governess's last interview, after Flora's delirium, with little Miles:

> Our meal was of the briefest—mine a vain pretense, and I had the things immediately removed. While this was done Miles stood again with his hands in his little pockets and his back to me—stood and looked out of the wide window through which, that other day, I had seen what pulled me up. We continued silent while the maid was with us—as silent, it whimsically occurred to me, as some young couple who, on their wedding-journey, at the inn, feel shy in the presence of the waiter.

The simile strikes the governess as whimsical. Whimsical in reality is precisely what it is not, guiding us, as it does, straight into her soul and plucking out the mystery of her lacerated heart.

VIII

If anyone will take the trouble to read in the letters of Henry James, all the passages referring to *The Turn of the Screw*, I shall be surprised if he does not come away with the impression—which at any rate is emphatically mine—of a very charming and good-humored, but a nonetheless very unmistakable, side-stepping of questions or comments which had evidently been flung at him, touching his "bogey-tale," as he calls it, by H. G. Wells, F. W. H. Myers, and at least one other correspondent—a side-stepping to the effectiveness of which, without risk of offence to its victims, James's peculiar style was not less than gloriously adapted. He consistently deprecates his tale as a "very mechanical matter. . . . an inferior, a merely *pictorial*, subject, and rather a shameless pot-boiler." The element of truth in this is obvious. We need not question James's sincerity. But in the face of the long list of notable critics and readers who, with different turns of phrase, have characterized *The Turn of the Screw* as one of the most powerful things ever written, it will not do to dismiss it as a mere exercise in literary ingenuity. It is easier to believe either that the author had a reason for belittling it or that his genius builded better than he knew. And indeed when we read his comment on the tale in the preface to the twelfth volume of his collected works, we see that he had come, partly perhaps under the pressure of its reception, which clearly exceeded his "liveliest hope," to put a somewhat higher estimate on his quondam "pot-boiler." He still speaks of it as a piece of "cold artistic calculation" deliberately planned "to catch those not easily caught (the 'fun' of the capture of the merely witless being ever but small), the jaded, the disillusioned, the fastidious." But in the retrospect he does not disguise his satisfaction with the tale or his sense of having struggled successfully with its technical difficulties and dangers. "Droll enough," he confesses, referring to letters received after its publication, was some of the testimony to that success. He tells of one reader in particular "capable evidently, for the time, of some attention, but not quite capable of enough," who complained that he hadn't sufficiently " 'characterized' " the governess. What wonder that the author's "ironic heart," as he puts it, "shook for the instant almost to breaking," under the reproach of not having sufficiently characterized a figure to the penetrating and detailed setting forth of whose mental condition every sentence of the story (barring part of the brief introductory chapter), from the first one to the last, is dedicated! "We have surely as much of her own nature as we can swallow," he writes in answer to this critic, "in watching it reflect her anxieties and induction." He speaks of the necessity of having the governess keep "crystalline her record of so many intense anomalies and obscurities," and then adds,"—by which I don't of course mean her explanation of them, a different matter."

Now whether these various references to catching "those not easily caught," to the "droll" evidence of the success of his "ingenuity," to his "ironic heart" that "shook for the instant almost to breaking" under the reproaches of readers incapable of quite enough attention, whether all of these things, coupled with the clear, if casual, warning that the governess's "explanation" of her experiences is a "different matter" from a clear record of them, have any separate or cumulative significance, I will not pretend to say. In even hinting at anything of the sort, I may be guilty of twisting perfectly innocent statements to fit a hypothesis. They do appear to fit with curiously little stretching. But I do not press the point. It is not vital. It in no way affects the main argument. For in these matters it is always the work itself and not the author that is the ultimate authority.

EDNA KENTON

Henry James to the Ruminant Reader: The Turn of the Screw †

* * * Critical appraisement of The Turn of the Screw has never, indeed, pressed beyond the outer circle of the story where the children and ghosts dance together, toward any discerned or discernible inner ring where another figure may be executing some frantic dance of terror, toward any possible story behind the "story," toward any character protected by its creator to the very top of his sardonic, ironic bent. * * *

It is as if, wearied of devoted readers who boasted of their "attention of perusal" and their consequent certainties of perception—certainties, by the way, which James was never wont to disturb—he determined to write, in The Turn of the Screw, a story for "the world." He would write it of course primarily for himself and for that reader for whom he must always write—the reader not content to have the author do all of the work—but he would make this particular work a supreme test, of attention and of inattention alike. He would have his own private "fun" in its writing, his own guarded intention, his own famous centre of interest. But he would put about this centre, not only traps set and baited for the least lapse of attention, but lures—delights and terrors mingled—calculated to distract or break off short any amount of alert intentness. Let some singularly astute reader avoid one and yet another of these—others would lie hidden or beckon invitingly ten steps ahead. It would be, as he said ten years later,

† From *The Arts*, VI (November, 1924), 245–255.

"an *amusette* to catch those not easily caught." But to make the amusement more complete, he would see how far he might go, this single time, in catching not only the cunning but the casual reader, the latter too often not his prey, in the maze of an irresistible illusion. He would make a deliberate bid, not only for as much attention as possible, but for as little. Illusion, if it were based on some denominator common to mankind, could be irresistible, if the right emotional spring were only rightly touched. It would be amusing to see how far he might work on the cunning and the casual alike; it would be the very essence of irony if their reactions to the story were identical. As a little matter of critical history they were. And Henry James narrowly escaped writing a best seller.

* * * The children hounded by the prowling ghosts—this is the hard and shining surface story of The Turn of the Screw; or to put it more accurately, it is the traditional and accepted interpretation of the story as it has come down through a quarter of a century of readers' reactions resulting from "a cold, artistic calculation" on the part of its highly entertained author. As a tiny matter of literal fact, no reader has more to go on than the young governess's word for this rather momentous and sidetracking allegation. As a rather large matter of literal fact, we may know, with but a modicum of attention paid to her recital of these nerve-shattering affairs at Bly, that it is she—always she herself—who sees the lurking shapes and heralds them to her little world. Not to the chaming little Flora, but, behind Flora and facing the governess, the apparitional Miss Jessel first appeared. There are traps and lures in plenty, but just a little wariness will suffice to disprove, with a single survey of the ground, the traditional, we might almost call it lazy version of this tale. Not the children, but the little governess was hounded by the ghosts who, as James confides with such suave frankness in his Preface, merely "helped me to express my subject all directly and intensely." * * *

So, on The Turn of the Screw, Henry James has won, hands down, all round; has won most of all when the reader, persistently baffled, but persistently wondering, comes face to face at last with the little governess, and realizes, with a conscious thrill greater than that of merely automatic nerve shudders before "horror," that the guarding ghosts and children—what they are and what they do—are only exquisite dramatizations of her little personal mystery, figures for the ebb and flow of troubled thought within her mind, acting out her story. If the reader has won for himself a blest sense of an extension of experience and consciousness in the recognition that her case, so delicate, so complicated, so critical and yet so transparent, has never in its whole treatment been cheapened or betrayed; if he has had, in the high modern sense, all of his "fun,"

he has none the less paid; he has worked for it all, and by that
fruitful labor has verified James's earliest contention that there
was a discoverable way to establish a relation of work shared between the writer and the reader sufficiently curious to follow
through.

MARTINA SLAUGHTER

Edmund Wilson and *The Turn of the Screw* †

For thirty-six years after James published his instantaneously
popular *The Turn of the Screw*, the tale was generally read as a
marvelously contrived, but pure and simple, ghost-story. There
were dissenters from this proposition—principally Edna Kenton,
who in 1924 suggested that the center of the reader's attention
should be placed not on the haunted children, but on the governess who is "pathetically trying to harmonize her own dis-
harmonies by creating discords outside herself" (*The Arts*, VI,
November, 1924, 254). The tale, not at all a mere fairy-tale,
was a sophisticated amusette carefully designed to trick the unwary
reader. When Edmund Wilson in the spring of 1934 published
"The Ambiguity of Henry James" in *Hound & Horn*, VII (April-
May, 1934, 385-406), this minority view received a clear and
forthright annunciation.

I

Wilson found a base in Miss Kenton's suggestion of the governess's neuroticism. The governess is indeed disturbed, but
according to Wilson's Freudian point of view, the nature of her
trouble is explicitly sexual. She is one of James's familiar types—
"the frustrated Anglo-Saxon spinster" (*Hound & Horn*, VII, April-
May, 1934, 391)—and in the role of narrator actually rationalizes,
justifies, and screens her personal inadequacy. For Wilson, then,
the tale holds "another mystery beneath the ostensible one" (VII,
385). Her account of the ghosts is not distorted; the ghosts simply
do not exist. Wilson believed that "the young governess who tells
the story is a neurotic case of sex repression, and the ghosts are
not real ghosts at all but merely the governess's hallucinations"
(VII, 385). The tale has "a false hypothesis which the narrator
is putting forward and a reality which we are supposed to divine"
(VII, 395).

Wilson justified this psychological interpretation by saying

† Published for the first time. By permission of the author.

that "there is never any evidence that anybody but the governess sees the ghosts" (VII, 387). Miles and Flora never really admit their existence. In the final scene, it is not implausible to attribute Miles's reaction to confusion and fright. Mrs. Grose seemingly comes over to the governess's side, but it is impossible to determine whether she believes in the ghosts or is merely placating her superior. The hallucination theory, however, might falter over one question: if the ghosts are products of her own mind, how can she, independently and accurately, without any previous knowledge of him, describe the apparition as Quint? For the time being, Wilson rested with a rather inscrutable answer: evidently Quint and the master strongly resembled one another and the governess had merely confused the two (VII, 388).

As Wilson saw it, the governess's self-conceived apparitions were projections resulting from sexual desire and frustration. After she fell in love with her handsome employer, she nursed her feelings with fantasies and much of her later behavior is motivated by her desire to impress him. We are supposed to feel that there is something obsessive about her repeated attempts to prove herself to a man she has met only once and may never see again. Her latent sexual frustrations are further revealed in her strikingly possessive and intimate attitude toward little Miles. The final clue is given in several well-placed, significant Freudian symbols: Quint on the tower; Miss Jessel at the lake; Flora's toy boat, which she makes by pushing a stick into a small flat piece of wood (VII, 387).

According to Wilson, then, James had intentionally created the governess as an ambiguous, neurotic character. Behind the façade of the ghost-story was the real tale, "a study in morbid psychology" (VII, 390): the governess was intentionally created as an ambiguous, neurotic character. In its vexing blend of the psychological and supernatural, the tale belongs to a group of fairy-tales "whose symbols exert a peculiar power by reason of the fact that they have behind them, whether or not the authors are aware of it, a profound grasp of subconscious processes" (VII, 390-91).

II

The extremity of Wilson's position and his avowed Freudian bias stimulated a literary controversy which, over the years, has become itself almost as compelling as the tale. Forced by critical pressure to reconsider his interpretation, Wilson followed up the original essay with a series of revisions and retractions, so that almost as much attention has been devoted to Wilson as to James. The criticism has become almost as interesting as the work, the critic almost as central as the author.

When Wilson revised his essay four years later for inclusion in *The Triple Thinkers* (Harcourt, Brace and Co.: New York,

1938), he seems to have had some doubts about his original interpretation. In the revision, not "everything" but "almost every-thing" (p. 130) in the tale could be read in either of two senses. In the late forties, critical pressure continued to bear down. A. J. A. Waldock, in "Mr. Edmund Wilson and *The Turn of the Screw*," questioned the identification of Quint: "How did the governess succeed in projecting on vacancy, out of her own self-conscious mind, a perfectly precise, point-by-point image of a man, then dead, whom she had never seen in her life and never heard of? What psychology, normal or abnormal, will explain that? And what is the right word for such a vision but 'ghost'?" (*Modern Language Notes*, LXII, May, 1947, 333-34). Robert B. Heilman, among others, went outside the text to James's Preface to Volume XII of the New York Edition for evidence to refute Wilson ("The Freudian Reading of *The Turn of the Screw*," MLN, LXII, November, 1947, 433-45). And, in 1947, when the *Note-books* were first published, further evidence was offered which seemed to indicate that James did indeed intend to write a bona-fide ghost-story.

III

As an apparent result of this assault, Wilson in the second and expanded edition of *Triple Thinkers* (Oxford University Press: New York, 1948) restated his thesis, conceding that he had "forced a point" (p. 123) in his explanation of the identification of Quint, and backing away from his original contention that James had consciously intended the governess's tale to be ambiguous. Wilson now observed that the story was written at a time when the author's "faith in himself had been somewhat shaken" (p. 123): his self-doubts were unintentionally and unconsciously incorpo-rated into the character of the governess. James's personal and authorial blind spot was sex, and his inability to confront, perhaps even to understand, sexual feelings, was transformed into the ambiguity of the governess. Wilson concluded that "in *The Turn of the Screw*, not merely is the governess self-deceived, but that James is self-deceived about her" (p. 125).

IV

By 1959, however, relying mainly on an article by John Silver, "A Note on the Freudian Reading of 'The Turn of the Screw'," Wilson was partially able to resolve his ambiguity about James's ambiguity; Silver extricated Wilson from his difficulties over the governess's identification of Quint by arguing that she had learned of his appearance from the neighboring villagers (*American Lit-erature*, XXIX, May, 1957, 207-11). Then, focussing once more on the author's conscious use and manipulation of the first-person narrator in this tale and the other stories with which it is bound in Volume XII of the New York Edition, Wilson, in a short note appended to a reprint of the 1948 version of his essay, was again "convinced that James knew exactly what he was doing and that he intended the governess to be suffering from delusions." Her mind is "warped," the story she tells is "untrue" (*A Casebook on Henry James's "The Turn of the Screw,"* Thomas Y. Crowell Co.: New York, 1960, p. 153). He did not mention, this time, the possible sexual origin of the governess's distortion.

Wilson's original thesis no longer startles, but it and the controversy which followed it so changed the winds of Jamesian criticism that many critics today remain divided into two camps: that which sees a ghost-story and that which sees a psychological study. In a recent book, Krishna B. Vaid has pronounced the governess absolutely straightforward and reliable (*Technique in the Tales of Henry James,* Harvard University Press: Cambridge, Mass., 1964). But more recently, Thomas M. Cranfill and Robert L. Clark, Jr. have written a book to prove the opposite (*An Anatomy of The Turn of the Screw,* University of Texas Press: Austin, 1965).

ROBERT HEILMAN

"The Turn of the Screw" as Poem †

There is probably no other short work of fiction which has been the center, during the first fifty years of its life, of such regular attention and speculation as have been called forth by Henry James's *The Turn of the Screw*. The more obvious reasons for this phenomenon—those summarized, for instance, in Heywood Broun's rather uncomplex description of *The Turn* as "the thriller of thrillers, the last word in creeping horror stories"—actually explain almost nothing. For thrillers that exert a "hideous thralldom" are incontinently begotten and die, like movies, each year; and the continuing devotion to *The Turn* has hardly been that of the multitudes in search of hashish. That devotion is significant, indeed, because it has been critical; *The Turn* has elicted special comment from such writers as Edmund Wilson, Philip Rahv, F. O. Matthiessen, Katherine Anne Porter, Mark Van Doren, Allen Tate. Since the book first appeared, there has been a series of interpretations; as these come forth periodically, and as the alterations in them show the different decades endeavoring to adjust

† From *The University of Kansas City Review*, XIV (Summer, 1948), 277– 289. Reprinted by permission of the author and editor.

James's materials to new interpretative methods, what is unmistakable is that James has hit upon some fundamental truth of experience that no generation can ignore and that each generation wishes to restate in its own terms. For half a century sensitive readers have felt the story exert a pull that far transcends any effects springing from the cool manipulations of mystery-mongers. Mr. Matthiessen's remark that the story exhibits James's "extraordinary command of . . . the darkness of moral evil" suggests the nature of the almost unique reality with which the story is infused. For critical readers the problem has been the definition of the evil, and the identification of the methods by which the awareness of evil is brought to disturbing intensity.

It is probably safe to say that the Freudian interpretation of the story, of which the best known exponent is Edmund Wilson, no longer enjoys wide critical acceptance.[1] If, then, we cannot account for the evil by treating the governess as pathological, we must seek elsewhere an explanation of the story's hold. I am convinced that, at the level of action, the story means exactly what it says: that at Bly there are apparitions which the governess sees, which Mrs. Grose does not see but comes to believe in because they are consistent with her own independent experience, and of which the children have a knowledge which they endeavor to conceal. These dramatic circumstances have a symbolic import which seems not too difficult to get hold of: the ghosts are evil, evil which comes subtly conquering before it is wholly seen; the governess, Cassandra-like in the intuitions which are inaccessible to others, is the guardian whose function it is to detect and attempt to ward off evil; Mrs. Grose—whose name, like the narrator's title, has virtually allegorical significance—is the commonplace mortal, well intentioned, but perceiving only the obvious; the children are the victims of evil, victims who ironically, practice concealment —who doubtless must conceal when not to conceal is essential to salvation. If this reading of the symbolism be tenable, we can understand in part the imaginative power of the story, for, beneath the strange and startling action-surface, we have the oldest of themes—the struggle of evil to possess the human soul. And if this struggle appears to resolve itself into a Christian form, that impulse, as it were, of the materials need not be surprising.

1. Philip Rahv calls attempts to explain away the ghosts "a fallacy of rationalism," and asserts, I think correctly, that the Freudian view narrows and conventionalizes the story in a way that contradicts both James's intentions and artistic habits, and, I might add, our own sense that large matters are at stake. In their symposium in *Invitation to Learning*, Katherine Anne Porter, Mark Van Doren, and Allen Tate [radio broadcast by CBS, May 3, 1942; published in *The New Invitation to Learning*, ed. Mark Van Doren (New York, 1942) pp. 223–235] have all specifically denied the validity of the Freudian reading of the story. I have attempted, in some detail, to show how Wilson's account of *The Turn* runs afoul of both the story and James's preface (*Modern Language Notes*, 1947, pp. 433–45).

II

But the compelling theme and the extraordinarily vivid plot-form are not the entirety of *The Turn of the Screw*; there are other methods by which James extends and intensifies his meaning and strikes more deeply into the reader's consciousness. Chief of these is a highly suggestive and even symbolic language which permeates the entire story. After I had become aware of and begun to investigate this phenomenon, I found Mr. Matthiessen, in quite fortuitous corroboration of my own critical method, commenting on the same technical aspect of James's later works—his ability to "bind together his imaginative effects by subtly recurrent images of a thematic kind" and to "extend a metaphor into a symbol," and the fact that later in his career "realistic details had become merely the covering for a content that was far from realistic." In *The Turn* there is a great deal of recurrent imagery which powerfully influences the tone and the meaning of the story; the story becomes, indeed, a dramatic poem, and to read it properly one must assess the role of the language precisely as one would if public form of the work were poetic. For by his iterative imagery and by the very unobtrusive management of symbols, which in the organic work co-function with the language, James has severely qualified the bare narrative; and, if he has not defined the evil which, as he specified, was to come to the reader as something monstrous and unidentified, he has at least set forth the mode and the terms of its operation with fullness.

For a mature reader it is hardly necessary to insist that the center of horror is not the apparitions themselves, though their appearances are worked out with fine uniqueness, but is the children, and our sense of what is happening to them. What is happening to them is Quint and Jessel; the governess's awareness of the apparitions is her awareness of a change within the children; the shock of ghostly appearances is the shock of evil perceived unexpectedly, suddenly, after it has secretly made inroads. Matthiessen and R. P. Blackmur both refer, as a matter of course, to the corruption of the children; E. M. W. Tillyard, in a volume on Shakespeare, remarks incidentally that James "owes so much of the power with which evil is conveyed to showing it in the minds of children, where it should least be found." Perhaps two modern phenomena, the sentimentalizing of children and the disinclination to concede to evil any status more profound than the melodramatic, account for a frequent unwillingness to accept what the story says. James is not disposed to make things easier; he emphasizes that it is the incorruptible who have taken on corruption. He introduces no mere pathos of childhood catastrophe; his are not ordinary children. He is at pains to give them a special quality—by repetition which in so careful an artist can hardly have been a clumsy accident. As the repeated words achieve a cumulative tonal force, we can see the working of the poetic imagination.

Flora has "extraordinary charm," is "most beautiful." Miles is "incredibly beautiful." Both have "the bloom of health and happiness." Miles is "too fine and fair" for the world; he is a "beautiful little boy." The governess is "dazzled by their loveliness." They are "most loveable" in their "helplessness." Touching their "fragrant faces" one could believe only "their incapacity and their beauty." Miles is a "prodigy of delightful, loveable goodness." In midstory Flora still emerges from concealment "rosily," and one is caught by "the golden glow of her curls," by her "loveliest, eagerest simplicity," by "the excess of something beautiful that shone out of the blue" of her eyes, by "the lovely little lighted face." In both, "beauty and amiability, happiness and cleverness" are still paramount. Miles has still the "wonderful smile" and the "beautiful eye" of "a little fairy prince." Both write letters "too beautiful to be posted." On the final Sunday the governess sees still Miles's "beautiful face" and talks of him as "beautiful and perfect"; he smiles at her "with the same loveliness" and spars verbally with "serenity" and "unimpeachable gaiety." Even after Flora is gone, Miles is "the beautiful little presence" as yet with "neither stain nor shadow"; his expression is "the most beautiful" the governess has ever known.

James devotes an almost prodigal care to creating an impression of special beauty in the children, an impression upon which depends the extraordinary effectiveness of the change which takes place in them. In such children the appearance of any imperfection is a shock. The shock is emphasized when the governess wonders whether she must "pronounce their loveliness a trick of premature cunning" and reflects upon the possibility that "the immediate charm . . . was studied"; when Miles's "sweet face" must be described as a "sweet ironic face"; when his "happy laugh" goes off into "incoherent extravagant song"; and when, above all, the governess must declare with conviction that their "more than earthly beauty, their absolutely unnatural goodness [is] a game, . . . a policy and a fraud."

Is James, then laboriously overusing the principle of contrast, clothing the children with an astonishing fascination merely to accentuate the shock of their being stripped bare? Obviously not. Beneath the superficial clash we can already sense a deeper paradox. When James speaks of Miles's "beautiful fevered face" and says that he "lives in a setting of beauty and misery," he puts into words what the reader has already come to feel—that his real subject is the dual nature of man, who is a little lower than the angels, and who yet can become a slave in the realm of evil. The children's beauty, we have come to feel, is a symbol of the spiritual perfection of which man is capable. Thus the battle between the governess and the demons becomes the old struggle of the morality play in new dress.

III

But that statement of the struggle is much more general and abstract than the formulation of it made by the story itself. When James speaks of "any clouding of their innocence," he reminds us again of a special quality in their beauty which he has quietly stressed with almost thematic fullness. The *clouding* suggests a *change* in a characteristic brightness of theirs, a brightness of which we are made aware by a recurrent imagery of light. Flora, at the start, "brightly" faces the new governess; hers is a "radiant" image; the children "dazzle" the governess; Flora has "a lovely little lighted face," and she considers "luminously"; in his "brightness" Miles "fairly glittered"; he speaks "radiantly"; at his "revolution" he speaks with "extraordinary brightness." This light-giving quality of theirs is more than a mere amplification of a charm shockingly to be destroyed; it is difficult not to read it as a symbol of their being, as it were, at the dawn of existence. For they are children, and their radiance suggests the primal and the universal. This provisional interpretation is supported by another verbal pattern which James uses to describe the children. Miles has a "great glow of freshness," a "positive fragrance of purity," a "sweetness of innocence"; in him she finds something "extraordinarily happy, that, . . . struck me as beginning anew each day"; he could draw upon "reserves of goodness." Then, as things change, the governess remarks, on one occasion, that "He couldn't play any longer at innocence," and mentions, on another, his pathetic struggles to "play . . . a part of innocence." To the emphasis upon beauty, then, is added this emphasis upon brightness and freshness and innocence. What must come across to us, from such a context, is echoes of the Garden of Eden; we have the morality play story, as we have said, but altered, complemented, and given unique poignance by being told of mankind at its first radical crisis, in consequence of which all other morality stories are; Miles and Flora become the childhood of the race. They are symbolic children as the ghosts are symbolic ghosts. Even the names themselves have a representative quality as those of James's characters often do: Miles—the soldier, the archetypal male; Flora—the flower, the essential female. Man and woman are caught even before the first hint of maturity, dissected, and shown to have within them all the seeds—possible of full growth even now—of their own destruction.

James's management of the setting and of other ingredients in the drama deepens one's sense of a story at once primeval and eternal, lurking beneath the surface of the action. Bly itself is almost an Eden with its "lawn and bright flowers"; the governess comments, "The scene had a greatness. . . ." Three times James writes of the "golden" sky, and one unconsciously recalls that Flora was a "rosy sprite" with "hair of gold." Miss Jessel first appears "in the garden," where "the old trees, the thick shrubbery, made a great and pleasant shade. . . ." Here, for a time, the three "lived in a cloud of music and love . . ."; the children are "extraordinarily at one" in "their quality of sweetness." Now it is significant that James uses even the seasons to heighten his drama; the pastoral idyl begins in June, when spring is at the full, and then is gradually altered until we reach the dark ending of a November whose coldness and deadness are unobtrusively but unmistakably stressed, ". . . the autumn had dropped . . . and blown out half our lights" (a variation of the light-pattern); the governess now notices "grey sky and withered garlands," "bared spaces and scattered dead leaves." What might elsewhere be Gothic trimming is here disciplined by the pattern. When, on the final Sunday night, the governess tries hard to "reach" Miles, there is "a great wind"; she hears "the lash of the rain and the batter of the gusts"; at the climax there is "an extraordinary blast and chill," and then darkness. The next afternoon is "damp and grey." After Flora's final escapade at the pond, James stresses the governess's feelings at the end of the day; the evening is "portentous" without precedent; she blows out the candles and feels a "mortal coldness." On the final day with Miles she notices "the stupid shrubs," "the dull things of November," "the dim day." So it is not merely the end of a year but the end of a cycle: the spring of gay, bright human innocence has given way to the dark autumn—or rather, as we might pun, to the dark *fall*.

And in the darkness of the latter end of things we might note the special development of the light which, to the sensitive governess, the children seem actually to give off. It is, I think, more than a coincidence that, when the governess mentions Miss Jessel, Flora's face shows a "quick, smitten glare," and that, in the final scene, Miles is twice said to be "glaring"—the same verb which has been used to describe Quint's look. All three characters, of course, look with malevolence; yet *glare* must suggest, also, a hard, powerful, ugly light—an especially effective transformation of the apparently benign luminousness of the spring.

The same movement of human experience James portrays in still another symbolic form. As the light changes and the season changes and the children's beauty becomes ambiguous, another alteration, takes place in them. Their youth, of course, is the prime datum of the story, and of it we are ever conscious; and

at the same time we are aware of a strange maturity in them—
in, for instance, their poise, their controlled utilization of their
unusual talents to give pleasure. Our sense of something that
transcends their youth is first defined overtly late in the story
when the governess speaks of her feeling that Miles is "accessible
as an older person." Though she does not speak of change, their
is subtly called forth in us a conviction that years have been
added to Miles. So we are not surprised when the governess assures
Mrs. Grose, and goes out of her way, a little later, to remind her
of the assurance, that, at meetings with Miss Jessel, Flora is "not
a child" but "an old, old woman"—an insight that receives a
measure of authentication, perhaps, by its reminiscence of the
Duessa motif. The suggestion that Flora has become older is skill-
fully conveyed, in the pond scene, by her silence (and silence itself
has an almost symbolic value throughout the story), by her quick
recovery of her poised gaiety, and especially by the picture of
her peeping at the governess over the shoulder of Mrs. Grose,
who is embracing her—the first intimation of a cold adult cal-
culatingness which appears in all her remaining actions. The
governess says, ". . . her incomparable childish beauty had suddenly failed, had quite vanished . . . she was literally . . . hideously,
hard; she had turned common and almost ugly." Mrs. Grose sums
up, "It has made her, every inch of her, quite old." More effective,
however, than any of this direct presentation of vital change is a
delicate symbol which may pass almost unnoticed: when she is discovered at the pond, Flora picks up, and drops a moment later,
"a big, ugly spray of withered fern"—a quiet commentary on the
passage of symbolic spring, on the spiritual withering that is the
story's center. When, at the end of the scene, the governess looks
"at the grey pool and its blank, haunted edge," we automatically
recall, "The sedge has withered from the lake"—the imagery used
by Keats in his account of an ailing knight-at-arms in another bitter
autumn.

Besides the drying of foliage and the coming of storms and
darkness there is one other set of elements, loosely working together and heavy with implications, which suggest that this is a
story of the decay of Eden. At Quint's first appearance Bly "had
been stricken with death." After Miles's nocturnal exploit the
governess utters a cliché that, under the influence of the context,
becomes vigorously meaningful: " . . . you . . . caught your death
in the night air!" There are further, some arresting details in the
description of Quint: "His eyes are sharp, strange—awfully; . . .
rather small and very fixed. His mouth's wide, and his lips are
thin, . . ." These are unmistakably the characteristics of a snake.
James is too fine an artist to allegorize the point, but, as he has

shaped the story, the coming of Quint is the coming of the serpent into the little Eden that is Bly (both Miss Porter and Mr. Tate have noted other physical characteristics of Quint which traditionally belong to the devil). Quint's handsomeness and his borrowed finery, by which he apes the gentleman, suggest, perhaps, the specious plausibleness of the visitor in the Garden. As for the "fixed eyes": later we learn that Miss Jessel "only fixed the child" and that the apparition of Quint "fixed me exactly as it had fixed me from the tower and from the garden." Of Quint's position at Bly Mrs. Grose says, "The master believed in him and placed him here because he was supposed not to be well and the country air so good for him." The master, in other words, has nourished a viper in his bosom. The secret influence upon Miles the governess describes as "poison," and at the very end she says that the demonic presence "filled the room like the taste of poison." In the first passage the governess equates "poison" with "secret precocity"; toward the end she emphasizes Miles's freedom and sorrowfully gives up "the fiction that I had anything more to teach him." Why is it a fiction? Because he already knew too much, because he had eaten of the fruit of the tree of knowledge? We have already been told of the "dark prodigy" by which "the imagination of all evil *had* been opened up to him," and of his being "under some influence operating in his small intellectual life as a tremendous incitement."

IV

We should not press such analogies too hard, or construct inflexible parables. Our business is rather to trace all the imaginative emanations that enrich the narrative, the associations and intimations by which it transcends the mere horror story and achieves its own kind of greatness. But by now it must be clear from the antipodal emphases of the story that James has an almost religious sense of the duality of man, and, as if to manifest an intention, he makes that sense explicit in terms broadly religious and even Christian. The image of Flora's "angelic beauty" is "beatific"; she has "the deep, sweet serenity . . . of one of Raphael's holy infants"; she has "placid heavenly eyes." In Miles there is "something divine that I have never found to the same degree in any child." In a mildly humorous context the children are called "cherubs." Seeing no signs of suffering from his school experience, the governess regards Miles as an "angel." Mrs. Grose imputes to Flora a "blessed innocence," and the governess surrenders to the children's "extraordinary childish grace"—a noun which in this patterned structure can hardly help being ambivalent. In mid-story Flora has still a "divine smile"; both children remain "adorable." This verbal pattern, which is too consistent to be coincidental, irresistibly makes us think of the divine in man, of his capability of salvation. Now what is tragic and terrifying in man is that to be capable of salvation is to be capable also of damnation—an equivocal potentiality suggested early by the alter-nation of moods in the newly arrived governess, who senses imme-diately a kind of wavering, a waiting for determination, at Bly. And James, to present the spiritual decline of the children, finds terms which exactly balance those that connote their spiritual capabilities.

We are never permitted to see the apparitions except as moral realities. Miss Jessel is a figure of "unmistakeable horror and evil . . . in black, pale and dreadful." She is a "horror of horrors," with "awful eyes," "with a kind of fury of intention," and yet "with extraordinary beauty." Again she is described as "Dark as midnight in her black dress, her haggard beauty, and her unutterable woe. . . ." It is brilliant to give her beauty, which not only iden-tifies her with Flora and thus underscores the dual possibilities that lie ahead of Flora, but also enriches the theme with its re-minder of Milton's fallen angels who retain something of their original splendor—"the excess / Of glory obscured." So, with the repeated stress upon her woe, we almost expect the passage which tells us that she "suffers the torments . . . of the damned": she is both damned and an agent of damnation—another reminiscence of the Miltonic myth. She is called later a "pale and ravenous demon," not "an inch of whose evil . . . fell short"—which reminds us of James's prefatory insistence that the apparitions were to be thought of as demons. Again, she is "our infernal witness"; she and Quint are "those fiends"; "they were not angels," and they could be bringing "some yet more infernal message." "And to ply them with that evil still, to keep up the work of demons, is what brings the others back." They are "tempters," who work subtly by hold-ing out fascinating "suggestions of danger." In the last scene Quint presents—the phrase is used twice—"his white face of damnation."

By this series of words, disposed throughout the story yet com-bining in a general statement, James defines as diabolic the forces attacking the children of whose angelic part we are often reminded. Now these attacking forces, as often in Elizabethan drama, are seen in two aspects. Dr. Faustus has to meet an enemy which has an inner and an outer reality—his own thoughts, and Mephistoph-eles; James presents evil both as agent (the demons) and as effect (the transformation in the once fresh and beautiful and innocent children). The dualistic concept of reality appears most explicitly when Mrs. Grose asks, "And if he was so bad there as that comes to, how is he such an angel now?" and the governess replies, "Yes, indeed—and if he was a fiend at school!" By the *angel-fiend* antithesis James underscores what he sees as a central human contradiction, which he emphasizes throughout the book by his chosen verbal pattern. The governess speaks of the children's "love of evil" gained from Quint and Miss Jessel, of Miles's "wickedness" at school. In such a context the use of the word *revolution* to describe Miles's final taking matters up with the governess—a move by which, we should remember, he becomes completely "free"—cannot help calling to mind the Paradise and Eden revolutions of Judæo-Christian mythology. The revolutionary change in character is nicely set forth by the verbal counterpoint in one passage. "He found the most divine little way," the governess says, "to keep me quiet while she went off." " 'Divine'?" Mrs. Grose asks, and the governess replies, "Infernal then!" The divine has paradoxically passed into the infernal. Then we see rapidly the completed transition in Flora: she turns upon the governess an expression of "hard, fixed gravity" and ignores the "hideous plain presence" of Miss Jessel—"a stroke that somehow converted the little girl herself into the very presence that could make me quail." In Miles, by contrast, we see a protracted struggle, poignantly conveyed by a recurrent metaphor of illness. Early in the story Miles is in "the bloom of health and happiness," but near the end he seems like a "wistful patient in a children's hospital," "like a convalescent slightly fatigued." At the end he shows "bravery" while "flushing with pain"; he gives "a sick little headshake"; his is a "beautiful fevered face." But the beauty goes, the fever gains; Miles gives "a frantic little shake for air and light"; he is in a "white rage." The climax of his disease, the binding together of all the strands we have been tracing, is his malevolent cry to the governess—"you devil!" It is his final transvaluation of values: she who would be his savior has become for him a demon. His face gives a "convulsive supplication"—that is, actually, a prayer, for and to Quint, the demon who has become his total deity. But the god isn't there, and Miles despairs and dies. We need not labor the dependence of this brilliant climax upon the host of associations and evocations by which, as this outline endeavors to show, James prepares us for the ultimate resolution of the children's being.

There are glimmerings of other imaginative kinships, such as that already mentioned, the Faustian. Miles's "You devil" is in one way almost identical with Faustus's savage attack, in Marlowe's play, upon the Old Man who has been trying to save him; indeed James's story, in its central combat, is not unlike the Faustus story as it might be told by the Good Angel. But whereas Dr. Faustus is a late intellectualist version of Everyman, James, as we have said, weaves in persuasive hints, one after another, of mankind undergoing, in his Golden Age, an elemental conflict: thus we have the morality play, but in a complicated, enriched, and intensified version. When the governess first sees Quint, she is aware of "some challenge between us"; the next time it seems "as if I had been looking at him for years and had known him always"; near the end she says, "I *was* . . . face to face with the elements," and, of the final scene, "It was like fighting with a demon for a human soul."

V

What, then, does the story say about the role of the governess, and how does this contribute to the complex of the impressions built up in part by James's language? From the start the words used by the governess suggest that James is attaching to her the quality of savior, not only in a general sense, but with certain Christian associations. She uses words like "atonement"; she speaks of herself as an "expiatory victim," of her "pure suffering," and at various times—twice in the final scene—of her "torment." Very early she plans to "shelter my pupils," to "absolutely save" them; she speaks variously of her "service," "to protect and defend the little creatures . . . bereaved . . . loveable." When she fears that she cannot "save or shield them" and that "they're lost," she is a "poor protectress." At another time she is a "sister of Charity" attempting to "cure" Miles. But by now what we cannot mistake is the relation of pastor and flock, a relationship which becomes overt when the governess tells Miles, "I just want you to help me to save you." It is in this sense that the governess "loves" Miles—a loving which must not be confused, as it is confused by some critics, with "making love to" or "being in love with" him. Without such pastoral love no guardian would consider his flock worth the sacrifice. The governess's priestly function is made still more explicit by the fact that she comes ultimately to act as confessor and to use every possible means to bring Miles to confession; the long final scene really takes place in the confessional, with the governess as priest endeavoring, by both word and gesture, to protect her charge against the evil force whose invasion has, with consummate irony, carried even there. In one sense the governess must elicit confession because, in her need for objective reassurance, she will not take the lead as accuser; but securing the confession is, more importantly, a mitigation of Miles's own pride, his self-will; it could soften him, make him accessible to grace. The experience has a clear sacramental quality: the governess says that Miles senses "the need of confession . . . he'll confess. If he confesses, he's saved." It is when he begins to break and confess that "the white face of damnation" becomes baffled and at a vital moment retreats; but it returns "as if to blight his confession," and it is in part through the ineptitude of the governess-confessor-savior, we are led to understand, that Miles is lost.

It is possible that there are even faint traces of theological speculation to give additional substance to the theme of salvation and damnation which finally achieves specific form in the sacramentalism of the closing scenes. Less than halfway through the story the governess refers to the children thus: "blameless and foredoomed as they were." By *blameless* she can only mean that she does not have direct, tangible evidence of voluntary evil-doing on their part; they still look charming and beautiful; she does not have grounds for a positive placing of blame. Why, then, "foredoomed"? May this not be a suggestion of original sin (which Miss Porter has already seen as an ingredient in the story), an interpretation consistent with the view of Bly as a kind of Eden? Three-quarters of the way through the story the governess again turns to speculation: ". . . I constantly both attacked and renounced the enigma of what such a little gentleman could have done that deserved a penalty." *Enigma* is perhaps just the word to be applied to a situation, of which one technical explication is the doctrine of original sin, by an inquiring lay mind with a religious sense but without precise theological tools. What is significant is that the governess does not revolt against the penalty as if it betokened a cosmic injustice. And original sin, whether it be natural depravity or a revolt in a heavenly or earthly paradise, fits exactly into the machinery of this story of two beautiful children who in a lovely springtime of existence already suffer, not unwillingly, hidden injuries which will eventually destroy them.

VI

This summary of the imaginative overtones in *The Turn of the Screw* has taken us rather deeply into a view of the book as strongly religious in cast. Yet this very moving impression is produced by agencies that quietly penetrate the story, not by devices that stick out of it, so to speak, and become commanding guideposts. There are no old familiar signs announcing a religious orientation of experience. There is nothing of the Bible overtly; there are no texts, no clergymen; there are no conventional indices of religious feeling —no invocations or prayers or meditations; all there is is a certain amount of church-going of a very matter-of-fact sort, and otherwise the context is ostensibly secular. Thus the story becomes no bland preachment; it simply "has life"—to use James's criterion of excellence—and it is left to us to define the boundaries and extensions and reverberations of that life. Right where we might expect the most positive assistance, perhaps, in seeking that definition, we find least. Yet even in a few dry and casual ecclesiastical mementoes we sense some ever-so-mild symbolic pressures, as of a not-very-articulate wispish presence that quietly makes itself felt. These intimations of a presence would not be magnified into a solid "character" who demands our attention. But in their small way they collaborate with other intimations. The reading of the story, for instance, takes place during the Christmas season; the framework action begins on Christmas Eve. Quint appears for the second time on a Sunday, a grey, rainy Sunday, just before the governess is about to go to the late church service with Mrs. Grose; after that she is, she says, "not fit for church"; and their only service is then "a little service of tears and vows, of prayers and promises, . . ." This is the important occasion on which Mrs. Grose identifies the apparition with Quint. As the governess reflects on the situation, she speaks of the "inconceivable communion" of which she has learned—a Black Mass, as it were. The event next in importance to the identification of Quint also occurs on a Sunday—Miles's "revolution." Miles and the governess are "within sight of the church"; she thinks "with envy" of the "almost spiritual help of the hassock." After they enter the churchyard gate, Miles detains her "by a low, oblong, table-like tomb"—a reminder that Bly was "stricken with death" on the first appearance of Quint. Then Miles threatens to bring his uncle down, and it is he, with fine irony, who "marched off alone into church," while the governess can only walk "round the church" and listen "to the sounds of worship." Here, for once, what we may call the Christian apparatus is out in the open, with a clear enough ironic function. From this we go on to the most tantalizing body of suggestion in the whole book, less a body than a wraith, indeed, and yet the more urgent for its not falling within the every-day commonplaces of fictional method. Miles's revolution introduces a straight-line action which continues with remarkably increasing tension to the end of the story. James allots forty percent of his total space to this action, which—and here is the notable point—takes only three days. Thus he puts the heaviest emphasis on those three days—Sunday, Monday, and Tuesday. During those three days the governess, the clergyman's daughter, undertakes her quasi-priestly function with a new intensity and aggressiveness. On Sunday night she enters upon a newly determined, if still cautious, effort to bring Miles to confession; she openly asserts her role as savior. On Monday she tries to shock Flora into spiritual pliability—and fails. All her will to redeem, she now turns upon Miles; in the final scene she fights the adversary directly. She succeeds to an extent: Miles cannot see Quint. But the end of the climactic triduum of her ordeal as savior is failure: Quint comes again, as if to "blight" Miles's confession; Miles still cannot see him—and dies. The would-be redeemer of the living is called "devil"; in Quint we see one who has risen again to tempt the living to destruction

—that is, the resurrection and the death. Here, Sunday does not triumphantly end a symbolic ordeal that had begun in apparent failure on Friday; rather it hopefully initiates a struggle which is to end, on the third day, in bitter loss. We have, then, a modern late-fall defeat patterned on the ancient springtide victory. To transmit its quality and to embrace all of its associations, may we not call it a Black Easter?

VII

If this interpretation will hold up, it will crown the remarkable associational edifice which is both a part of and an extension of the dramatic structure of the story, an edifice which figures forth man's quality, his living, so to speak, as a potentiality which may be fulfilled or may paradoxically be transformed into its radical opposite. This we are told, by implication, through the beauty which can become ugliness, the brightness which becomes darkness, the innocence which can become sophistication, the spring which becomes fall, the youth which becomes age, the Eden which can be stricken with death, the angelic which becomes diabolic; and through the pictured capacity, whether it be understood as original sin or otherwise, for revolt, for transvaluation of values, for denial of the agency of salvation. And this truth comes to us with peculiar shock because we see enacted, not that imperceptible movement by which man's advance in age and in corruption becomes endurable, but the transformation from one extreme to the other in pure state, in essence, in symbolic immediacy. In this poem about evil, youth is age.

James deliberately chose to omit certain matters from his narrative statement. But in his poetic statement he has elaborated upon his story and given adequate clues to the metaphysical foundations of his plot. The universality which has stimulated many critics is the Christian dualism of good and evil; this substance James has projected by poetic method into numerous details of symbolic language and action of which the implications may, in their subtlety, almost be missed. For, like all poetic statements, James's is not direct; even in prose medium it eschews a conventional prose logic; it endows his tale with an atmosphere in which we sense the pressure of so much more imaginative force than meets the casual fiction-reading eye. In attempting to state schematically the origins of that pressure, we fall into much more blunt statements than we ought to make. We say, too forthrightly, that Bly "becomes" a Garden of Eden. As in studying all good poetry, we must resist the impulse to line up, on a secondary level of meaning, exact equivalents for the narrative elements, for such a procedure stems from the rude assumption that every part of the story is a precision-tooled cog in an allegorical machine. But we must be sensitive to parallels, analogies, intimations; thus, while preserving the fullness and flexibility of the work, we can investigate its extraordinarily moving tonal richness. And in accounting for tone we necessarily move toward a definition of structure. The verbal and imagistic patterns which have been described do not have the structural finality that they would have in lyric verse. Yet these patterns, which overlap and interfuse in a way badly obscured by the clumsy analytical process, are unquestionably important in the formation of the story and the qualifying of its meaning; they are one of the ways in which the esemplastic imagination, as Coleridge called it, works; and they collaborate closely with the larger structural units—the parts of the narrative as such—in defining this version of the struggle between good and evil.

LEON EDEL

The Point of View †

There are, on the long Jamesian shelf, two pieces of fiction which admirably illustrate the novelist's cunning experiments with the point of view. One of them, *The Turn of the Screw*, has become the subject of a long and rather tiresome controversy arising from a discussion of the circumstantial evidence in the narrative, with the participants, however, failing to examine the technique of the story-telling, which would have made much of the dispute unnecessary. The second has met with general critical bafflement. I refer to *The Sacred Fount*, written in 1900, just before *The Ambassadors*. * * *

When criticism throws up its hands in bewilderment over the work of an artist or wavers between such extremes, it is reasonable to inquire whether the work in question is really art. Has there been a failure in communication or a failure in perception—or both? For us the question is pertinent, since in both these works James came closest to creating that type of bewilderment which contemporary novel readers feel at first, say, when they open *The Sound and the Fury* and are plunged into the shifting consciousness of Benjy. Dostoevsky had preceded James in a remarkable story, *Letters from the Underworld*, but there, in the first paragraph, he had semaphored the reader, not with flags but with klieg lights that here was the mind of an eccentric, if not a madman. There is no such

† From Chapter III, *The Psychological Novel: 1900–1950* (J. B. Lippincott Co.: New York, 1955), pp. 56–68. Pp. 72–73 reprinted by permission of the author and the William Morris Agency, Inc.

obvious signalling in *The Turn of the Screw* or *The Sacred Fount*. In both of these works the reader is led unsuspectingly to accept the narrator in good faith, and this may have been what James meant when he said he had set "a trap for the unwary." In *The Turn of the Screw* James even provides an elaborate testimonial to the good character of the unnamed governess, who is the first-person narrator. Yet in both cases, if the reader reads attentively, he will discover that he is tied down by the limitations James imposes upon him. The data go only so far: beyond, he can have recourse only to his own imagination.

There are, so to speak, three narrators in *The Turn of the Screw*. The first is the individual, perhaps James himself, who begins by telling us, "The story had held us, round the fire. . . ." This un-identified First Narrator goes on to mention a second personage named Douglas. Douglas now briefly takes over the narrative; he tells of a ghost story with a special "turn of the screw." It is related in an old manuscript. Douglas is thus, in a certain sense, Second Narrator, but not technically, since his account is at first being quoted or summarized by the First Narrator. Then, finally, Douglas begins to read the manuscript and the Principal Narrator, the governess, takes over. The story we are finally given is hers, and it is told in the first person. Douglas and the First Narrator disappear, never to return.

Readers often become so wrapped up in the ghosts and the children of *The Turn of the Screw* that they forget this elaborate setting. In it a great deal of significant information is given to us. Each narrator provides a set of facts, not, however, evaluated for us. We are told the governess has been dead for twenty years. She sent the manuscript to Douglas before she died. Douglas tells us she was ten years older than he was and that she was his sister's governess. "She struck me as awfully clever and nice . . . I liked her extremely." She was twenty when the events described in the manuscript occurred. We are told that forty years have elapsed since her death. Douglas says "it was long ago" that he knew her and "this episode was long before." In fact, he was at Trinity College "and I found her at home on my coming down the second summer." This means that Douglas must have been eighteen or perhaps twenty when he had completed his second year at the university; and the governess, ten years older, would be about thirty when Douglas met her and found her "nice." And the meeting was ten years after the events described in her manuscript.

This is an elaborate and careful time-scheme for James to have set down, and he did so not merely through whim. We know from his working notebooks the care with which he placed every detail in his fictions. The time-scheme is extremely important in this story.

It establishes, for one thing, that Douglas's testimony is based on the personality of the governess as it was ten years *after* the events of the story. By that time we can presume she had learned the ways of the world. We are explicitly told that at twenty she knew little of the world; she had emerged from a cloistered Hampshire vicarage, the youngest of several daughters of a poor and—as she describes him—erratic country parson. The narrative itself emphasizes her rusticity and unworldliness: she had never seen herself in a full-length mirror; she had never read a novel (and at Bly she reads Fielding's *Amelia*, which has the word "rape" and the word "adultery" on its first page); she has never seen a play. If we add to these little details the significant fact that she has received her position from a mysterious and handsome gentleman in Harley Street who sends her to Bly to take care of his nephew and niece with only a maid and an ignorant but well-meaning housekeeper (her name, Mrs. Grose, suggests the quality of her mind) for company, it becomes clear that she has ample reason to be nervous about the duties and responsibilities conferred on her. Moreover, she is given *carte blanche:* she must make her own decisions and may not communicate with her employer. These are circumstances enough to make for nervousness and anxiety in a young girl taking her first job. In effect, she has jumped from a humble parsonage to the role of mistress of a country house and to vicarious motherhood of two beautiful children.

What happens thereafter, by her own account, is a story of her throbbing sense of insecurity and her unbridled speculations about the governess who preceded her and the valet with whom that governess was friendly—both of whom are dead. Her daydreams are filled with the figure of the man in Harley Street; she takes evening walks hoping to meet him. She encounters instead her first vision of Peter Quint. He is on the tower; he wears the clothes of the man in Harley Street; she sees him only from the waist up.

The governess's account of her stay at Bly is riddled with inconsistencies which the many critics who have discussed the story have never sufficiently perceived. There are moments when she is, in a less mad way, doing what the retired civil servant does in Dostoevsky's *Letters from the Underworld*. She speculates and she assumes —and what she first states as fancy she later states as fact. Most readers have tended to accept her story as "fact" partly because Douglas has given her such a good character at the outset and particularly because of the cunning which James has employed in telling the story.

Let us glance at the second occasion on which the governess sees Quint, that is on the day he appears looking through the window of the dining-room. She does not know that it is Quint, or that he is a ghost. She sees him again from the waist up.

On the spot there came to me the added shock of a certitude that it was not for me he had come there. He had come for someone else.

The flash of this knowledge—for it was knowledge in the midst of dread—produced in me the most extraordinary effect, started, as I stood there, a sudden vibration of duty and courage.

We must remember that we are receiving from the governess her story and *her* interpretation of what she saw or imagined. We are entirely in her mind. She had seen a strange man and she does not at this moment know that he is anything but a palpable man; he resembles the man seen on the tower. But she has the "shock of a certitude" that "it was not for me he had come there." He had come for "someone else." This is to say the least an assumption. But the governess promptly appropriates it as "knowledge in the midst of dread." It is "certitude."

There follows the first vision of the woman, Miss Jessel, or a person the governess believes to be Miss Jessel. She is seen by the governess, or rather *felt*, on the other side of the pond which they have named, in Flora's geography lesson, the Sea of Azof.

I became aware that, on the other side of the Sea of Azof, we had an interested spectator. The way this knowledge gathered in me was the strangest thing in the world—the strangest, that is, except the very much stranger in which it quickly merged itself.

She describes how she had sat down with a piece of sewing on a stone bench beside the pond and "in this position I began to take in with certitude, and yet without direct vision, the presence, at a distance, of a third person."

There was no ambiguity in anything; none whatever, at least, in the conviction I from one moment to another found myself forming as to what I should see straight before me and across the lake as a consequence of raising my eyes.

She does not, however, raise her eyes. She continues her sewing in order to steady herself while she is deciding what to do.

She says that while she was sewing she knew "there was an alien object in view" across the pond, and this, she is convinced, is true, even though she tells herself it might be "a messenger, a postman, or a tradesman's boy," one of the men about the place. "That reminder had as little effect on my practical certitude as I was conscious—still even without looking—of its having upon the character and attitude of our visitor. Nothing was more natural than that these things should be the other things they absolutely were not." The young lady, we see, always has an abundance of "certitude." Although she has not yet looked, she would get the "positive identity of the apparition"—she tells herself—"as soon as the small clock of my courage should have ticked out the right second." She has already decided, we see, that it is an apparition. Meanwhile, she glances at little Flora. The girl is ten yards away—we are given the distance—and she expects her to cry out or to show some "sudden innocent sign either of interest or of alarm." It is difficult to understand why, since the child has her back to the water and hence her back to the "visitor" on the other bank. The girl has other things to think of; in her play she is trying to put together two pieces of wood to form a boat.

> My apprehension of what she was doing sustained me so that after some seconds I felt I was ready for more. Then I again shifted my eyes—I faced what I had to face.

This is all the evidence we have. And we are at the end of the chapter.

The first paragraph of the next chapter tells us:

> I got hold of Mrs. Grose as soon after this as I could; and I can give no intelligible account of how I fought out the interval. Yet I still hear myself cry as I fairly threw myself into her arms: "They *know*—it's too monstrous: they know, they know!"

Mrs. Grose, naturally, wants to know what they know.

"Why, all that *we* know—and heaven knows what else besides!" And she adds, "Two hours ago, in the garden . . . Flora *saw!*"

A supposition has now become a fact, for this is clearly not what the governess previously described. Her own fancy has quite carried her away. After telling us that Flora had her back to the Sea of Azof and was preoccupied with two pieces of wood, she nevertheless tells Mrs. Grose that the girl *saw* what was on the other shore.

Mrs. Grose, true to her name, is down to earth about such matters. "She has told you?" she asks.

"Not a word—that's the horror. She kept it to herself! The child of eight, *that* child!"

Mrs. Grose persists. Her logic is sound enough: "Then how do you know?"

"I was there—I saw with my eyes: saw that she was perfectly aware." This is a significant shift of ground—from *seeing* to her knowledge of *awareness*. She then tells Mrs. Grose that she saw across the pond a woman who was Miss Jessel.

"How can you be sure?" Mrs. Grose asks.

The governess says: "Then ask Flora—*she's* sure!"

But she has an afterthought. "I had no sooner spoken than I caught myself up. 'No, for God's sake, *don't!* She'll say she isn't —she'll lie!' "

Mrs. Grose rebels at this. "Ah, how *can* you?"

"Because I'm clear. Flora doesn't want me to know."

"It's only then to spare you."

"No, no—there are depths, depths! The more I go over it, the more I see in it, and the more I see in it the more I fear. I don't know what I *don't* see—what I *don't* fear!"

The governess's imagination, we see, discovers "depths" within herself. Fantasy seems to be reality for her. Anything and everything can and does happen, in her mind. The attentive reader, when he is reading the story critically, can only observe that we are always in the realm of the supposititious. Not once in the entire story do the children see anything strange or frightening. It is the governess's theory that they see as much as she does, and that they communicate with the dead. But it is the governess who does all the seeing and all the supposing. "My values are positively all blanks save only so far as an excited horror, a promoted pity, a created expertness," James explained in his Preface. But we have one significant clue to the author's "blanks." In his revision of the story for the New York Edition he altered his text again and again to put the story into the realm of the governess's feelings. Where he had her say originally "I saw" or "I believed" he often substituted "I felt."

We have here thus in reality two stories, and a method that foreshadows the problems of the stream-of-consciousness writer. One is the area of fact, the other the area of fancy. There is the witness, in this case the governess and her seemingly circumstantial story, and there is the mind itself, the contents of which are given to the reader. The reader must establish for himself the credibility of the witness; he must decide between what the governess *supposed* and what she claims she saw. Read in this fashion, *The Turn of the Screw* becomes an absorbing study of a troubled young woman, with little knowledge or understanding of children, called upon to assume serious responsibilities for the first time in her life. She finds support for her own lack of assurance by telling herself she is courageous and "wonderful." Yet in reality and by her own admission, she is filled with endless fears: "I don't know what I *don't* see—and what I *don't* fear!" The life she describes at Bly is serene enough outwardly: the servants are obedient and devoted to their master and the children. The children are on the whole well behaved at Bly—and sufficiently normal to indulge in a measure of mischief. It is the governess who sees ghosts and reads sinister meanings into everything around her. It is she who subjects the children to a psychological harassment that in the end leads to Flora's hysteria and Miles's death.

In the controversies that have raged about this work, certain critics have argued that James was telling us a ghost story pure and simple, and that there *are* ghosts in the tale, and that to attempt to explain the governess is to be "over-rationalistic." The ghosts, of course, are there: they belong to the experience of the governess. But to attempt to dismiss any weightier critical consideration of the tale on grounds of too much "rationalism" is to overlook the art of the narrator. Regardless of what any clinical diagnosis of the governess might be, or any judgment of her credibility as a witness, there remains her sense of horror and the extent to which it is communicated to the reader. And it is because there is this question of her feeling, and its communication to the reader, that there has been so much critical argument: for each reader feels the story differently and fills in the Jamesian blanks in accordance with these feelings. In describing Balzac's Valérie Marneffe, James spoke of the French novelist's giving her "the long rope, for her acting herself out." The governess acts herself out, that is the essence of the art used in this story. As in the case of Isabel Archer, we are made aware of her "relation to herself." And by this, *The Turn of the Screw* foreshadows the psychological fiction of our century.

* * * These two works are not isolated on the long shelf of Henry James's fiction. From 1896 to the century's turn he wrote a series of studies of persons seeking to fathom the world around them, and so arranged the telling of the stories that the reader must actively fathom it with them. If this is the method of the drama, it is also the method of the traditional detective story. The works follow in a logical progression: *What Maisie Knew*, in which the reader must determine how much a "light vessel of consciousness," a little girl, knew of the world of divorce and adultery into which she was thrown; *The Turn of the Screw*, with the governess seeking to fathom the world at Bly largely created by herself; the little telegraph girl of *In the Cage*, piecing together from her limited angle of vision the meanings of the messages she dispatches in her capacity as clerk in a telegraph office; *The Awkward Age*, in which the heroine, emerging from late adolescence, tries to put together the meaning of the adult world into which her mother prematurely thrusts her; and finally, *The Sacred Fount*. James admitted that these characters all possess a "rage of wonderment." The reader must acquire the same "rage," for in each case, with the exception of *The Awkward Age*, we remain largely within the given "point of view." The reader's mind is forced to hold to two levels of awareness: *the story as told*, and *the story to be deduced*. This is the calculated risk Henry James took in writing for audiences not prepared to read him so actively. The writer of stream of consciousness takes the same risk.

Recent Criticism

Leon Edel's focus on technique rather than on content has permitted recent criticism to go beyond the simple question, "are the ghosts real?" To be sure, in 1959, after reviewing practically every piece of criticism of the tale, Alexander E. Jones (see Cargill, note #3, above, p. 160) returns to the earliest view of the tale—a sane and sound young governess has to face evil spirits. But for the most part, criticism has now moved away from mere rehashing of old arguments, as the following selection demonstrates. Unfortunately, space limitations prevented the publishing of other fine essays; however, the reader should consult the annotated, chronologically arranged Bibliography, section III.

IGNACE FEUERLICHT

"Erlkönig" and The Turn of the Screw †

Certain aspects of The Turn of the Screw remind one of Goethe's "Erlkönig." Although it can hardly be attempted to establish the direct "influence" of the widely known German ballad on James's story, a comparison of the two reveals a significant number of common traits and may deepen the understanding of both.

There is above all the unity of actors: the child, the adult in charge of it, and the spirit; though in The Turn of the Screw, because of the "other turn of the screw," the number is multiplied by two and we have two children, two adults, and two spirits. The story and the ballad also have the same basic theme: An evil spirit tries to get hold of a beautiful child whom an adult tries to protect. At the end, the child dies mysteriously in the arms of his protector.

Henry James in one of his prefaces, a *post mortem* to be sure, seems almost to point at Goethe's alluring king of elves, whose daughters dance during the night: "Peter Quint and Miss Jessel are not 'ghosts' at all, as we now know the ghost, but goblins,

† From the *Journal of English and Germanic Philology*, LVIII (January, 1959), 68–74. Reprinted by permission of the author and publisher. Notes 5, 6, and 7 have been renumbered.

elves . . . if not . . . fairies, wooing their victims forth to see them dance under the moon." [1]

James claimed that *The Turn of the Screw* had the "unattackable ease of perfect homogeneity," [2] that it was "simple." [3] Yet this alleged ease has sometimes baffled and divided interpreters and for some observers the homogeneity has given way to different colors, levels, and meanings. In which direction does the elusive screw turn? Does it turn only twice? Is this short novel not pure strangeness, couched in mystery, wrapped up in ambiguity?

The Turn of the Screw has achieved its great popularity as a ghost story. Yet some critics do not believe in James' ghosts, and explain them as hallucinations of the frustrated and perverted governess, who alleges seeing those ghosts. This is parallel to the reception of "Erlkönig," which achieved its great fame as a naïve ballad in which the evil king of the elves kills the innocent little boy, but which most critics have interpreted as based on the hallucinations of the sick child.[4]

* * *

In the two stories there is a strong link between beauty and perversion. The homosexual note in *The Turn of the Screw* is recognized by some critics of James. The Goethe philologists, on the other hand, seem to be unaware of the homosexual motive in the ballad or unwilling to concede it. Goethe, however, in his later years again used the theme of an evil demon attracted to "beautiful boys" (*Faust*, ii, 11, 769). Most readers would agree that the erlking's advances arouse no kindred response in the child. Yet such an authority on pederasty and expert on Goethe as André Gide could read in the "Erlkönig," though where is hard to tell, that the child is more charmed than terrified, that he is yielding to the mysterious seduction in the beginning, and that only the father is frightened.[5]

An erotic relation between supernatural beings and a "lovely" as well as "loved" boy is, incidentally, also a motive in *A Mid-summer-Night's Dream*, a link which perhaps may help to account for the curious similarity of names—Peter Quint and Peter Quince.

Considering the beauty of the children in "Erlkönig" and *The Turn of the Screw*, one is reminded of another similarity between the two tales. Before writing his story, James "was charmed by a young boy. . . . The child, aged six or seven, had eyebrows 'six inches long.' " [6] Goethe was likewise inspired to his ballad by the

1. Henry James, *The Art of the Novel* (New York, 1946), p. 175.
2. *Ibid.*, 169.
3. *The Notebooks of Henry James*, ed. by F. O. Matthiessen and K. B. Murdock (New York, 1947), [p. 115].
4. Ignace Feuerlicht, "Goethes Bal-

laden," *Monatshefte, XLV* (December 1953), 424 f.
5. André Gide, *Journal, 1889–1934* (Paris, 1949), p. 873.
6. *The Ghostly Tales of Henry James*, ed. by Leon Edel (New Brunswick, 1948), p. 431.

beautiful body of a six-year-old boy, the little Fritz Stein, whom he admired and whom he took out one evening on a horseback ride.[7]

Critics who do not think that Goethe and James wanted their readers to believe in the reality of the erlking and Quint and their evil intentions and powers, are hard put to explain the sudden death of the children. The rationalizing Goethe commentators dream up the boy's feverish sickness. The psychoanalyzing James critics argue that the neurotic and crazed governess has frightened Miles to death. The death of a healthy child from mere mental shock seems, however, to be such a rare occurrence in medical history as to make it almost as unbelievable as the existence of evil ghosts.

Miles' "little heart," as the governess says,—this, by the way, is the moving style of a loving and lovable person, not of a lunatic or a sadist—has stopped because it has been "dispossessed." It is a case parallel to one at the end of the Yiddish play, *The Dybbuk*, where a girl dies because the spirit of her lover has been exorcised out of her. The girl and Miles die when they have to give up the ghost, as the boy in "Erlkönig" dies because the ghost has to give him up.

Thus, there are striking similarities between Goethe's ballad and James' story: in the mood of "old sacred terror," in the basic themes, in the reality of the "apparitions," in the motives of supernatural evil, of extraordinary beauty of children, of sexual perversion, and of sudden and mysterious death, and in the abrupt ending.

ERIC SOLOMON

The Return of the Screw †

This article on Henry James' *The Turn of the Screw* is unique for two reasons. There is no opening paragraph that includes a rich cluster of footnotes referring to the classic controversies over the short novel; it is taken for granted that the readers are familiar with the two basic interpretations—either the governess is a villainess (conscious or unconscious) and there are no ghosts; or there are ghosts, and the children may be villains or innocents, but the governess is an innocent struggling against supernatural evil. Nor will this essay recount the many refinements of Freudian, mythic, or pastoral readings James' story has received. Secondly,

7. F. Sintennis, "Zum Erlkönig," *Goethe Jahrbuch*, XXII (1901), 260.
† From *The University Review—Kansas City*, XXX (Spring, 1964), 205–211. Reprinted by permission of the author and the publisher.

this article is definitive and provides the one, incontrovertible explanation for the strange happenings at Bly. Never again need there be another explication of *The Turn of the Screw*.

If only the governess had realized that the "dreadfulness" at Bly called for expert attention, she would have turned, as many of her compatriots did at this time, to the services of a master-detective. Sherlock Holmes, for example, would have cleared up the horrible crimes at Bly—for crimes they were—in an instant. He would simply have asked three questions familiar to all readers of mysteries: "Who is the least obvious suspect? What is the motive? What is the nature of the crime, and how did it take place?" Lacking the Holmesian advantage of on-the-spot investigation (for he would have rushed Watson onto the first train from Paddington), we must apply our investigative powers to the governess' manuscript. A careful reading of this deposition can leave no doubt. The least obvious suspect, and the criminal, is the housekeeper, Mrs. Grose; the motive is greed; the crime is murder, more than one murder! Let us read the governess' story with the care we would apply to, say, *The Hound of the Baskervilles* and watch the incredible become elementary.

Our first introduction to Mrs. Grose, presented with typical Jamesian irony, provides the key. The master had "placed at the head of the little establishment—*but below stairs only*—an excellent woman, Mrs. Grose, whom he was sure his visitor would like and who had formerly been maid to his mother. She was now housekeeper and *was also acting for the time as superintendent to the little girl*, of whom, without children of her own, she was by good luck, *extremely fond*." [My italics.] Motive? Love and ambition. Mrs. Grose has already risen from maid to housekeeper—why not to governess? Her obstacle is this young lady "who should go down as governess [and] would be in supreme authority." Thus the governess, who has the proper credentials for her role, replaces the housekeeper who, despite her lack of education, has had Flora for her own *since the death of the previous governess*. When the new governess' ordeal has ended, there will have been another death, and Mrs. Grose will again have control of Flora. How easily Holmes could have prevented this second tragedy!

Flora, of course, "the most beautiful child I had ever seen," would have tempted one less evil than Mrs. Grose. At the start, the governess herself is disturbed about the housekeeper whose position is being usurped. The governess has the sense to brood in the coach over the forthcoming relationship with the woman she is going to replace, but Mrs. Grose's decent curtsy, her appearance as a "stout, simple, plain, clean, wholesome woman," allay the governess' suspicions. Yet the curtsy is ironic, "as if I had been the mistress or a distinguished visitor"; Mrs. Grose seems "positively on her guard" against showing how glad she is to see the new governess. If only the governess had sustained her original misgivings, all might have been well. The evidence is there for the reader, however. "I wondered even then a little why she should wish not to show it, and that, with reflection, with suspicion, might of course have made me uneasy."

Once alerted to the possibility of duplicity in Mrs. Grose's actions, we see it in her every word and deed. She is supposed to be gratified that Flora will now sleep with the new governess instead of with her old friend. And the simple young girl is completely taken in. "Oh, she was glad I was there!" Glad, when every move of the new governess brings pain to Mrs. Grose: first the loss of Flora; then having it thrown in her face that she cannot read ("I winced at my mistake") and that she is stupid (" 'To contaminate?'—my big word left her at a loss.") But even at this stage Mrs. Grose gets a little revenge. She raises a curiosity in the governess about Miles that "was to deepen almost to pain. Mrs. Grose was aware, I could judge, of what she had produced in me . . ." The naive governess continues to push Mrs. Grose, only "fancying" that "she rather sought to avoid me."

The tone of *The Turn of the Screw* becomes more sinister. Mrs. Grose's reply to a question about the previous governess is virtually a threat. " 'The last governess? She was also young and pretty— *almost as young and almost as pretty, Miss, even as you.*' " [My italics.] The mystery thickens as the two women misunderstand each other. When the governess says, " 'He seems to like us young and pretty,' " referring to the Harley Street master, Mrs. Grose's mind turns on Peter Quint, the previous butler. " 'Oh, he *did* . . . it was the way he liked everyone.' She had no sooner spoken indeed than she caught herself up."

Soon she blushes and becomes silent. Clearly she resented Quint's way with young and pretty women. Why? What was Quint to her? Why is Quint uppermost in her mind? Why is the "open" Mrs. Grose suddenly careful? " 'Did she die here?' 'No—she went off.' I don't know what there was in this brevity of Mrs. Grose's that struck me as ambiguous." But Mrs. Grose will not give herself away. " '. . . please, Miss,' said Mrs. Grose, 'I must get to my work.' " And we shall see just what is the nature of Mrs. Grose's work.

Although she may not be able to read, Mrs. Grose is extremely acute. The governess has only to make a vague statement and "She promptly understood me." With understanding, the governess thinks, must come affection, and the women embrace like sisters. Mrs. Grose's "work," then, is to gain the governess' confidence, and this the housekeeper does perfectly. For when the governess sees the figure on the battlements and at the window and, supposedly, describes Peter Quint, Mrs. Grose controls the whole episode. This crux of the story has given even Edmund Wilson pause, yet, when properly understood, it is not in the least confusing.

How can the governess describe Peter Quint unless he really exists? Only if Mrs. Grose, cleverly working on her victim's imagination, tells her that what she has seen is Peter Quint. After seeing the figure, the governess rushes to her friend, is convinced Mrs. Grose knows nothing, but "Scarce anything in the whole history seems to me so odd as this fact that my real beginning of fear was one, as I may say, with the instinct of sparing my companion." Although some instinct warns her about Mrs. Grose, the young lady misinterprets the warning. Henry James, however, gives the perceptive reader the only clue necessary. Someone, the governess thinks, is practising upon her. But who? She does not know. "There was but one sane inference: someone had taken a liberty rather *gross*." [My italics.] Even Dr. Watson would catch the clue.

The governess has her second vision, and once again Mrs. Grose is immediately on the scene. This time, however, she appears frightened. "I wondered why *she* should be scared." Perhaps she thinks that the governess is on to her game, but after seeing the younger woman's face, she regains her confidence and returns to her work —of driving the governess mad. " 'You're white as a sheet. You look awful.' " The ensuing dialogue between Mrs. Grose and the governess is a prime example of what the modern psychologist would call non-directive:

> "It's time we should be at church."
> "Oh, I'm not fit for church!"
> "Won't it do you good?"
> "It won't do *them*—!" I nodded at the house.
> "The children?"
> "I can't leave them now."
> "You're afraid—?"

Pushing the governess more deeply into her fears, Mrs. Grose manipulates her victim—who only vaguely suspects with whom she is dealing. "Mrs. Grose's large face showed me, at this, for the first time, the far-away faint glimmer of a consciousness more acute. . . ." The dialogue is a masterpiece of dramatic irony: " 'I have my duty.' 'So have I mine,' she replied." Now the governess describes the man she has seen, partly like the devil, partly like the master. What is as important as a dog barking in the night, what a detective should grasp at once, is the fact that the governess—and the reader—*has only Mrs. Grose's word for it that the apparition is Peter Quint!* The governess might have been frightened into describing a club-footed midget, and Mrs. Grose could *still* have cried, "Quint!" She presses her advantage; Quint was alone in charge of Bly last year (as the governess is this year), " 'alone with *us.*' " [Mrs. Grose's italics.] And what happened? " 'He died.' 'Died?' I almost shrieked." Mrs. Grose's work is off to a good start.

Henry James makes abundantly clear that the housekeeper dominates the situation. The governess realizes "my dreadful liability to impressions of the order so vividly exemplified, and my companion's knowledge . . . of that liability." James' irony is manifest. Mrs. Grose, the "honest ally," accepts what the governess says "without directly impugning my sanity." Not directly, but surely non-directly.

The reader-detective may wonder at this point why Mrs. Grose is intent on driving the governess mad. The answer clearly lies in the description of Mrs. Grose's relations with the late Peter Quint. " 'Quint was much too free.' " Too free with Miles? wonders the governess. " 'Too free with everyone!' " exclaims Mrs. Grose, dropping her mask for the moment. The innocent governess assumes that Quint was too free perhaps with the maids or with Miss Jessel —but the reader wonders how free a younger Quint had been with a younger Mrs. Grose.

Added to this possibility is the certainty that Mrs. Grose was bitterly jealous of Quint because he was in charge of "her" children. " 'So he had everything to say . . . even about *them.*' " James' ironic stance plainly shows through the remainder of this essential dialogue. " 'Them—that creature?' I had to smother a kind of howl. 'And you could bear it!' 'No. I couldn't—*and I can't now!*' " [My italics.] Meaning not only that she couldn't stand Quint's control of the children, particularly Flora, *and* Mrs. Grose can't stand the present situation either. The governess is too obtuse to take warning—even though she faintly suspects the worst, she cannot face the truth.

The truth is, obviously, that despite Mrs. Grose's regained "rigid control" the next day, she has revealed herself as a passionate, jealous woman. And the governess, as well as the aware reader, is "still haunted with the shadow of something she had not told me." How did Peter Quint die?

Peter Quint was found, by a labourer going to early work, stone dead on the road from the village: a catastrophe explained—superficially at least—by a visible wound to his head; such a wound as might have been produced—and as, on the final evidence, *had* been—by a fatal slip, in the dark and after leaving the public house, on the steepish icy slope, a wrong path, altogether, at the bottom of which he lay. The icy slope, the turn mistaken at night and in liquor, accounted for much—practically, in the end and after the inquest and boundless chatter, for everything; but there had been matters in his life—strange passages and perils, secret disorders, vices more than suspected—that would have accounted for a great deal more.

"Superficially"; "might have"; "accounted for much"; the missing link is obvious. Peter Quint was murdered, murdered by a Mrs. Grose who would stick at nothing to regain control of Flora. Whether the ghosts exist or not is unimportant. If they don't exist, Mrs. Grose is using the illusion to destroy the governess; if they do exist, they have come to see Mrs. Grose, but that hard case is still capable of handling them, in death as in life, and in using them for her own supreme purpose—to retain little Flora.

Mrs. Grose merely has to keep digging at the governess' apprehensions, which are doubled after Mrs. Grose has implanted the idea of Miss Jessel. Once more the mask slips, and we see Mrs. Grose's envy of Miss Jessel. Practically mesmerizing the governess —"She once more took my hand in both her own, holding it as tight as if to fortify me against the increase in alarm . . ."—she tells of Miss Jessel's beauty, infamy. For her part, the governess angers Mrs. Grose for the same reasons Miss Jessel had. The governess wonders at the relationship between Quint and her predecessor, " 'In spite of the difference . . . she was a lady.' 'And he so dreadfully below,' said Mrs. Grose," completing the governess' implied insult to the housekeeper. Although she lost Quint to a "lady," although she must always lose Flora to a lady, Mrs. Grose will never give in. Miss Jessel, the housekeeper remarks, " 'paid for it!' " by her death. The governess, as we learn from Douglas' introduction to the story, pays for it by a shattered life, post-Bly.

The two women continue their talks. And just in case the reader has missed James' first hint as to how the governess was able to describe the ghost, he reiterates: the governess gives a picture of the two—"a portrait on the exhibition of which she [Mrs. Grose] had instantly recognized and named them." That Mrs. Grose is the villain should be obvious from her very omnipresence, an element of the case rarely noticed. She is always at the governess, digging, probing, hinting. "She had told me, bit by bit, under pressure, a great deal; but a small shifty spot on the wrong side of it all still sometimes brushed my brow like the wing of a bat . . . 'I don't believe anything so horrible. . . .' " But she will. Mrs. Grose will see to that by perpetually adding to the horror.

The governess continually adds fuel to Mrs. Grose's anger. " 'You remind him that Quint was only a *base menial?*" 'As *you* might say!' " [My italics.] Her naïveté is remarkable; this timid, inexperienced girl can say to her elder, "'. . . you haven't my dreadful boldness of mind, and you keep back, out of timidity and modesty and delicacy. . . .'" These words applied to Mrs. Grose! If the governess does not understand, the author, behind the narrative, certainly does: ". . . if my pupils practiced upon me, it was surely with the minimum of grossness. It was all in the other quarter that after a lull, the grossness broke out."

The governess continues to see the ghosts; Mrs. Grose obstinately refuses to see them. "At that moment, in the state of my nerves, I absolutely believed she lied. . . ." Everything that she tells Mrs. Grose, by now her confidant and mentor, is received with that lady's "smooth aspect." Ironically, the governess thinks Mrs. Grose lacks imagination because of the "serenity in all her look," serenity because her plans are moving well. She assents to all the governess' changes of mood and shifting interpretation of the spirits' motives. And she plants the next seed in the governess' mind: she must write to the master. The governess assumes that Mrs. Grose misses the point: such a letter would mean either that the master might consider the governess mad, or she would feel it necessary to "'leave, on the spot. . . .'" A conclusion devoutly to be wished for, on Mrs. Grose's part.

The strain of Bly, the governess' shaky heredity, her inexperience —all make her an easy mark. She is tempted to run away, but she remains, despite her growing uneasiness about "Mrs. Grose's odd face." "So I see her still, so I see her best," remembers the governess when writing her report, "facing the flame from her straight chair in the dusky, shining room. . . ." A sinister figure, surely. And a pathetic one withal, at times tempted to confess ("'The fault's mine!' She had turned quite pale . . .") and then having her resolution stiffened by the constant reminders of her place, her illiteracy that must keep Flora in the hands of such as Miss Jessel and her successor—"My question [as to why Mrs. Grose does not write the master] had a sarcastic force that I had not fully intended."

The climax comes almost without Mrs. Grose's active participation, so well has she prepared the way. The frantic governess continues to put pressure on the children; Mrs. Grose continues to get "possession of my hand" and to insist upon the letter being sent, when matters work out even better than Mrs. Grose has hoped. She accompanies the governess to the lake where the latter avers that Flora will meet the ghost of Miss Jessel. Note that this excursion is described as one of the rare moments when Flora has been out of the governess' sight. How deprived Mrs. Grose must have felt! Once at the lake, Mrs. Grose forgets the governess: "She threw herself on her knees and, drawing the child to her breast, clasped in a long embrace the little, tender yielding body." Confident that Flora is hers, that the governess has gone too far and sent the letter, Mrs. Grose "kept the child's hand."

Indeed, the governess goes farther than Mrs. Grose expected. Insisting on Miss Jessel's visibility, the governess terrifies Flora, and Mrs. Grose turns on her superior "very formidably," with "her loud, shocked protest, a burst of high disapproval." Ghost or no ghost, Mrs. Grose is holding on to Flora and looking at the governess with "negation, repulsion." Quick to grasp her victory, to settle the governess for good, Mrs. Grose unites with Flora "in pained opposition." We hear the note of triumph. " 'She isn't there, little lady, and nobody's there—and you never see nothing, my sweet! How can poor Miss Jessel? when poor Miss Jessel's dead and buried? We know, don't we, love? . . . It's all a mere mistake and a worry and a joke—and we'll go home as fast as we can!' " And, the reader might add, we'll get away from this governess who threatened us as much as the others, but who was easier to handle. Flora is convinced; she begs Mrs. Grose to keep the governess away. Mrs. Grose's victory is complete. She is "mutely possessed of the little girl," and Flora spends the night in Mrs. Grose's bedroom—"the happiest of arrangements" for her.

The next morning, Mrs. Grose confidently solidifies her position. Having "girded her loins to meet me once more," the vindictive housekeeper really turns the screw on the governess. Flora now fears only her present governess and will never speak to her again, reports Mrs. Grose, cruelly—"with a frankness, which, I made sure, had more behind it." When the governess wails that Flora will give a bad report to the master, Mrs. Grose gleefully agrees, " 'And him who thinks so well of you!' " Flora wants " 'Never again to so much as look at you.' " And although matters do not work out exactly according to Mrs. Grose's plans—the governess sends her and Flora away to London instead of leaving herself—Mrs. Grose is satisfied. She has Flora. " 'I'll go—I'll go. I'll go this morning.' " When the governess falters, " 'If you *should* wish still to wait . . .' " Mrs. Grose thinks quickly and throws the governess a sop: Flora does speak horrors, there must have been a ghost, the governess is justified—anything to assure the housekeeper's escape with Flora. The governess still tries to hold Mrs. Grose; there is no need to go, the letter will have given the alarm. Mrs. Grose is equal to this final obstacle. The letter, she says, never went; Miles must have stolen it. This desperate lie would be patent to anyone except the shattered governess who scarcely notices that "it was Mrs. Grose who first brought up the plumb with an almost elate 'you see!' " in order to make her departure.

The climax to Mrs. Grose's villainy comes when she and Flora roll out of the gates, reunited. The anticlimax, and a very serious one it is, would surely have been avoided if only Sherlock Holmes —or even Lestrade or Gregson—had been called in. The governess has been maddened by her experiences, which she believes to be the result of either Miles' and Flora's sins or to be supernatural effects. She frightens Miles to death by her fears of the ghosts. She never realizes, as the thoughtful reader must, that she, and Miles, and, indeed, Miss Jessel and Peter Quint, have all been the victims of that most clever and desperate of Victorian villainesses, the evil Mrs. Grose.

MARK SPILKA

Turning the Freudian Screw: How Not to Do It †

My concern in this paper is with the imaginative poverty of much Freudian criticism, its crudeness and rigidity in applying valid psychological insights, its narrow conception of its own best possibilities. I would like to expose that poverty and reveal those possibilities by reviewing three contentions about Henry James's popular thriller of 1898, *The Turn of the Screw*. Over the past four decades Freudian critics have made James's tale a *cause célèbre*. The tale sustains the *"cause"* through erotic ambiguities. Since it also arouses childhood terrors, and perhaps arises from them, we may say that the Freudian approach works here or nowhere. Yet opponents charge that Freudian critics have reduced the tale to a "commonplace clinical record." [1] Though they are perfectly correct, my own charge seems more pertinent: these Freudian critics have not been sufficiently Freudian.

Most of them argue that the governess, in James's tale, is neurotic or insane and sees no apparitions: she merely records her own hallucinations and their damaging effect on two innocent children. In the best recent reading, John Lydenberg drops the hallucination theory and holds, more sensibly, that the ghosts are somehow real, that they symbolize some "generalized evil" which the governess exacerbates for neurotic ends. She is, says

† From *Literature and Psychology*, XIII (Fall, 1963), 105–111. Reprinted by permission of the author and publisher. [The reader might wish to see John Lydenberg's "Comment on Mr. Spilka's Paper," and "Mr. Spilka's Reply," *Literature and Psychology*, XIV (Winter, 1964), 6–8, 34.]
1. Robert Heilman, "The Freudian Reading of *The Turn of the Screw, Modern Language Notes*, LXII (November 1947), 443.

Lydenberg, an "authoritarian character: hysterical, compulsive, sado—masochistic," who makes active, effective, dominant what might have remained quiescent." [2] Here Lydenberg rightly sees that the ghosts' reality does not preclude neurosis but may in fact provoke it; yet, like other Freudians, he fails to allow for subtle provocations. If James's governess is neurotic, she is still a Jamesian governess: the intensity and degree of her neurosis must be less harshly defined. Suppose, as I do, that she is chiefly prurient, that she possesses in supreme degree a prurient sensibility. She is not merely more sensitive than the housekeeper, Mrs. *Grose*, to evil apparitions: she is sensitive to sex-ghosts, especially those who appear to children; hence she is admirably suited for the author's carefully stated purpose:

> Only make the reader's general vision of evil intense enough, I said to myself—and that already is a charming job—and his own experience, his own imagination, his own sympathy (with the children) and horror (of their false friends) will supply him quite sufficiently with all the particulars. Make him *think* the evil, make him think it for himself, and you are released from weak specifications.[3]

James's "charming job" here is to make us think about sexual corruption in children, to make us specify, *from our own experience and imagination*, the particular depravities they absorb from evil friends. Among the tale's many critics, only Peter Coveney has seen this job for what it is: a frank appeal to prurient speculation, an invitation to think dirty thoughts so as to release the author from "expatiation." Coveney accuses James of "psychic dishonesty" in this regard:[4] and yet prurience is the condition which his tale records, especially as it relates to saintliness, for which combination his governess becomes the perfect medium. Her sympathy and horror, her saintliness and prurience, give the novel its appropriate texture: through her defining sensibility we experience those conflicting cultural attitudes which James was then exploring.

In the tales which flank *The Turn of the Screw* (*What Maisie Knew* appeared in 1897, *The Awkward Age* in 1899) James had assailed prurience from different angles. Maisie Farange is an innocent girl who knows all about illicit love among her elders. Discerning adults admire her, curiously, for combining saving innocence with precocious sexual knowledge. [5] In *The Awkward*

2. John Lydenberg, "The Governess Turns the Screw" [*Nineteenth-Century Fiction*, XII (June 1957), 37–58].
3. Henry James, "Preface to *The Aspern Papers*," [p. 124].
4. Peter Coveney, *Poor Monkey: The Child in Literature* (London: Rockliff, 1957), pp. 166–67.
5. As Stephen Spender observes (I

think correctly), ". . . there is something particularly obscene about *What Maisie Knew*, in which a small girl is, in a rather admiring way, exhibited as prying into the sexual lives of her very promiscuous elders." Quoted by Coveney (who disagrees), *Poor Monkey*, p. 160.

Age a somewhat older heroine, Nanda Brookenham, is admired
for the same prurient capacities, once more combined with saving
innocence. That James himself admired these heroines seems clear,
and that the governess belongs between them on the prurient spec-
trum seems equally clear. As sensitive narrator, she enables James
to make his most psychologically *honest* ordering of a vital problem:
the impasse in Victorian attitudes toward sex and innocence.
Where Maisie escapes with her Dickensian nanny, Mrs. Wix, and
Nanda with her sexless sexagenarian, Mr. Longdon, the governess
is left with a dead boy in her arms. She alone confronts an un-
resolved dilemma, braves it out with ironic pride, and so reveals
its ugly implications.

Consider in this light her own romantic yearnings. In her
early days at Bly she dreams about the children's future:

> I used to speculate . . . as to how the rough future (for all
> futures are rough!) would handle them and might bruise them.
> They had the bloom of health and happiness; and yet, as if I
> had been in charge of a pair of little grandees, of princes of the
> blood, for whom everything, to be right, would have to be
> enclosed and protected, the only form that, in my fancy,
> the afteryears could take for them was that of a romantic, a
> really royal extension of the garden and the park.[6]

In other words, she wants to extend the Edenic bliss of childhood
into adulthood, But at this point the intruding ghost appears on a
tower which had often stirred her romantic fancies. The intruder
supplants another object of romantic fancy, her master and the
children's uncle, whom she dreams of meeting now on the path,
smiling and approving, as in a "charming story." Instead she
sees the sex-ghost, Peter Quint. Edmund Wilson argues that she
projects her repressed sexual feeling for the master here. Robert
Heilman says no: her "feelings for the master are never repressed:
they are wholly in the open and are joyously talked about." [7]
But Wilson is right about repression, if not about projection, and
Heilman is culturally off-base. Romantic love was identified by
Victorians with affection: its sexual side was severely censored,
hence the object of much furtive interest. The governess's feelings
for the tower, the children, her master, all loosely enveloped in
a romantic haze, are fully primed for prurient attunement. Now,
more than ever, she is sensitive to sexual evil, the fearsome side
of romantic love, the disruptive threat to the world of garden and
park which the governess, like the children, must outgrow.

Quint's second intrusion helps to reinforce the point. He
appears one Sunday evening at the window of the "grown-up" din-

6. [Pp. 14–15].
7. Edmund Wilson, "The Ambiguity
of Henry James," * * *; Heilman,
"Freudian Reading" p. 436.

ing room, "that cold, clean temple of mahogany and brass" reserved for Sunday tea. "He remained but a few seconds," says the governess, "but it was as if I had been looking at him for years and had known him always." [8] If this is the sexual bogeyman who haunts the "grown-up" parlor, she has indeed known him always. The guilt-laden atmosphere of that site is an emotional fact of Victorian childhood. Dickens records it sharply, in *David Copperfield*, when Murdstone appears in the Sunday parlor which David associates with his father's funeral, and David feels that his father's ghost has somehow risen. From her own "smothered life" in a country parsonage the governess seems to know the ghostly feel of "cold, clean temples." Like the children, she lives in a culture where sexual "horrors" are invested with religious dread, and the term "horror" connects natural with infernal realms. The sex-ghosts connect them still more firmly as the governess records and explains their brief appearances through fears and sympathies which the ghosts alert. Thus prurience accounts for her perceptions as well as hallucination and keeps more faith with the childhood theme. Witness, the opening case in the prologue—"an appearance, of a dreadful kind, to a little boy sleeping in the room with his mother and waking her . . . to encounter . . . the same sight that had shaken him."

The appearance of such ghosts to children suggests one of the most basic Freudian principles, that of infantile sexuality, which James clearly anticipates. The spectacle of Freudian critics ignoring or minimizing that principle, while conventional critics defend it, is bizarre enough: but then conventional critics ignore it too. They speak consistently of generalized Evil, a capitalized abstraction, as opposed to generalized *sexual* evil, and so avoid "weak specifications." Heilman's view of the tale as a morality play, his grandiose allusions to *Faust* and *Paradise Lost*, his more recent retreat to "the lure of the demonic," suggest their line of evasion.[9] The Freudians seem oddly Rousseauistic: they believe in Original Innocence, in adult harassment of passive or unwilling victims without positive desires. Hence they minimize or rationalize Miles's dismissal from school, Flora's verbal horrors, and the reports of earlier evils, as childish peccadilloes. Along with precocious sexuality, they ignore the clear signs of extreme repression in Miles's illness, Flora's aging, her "quick, smitten glare" at the lake, which the governess likens to "the smash of a pane of glass," and Miles's suffering in the final scene, when his answers to the governess come slowly, painfully, as if rising from "the bottom of the sea." Or, to account for these details, they invent scenes in

8. [P. 20].
9. Heilman, *"The Turn of the Screw as Poem,"* * * *; "The Lure of the Demonic: James and Durrenmatt," *Comparative Literature*, XIII (Fall 1961), 346–357.

which the governess pumps the children full of horrors which she later pumps out. Yet the children's radical self-division precedes her arrival: their heightened innocence, their silence on the immediate past, their initiation then by Quint and Jessel, are fairly evident points.

A second Rousseauistic notion, that the governess exacerbates quiescent evils, seems equally untenable. So far as one can see, neither the ghosts nor the children need incitement. What the governess does, out of egoistic righteousness, is to force rather than ease two drastic confrontations. Her flaw is one of character, not compulsion; in her devotion to Victorian virtues—those of duty, sacrifice, and sexless love—she takes exorbitant pride in her own saving powers. But in doing so she enables James to establish something more important: the inevitable failure of Victorian domestic sainthood in coping with erotic horror. The governess may postpone that horror, she may assuage its impact; but at some point in their lives Victorian children will meet their sex-ghosts: there is no real alternative in the tale, no way to save them from damage or destruction. If this is so, we are scarcely meant to condemn the egoistic savior: we are meant, rather, to grasp the cultural impasse of which Miles and Flora, and the governess herself, are victims.

John Lydenberg is the only critic, Freudian or otherwise, to discuss the story's cultural implications. He allows that the governess may be taken, sympathetically, as a Puritan savior who cannot save, and that James may have seen her in this light. He argues, however, that readers without "a predilection for this variant of Christianity will almost certainly see the governess differently, and believe that James saw her differently"; and he conceives the tale himself "as a covert, if unconscious attack" on that New England Puritanism with which James was most familiar (transposed, apparently, to Victorian England).[1] With this odd confession of subjective bias Lydenberg supplants an objective possibility with his own predilections, which he then imposes on the author. This kind of imposition could be demonstrated in Cargill, Wilson, Goddard, and other Freudians, who confidently assume that James adopts their modern attitudes. It seems more likely, however, that contemporary attitudes have obscured the story for such critics. Heilman in particular speaks of an "intellectual climate," primarily scientific, which distorts critical perception. He belives that "scientific prepossession may seriously impede . . . imaginative insight" in this and similar cases, though scientific *truth* may ideally "collaborate with, subserve, and even throw light upon imaginative truth."[2] We

1. Lydenberg, [*Nineteenth-Century Fiction*, XII (June, 1957), 58].

2. Heilman, "Freudian Reading," p. 444.

must agree, I think, that Freudian critics of the tale are strongly prepossessed; yet Heilman himself seems bound by scientific assumptions which obscure the story: he reads the tale hermetically as verbal object, ignores its human sources and dimensions, and so spirals off in abstruse fancies. If James's tale is to receive its due, we must approach it with more genuine imagination than either side exhibits, and with more fidelity to Victorian culture. For the tale matters, finally, precisely as it orders and expresses the intense domesticity of Victorian times.

The Victorian home may be seen, in this light, as a defensive reaction against those inroads on family life which later produced our own domestic freeways. Victorian middle-class homes were, by contrast, domestic sanctuaries, sacred castles or fortified temples, protective bulwarks against an increasingly hostile world of ruthless commerce, poverty and industrial blight, child and sweatshop labor, prostitution and crime. But in the home adults might immerse themselves in family life and salvage some humanity. Unfortunately, their normal affections were intensified by close confinement and overstimulation.[3] The result was a hothouse atmosphere of intense domestic feeling; and within that hothouse certain exaggerated values flourished.

The triumphant spread of science and materialism had created something like a religious vacuum in society. But in the home women assumed the moral and religious roles once held by churchly figures: mothers and sisters were seen as saints and angels, vessels of spiritual perfection, guardians of faith, virtue, and affection; children too, under the aegis of Rousseau, were considered pure and untainted, though little girls had an apparent edge in purity; fathers, in their awareness of urban vices, took on added harshness as disciplinarians and patriarchal protectors. For evil existed outside the home, and children had to be preserved from it by feminine example and paternal sternness. And evil, in the Victorian age, tended to be largely identified with sex: the home might tolerate commercial hardness and impiety in the world outside, but it could not accommodate sexual license.

As we now understand, Victorian prudery developed partly in reaction to Regency license, partly to the alarming spread of prostitution, promiscuity, free-love cults, and salacious novels.[4] The prudery was founded on real fears; but whatever its justification, the attitude was there as part of the mixture of feeling in

3. "In the reaction from a heartless world," writes Walter Houghton, "the domestic emotions were released too strongly and indulged too eagerly," *The Victorian Frame of Mind* (New Haven: Yale, 1957), p. 346.

4. *Ibid.*, pp. 359–366.

the domestic hothouse. On the one hand, domestic affections were cooked up to a high pitch; on the other, sexual feeling was severely repressed and talk about sex forbidden, the whole matter kept under strict taboo. In the meantime prostitution flourished in the city and, in covert and open ways, prurience seems to have flourished in the home.

Consider too the effect on children of extreme affection and repression. Conditions were just about perfect for producing sexual neurosis, if we can agree with Freud that every child tends normally to love his parents or siblings of the opposite sex, and to hate those of the same sex as rivals. The Victorian home so intensified that normal conflict as to thwart or impede its eventual resolution. It seems obvious, even without Freud's theory, that Victorian sons and daughters identified affection with the whole of love, had no way to account for sex except as sinful, and so felt intensely guilty when love was combined with sex in marriage. Affection too was so familial in quality as to give an incestuous tinge to married love.

Yet marriage and home had seemed Edenic, overtly and by nostalgic selection, in childhood, and many Victorians now longed to return to that period, when sexual guilt remained unconscious and faith and affection were shielded from science and commercial hardness. The cult of childhood innocence flourished, abetted by writers like Dickens, Eliot, Carroll, Spyri, and Barrie. At Oxford in the 'eighties students invited little girls (as opposed to big ones) to their rooms for tea. Art critic Ruskin, unable to consummate his marriage, worshipped a severely religious girl of fourteen; poet Dowson worshipped one of twelve while at the same time going to prostitutes; bachelor Dodgson doted all his life on little Alices; and bachelor James, always fond of a sister who went mad and a cousin who died young, wrote a first novel (*Watch and Ward*) in which a young man in his twenties adopts and raises a girl of twelve to be his wife.

We need not rehearse the rivalries and affections of James's childhood, the mysterious accident in his youth, his inveterate bachelorhood and secretiveness, to place him in this cult. We know that he produced a body of fiction in which sex is often identified with evil and affection with the whole of love; that his nubile maidens and pubescent boys tend to die when faced with sexual evil; that his heroines often renounce marriage altogether or enter into sexless compacts; that they show exceptional concern with sheer *perception* of adult sexuality. We know, in short, that he suffered from the peculiar tensions of Victorian childhood (New York brownstone styles). But like many writers of his time, he was able to find adequate ways to express those tensions in his works. Endowed with an exquisite sensibility, fortunate in the assurance that his social background fostered, he could richly mine a small vein of human experience, the vein of personal relations in genteel Europe and America of the late nineteenth century. Through powers of sensibility alone he could create stories in which seeing rather than acting is the paramount experience; or he could explore experiences in which renunciation, or the decision not to act, is the characteristic gesture, so that seeing and sacrificial idealism came to be his primary values. But by the 1890's James had begun to sense the limits of idealism, the limits too of his belief that experience is a vast web of sensibility, "a huge spider-web of the finest silken threads suspended in the chamber of consciousness . . . the very atmosphere of the mind." [5] He began to see that experience is something more than apprehension, that it involves action and engagement, doing as well as seeing, embracing as well as renouncing, and in tales like *The Spoils of Poynton* and *The Turn of the Screw* he could record the failure of cherished values. By the new century he could write too of the need to live, only to live, to get beyond perception to engagement and involvement, and, interestingly enough, to get beyond affective innocence to the sexual basis of adult experience. In the great recognition scene in *The Ambassadors*, when Strether sees the boat carrying two lovers enter the frame of his aesthetic perception, the perfect picture of pastoral romance, he comes to accept sex as the necessary source of charm and loveliness in a relation he had tried to see in terms of sexless virtue.

The Turn of the Screw can be seen as a step toward that acceptance, a recognition of the impossibility of an adult life which excludes sexuality in the name of ideal innocence, a recognition of the impasse which his own cultural assumptions made inevitable. Using a few hints from a tale told by a friend, James invented a fable of a nineteenth century home (circa 1840) in which two lovely children, their protective parents being dead, are exposed to outside evil in the form of sex-ghosts; but to their rescue comes a maternal young lady, full of domestic affection and attuned to sexual evil, saintly and prurient in the Best Victorian manner. The young woman proceeds to fight the invading evil in the name of hothouse purity and domestic sainthood. That she destroys the children in saving them is understandable: her contemporaries were doing so all around her, and would do so for the next six decades. That James valued her saintliness and recognized the reality of what she fought, yet foresaw her inevitable failure, is a tribute

5. Henry James, "The Art of Fiction," *Approaches to the Novel* ed. Robert Scholes (San Francisco: Chandler, 1961), p. 299.

to his artistic grasp of his materials. It was a battle often fought and lost in his time; and, in the guise of a fable about ghosts and children and saintly saviors, he accurately caught the order and texture of the intense struggle. The governess's smothering kisses and accompanying sobs of atonement, her strong preference for Miles based on her old idolatry of little brothers, her religious conception of an essentially natural conflict, her attempt to perpetuate sexless love in angelic children and their strong desire to penetrate satanic realms, the atmosphere of extreme affection and repression in which she struggles, the romantic castle besieged by outside evil—all these reflections of the Victorian hothouse are rendered in the story; and all are nicely focussed by the device of ghosts who appear alike to children and adults: the sexual bogeys of Victorian childhood.

Freudian critics, whatever their faults, have at least sensed the tale's erotic ambiguities: they have rightly rejected James's evasive labels—"a fairy tale pure and simple," "a piece of ingenuity pure and simple," an "irresponsible little fiction," "an *amusette* to catch those not easily caught." For the tale is neither pure nor simple nor safely irresponsible; and whatever its amusing ambiguities in structure, the author has caught, himself, his culture, and his readers in a serious dilemma.[6] By turning the opposing screws of sexual horror and idolatrous virtue, he has poignantly revealed the moral and psychic cost of hothouse life. The Freudians err in the right direction, then, by suspecting his ambiguous preface: their methods, more flexibly and relevantly applied, help us to save the tale from its evasive author and to place it in perspective as an impressive domestic parable. In their fidelity to a system crudely applied and narrowly conceived, they have themselves failed to "throw light upon imaginative truth." More specifically, they have failed to allow for secondary elaboration, for infantile sexuality, for civilization and its discontents—for those Freudian principles, in short, which *can* be made to subserve imagination in appraising James's story. As I hope this paper attests, such principles can be of enormous service to criticism, especially with the literature of the last two centuries. With them we may reduce literature to clinical cases, as purists often say; but without them we may reduce imagination to sterile fancy, as purists sometimes do. Perhaps we will eventually learn how to avoid both pitfalls—how *not* to do it.

6. There are two forms of ambiguity in the tale which are seldom distinguished: the dramatic ambiguity of the ghosts' reality and the governess's sanity, which justifies the label, "*amu-*sette"; and the moral ambiguity of the children's depravity, which engages James and the reader in serious issues —his evasive preface to the contrary notwithstanding.

S. P. ROSENBAUM

A Note on John La Farge's Illustration
for Henry James's *The Turn of the Screw* †

The controversies—they concern not simply the reality of the ghosts but also and independently the moral natures of the children and the governess—surrounding the ambiguities in *The Turn of the Screw* are now some forty years old. The most trivial facts in the text have been scrutinized and transformed into clinching evidence for one interpretation or another. Even non-facts—such as the governess's putative interviews with the villagers—have been offered and accepted as proof. Relatively little, however, has been done with possible evidence that lies outside the text itself. James's remarks in his notebooks, letters, and prefaces have as often as not been taken into account by critics, yet practically none has considered James's revisions of the story (until now there has been no published record of them) or the circumstances accompanying the various appearances of the tale in James's lifetime. There has been some misleading comment about the significance of the story's location between *The Aspern Papers* and "The Liar" in the collected New York Edition of James's work, though the story's prior appearance along with "The Covering End" in a book entitled *The Two Magics* has been rather awkwardly ignored by the same commentators. The conditions of publication rarely offer conclusive evidence for criticism; yet when interpretations are based on the non-existent or the misleading, then the unimportant is at least worth mentioning—if only to forestall its becoming grist for some new critical grinding of the story.

One such condition of the original publication of *The Turn of the Screw* is the illustration done for the story by John LaFarge when James's tale first appeared as a serial of twelve installments, running from January to April, 1898, in *Collier's Weekly, An Illustrated Journal.* How the story came to be published along with La Farge's illustration in such an unlikely place as the ancestor of the recently defunct *Collier's* was revealed by the son of the magazine's immigrant founder. Robert J. Collier took over his father's magazine and tried to raise the declining circulation by offering culture for mass consumption—an idea apparently too far ahead of his time. Collier's comment on the result of his effort suggests perhaps why his later success in popular journalism lay

† Printed for the first time. By permission of the author.

squarely in his own time with his exploitation of The Spanish-American War:

> I had just come from Harvard with the idea that popular journalism needed a little true literary flavor. I showed my judgement of the public taste by ordering a serial story by Henry James. The illustrations were by John La Farge, and I have never yet discovered what either the story or the pictures were about.[1]

By the 1890's James was having increasing difficulty in serializing his fiction. An offer from *Collier's Weekly* must have been welcome, even though it entailed the custom of illustration that he so detested. Just two months after *The Turn of the Screw* was serialized, James observed to his English public that the character of American magazines as well as "the temper of the public, and the state of letters" was displayed in those magazines' being so "copiously 'illustrated.'" This was splendid for "the art of illustration," James concluded; only a "fanatic" such as himself would hold that "good prose is itself full dress" and resent the additional costume that magazines tended to superimpose.[2] The only kind of illustration that James could tolerate is described in his preface to *The Golden Bowl*, where he discussed the photographic frontispieces to the New York Edition and commented on their not competing with the text but being rather "mere optical symbols or echoes, expressions of no particular thing in the text, but only of the type or idea of this or that thing."[3]

An illustration by John La Farge was another matter, however. One of America's most versatile and distinguished artists, La Farge was an accomplished landscape and portrait painter, magazine illustrator, worker in stained glass, and religious muralist; he was also considered to have one of the most cultivated and subtle minds of his time, or so at least thought his close friend Henry Adams whose study of Chartres began with an interest in La Farge's stained glass work.[4] Antedating his friendship with Adams was La Farge's close relationship with Henry James himself. Chapter IV of James's autobiography, *Notes of a Son and Brother*, is largely given over to describing this relationship and its setting at Newport in the late 1850's and early 1860's. La Farge was eight years older than James, he was familiar with recent English and

1. Quoted in Frank Luther Mott's *A History of American Magazines: 1885–1905* (Cambridge, Mass., 1957), p. 455; Collier's remarks were originally reported by Cecil Carnes in *Jimmy Hare, News Photographer* (N. Y., 1940), p. 257. La Farge actually made only one illustration for the story. Five other illustrations that appeared with the serial were done by Eric Pape. Despite his mystification, Collier took three more of James's stories, all illustrated, but not by La Farge.
2. *The American Essays of Henry James,* ed. Leon Edel (N. Y., 1956), pp. 234, 237; James's remarks originally appeared in *Literature*, June 11, 1898.
3. *The Art of the Novel: Critical Prefaces by Henry James,* ed. Richard P. Blackmur (N. Y., 1934), p. 333.
4. *The Education of Henry Adams* (N. Y., 1931), p. 371.

French literature, and he had studied painting in Paris before coming to study at Newport with William Morris Hunt, another of whose pupils was William James. La Farge's European culture gave him, for Henry James, an authority that took years to be undermined.[5] La Farge encouraged Henry with his attempts at painting [6] and introduced him to the work of such writers as Balzac and Browning. "That was the luxury of the friend and senior with a literary side—" James recalled half a century later, "that if there were futilities that he didn't bring home to me he nevertheless opened more windows than he closed." [7] Among those futilities appears to have been James's talent for painting, but among the "windows" that La Farge later recalled he had helped to open was writing:

> The novelist had, [LaFarge] said, the painter's eye, adding that few writers possessed it. In La Farge's opinion the literary man did not so much see a thing as think about it. In those old days he advised Henry James to turn writer, but, he said, he did not offer his counsel dogmatically. He simply felt vaguely that in the conflict between the two instincts in his friend the writing one seemed the stronger.[8]

Something not too remote from the conflict of instincts that La Farge had recognized in James was perceived by James's "painter's eye" in La Farge's work. Reviewing an exhibit of paintings in 1875, James found La Farge "a complex and suggestive [artist] . . . whose pictures are always a challenge to the imagination and the culture of the critics," and he contrasted him with Winslow Homer.

> Mr. Homer's pictures . . . imply no explanatory sonnets; the artist turns his back squarely and frankly upon literature. In this he may be said to be typical of the general body of his fellow artists.

James's conclusion about the differences between La Farge and Homer was not invidious, however, for he said then about painting what he was to say later about fiction: "In the Palace of Art there are many mansions!" [9]

5. *Notes of a Son and Brother* in *Henry James: Autobiography,* ed. F. W. Dupee (N. Y., 1956), p. 289.
6. La Farge also painted James. His portrait appears as the frontispiece for Robert C. LeClair's *Young Henry James* (N. Y., 1955). The result has been described by F. W. Dupee as "a mystifying likeness. A handsome world-weary youth with an elegant large nose, full lips and a brooding shadow around his eyes, he might already be the well-known author of a distinguished tragedy in verse, preferably in French alexandrines," *Henry James* (N. Y., 1956), p. 31.
7. *Notes of a Son and Brother,* p. 294.
8. Royal Cortissoz, *John La Farge, A Memoir and A Study* (Boston, 1911), p. 117.
9. *The Painter's Eye: Notes and Essays on the Pictorial Arts by Henry James,* ed. by John L. Sweeney (London, 1956), pp. 91, 97. Probably one of the main reasons for the obscurity of La Farge's present reputation, compared to Homer's, is the literary nature of his painting.

The results of the "painter's eye" can easily be found throughout James's fiction. The importance of what he termed "picture" to his earlier work is modified only by his later effort to balance this element in the art of fiction with the "scene" of drama. Yet in a work as late as *The Turn of the Screw* James felt that the pictorial dominated the dramatic, or so he said in his letters. To one of the founders of The Society for Psychical Research who evinced interest in the story, James wrote deprecatingly that it was "a very mechanical matter, I honestly think—an inferior, a merely *pictorial*, subject and rather a shameless pot-boiler." James went on to say that what he most wanted to picture in the tale was the condition of the children exposed to evil.[1] And to another correspondent who had perhaps inquired about the tale's moral, James replied, again in words that recall La Farge's description of him,

> It is the intention so primarily, with me, always, of the artist, the *painter*, that *that* is what I most, myself, feel in it—and the lesson, the idea—ever—conveyed is only the one that deeply lurks in any vision prompted by life.[2]

What kind of illustration, then, did the complex, cultured, literary La Farge do for the ambiguous story by his old friend whose "painter's eye" was to see his own tale as "merely *pictorial*"? As reproduced in *Collier's Weekly* above the title of all the installments except the eleventh, La Farge's illustration shows the half-length figures of the governess and Miles. They stand side by side, their faces turned toward each other, and the attractive, slightly matronly governess has her hand around Miles's shoulder. Her face shows kindly concern as she talks to him; Miles regards her pleasantly but enigmatically, and his turned head reveals *another* darker hand cradling the back of his head. Curving across the top of the picture is a filmy streak that blends with a thick curl of fog-like substance separating Miles from a shadowy giant face, half of which is visible at the side of the picture. All that is clearly present of the face are its thin lips and a one huge staring eye. The drawing, eight and three-eighths inches wide and three and a half inches high, is formally bordered on each

1. *The Letters of Henry James*, ed. Percy Lubbock (N.Y., 1920), [p. 112–113]. James had earlier dubbed the story a pot-boiler in writing to H. G. Wells, adding that it was also a *jeu d'esprit* (*Letters*, [p. 112]). It is a little surprising how often critics soberly questing for the smallest ambiguity in or around the story have ignored the pun.
2. *Letters*, [p. 110]. In his preface to *The Turn of the Screw*, which he wrote nearly ten years later, James publicly appears to think more of the story than in his earlier, private letters. He also came to appreciate the dramatic nature of the story, noting that it was "an action desperately, or it was nothing" (*Art of the Novel*, p. 174). For James "action" is close in meaning to the Aristotelian sense in which tragedy is defined as an imitation of an action. Together, James's comments in his letters and his preface emphasize both the picture and scene aspects of the story.

side by an ornamental monster that somewhat resembles a toad standing on its hind legs and presenting half a dozen long, somewhat wavy fangs. In the lower right-hand corner is written "La Farge 98."

La Farge's picture, unlike the four full-page and one double-page drawings of Eric Pape that appeared with *The Turn of the Screw* as it was serialized, is of no particular scene or event in the text, though it corresponds more specifically to the human and non-human characters in the story than a mere optical echo or symbol might. Pape's illustrations depict various key scenes in the tale, such as the governess's early discovery of a figure on the battlement. In that particular picture the figure is clearly visible as the governess regards it, her back turned to the reader. The ambiguous nature of James's ghosts clearly presented no challenge to this artist. While not actually detracting from the story, Pape's drawings are distracting to the reader, and it is not difficult to understand why James usually flinched from the illustration of his fiction. In La Farge's headpiece, however, there is something of James's own intention, as he noted later in his preface, to encourage the reader to summon up his own vision of terror:

> Only make the reader's general vision of evil intense enough, I said to myself—and that already is a charming job—and his own experience, his own imagination, his own sympathy (with the children) and horror, of their false friends) will supply him quite sufficiently with all the particulars. Make him *think* the evil, make him think it for himself, and you are released from weak specifications.[3]

Such an idea for evoking terror certainly fits with La Farge's idea that writers think about things rather than see them. Yet given the effectiveness of James's evocation of terror, there is a danger to the whole conception of the story in illustrating it as seen rather than thought. This is evident in the "weak specifications" of Pape's drawings, while La Farge's illustration preserves something of the ambiguity of the ghosts—except for the quite unambiguous bordering monsters. Their appropriateness might be found in James's rather old-fashioned ghosts which, he explained later, were more akin to "goblins, elves, imps, demons" than to more modern psychic phenomena.[4]

James never mentioned La Large's collaboration in *The Turn of the Screw*, and there are no published letters between the two that throw more light on the genesis of the illustration, the meanings of the story, or the intentions of the author. About James's conscious intentions concerning the reality of the ghosts, we have

3. *Art of the Novel*, p. 176.   4. *The Art of the Novel*, pp. 169, 175.

all we need—if not in his public preface and in his letters, then in his private aside to himself, two years later in his notebooks, that he wanted now to write "something as simple as *The Turn of the Screw*, only different and less grossly and merely apparitional." [5] What La Farge's illustration and the recoverable story behind it do show is how a subtle and cultivated contemporary and friend of the author interpreted his now so famous and controversial story for its magazine public, and how another less cultivated contemporary reflected the popular taste of the time in his arrangements for and comprehension of the illustration and the story.

JOHN J. ENCK

The Turn of the Screw & the Turn of the Century †

I

"In or about December, 1910, human character changed": whether one accepts Virginia Woolf's casual dictum or not, to regard *The Turn of the Screw* as part of an international revolt in aesthetics might provide a context for interpreting James's enigmatic masterpiece. Rather than having predicted toward the end of this same essay, "Mr. Bennett and Mrs. Brown," read in 1924, that, "we are trembling on the verge of one of the great ages of English literature," she should, however, it now seems, have declared the goal achieved by 1922, the *annus mirabilis* for modern art. Commensurately, one might thus, pushing the crucial moment for "change" back to, roughly, the turn of the century, locate the favorable climate between the symbol and the surreal or in late art nouveau through cubism. (Far from pretending to absolute validity, such boundaries can modestly sketch mere general tendencies because, self-evidently, within this same span Victorian holdovers persisted and quasi-experiments—those favored, for example, by Arnold Bennett, whom Mrs. Woolf singled out to ridicule [along with H. G. Wells and John Galsworthy]—lagged behind new developments.) Although genres continued, as they have for centuries, their former ranges were expanded or altered to accommodate fresh possibilities. Also, another aspect which establishes this distinctive style arises from its having graced neither one country only nor a single art but having won an international

5. *The Notebooks of Henry James,* ed. F. O. Matthiessen and Kenneth B. Murdock (N.Y., 1947), [p. 115].

† Published for the first time. By permission of the author.

sway over culture. Finally, unless one posits measurable differences, the recent delusions popular among literary historians—really moralists *manqué*—that twentieth-century artists just perpetuate, often less effectually, outlooks inherited from the nineteenth culminate in futile squabbles such as those fought over *The Turn of the Screw*.

Rather than plunge into that *nouvelle* at once, warned by the many clashes which direct assaults have produced, one had better proceed obliquely and isolate the major trends which it illustrates. The first principle derives from the self-conscious awareness that true art does not, cannot, incorporate "reality" (or life) but, instead, refers to itself and its own nature. Concomitantly, the experimenters, shunning earlier romantics' empty phantasies, teasingly drew upon clichés from literature, or experience, or legends, or society but inverted or caricatured them. Upon these complementary bases by exploiting all inherent segments, many dismissed as self-contradictory or tabu before, they further refined their intricate artifacts purified of all personal and explanatory touches. To offer these constructs in full rigor artists stressed not the subject but the media in which they worked: paint, notes, marble, or words. Thus, the façades opened no vistas upon "life" —much less antiquated allegories unlocked with a single key—but through the stylized surfaces offered dramatized objects. Finally, the total impact, balanced by the uncommitted ambiguities, sought not to reassure but to disturb. The masters of this technique, which, as sketched, extends to disparate groups, apparently discovered it for themselves; even if in or about December, 1900, human character did not spontaneously change, what amounts to the same thing—artists' ways of seeing and showing it—did. The older ones came upon the knowledge in mid-career, and the younger, who may have started with it, in some instances now and then abandoned it. Nevertheless, the practitioners include Eliot, Giraudoux, Joyce, Pirandello, Proust, Rilke, Stevens, Valéry, Mrs. Woolf, Yeats, and, of course, James, but not Shaw, Frost, Hemingway, or Lawrence. For an indicative model here, however, a very remote parallel to *The Turn of the Screw*, one beyond any Jamesian influence and without any similarity in plot, genre, tone, or language will serve best. The distance, in view of the hypnotic force which the *nouvelle* exerts, lends a salutary disenchantment.

In the United States, where opera, more than any other art, must struggle against forces hostile to innovations, *Ariadne auf Naxos*, although produced in several cities, remains almost unknown. Because, having first been given in 1912, it can illuminate aspects of the qualities listed above, considering briefly Hugo von Hofmannsthal's libretto, even at the expense of Richard Strauss' score, may offer preliminary clues through a maze. The prologue to the one-act opera shows the usual activity backstage, here in a private eighteenth-century theater before the curtain rises. The major-domo's announcement that his master has whimsically commanded that the opera seria, *Ariadne auf Naxos*, and a commedia dell'arte troupe led by Zerbinetta must follow one another rather than be separated by the planned fireworks aggravates the already clashing temperaments. Particularly, the young composer of the opera objects, and, scarcely reconciled, upon a new order from the patron that the serious and comic dramas must, somehow, be performed simultaneously he threatens to withdraw in protest. Zerbinetta, however, who always acts the same role, can quickly accept the bizarre scheme. By coquettishly confiding to the composer her secret—that her frivolity conceals a search for true love—she wins him to accept the compromise. The prologue ends with his dedicating himself to his sacred art, music. For the opera itself, after an intermission, with the most effective décor the stage seems to have turned a hundred and eighty degrees so that a modern audience becomes the one which first witnessed the eccentric entertainment. Ariadne, abandoned by her beloved Theseus on Naxos and taking no comfort in nature, represented by the voices of Naiad, Dryad, and Echo, wishes only to die. Zerbinetta, explaining facilely that she happens to be passing through, vainly reassures Ariadne that she has herself enjoyed many lovers, who differ from each other not at all. With her four companions, Arlecchino, Scaramuccio, Brighella, and Truffaldino, she dances through an exemplary sketch. Suddenly Bacchus, a young god as yet unsure of his identity, arrives, but to Ariadne he personifies the death she seeks. Love, however, mysteriously transforms both; they leave the island together while Zerbinetta comments that this new "god" resembles all the others.

Strauss, frequently perplexed by his collaborator's subtleties, oversimplified the theme to his own satisfaction: a woman who cannot forget one man and a woman who cannot remember any. Obviously the complete opera, by drawing upon the interplay between appearance and reality inherent in western drama, exceeds this easy formula. Many of its ambiguities suggest those in *The Turn of the Screw*, whose plot now scarcely requires a separate outline. For both a prologue ushers in the self-contained episode on which the action ends, so that in the opera one learns no more about the composer, in the *nouvelle* no more about Douglas. The two prefaces, moreover, depict aimless pastimes, waiting for a curtain call or telling ghost stories, while the final parts revel in the intricacies of art. For the finished tales, however,

Hofmannsthal and James pointedly revivified suitable stereotypes: the former, Greek myths and Italian commedia dell'arte; the latter, Gothic settings and British nurseries. Within these artificial milieux the supernatural, an elusive quality since the seventeenth century, whether projected as gods or ghosts, deepens the problems. Ariadne, almost to the end, believes Bacchus really Death, while Zerbinetta, allowed the last human word, always counts him a god only in a manner of speaking. Peter Quint and Miss Jessel have inspired no less divergent opinions. In drawing conclusions about a single "truth" one runs the same risks as well. While fatuous singers embody the ideal lovers, Ariadne and Bacchus, Zerbinetta's frivolity stays constant, almost sincere, unless, of course, her confession to the composer betrays her genuine belief. Further speculations come to mind, but for a final one here, which exceeds a bit the limits of conscientious criticism: were "Zerbinetta" as a character to set down her own account of what happened on Naxos—as the real (?) Zerbinetta does briefly in the prologue—how would one "understand" Ariadne and Bacchus?

II

From this much, then, it should have become evident that one can read *The Turn of the Screw* not to discern whether the governess *either* tells objectively what happens *or* occasionally deceives herself but, rather, simultaneously for both likelihoods. Controversies about who sees what lead to only two verdicts: either James, who scrupulously worried about every detail, here overlooked one complete, consistent half of his story or many otherwise intelligent critics have quite floundered on this *nouvelle* —and this either/or, unlike the one in the preceding sentence, cannot admit both possibilities. (True, debates have raged over the centuries about other works: *Hamlet*, for the inevitable example. Suppose, however, the drama unfolded so that Hamlet's vision, like Macbeth's, might proceed from a heat-oppressed brain and that Claudius might have had nothing to do with the murder—the sort of dual structure which does inform *Troilus and Cressida*—then problems comparable with those about *The Turn of the Screw* could confront one.) With James (and Shakespeare) an initial mistake derives from an unwarranted emphasis upon the consistency of "human character," as though it could never change or as though it always usurped authors' identical concerns. Instead of envisaging the governess, Miles, and Flora as "rounded" figures, one might more profitably borrow another simile from sculpture; less like objects rendered in the round, they resemble elements of a mobile whose relationships, if restricted, constantly shift or, for a turn-of-the-century metaphor, commonplace items depicted abstractly and from several angles cubistically. Should such comparisons throw an anachronistic and incongruous pall over a literary work, for fiction which undeniably presents its subjects in a double perspective, one might recall that Stevenson's *Dr. Jekyll and Mr. Hyde* had appeared some years earlier and Hofmannsthal's fragmentary *Andreas* some years later.

In showing noncommittally at least diametric aspects of both the governess and the children James scrupulously had to limit the avenues for conjectures; otherwise, unredeemable chaos would ensue. With his accustomed probity in this regard he implies some limits. The authorial voice in the prologue—what it attributes to Douglas and the others—indulges in no masquerade. Also, honoring the rules of the game, as persona in the first-person narrative, he withholds no essential facts; all that a reader requires is given or can be inferred. At the same time, no detail exists merely for its own sake, and potentially each aspect may aid (or addle) comprehension. To stray outside all bounds, however, to fancy, for example, Mrs. Grose a disguised medium, would convert the plot into an outright farce like Noël Coward's *Blithe Spirit*, the basis for a musical such as *High Spirits* rather than the source for the opera by Benjamin Britten. Nevertheless, not all "facts" rest on verifiable evidence, and, although degress of reliability fade into one another, four principal strata emerge: those which admit little room for doubt, such as setting, season, external traits of character, and the background; those which the governess perhaps misinterprets, such as her own feelings or the tone in dialogue; those highly suspect, such as the extent of Miles's and Flora's depravity; those which could be downright wrong, such as the ghosts. While investigating these four levels in the next paragraphs, one should remember that on all of them through his usual stylistic devices James conscientiously permits readers to follow until, suddenly, the obviously objective dissolves in misstatements. Constantly in addition to heeding the governess one must catch Miles's and Flora's accents as a kind of chorus and then the woman's perhaps malevolent keening which floats over them. The effect, no more than in atonal compositions which likewise found congenial the tempo at the turn of the century, becomes not a cacophony but releases new harmonics.

James increasingly, if less vigorously than sometimes assumed, managed the point of view for maximum dramatic suspense. With a first-person narrator especially, a device about which in the preface to *The Ambassadors* he expressed decidedly mixed feelings for longer works, he went to great lengths to prevent the subject from fusing loosely with the object. Consequently, no matter what one's convictions about the governess' reliability, part of her account stays questionable on all the four levels, even the largely factual. Two casual details unexceptionable by themselves when juxtaposed form a disturbing design. An early exercise, "I had established [Flora] in the schoolroom with a sheet of white paper, a pencil, and a copy of nice 'round O's,' " [1] predicts a pattern before Miss Jessel's appearance across the water: "[Flora] had picked up a small flat piece of wood which happened to have in it a little hole that had evidently suggested to her the idea of sticking in another fragment that might figure as a mast." Doubts whether these represent a charm used by Flora, an unsuppressible phallic phantasy on the governess' part, or a banal coincidence help make the surfaces unstable. Another series: "the long glasses in which, for the first time, I could see myself from head to foot" serves as an overture to Peter Quint's first two manifestations: "the man who looked at me over the battlements was as definite as a picture in a frame," and "seen, this time, as he had been seen before, from the waist up." Do the later, fuller encounters hint at the ghosts' or the governess' swelling threats: the former case to her, in the latter to herself? Indeed, repeated references to mirrors, frames, reflections, and doublings darken the shadowy atmosphere. Her first sentence establishes the rhythm: "a succession of flights and drops, a little see-saw of the right throbs and the wrong." The governess, then, even when a nearly neutral watcher eyes events from her see-saw. Douglas' later praise need not rule out of her unconscious drives the fear which W. H. Auden attributes to "Voltaire at Ferney: "still all over Europe stood the horrible nurses/Itching to boil their children."

The governess, so frequently accused and defended, when describing herself exhibits skills identical with those which she brings to external matters, although one's suspicions increase. Her position initially accommodates all the trite aspects which usually enhance such a figure: a touch of Cinderella, an enchanted house, charming security in the classroom, and a charitable loyalty to a master. By a few breathtaking strokes James neatly undercuts the clichés and so invests them with a sinister power. This very surprise, tending to make the reader wonder about her, highlights the two faces which she presents. Nevertheless, steadily as one contemplates her, even to the point—surely mistaken—of deciding whether ghosts haunt the children or, being an imago, express her own hysteria, all verdicts run risks. While she repeatedly stresses her frantic grimaces, her firmness with Mrs. Grose, her courageous independence, and her constant fidelity something less (or more) than she claims to reveal about herself emerges between the lines.

1. All quotations are from the text in the present Norton Critical Edition of the New York Edition.

By now, of course, all those absolute "proofs" which would exile the ghosts from a subjective derangement and to which she so shrilly alludes have had expert scrutiny and dismissal. Goddard's early essay, particularly, answers those who from inexplicable prejudices boggle at a Freudian analysis. Some slight but indicative details best isolate the pervasive duplicity. Just before Peter Quint's second materialization: "I remembered a pair of gloves that had required three stitches and that had received them—with a publicity perhaps not edifying—while I sat with the children at their tea." The coy apology from an eccentric parson's daughter accustomed to English Sundays verges upon indecent exposure. Similarly, while discerning what Flora stares at on the lawn, she describes the spying place: "a large, square chamber, arranged with some state as a bedroom, [of] extravagant size. . . . I had often admired it and I knew my way about in it"—not a privately edifying practice. Indeed, her vainly repeated "There, there, *there*" to Flora pointing out Miss Jessel and the same words directed at Miles for Peter Quint mark her as seldom auspiciously enlightening. Her momentary doubt, "if he [Miles] *were* innocent what then on earth was I," does not in terms of the ghosts italicize the most baffling phrase: what *on earth* indeed?

With the governess as narrator, the children can never speak for themselves: according to her they at first appear cherubic, later fiendish. Indicatively, the one positive trait which makes them lower than angels depends upon their aping vocabulary. Mrs. Grose condemns Flora: " 'On my honour, Miss, she says things—!' " Miles, likewise, pleads guilty to his obscure behavior at school: " 'Well—I said things.' " Among the many pseudo-facts of Victorian life, one genteel standard denied that any but social outcasts bandied forbidden words. Of course, upper-class children cared for by lower-class servants picked up indelicate Anglo-Saxon monosyllables from the cradle. (The middle class supervised hired help and children more closely, and that pillar of dullness, Mrs. Grose, ironically by her name marks the strata among domestics.) With her countenancing a stitch in time, even on Sundays, the governess thus can genuinely believe that Peter Quint and Miss Jessel have by this much permanently contaminated her charges. Whether the children's depravity goes deeper and to what level and, if so, whether the governess' methods of education (or exorcism) prove most edifying, the story does not affirm. In other ways, however, Miles and Flora, by their deceiving her harmlessly, prove their greater candor and knowledgeability. If they believe her only naïve, the tone often allows them a precocious charm; if her erratic conduct so frightens them that their entertainments for her do resemble "David playing to Saul," then their failure to placate her verges upon tragedy. On the other hand, should Peter Quint's and Miss Jessel's baleful influence not have stopped with words but still actively reach from beyond the grave, then later twentieth-century theories which consider children savages pale in comparison. In their charade, broken by the scattered dialogues assigned them, they wander more tantalizingly uncommitted than she. Miles's guarded aloofness during the final scene, with its erotic intensity introduced by the governess, even out of context—removed from all preceding "unnatural" manifestations—can uncannily disturb. "We continued silent while the maid was with us—as silent, it whimsically occurred to me, as some young couple who, on their wedding-journey, at the inn, feel shy in the presence of the waiter. He turned round only when the waiter had left us. [The maid not at all whimsically becomes a waiter, thus shifting the scene and the sexes.] 'Well—so we're alone!' "

Of course, no one in *The Turn of the Screw* long remains alone, the ghosts themselves being not immune from the governess' intrusions. To read and reread the *nouvelle* while keeping suspended the multiple possibilities for reversals among themes and characters yields the most satisfying variety. Furthermore, James's increasing assurance about his mastery over several spheres in his craft confirms the wisdom of not fixing guilt. His considerable number of shorter works reported in the first person had sometimes mocked the narrator. *The Sacred Fount*, in ways less clear-cut than *The Turn of the Screw*, if only because it presents more facets, exemplifies through a novel the most confident attainment with such données. Moreover with *What Maisie Knew* and *The Awkward Age* James brilliantly discerned how to evade Wordsworthian fallacies and to portray children. For comparisons one might recall the appallingly undisciplined Randolph C. Miller or the simply appalling Pansy Osmond. Indeed, the adolescent trauma of initiation into a dishonest mature world from a barbarous yet honest childhood has never had so scrupulous a chronicler. In addition to incorporating James's new assurance with first-person narrators and children, *The Turn of the Screw* profits from two other kinds of discoveries. For James, as for Hofmannsthal, manners were always symbolic, and his search for them and their equivalents lead him from the United States to Europe. The widening split between the outward gesture and the inner nuance—sometimes hollowness—behind it, terminating in a pervasive hypocrisy, preoccupied him increasingly. The end of *The Awkward Age* where the finally disillusioned Nanda gracefully practices all proprieties to conceal her genuine injuries—a blending of stylization and pathos unmatched in English except the climax which Ford contrived for *The Broken Heart*—unsentimentally depicts the honorable individual lost amid masked cruelties.

The awareness that bad good manners tend chiefly to stifle but that without customs all society collapses ushers in the three last novels: *The Ambassadors, The Wings of the Dove,* and *The Golden Bowl.* In these one character, at the risk of losing all, through sacrifices and on his own authority, braves anarchy by relying upon his own insights. Terror as well as grandeur accompanies these defiant codes, which for James dare never call notice to themselves by outwardly departing from the conventional norms. Whether this existential morality engenders a more creative order or a selfish tyranny—or a disturbing mixture of both—each book itself must show because the mistrust of absolutes extends to all matters. The governess, consequently, partakes of the frightening lucidity, which may yet deceive itself, shared by Strether, Milly Theale, and Maggie Verver. Finally the theme which James bravely confronted even in his earliest writings and from which he never averted his gaze—the potential destructiveness of love—here reaches as far as it can. Seemingly generous emotions can shield a desire for total surrender which annihilates one or both of the lovers. No matter the causes, under the circumstances the governess' final triumph, " 'What does he matter now, my own?—what will he *ever* matter? I have you . . . but he has lost you for ever!' " awfully parodies all similar sincere vows of devotion.

Despite the strands traceable forward or backward from James's other works, or those by contemporaries, into *The Turn of the Screw,* the *nouvelle* must stand by itself. Nevertheless, the fact that James, like most important twentieth-century authors, described his books not at all or inscrutably, has not deterred a number of critics from trying to spell out his "intentions," as though these could matter beyond what the text itself contains. If one requires added proof about the uselessness of such pseudo-research, *Ariadne auf Naxos* provides it. Strauss himself, despite repeated protests that audiences would find the metaphysical libretto as incomprehensible as he did, nevertheless composed a score which interlocks tellingly with the action. Moreover, in the prologue the composer cannot quite explain to himself the power which transforms Ariadne. To unearth a source offers no crutch for understanding either: again, the tangled history of the Hofmannsthal-Strauss opera, including its having complemented Molière's *Bourgeois gentilhomme* at one point, will not declare either Ariadne or Zerbinetta right. James throughout his career sought in isolating his "germ" not for ponderous exterior ideas but for materials just tensile enough to bear the full strain put upon them. Controversies about certitudes in *The Turn of the Screw* persist, however, and recently in a book of stultifying length, Wayne C. Booth, after three hundred and fourteen pages (and fifty-four epigraphs), lamely decides: "I may as well begin by admitting—reluctantly since all of the glamor is on the other side—that for me James's conscious intentions are fully realized: the ghosts are real, the governess sees what she says she sees." [2] Because James said little explicit about this work, except to place a slight value upon it, citing his intentions implies that he hoped, in an analogy from music, to compose a hummable tune, for example "Bewitched, Bothered, and Bewildered," but luckily ended with a double inverted fugue on his fumbling hands. When, however, the governess receives a pat on her brave little back from Professor Booth, "she behaves about as well as we could reasonably expect of ourselves under similarly intolerable circumstances," (p. 314) the mind reels more violently in perplexities about unchanging human character than at anything in *The Turn of the Screw* itself.

The *nouvelle* by engendering that exhilaration which the apparently effortless triumph over recalcitrant materials alone produces needs no excuse beyond its aesthetic perfection. That so high a standard has now almost disappeared except for a few practitioners such as Nabokov, that since the Second World War most novelists have settled on less demanding techniques neither lessens the impact nor invalidates the nobility in the main artistic impetus from the turn of the century until the late nineteen-thirties. If, however, pedants go on insisting that literature must edify one about "life," James in the preface to the New York Edition strikes the right note: "Only make the reader's general vision intense enough. . . . Make him *think* the evil, make him think it for himself." Once again, as Valéry liked to note, Peter's opinion about Paul tells more about Peter than Paul. *The Turn of the Screw* implacably tempts everyone into judgments—rash or laboriously reasoned. Nevertheless, as with most of James's later books, the closer the reading, the more one's sensitivity increases about the difficulty of all decisions: how very tenuous one's estimate of others—and one's self—must in civilized fairness be. The most solid appearance may dissolve as illusory to unmask irremediable horrors; an impeccable worship of "truth" (or "goodness" or "beauty") can conceal a temple to evil. One looks back at Bly and its unconventional inhabitants

2. *The Rhetoric of Fiction* (The University of Chicago Press: Chicago, 1961), p. 314. From one who tiresomely insists upon a clear "communication" between author and reader, the words inside the dashes provide an instructive paradox. Does Professor Booth use "glamor" in its primary sense of "magic; a spell or charm"? No, clearly, the magic belongs to the children and him. Has he unprofessorially lapsed into the distortion given currency by press agents of Hollywood? If so, do "reluctantly" and "all" hint at a surreptitious boredom with his earnest pursuit of platitudes? Or, has he recklessly indulged in a pun, granted a heavy-handed one? When anyone so hot for certainties in art casually throws about a double meaning, especially when neither makes any particular point, he risks irresponsibility. That last phrase, however, "on the other side" stays in character; a criterion like this one insists on labeling the good and the bad sides so it can smugly proclaim its righteous choice.

repeatedly because one cannot, dare not, make the final pronounce-
ment. Whatever anxiety such hesitancy causes disappears in part
because of the wholeness which art alone provides; one learns enough
to suspend judgment. Experience itself necessarily offers less and
thus lures one into facile verdicts. One consequently almost accepts
the heavy burden which accompanies admitting the likely ultimate
uniqueness of each situation and the frequent need for evaluating it
existentially on its own terms, perilous as that experiment may
appear. Any standard more passionately championed may betray
one and others into positive error and evil. Should anyone insist
that responsible art must incorporate more positive nostrums, let
him heed the muted challenge in Miles's final cry, " 'Peter Quint—
you devil. . . . *Where?*' " The governess has (diabolically?) long
since made up her mind *where*; the conscientious reader should
keep questioning. Finally, what better describes the two attitudes
in the *nouvelle* toward the ghosts, the two sides among critics of
The Turn of the Screw, the two antagonistic "cultures" in Western
society, and the two hostile ideologies dividing the earth than
Hofmannsthal's summary for Strauss about *Ariadne auf Naxos*: "So
the two worlds are, in the end, connected ironically by non-compre-
hension"? Of course, each reader's intelligence composes the irony
of the opera and the *nouvelle* in aesthetic harmonies. At present,
long after the turn of the century it seems even less likely than at
that time it may have that the one apparently unchangeable part
of human character will long in life itself tolerate between inflexible
prejudices a verb so peaceful as *connected*—quite the opposite.

ROBERT GINSBERG

["James's Criticism of James"] †

* * * And now let us consider in outline the critical contribution
to "The Turn of the Screw" made by the most formidable of Jamesian critics, an aesthetic and artist of high caliber, Henry James. It has
been an easy matter for critics to tell us what James's approach and
conclusions were, but we must exercise a certain willing disbelief in
their analyses for the reason that they do not agree as to what
James meant, and each explanation is peculiarly appropriate to the
approach or interpretation of the particular critic. The controversy

† From "Criticism, Jamesian Criticism,
and James's Criticism of James: 'The
Turn of the Screw'," *Criticism and
Theory in the Arts*, ed. Robert Ginsberg, Paris, 1963, pp. 20–37. Pp.
33–36 reprinted by permission of the
author and publisher.

has manifested an obstinate disregard of the differences between what an artist does as an artist (in this case, writing and on two occasions slightly rewriting "The Turn of the Screw"), what he does as a critic (in this case composing his Preface), and what he does in other domains of his private and professional life, such as writing letters to friends or admirers, such as coping with readers who come up to him with comments about his story, such as making notes in a workbook, such as arranging the publication of his story together with others in the same volume or edition. What James says about the story in his Preface thus becomes inseparable from what James was as a person, and what his letters, conversation, notebooks, revisions, works of fiction, and "The Turn of the Screw" itself mean. Many arguments, after all, may be found for correcting the distortions and ambiguities that creep into the Preface, for when a man criticizes his own work he may be too modest, ashamed, vain, superficial, mysterious, proud, subjective, objective, disappointed, elusive, confused, disinterested, hallucinated, disillusioned, equivocal, or hypersensitive. Anything the artist says may be used against him. But even if the critical Preface is accepted at face value as a critical Preface (Richard P. Blackmur has gathered the Prefaces of the New York Edition into one volume which is entitled *The Art of the Novel: Critical Prefaces,* New York: 1948), James's criticism is reorganized by the perspectives of other approaches rather than being considered as James organized it. A very simple and universal method is used to interpret James. It consists in reading with a pair of scissors in one hand and a jar of paste in the other; each time one finds a sentence in the text (in the case of James half a sentence will do) that supports the view one has of the tale or the view that one would like James to have—these are generally the same—one clips it out of its context and glues it on a fresh sheet of paper; after a while an impressive array of such authoritative phrases linked together with a few words of one's own may be displayed as "James's criticism of James." This is the thematic-imagistic approach in criticism applied to criticism; it may work on impressionistic critics whose structures are precisely strings of phrases about a work, but James does not fall into this category unless he is pushed.

James begins his discussion of "The Turn of the Screw" in the Preface [pp. 118–119] by indicating the anecdote which became the germ of the work. There should be no surprise about such a beginning. In his very first Preface James indicates the significance of the accessory facts of composition of his stories, including the germ: they mark a station in the growth of the artist's operative consciousness, they indicate the continuity of his endeavor, the unfolding of his whole creative process (Blackmur p. 4). Let it be noted that Richard P. Blackmur in his introduction to the Prefaces takes James's statement as applying to the Prefaces themselves rather to notes and memories. In the successive Prefaces James will unearth the germ as far as is possible, for it lies at the start of the creative operations, he will then trace and judge the transformations and flowerings that followed. The problems, then, that James discusses one after the other in his Preface indicate both the path of the creative process and the points for appraisal in the result. James indicates in his first Preface that the private character drops out of sight in the consideration of the accessory facts, that is, the personal interest of the author in the fact is not as significant as the aesthetic implications of the fact for his art, and so it is that James qualifies the anecdote related to him as the private source of "The Turn of the Screw." Although identifying the "source" of the work, James indicates how the story originated in his own creative operations. Rather than causing the work, the anecdote is merely the starting point within the art that causes the work. The first problem James faced was the need to allow freedom to the imagination (his own) and yet to sufficiently curtail it for singularity of form [pp. 119–120]. The appropriate form he hits upon is the fairy-tale. The next problem discussed is the picturing of the governess's character without having to shove too much down the reader's throat [pp. 120–121]. The governess as narrator-character has two functions: telling and explaining. James endeavored to knead the *subject* of the narrator's mystification on one hand, while on the other, making the *expression* of it so fine and clear that beauty results. Next is the selection of ghosts appropriate to the effects to be achieved [pp. 122–123]. It is here that James had to choose between modern ghosts who just stood around and did nothing and old fashioned "non-scientific" ghosts who could chill the blood. He cast his lot with pure romance in picking the latter who do not conform to our sense of the way things happen (for the definition of romance see Prefaces, pp. 31–32). The final problem is to create a sense of portentous evil without specifying what the ghosts had in mind concerning the children, by relying on the reader's imagination [pp. 123–124].

The continuing concern in each stage of the process is the effect to be achieved: (1) the suggestiveness of horror in the germ, (2) the controlling of form so that its effect would not be lost, (3) the facilitation of horror by the proper narrator-character, (4) its facilitation by the ghosts who enter into the action, (5) its strength attained by a lack of certain explanations. James notes that his story is an *amusette* to catch readers. Stating this otherwise, he says it achieves a tone of mystification: it is the subject of the narrator's mystification that is worked on. James does not say here [pp. 121–

122] that he has tricked or deceived the reader, he speaks of capturing, catching him. In the context of the particular stage of the process James discusses, this might mean that although the form of "The Turn of the Screw" is simple—a fairy-tale—it is capable nonetheless of working its effects of horror even on the most mature or sceptical of readers, one of its means being the "tragic" mystification of the subject in conjunction with the "exquisite" mystification of the expression. An *amusette* is a child's play just as fairy-tales are children's literature, but James is working for an adult audience and he doesn't fail to bring out the irony of horror producible from children's materials.

James does not say that the ghosts exist only for the governess or that they exist for the children too. He is interested in their action in the story, their causing situations to lead to certain effects. Although James says the ghosts imply Evil, he does not say the governess stands for Good. He does speak of his story as "good," however, and by this he means producing the impression of the dreadful, his designed horror [pp. 123–124]. The reader is caught by the play between the governess's *explanation* of things and the obscure and anomalous nature of them, and the reader is led to provide his own *explanation* of the evil the ghosts intend for the children. It is not mystification that is ultimately aimed at but horrification, for the governess who faces the horror is able to reason out the mysteries, and the ghosts' evils are not indicated in order to create the feeling of the greatest possible horror they could cause.

James's approach to "The Turn of the Screw" as a work of art designed to produce horror has been partially followed by a number of critics, and many eloquent testimonies have been made to the superlative horror of the story. but one must be cautious, for the exact emotional effect varies enormously depending on how it is mixed up with such things as mystification, moral indignation, disbelief, and confusion, as well as what the chief causes of the horror are: the governess's illness, the diabolical intentions of the ghosts, the Evil of the world, the innocence or corruption of the children. Most critics, indeed, have sought in one way or another to advance James's analysis of the horror story by exposing the techniques he used to accomplish his intentions. Each of the aesthetic problems focused on by James in his Preface is discussed in turn by the critics in great detail, with the relationship between the problems ignored, with new intermittent stages expounded, and with the leaving out of certain steps. James is only apparently in a unique position as critic of his own story, tracing its formation, for the inside information that he possesses may, despite his memory and candor, be inaccurate or false. In short, critics have substituted other versions of James's process of creation of "The Turn of the Screw."

There is, finally, no impulsion to model one's approach to the work on James's, as there is no requirement that one's conclusions about the story must be the same as the author's. James stands as only one among many critics and their ranks swell from year to year while James's approach, commensurate with his conception of fiction as an art of representation in which form is created in terms of characters and actions, and in which narrative means are specially designed for the representation desired and its effect, tends to be neglected, misunderstood, underestimated, disproved, disapproved, interpreted, or, more frequently, chopped up into fragments and blown away by the hot winds of debate.

Bibliography

In the following lists no mention is made of collections, books, studies, or articles already quoted from or referred to in the footnotes of the preceding sections.

I. CHECK LISTS

For early reactions, see Richard N. Foley, *Criticism in American Periodicals of the Works of Henry James from 1866 to 1916* (The Catholic University of America Press: Washington, D. C., 1944). For a full but dated bibliography, see Lyon N. Richardson, *Henry James* (American Writers Series, American Book Company: New York, 1941). More recent is the bibliography of Maurice Beebe and Wm. T. Stafford in the special James number of *Modern Fiction Studies,* III (Spring, 1957), 73–94. Fullest and most recent is the annotated bibliography of Thomas M. Cranfill and Robert L. Clark, Jr., *An Anatomy of THE TURN OF THE SCREW* (University of Texas Press: Austin, 1965).

II. GENERAL STUDIES

Dupee, F. W., *Henry James* (Doubleday Anchor Book: New York, 1956). Revised version of a 1951 American Men of Letters volume; good general biography with critical observations.

Edel, Leon, *Henry James: The Untried Years, The Conquest of London, The Middle Years* (Lippincott: Philadelphia, 1953–62). The first three volumes of what will be the definitive biography; 1897–1898, the years of *The Turn of the Screw,* are not yet covered.

————, *Henry James* (University of Minnesota Press: St. Paul, 1960). Number 4, in the University of Minnesota Pamphlets on American Writers.

Geismar, Maxwell, *Henry James and the Jacobites* (Houghton Mifflin: Boston, 1963). Tries to prove that James owes his status more to his critical admirers than to his craft.

Jefferson, D. W., *Henry James* (Writers and Critics Series, Oliver and Boyd: Edinburgh and London, 1960). Short but full critical survey, with bibliography.

Nowell-Smith, Simon, *The Legend of the Master* (Constable: London, 1947). A biography made up of reactions to and recollections of James.

Richardson, L. N. (see above, section I).

Zabell, Morton Dawen, "Henry James: The Art of Life," *Craft and Character: Texts, Method, and Vocation in Modern Fiction* (Viking Press: New York, 1957), pp. 114–143. Excellent introduction to James.

III. STUDIES IN TECHNIQUE

Beach, Joseph Warren, *The Method of Henry James* (Albert Saifer: Philadephia, rev. ed. 1954, first pub. 1918).

Gale, Robert L., *The Caught Image: Figurative Language in the Fiction of Henry James* (University of North Carolina Press: Chapel Hill, 1964).

Hoffman, Charles G., *The Short Novels of Henry James* (Bookman Associates: New York, 1957).

Leavis, F. R., *The Great Tradition: A study of the English Novel* (Doubleday Anchor Book: New York, 1954, first pub. 1948).

Lubbock, Percy, *The Craft of Fiction* (Viking Press Compass Book: New York, 1957, first pub. 1921).

Matthiessen, F. O., *Henry James: The Major Phase* (Oxford University Press: New York, 1944).

McCarthy, Harold T., *Henry James: The Creative Process* (Thomas Yoseloff: New York and London, 1958).

Sharp, Sister M. Corona, O.S.U., *The Confidante in Henry James: Evolution and Moral Value of a Fictive Character* (University of Notre Dame Press: Notre Dame, Indiana, 1963).

Ward, Joseph A., *The Imagination of Disaster: Evil in the Fiction of Henry James* (University of Nebraska Press: Lincoln, 1961).

Winters, Yvor, "Maule's Well, or Henry James and the Relation of Morals to Manners," *In Defense of Reason* (University of Denver Press: Denver, 1947, first pub. in 1938, in *Maule's Curse*).

IV. SPECIAL STUDIES (chronologically arranged)

Liddell, Robert, "The 'Hallucination' Theory of *The Turn of the Screw*," Appendix II, *A Treatise on the Novel* (Jonathan Cape: London, 1947). A refutation of Edmund Wilson.

Stoll, E. E., "Symbolism in Coleridge," *PMLA*, LXIII (March, 1948), 214–233. Defends the actuality of the ghosts.

Reed, Glenn A., "Another Turn on James's 'The Turn of the Screw'," *American Literature*, XX (January, 1949), 413–423. Another refutation of the pyschological interpretation.

Evans, Oliver, "James's Air of Evil: 'The Turn of the Screw'," *Partisan Review*, XVI (February, 1949), 175–187. "Without the possession theme, * * * there is simply no conflict, no drama, no *story*."

Bewley, Marius [and F. R. Leavis], "Appearance and Reality in Henry James"; "*What Masie Knew:* A Disagreement by F. R. Leavis"; "Maisie, Miles, and Flora, the Jamsian Innocents: A Rejoinder"; "Comment by F. R. Leavis"; [and] "The Relations between William and Henry James"; *The Complex Fate* (Chatto and Windus: London, 1952), pp. 79–149. A reprint of an essay by Bewley in *Scrutiny*, XVI (Summer, 1950) along with rejoinders back and forth between the author and editor, F. R. Leavis, arguing over James's techniques and the question of the innocence or guilt of the children.

Collins, Carvel, "James's 'The Turn of the Screw'," *Explicator*, XIII (June, 1955), item 49. Douglas is Miles grown up.

Firebaugh, Joseph, J. "Inadequacy in Eden: Knowledge and 'The Turn of the Screw'," *Modern Fiction Studies*, III (Spring, 1957), 57–63. The Governess is "the inadequate priestess of an irresponsible deity—the Harley Street uncle. * * * She destroys the [innocent] children by imposing on them images of evil formed in her conviction of the essential sinfulness of mankind."

Costello, Donald P., "The Structure of *The Turn of the Screw*," *Modern Language Notes*, LXXV (April, 1960), 312–321. Through a detailed structural analysis, Costello concludes that James wanted the reader both "to accept the ghosts" and "to doubt the ghosts" by simultaneously evoking "a feeling of horror" and "a feeling of mystification."

Gargano, James W., "*The Turn of the Screw*," *The Western Humanities Review*, XV (Spring, 1961), 173–179. The governess is utterly reliable in all that she reports.

Krook, Dorothea, "*The Turn of the Screw*," [and] "Edmund Wilson and Others on The Turn of the Screw," *The Ordeal of Consciousness in Henry James* (Cambridge University Press: Cambridge, England, 1962), pp. 106–134 and 370–389. In a chapter on *The Turn*, Krook concludes that the moral ambiguity of the tale expresses a mysterious and inexplicable phenomenon of "copresence of good and evil, innocence and guilt, in the children and in the governess; and the final baffling, tormenting impossibility of determining the degree of innocence in the guilt and of guilt in the innocence." In an appendix, the author takes on Edmund Wilson, Robert Heilman, and H. C. Goddard.

MacKenzie, Manfred, "The Turn of the Screw: Jamesian Gothic," *Essays in Criticism*, XII (January, 1962), 34–38. Places the tale in the tradition of "gothic" stories and novels.

Slabey, Robert M., " 'The Holy Innocents' and *The Turn of the Screw*", *Neueren Sprachen*, XII (1963), 170–173. Douglas begins reading the manuscript on December 28th, the day of "the Feast of the Holy Innocents, the commemoration of Herod's massacre of the boys in Bethlehem and its neighborhood who were two years old or younger."

Rubin, Louis D., Jr., "One More Turn of the Screw," *Modern Fiction Studies*, IX (Winter, 1963–64), 314–328. "Douglas *is* Miles."

Lang, Hans-Joachim, "The Turns in *The Turn of the Screw*," *Jahrbuch für Amerikastudien*, IX (1964), 110–128. In "gothic" tradition, the ghosts belong both to the house as symbols of past evil and to the governess because she activates them; the tale is more pictorial and dramatic than psychological.

Banta, Martha, "Henry James and 'The Others'," *The New England Quarterly*, XXXVII (June, 1964), 171–184. Traces James's interest in the supernatural, both in life and in art.

Vaid, Krishna Baldev, "The Turns of the Screw," *Technique in the Tales of Henry James* (Harvard University Press: Cambridge, Mass., 1964), pp. 90–122. The governess is completely reliable; in fact, "her intuitive faculty is more highly developed than that of any other Jamesian narrator, except perhaps the narrator of *The Sacred Fount*."

West, Muriel, *A Stormy Night with The Turn of the Screw* (Frye & Smith: Phoenix, 1964). A far ranging critical exploration of the tale using various approaches and exploiting various points of view, done through a fictive mode, and ending up rather "on the side of the 'hallucinationists'—but with differences and modifications." See also Miss West's "The Death of Miles in *The Turn of the Screw*," *PMLA*, LXXIX (June, 1964), 283–288, in which she concludes that at the end "the governess indulges in an exuberant debauch of violence that contributes to the sudden death of little Miles—or dreams that she did."

Cranfill, Thomas M. and Robert L. Clark, Jr., *An Anatomy of THE TURN OF THE SCREW* (University of Texas Press: Austin, 1965). Could be entitled "An Anatomy of the Governess" so unrelentlessly do the authors dissect her, coming to the conclusion that there are no ghosts, only a sick heroine. A chapter on Mrs. Grose appeared in *Texas Studies in Literature and Language*, V (Summer, 1963), 189–198, and one on James's revisions, in *Nineteenth-Century Fiction*, XIX (March, 1965), pp. 394–398.

Clair, John A., *"The Turn of the Screw," The Ironic Dimension in the Fiction of Henry James* (Duquesne University Press: Pittsburgh, 1965), pp. 37–58. The uncle and Miss Jessel are probably the parents of the children, but Miss Jessel has gone mad, has been locked up in the tower under the guard of Quint, but escapes from time to time because she wants her children back. The one really in charge at Bly, manipulating all, is the devious, dishonest Mrs. Grose.

Trachtenberg, Stanley, "The Return of the Screw," *Modern Fiction Studies*, XI Summer 1965), 180–182. Douglas is Miles who after 50 years of silence confesses by means of the story his childhood guilt, the source of which is "unspecified"; the end effect is "a symbolic deathbed confession, while the attending guests perform a priestlike absolution around the cleansing fire of the hearth."